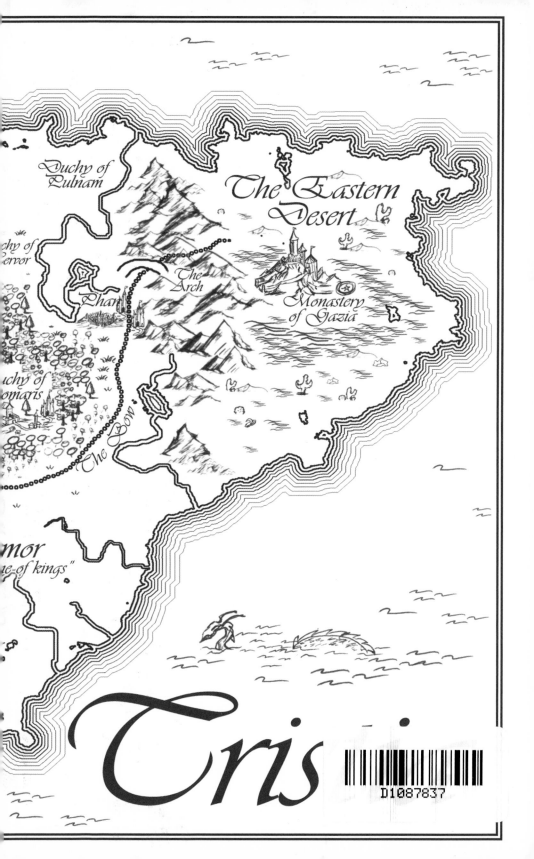

Duchy of
Pulnam

chy of
ervor

The Eastern
Desert

The
Arch

Phar

Monastery
of Gazia

chy of
omaris

The Bow

mor
e of kings"

Cris

D1087837

SAINT'S BLOOD

ALSO BY SEBASTIEN DE CASTELL

Traitor's Blade
Knight's Shadow

SAINT'S BLOOD

SEBASTIEN DE CASTELL

Jo Fletcher

New York • London

Jo Fletcher Books
New York • London
an imprint of Quercus Editions Ltd.

© 2016 by Sebastien de Castell
Map copyright © 2014 Morag Hood
Author photo © Pink Monkey Studios
First published in the United States by Quercus in 2016

ISBN 978-1-681-44489-5

Library of Congress Control Number: 2016010983

Distributed in the United States and Canada by
Hachette Book Group
1290 Avenue of the Americas
New York, NY 10104

Manufactured in the United States

10 9 8 7 6 5 4 3 2 1

www.quercus.com

For my wonderful sister-in-law, Terry Lanthier,
the closest most of us will ever come to
meeting an actual Saint . . .

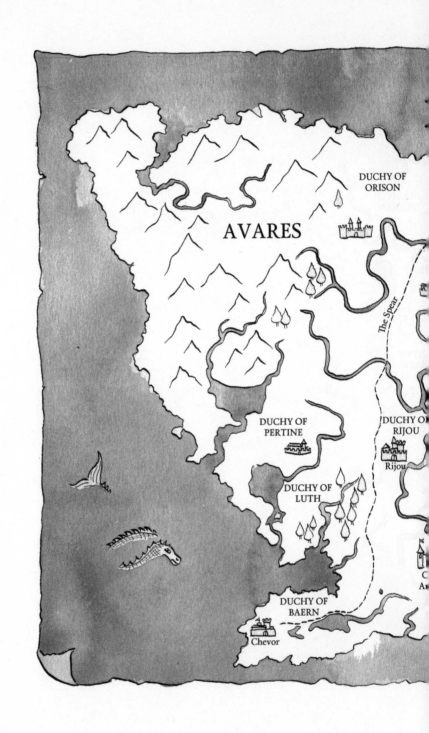

DUCHY OF
ORISON

AVARES

DUCHY OF
PERTINE

DUCHY OF
RIJOU

Rijou

DUCHY OF
LUTH

The Spear

DUCHY OF
BAERN

Chevor

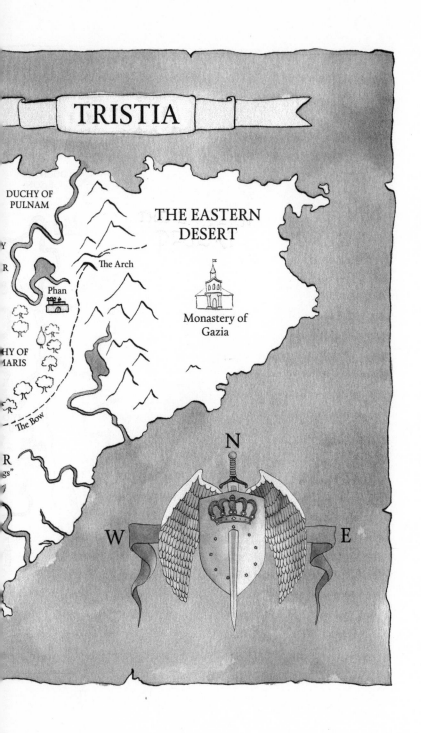

CONTENTS

CHAPTER ONE

ON THE MORNING OF YOUR FIRST DUEL

On the morning of your first duel, an unusually attractive herald will arrive at your door bearing a sealed note and an encouraging smile. You should trust neither the note nor the smile. Dueling courts long ago figured out that first-time defendants are less prone to running away if it means embarrassing themselves in front of beautiful strangers. The practice might seem deceptive, even insulting, but just remember that *you* are the idiot who agreed to fight a duel.

Don't bother opening the envelope. While the letter might start out with extravagant praise for your courage and dignity, it quickly descends into a lengthy description of the punishment for failure to show up at court. In case you're wondering, the penalty in Tristia for attempted flight from a lawful duel is roughly the same as that of attempted flight from the top of a tall tree with a rope tied around your neck. So just take the unopened envelope from the herald, crumple it in your hands and toss it into the fire. It helps if you do this while uttering a dismissive snort or even a boisterous "huzzah!" for best effect. Then as the flames feast upon the details of your upcoming demise, place your hands on your hips and strike a confident pose.

The herald might, at this point, suggest you put on some clothes.

Choose trousers or breeches made of a light, loose fabric, with plenty of room to move. There's nothing quite so embarrassing as having your lunge come up short at the precise moment that your enemy is counterattacking, and he drives his blade deep into your belly just as your seams split at the crotch.

"But wait!" you say. "I haven't done anything wrong! How did I end up in such dire circumstances when I don't even know how to hold a sword properly?"

The herald will laugh brightly, as though firmly of the belief that you're merely jesting, before ushering you out the door and escorting you to the courthouse to meet your *secondier*.

The law in Tristia, observed in all nine Duchies, requires that every duelist be supported by a second—for otherwise, who would go back and forth between you and your opponent to deliver the necessary scathingly droll insults? If you have no one of your acquaintance willing—or able—to fulfill this sacred duty, and you are too poor to hire a suitable candidate, then you can count on the local Lord or Duke to provide a secondier for you. That's right: you live in a country so feckless and corrupt that those same nobles who would gladly stand aside as you starve to death would never, *ever* consider allowing you to be skewered by the pointy end of a blade without a second standing proudly beside you.

Make your way past the twin statues of the Gods of Death and War that guard the double doors leading into the courthouse and through to the large central room littered with exquisite architectural features, none of which you'll notice, for by now your eyes will be fixed on the dueling court itself. The classical form is a simple white circle, roughly ten yards across, however, in these modern times you may instead find yourself in a pentagon or hexagon or whatever shape is deemed to be most blessed by the Gods in that particular Duchy. Once you're done admiring the architecture, take a look at the person standing on the opposite side of the dueling court. This is the moment to remember to clench all the muscles in your lower body to prevent any . . . *accidents*.

Your opponent—likely a highly skilled Knight, or perhaps a foreign mercenary—will smile or grimace, or possibly spit at your feet, and then immediately turn away and pretend to be engaged in a thoroughly witty conversation with a member of the audience. Don't worry too much about this part—they're only doing it to unnerve you.

The clerk of the court will now announce the terms of the duel. You might be tempted to take heart when you hear that this duel *isn't* to the death, but that would be a mistake. Whichever Lord or Lady you offended has almost certainly instructed their champion to first humiliate you, then bloody you, and finally—and with a grand flourish that will bring the audience to their feet, roaring with applause—kill you.

When this happens, you can rest assured that the presiding magistrate will undoubtedly make a great harrumphing noise over this gross violation of the rules, and will immediately fine said Lord or Lady, although that will be roughly equivalent to the cost of the wine in the goblet they'll be drinking while watching you bleed out on the floor.

Not really your best day, is it?

Well, that's for later. For now, take a good, long look at your opponent standing across from you in the dueling court, because this is the part where you learn how to *win*.

Your enemy is almost certainly a great fencer—someone with speed, strength of arm, exceptional balance, lightning reflexes, and nerves of steel. A great fencer spends years studying under the finest masters in the country. You, regrettably, aren't likely to have had the benefit of any of those fine qualities, and there's a good chance that your only fencing master was your best friend when the pair of you were six years old, play-fighting with sticks and dreaming of growing up to be Greatcoats.

But you don't need to be a *fencer* right now; you need to be a *duelist*.

A duelist doesn't care about technique. A duelist won't be walking into that circle hoping to impress the audience or curry favor with their nobles. A duelist cares about one thing only, that most ancient and venerable of axioms: *Put the pointy end of the sword into the other guy first.*

So as the clerk strikes the bell signaling the beginning of the duel and your opponent begins his masterful display of skill to the appreciative *oohs* and *ahs* of the audience, forget about life and death or honor and cowardice; forget about everything except finding that one opportunity—that single moment—when you can push the top three inches of your blade into your opponent's belly.

In Tristia we have a saying: *Deato mendea valus febletta. The Gods give every man a weakness.*

Remember this, and you might just survive the day. In fact, over the years that follow, you might even go on to win other duels. You might even become known as one of the deadliest swordfighters of your generation. Of course, if that does turn out to be the case, then it's equally likely that one day—perhaps even today—that great swordfighter who's about to lose the duel?

It could be you.

CHAPTER TWO
THE SANGUINIST

"You realize you're losing quite badly, Falcio?" Brasti asked, leaning against a column just outside the seven-sided dueling court of the Ducal Palace of Baern.

"Shut up, please," I replied.

My opponent, whom I'd been informed was undefeated in court duels but whose name I'd forgotten, gave me a little smirk as he flicked the point of his smallsword underneath the guard of my rapier. I swung my own blade down in a semicircle to keep him from stabbing my thigh, but at the last instant he evaded my parry by flipping his point back up. He extended his sword arm and pushed off his back leg in a quick lunge. Had there been any justice in the world, he shouldn't have been able to reach me.

"Saint Zaghev's balls," I grunted, the tiny cut burning into my right shoulder: a reprimand for misjudging the distance.

Why do I always let myself get tripped up by smallswords?

Despite the name and the delicately thin blade, smallswords are deceptively long. My opponent's was only a couple of inches shorter than my own rapier, and he'd made up the difference with an extravagantly long lunge of the sort immortalized in the illustrations of the more imaginative fencing manuals.

From the far side of the dueling court Kunciet, Margrave of Gerlac, the rotund, fetid bastard who'd engineered this duel, shouted, "Bravasa!" at his champion. Twenty or so of the Margrave's retainers joined in the cheer, adding a few sprinkles of "Fantisima!," "Dei blessé!," and other misapplied fencing terms.

However much this annoyed me, it is accepted practice for a duelist's supporters to cheer them on—in fact, I was entitled to similar outbursts from my own admirers.

"This Undriel fellow really is remarkably skilled," Kest remarked.

Undriel. That was the bastard's name.

Brasti came to my defense, after a fashion. "It's not Falcio's fault. He's getting old. And slow. Also, I think he might be getting fat. Just look at him—barely four months since he beat Shuran and already he's half the man he once was."

Always nice to have friends nearby in troubled times, I thought, batting at Undriel's blade with a clumsy parry that was testament to my increasing exhaustion.

"Don't distract him," Ethalia said.

I started to glance over to give her a reassuring smile, but instead felt the heel of my right boot slip on the slick floor and stumbled several steps back, trying to catch my balance.

Idiot! Reassure her by not dying.

Undriel and I circled each other for a few seconds, eyeing each other for signs of any growing weaknesses that could be exploited.

Gods, but I'm tired. Why doesn't he look tired?

The sound of someone sipping tea drew everyone's attention: Ossia, the rake-thin, elegantly aged Duchess of Baern was sitting upon her high-backed throne at the head of the courtroom. Aline, heir to the Crown of Tristia, and Valiana, Realm's Protector, sat on either side, perched on considerably smaller chairs, like children made to attend their aunt. Aline periodically looked up at the Duchess in irritation, but Valiana's barely contained fury was reserved entirely for me.

I couldn't really blame her.

What had started as a largely ceremonial event meant to introduce Aline to the various minor nobles of the Duchy had taken an unexpected turn when the Margrave of Gerlac, one of six men hoping to replace the aging and childless Duchess Ossia, took advantage of our presence to launch a legal dispute against the Crown. Through a torturous process of twisted judicial logic, he'd claimed he'd merged his properties with those of the churches on his lands and thus was now—despite still occupying those lands—exempt from paying taxes. He'd even brought in a few token clerics in impressively ornate robes to confirm his story.

Duchess Ossia, ever the diplomat, had elected to defer judgment of the issue to Valiana, who, as Realm's Protector, had patiently listened to every argument, reviewed every document, and then promptly declared the case invalid. Kunciet, as such men do on those rare occasions when they don't get their way, threw a hissy fit. He began by questioning the validity of the verdict, then Valiana's standing as Realm's Protector, and then, right in front of us, started making not-very-subtle threats against Aline.

That was when I took over.

Less than six months ago I'd bled buckets to keep Shuran and his Black Tabards from taking over the damned country. I'd risked not just my own life but those of the people I loved best to save those same Dukes who'd been spending a considerable portion of their spare time trying to have me killed. I'd been beaten, tortured, and brought to the very edge of death, and all of it so that the daughter of my King could one day take her rightful place on the throne.

Did anyone seriously believe that I was going to let some noxious backwater nobleman like Kunciet make public threats against her?

The hells for that.

Undriel made a rather stunning and unexpected dive below my blade, rolling on the ground and coming up on my left side, then skipping away before I could cut him. In the process, he tagged me again, this time on my left shoulder.

"Should've worn your coat, Falcio," Brasti said.

"Shut up," I repeated.

Armor is forbidden in judicial duels, but most legal interpretations limit the prohibition to chain mail or plate. Since our greatcoats are made of leather, albeit with bone plates sewn inside, they've never been considered armor, not in the technical sense. After all, that was part of the design consideration behind the coats in the first place.

So why wasn't I wearing mine? Because Kunciet, Margrave of Gerlac, had declared such protection "cowardly," and because Kest had, through a combination of raised eyebrows and light coughs, apparently agreed with him. *In other words, because I'm an idiot and my friends are trying to kill me.*

A line of red began to stain the left shoulder of my white linen shirt, an almost perfect match to the one on my right. Evidently Undriel was using me as a canvas and wanted to balance his composition.

The son of a bitch is trying to bleed me to death.

Undriel is what we call in the dueling business a sanguinist: a fencer whose primary strategy is to go for little cuts—wounds that sting and bleed and distract you, until you start to slow down without even realizing it. Sanguinists take their time, pulling you apart bit by bit, until they can end the fight with a single, brilliant flourish—they usually go for an artery so that you end by bleeding out spectacularly all over the floor. It can create quite a stunning tableau for the audience.

I hate sanguinists.

The wounds themselves were more annoying than anything else. Later, assuming I didn't die, Ethalia would use one of her almost magical ointments to treat the wound, followed by a sticky salve to seal it. One of the many reasons I should already have asked her to marry me was the gentle way she'd pass her finger over the wound to wipe away the extra salve. That experience was so oddly sensuous it almost made you think getting a few more cuts wouldn't be so bad . . .

I let out an inadvertent and embarrassingly high-pitched yelp as the tip of Undriel's blade scored another nick, this time on the left side of my jaw.

Focus, idiot. He's doing a fine job of bleeding you without your help.

Undriel pressed his advantage in a whirling attack, moving the point of his blade in a figure-eight motion, then suddenly striking out toward me like a snake, only to pull back the instant I tried to parry him.

Dashini, I thought suddenly, barely able to keep myself from fleeing the dueling circle. *He's using* Dashini *tactics.*

Undriel caught the look of fear on my face and, smiling, increased the speed and ferocity of his attack. I swung my own blade in a clumsy counter-pattern to keep him from getting too close, but my heavier weapon made it a tiring exercise on my part. I was sweating now, and not just from exertion.

Stop being a fool! The Dashini are dead, and even if they weren't, there's no way this prancing pony is one of them. He's just practiced their style to throw you off guard.

"So it's true, what I've heard about you," Undriel said. It was the first time he'd spoken and his voice was as relaxed as if he'd just gotten out of bed.

"If what you've heard is that I'm going to knock you on your ass so hard you won't be able to sit a horse for a year, then yes, it's all true." My bravado would have sounded more convincing had my lungs not been pumping like a bellows.

"Rumor has it that since the Lament you wake up screaming every night, begging for the torment to stop."

"I wouldn't know," I said. "I've been having quite a lot of sex lately so I'm usually too tired to remember my dreams."

Why did I say that? I sound like an idiot. Gods, what did Ethalia do to deserve me?

I swung my rapier in a low arc with enough force to smash the bones in Undriel's knee, but he skipped out of its path with the easy grace of a dancer before repeating the Dashini pattern that was so unnerving me.

Why was I letting him get to me? More to the point, how was he so good at doing it?

Pieces of a puzzle started to form in my mind: Undriel was intentionally stretching the duel out for far too long. Normally this wouldn't have been a problem, except that I still tired quickly, the result of the injuries I'd suffered months before. He'd chosen a smallsword, but for the past several years I'd been facing Knights and soldiers who used heavier—and slower—weapons, like warswords and maces. And the Dashini forms, even though they might not be particularly effective when performed with a smallsword, were making me jumpy and clumsy. In other words, he was the perfect opponent to put against me. So what were the odds that Kunciet just *happened* to have a champion at hand who just *happened* to incorporate all these disparate tactics into one unique style?

The bastard's been training for this very fight.

Undriel grinned as if my thoughts were written across my face and came straight for me, and as I stumbled back, struggling to keep out of the way of his swift, dancing attack, the rest of the pieces fell into place. Kunciet hadn't lost his temper today. He didn't care about his damned taxes. This whole case had been nothing more than a pretext for him to pick a fight with the Crown and trick me into accepting an unnecessary duel.

What better way to make your bid to become the next Duke of Baern than by killing off a Greatcoat and defying the Realm's Protector in front of your fellows, all without breaking a single one of the King's Laws?

Better yet, Kunciet was doing it right in front of the current Duchess—a known ally of the heir—while she sat powerless to stop it.

That's how you stake your claim to a Dukedom.

In fact, there was only one way he could possibly make an even stronger case: don't kill just *any* Greatcoat, kill the future Queen's favorite. Kill the First Cantor.

That was me, by the way.

Undriel's smile widened: all the little cuts were starting to slow me down. A single thought went through my head: *I swear, I used to be good at this.*

CHAPTER THREE
THE LARK'S PIROUETTE

I once asked a doctor why it was that time seems to slow down at the exact moment someone is about to kill you. He told me that during moments of extreme danger, a certain organ in the body begins to excrete a fluid called the "vital humor" which increases strength in the limbs and speeds up the body's reactions. This has the effect of making it appear as if time itself has frozen, thus giving the soon-to-be-departed one last chance at survival.

One would think such a miraculous fluid would also focus the mind exclusively on the source of danger, but in my case it had the opposite effect. Even with the point of Undriel's smallsword darting at me, forcing me backward and keeping me off balance as he set me up for the final kill, I couldn't help but notice all the little things going on around me.

Brasti's eyes were narrowed in confusion, which told me that he was only now figuring out that I was actually in trouble. Kest's mouth was open, just a hair's-breadth, as if he'd been about to call out some obscure fencing tactic that might save me, only to realize there wasn't time. I could even see Valiana's hand twitch as though she were about to draw her sword and run to my defense. Ethalia, the woman I loved, the woman to whom I'd jokingly said, "You might as well stick around. This whole silly business will be done in a minute or two!," looked as pale as the dead.

Why hadn't I asked her to leave the courtroom? Why did I accept the damned challenge in the first place? The second we'd arrived in the south I should have picked Ethalia up into my arms, found the nearest boat and set sail for that tiny island she'd told me about a hundred times.

With a doomed man's fervor I beat back Undriel's blade and lunged, once, twice, thrice, each time sure I'd found an opening in his defense, each time proven wrong by his effortless parry, swiftly followed by another light cut to my arm or thigh or chest. I was using up my last reserves of strength just to stay in the fight.

It wasn't enough.

From the corner of my eye I saw Kunciet lean forward, wearing the patient smile of a man who has spent years tending a garden and is now watching the first rose bloom. His retainers began patting each other on the back. Ossia, Duchess of Baern, looked disappointed.

Well, I'm disappointed too, Your Grace. I was about to lose, and everyone knew it—everyone except Aline. Unlike the others, she watched me impassively, without the slightest widening of the eyes or trembling of the lips, as my opponent worked me like a puppet around the dueling circle.

She doesn't see what's happening, I realized, horrified. *She's seen me fight Knights and bully boys and even Dashini assassins and now she thinks I can't be beaten.*

That's the problem with people who aren't duelists: they don't understand that eventually, everyone loses.

The vaguely metallic taste on my tongue—I'd bitten my own lip— brought me back to the fight. *No. I won't die like this, not in front of the people I love. I swear, all you worthless Gods and Saints, I'm going to find a way to win, and then, after a suitable convalescence, I'm asking Ethalia to marry me.*

Undriel, no doubt promised a huge reward if he killed me, was ready to perform his grand finale. He delivered a quick cut against my right wrist—not deep, but enough to make me loosen my grip on my rapier—and followed up with a sudden hard beat of his sword's crossbar against my blade, sending my rapier flying up into the air above me.

I started to reach out with my left hand in a desperate attempt to grab the hilt as Undriel prepared a high slash meant to sever the artery in my neck. A thrust to the chest would have been a surer target, but it would have lacked the more artistic final flourish of a blood spray.

Arrogant bastard.

I kicked out at his knee, which he shifted out of reach, but that distraction gave me a precious moment to catch my falling rapier in my left hand even as Undriel scored another, deeper, cut against my right forearm. I could already feel it going numb from the pain.

Great, now I'm going to have to fight left-handed.

Having been deprived of his first attempt at a spectacularly stylish kill, Undriel dropped the guard of his weapon low and brought the blade straight up in a vertical line.

A lark's pirouette? He's going to end me with a fucking lark's pirouette!

The flowery name masks a deadly and precarious technique. The attacker leaps past his opponent, whirling his blade in the process—not to slash, but to parry the counterattack as he comes around the other side. He completes the move by landing in a perfect reverse-lunge, his rear foot and arm thrown back as the tip of his sword drives deep into his victim's kidney.

The lark's pirouette is devastating to behold: it's what you do when you want to show the world that you're a true master of the blade—but it's a move you use *only* when you're absolutely sure that your opponent has exhausted all his strength. Undriel could have killed me any number of simple, clean ways, but he wanted to break me first.

That realization sent a surge of anger through me. Death I could have lived with—but this? *You come here to humiliate the Greatcoats, to threaten the girl I've sworn to put on the throne, and you want to make a performance of it? You forgot the first rule of the sword, you son of a bitch.*

I fought the instinct to fall back and instead did something Kest and I used to practice as boys: I counter-windmilled *into* Undriel's blade. As he spun clockwise while leaping past me, I turned the other way, letting him knock my point out of the way even as I readied my free right hand to grab his blade. It was an outlandish, desperate tactic, but I was, at that moment, an outlandish, desperate man.

As we moved around each other like dancers on a stage, Undriel, suspecting what I was doing, began to pull his weapon away before I could get a solid grip on it, cutting into the palm of my hand in the process—of course, this is why most masters tell you *never* to counter a lark's pirouette this way. That's why the second part of my maneuver was to toss my own sword on the floor right between my opponent's legs as he was spinning. The hilt clattered against the marble and the blade became caught between Undriel's left calf and his right thigh, entangling his feet. He was already midway through his turn and it was too late for him to catch his balance. His eyes caught mine and went wide.

It was my turn to smile.

I stepped into him, bending my knees for leverage and holding his blade tightly in my bleeding right hand as I pressed my left against his chest and shoved with every last ounce of strength that remained in my limbs.

Undriel fell backward, his feet still caught in my blade, his attempts to regain his balance only making his situation worse. His desperate stumbling took him all the way outside the circle until he bashed the back of his head against one of the marble columns ringing the dueling court.

A satisfying crack echoed throughout the room, followed by the heart-warming sight of Undriel sliding, ever so slowly, down the length of the column until his bottom hit the floor with a loud thump. The blow to his head wouldn't be enough to kill him, but it was more than sufficient to draw a collective wince from the audience, followed soon thereafter by peals of laughter.

I took the deepest breath I could manage and let myself drop to my knees. I had, by the skin of my teeth, not only evaded a humiliating death that would have embarrassed the Crown and called into question the vaunted abilities of the Greatcoats, I had even defeated the Margrave's champion without killing him—and I'd done it in a way that would leave people believing I was the superior swordsman and had simply been playing along until it no longer amused me.

All of that would have been extremely gratifying, if only I wasn't absolutely positive that Undriel was better than I was. I had eked out the narrowest possible victory thanks to a childhood trick and an unexpected stroke of luck. Without those things, I would have been dead.

My name is Falcio val Mond, First Cantor of the King's Greatcoats. Not long ago I was one of the finest swordsmen in the world.

These days? Not so much.

CHAPTER FOUR

THE HEALERS

The funny thing about a duel is how little attention is paid to the opponents after it's over. Once one man drops, what follows is a furor of activity as audience members pay up or try to slip out before their creditors can catch up with them. Some cheer and boast of their predictions as if they themselves had fought the duel while others gripe and spit in their cups over the poor performances of the duelists.

And this is the point when the opponents, only now realizing just how badly they've been hurt, let forth a wide variety of moaning sounds as they crawl toward anything that looks remotely like a chair. Doctors or priests (depending on which is more urgently required) rush in to begin their work, but what I want most in those moments is for Ethalia to come and treat my wounds. However, the duelist for the Crown is always examined first by the royal physician, a heavyset man of middle years named Histus with whom I shared exactly one thing: we both hated him having to treat me.

"Are you sure you won this duel?" he muttered as he began prodding at my wounds.

I flinched. "Are you sure you don't work for the other guys?"

He brought out a flask of cleansing alcohol and poured it liberally over the cuts. "You know, I'm going to end up amputating one of your limbs if you keep this up."

"My wounds aren't infected."

"I never said it would be on medical grounds."

I glanced over at Undriel, lying on the floor next to one of the columns. Usually there's a sort of bond that forms between duelists when neither has ended up dead. I didn't expect that to be the case this time.

A number of Kunciet's retainers—notably, not the Margrave of Gerlac himself—were standing over Undriel, making noises of great concern, although not, as I might have expected, in reference to his personal well-being. Instead, I heard, "Do you think he'll *ever* be a champion again?" answered with, "Can't see how, not after *that* beating." This was followed by sage comments such as, "Lost his touch, he has. Knew it the second I saw him enter the court."

Maybe I was wrong about not feeling a shared bond.

Kunciet was busying himself with a different tradition: the one in which the losing plaintiff immediately starts hurling accusations of foul play and cheating. He launched into a steady stream of denouncements that began with the ungentlemanly conduct on my part (Laying a hand on an opponent during a duel? *Improper!*) and followed up with a charge that the dueling circle was not perfectly circular, descending into a rather convoluted accusation of dark sorcery involving Valiana, Aline, Kest, Brasti, and me performing some rather daring feats of sexual prowess as part of a ritual dedicated to Saint Zaghev-who-sings-for-tears.

The clerics, no doubt worrying that their financial arrangement with the Margrave was about to become null and void, were vigorously backing him up.

I thought about challenging the fat bastard then and there, until I realized even he could probably take me down at that precise moment. Fortunately, there was someone in the room even angrier than me.

"One more word from you, Margrave," Valiana said, her voice as cold as the North Wind, "especially one word aimed at the heir to the throne of Tristia, and I swear it will be you and me in the dueling circle next."

Kunciet made a sound that was probably meant to be a scoff but which ended up something considerably less dignified.

The thing you have to remember about Valiana is, yes, she's young, and yes, she was raised to be beautiful and vapid in equal measure. But that was *then*. She's long since shed those trappings and revealed herself to be smart, daring, and more than ready to lay down her life to protect Aline and defend Tristia. More importantly, despite the new title and the responsibilities that went with it, anyone who looked into her eyes would see she was a Greatcoat to the bone.

Kunciet saw that too.

Nobles don't like to be publicly embarrassed; when their fellows see them as weak it tends to create problems for them. As far as I could see, the Margrave's only hope now was for support from the Duchess Ossia . . .

. . . who looked up at him, her face expressionless. "Lovely to see you, Margrave," she said, sipping tea from her beautifully painted porcelain cup. "Your visits are always so diverting."

"*Outrageous*," Kunciet said finally, and apparently that one particular word was acceptable to Valiana because she allowed the Margrave and his retainers and clerics to withdraw from the courtroom.

Two of them were supporting the dazed Undriel until the Margrave growled at them, "Leave the bastard outside with the rest of the garbage. Let him crawl back to the filthy village I found him in."

I felt a brief sympathy for my former opponent. He'd find no other patron now; this was farewell to any chance of wealth and advancement. I imagined he was going to be a pretty unpleasant man to be around from here on out.

Kunciet scowled at me as he reached the double doors, but I'd taken more than my share of cuts already so I felt I'd earned the right to deliver one of my own. "Be sure to tell your friends, Margrave."

"Tell them what?" he spat.

"Tell them the Greatcoats are coming."

The word "outrageous" having been successful for him the first time, the Margrave of Gerlac elected to use it several more times on his way out.

"That man really needs to work on his vocabulary," Brasti observed blithely. "You can't properly storm off just repeating the same word over and over. He could have at least tossed in an 'unspeakable' or perhaps 'unpardonable.'"

"'Execrable'?" Kest suggested.

"'Aberrant' has more flair," Brasti countered.

"I think you mean 'abhorrent.'"

"Which one's 'aberrant' then?"

"The one that means something else."

Brasti tried to look indignant. "Fine. Can we settle on 'inconceivable'?"

"Now you're just being silly."

"Is it too late to bring Undriel back in and just let him kill me?" I groaned, pulling away from Histus, who was doing an admirable job of making me painfully aware of each and every cut on my body. Finally I spotted Ethalia, pushing through the crowd toward me.

The *Bardatti* tell us life is sweeter in those precious minutes after narrowly escaping death. In my experience, however, "life" during that particular moment mostly smells like sweat, drying blood and . . . other things. Ethalia, though? She was the exception. I felt a sudden desperate desire to hold her, to sink my face in her long black hair and breathe her in. Had my shirt not been covered in blood, and had I not been having the greatest difficulty standing, I would have run to her. Fortunately, she came to me.

Everything about Ethalia is in the eyes. They're pale blue, like the line where the sky meets the sea on the horizon, and beautiful, of course, but that's beside the point. It's the way she *looks* at me. When she first sees me there's this immediate flash of joy that brightens her irises, an effect so profound it completely contradicts all those people who firmly believe the world would be a better place if I were dead. Then comes the harder part, when she sees the results of my most recent foolishness. I see the first tears forming in the corners of her eyes, then concern and sorrow give way to determination as her eyes narrow and start moving from bruise to cut to scrape as she determines where to begin.

"Thank you, Doctor Histus," she said, picking up a chair and bringing it to me. "I'll take care of our patient now."

Histus had an unrelenting disdain for the training Ethalia had received in the Order of Merciful Light. Like far too many people, he considered her order to be nothing more than a brothel with high-priced prostitutes. I suspect it didn't help that Ethalia was a far better healer than he would ever be.

"Try not to give him an incurable infectious disease," Histus grumbled, closing his bag.

"I'll make sure his wounds are properly cleaned, Doctor."

"That's not what I meant," Histus said, and walked away.

Ethalia gave a laugh. "You can't fault the man's sense of humor."

"I can fault it a great deal," I countered.

She sat me down and helped me remove my shirt, then took out a dozen blue jars from her bag. They all looked the same to me, but I knew from bitter experience that they weren't. She set them in a line on the floor. "I know what he meant, Falcio. Do you think there's anything that Histus could say to me that I haven't heard since I was thirteen years old?"

Thirteen years old. Saints. What kind of world makes a—?

"Stop," she said. "You'll open your wounds again if you keep tensing your shoulders like that." She selected one jar, examined it, then exchanged it for the one next to it.

"I wish you'd give some of these to Histus. His salves don't do me any good at all."

"I'm afraid they wouldn't work very well for him." She scooped out a generous amount, closed her eyes and spread the salve on a large cut on my stomach that I hadn't even noticed during the fight but which had been stinging like a devil. "The salve is a bridge between the healer's heart and the patient's wound." The instant her fingers touched my stomach a surprisingly warm sensation spread along the cut, taking a good deal of the pain away.

"You know what I think?" I said, a little uncomfortable about how I was feeling, especially with so many people in the room. "I think you're making that up. You just have better drugs than Histus!"

"Shush," she said, "or I'll use the strongest of the salves."

"What does it do?" I asked.

Abruptly she reached her arms around me, buried her face into my neck and held me. "It makes a man come to his senses, Falcio," she said, crying softly. "It makes him admit that he's hurt, that he's haunted by memories of the past. It makes him stop trying to get himself killed just to prove he isn't scared. I'm not sure your foolish heart would survive it."

I reached up awkwardly with my right hand, holding her head as I ignored the pain in my shoulder. *Now, you idiot,* I told myself, *stop hesitating. Stop finding excuses. Ask her to marry you.*

I swear the words were about to leave my lips, but unfortunately, that's when the Realm's Protector's not inconsiderable patience came to an end.

CHAPTER FIVE

THE WOUNDED

"First Cantor," Valiana said, her voice flat as she approached us.

It's never a good sign when she addresses me as "First Cantor." I rose unsteadily to my feet. "Realm's Protector?"

Before Valiana could get to me, Aline ran in front of her and came in close to hug me. "You're getting a little slow, Falcio," she said.

I wrapped my arms around her. "I could've used a throwing knife in there, you know. Where were you when I needed you?"

Aline stepped back and gave a decent imitation of shock and dismay. "Falcio val Mond! You would ask your future Queen to help you cheat in a duel?"

"The First Cantor would never cheat in a duel," another voice said, with all the assured confidence that only a twelve-year-old boy can muster. Tommer, heir to the Ducal throne of Rijou, walked over to join us. In recent months he'd taken to wearing a long leather coat that looked suspiciously like my own, much to the chagrin of his father. Duke Jillard was at that moment chatting with Duchess Ossia; he glanced over briefly, just long enough to convey his ambivalence about the outcome of my duel.

"Falcio cheats all the time," Aline said, a little dismissively.

"Now you listen to me," I said. "I'm the First Cantor of the Great-coats and therefore a true magistrate and it's my considered legal opinion that it would be entirely proper for you to have tossed me a knife. Maybe even two or three."

"That," Aline said, grinning, "is probably why people aren't very keen to have the Greatcoats administer the King's Laws anymore, don't you think?"

I gave a mock growl and gently pushed her away. "Don't you have lessons in maritime geography or some such thing?" Aline winked and curtsied before backing away, taking Tommer with her. She'd done what she'd come to do, which was to delay Valiana long enough to give her time to calm down before starting on me. It was a nice thought. I felt Ethalia's hand slip into my own, both for support, and as a reminder that I should keep my temper.

"Your third duel in less than a month, First Cantor," Valiana said, and pressed her lips together so tightly that you might never have known that at one point she'd actually looked up to me. "Not once have you sought out my counsel, never mind my approval, before risking the reputation of the Greatcoats over a petty grudge."

Brasti stepped between us. "Now, sweetling, don't blame Falcio. The Margrave had the right to demand trial by combat in his appeal of your decision. Under the King's Third Law of Property we had no choice but to grant—"

"No, you idiot," she said, infuriated, "it's not the King's Third Law o—"

"Perhaps this is a conversation for a later time?" Kest suggested.

"No," Valiana said. "No. If I'm going to be forced to deal with the Crown's own magistrates fouling up my every effort to get the nobles under control then we're at least going to get the names of the damned Laws right!" She turned on Brasti. "The King's *Fifth* Law of Property deals with appeals. The King's *Third* Law governs agreements for sale and trade."

Brasti backed up a step. "Well, now you're just being—"

"Furthermore, the King's Fifth Law *doesn't* grant the Margrave of Gerlac the right to trial by combat. It only says he can request it,

and *only* in the event that there is insufficient evidence with which
to demonstrate the right of the case in either direction. I don't suppose you noticed when the Crown presented *three hours* of evidence
proving Kunciet had been withholding his taxes illegally?"

"Ah," Brasti said, "it's possible I wasn't paying attention during
that part."

It was Kest's turn to intercede. "There's still an argument to be
made that—"

"Don't *you* start," Valiana said. "Do you really think I'm so stupid
that I can't see how this works?" She pointed at me. "He goes off and
does something incredibly foolish, and the rest of you try to deflect
me until I'm forced into doing something of actual consequence for
the Kingdom."

Brasti grinned. "So it's working then?"

"*Kunciet had no case*," Valiana said to me, almost despairingly.
"There was no *need* for this duel. If you'd lost, then every other
nobleman in Tristia could have started making the same deals with
their churches to avoid paying taxes."

"Also, Falcio might be dead," Kest interjected.

"That possibility is bothering me less and less," Valiana said.

Darriana emerged from the shadows and said, "Maybe we should
be asking why the so-called 'greatest swordsman in the world' isn't
taking on these idiotic duels?"

"Easily answered," Kest replied, holding up his right arm, showing the stump where his hand used to be. "I would have lost."

It was a surprisingly effective way to stop the conversation. No
one wanted to ask the question *why?*, because by rights, Kest should
still have been the finest swordsman in the country. He'd spent years
perfecting his ambidextrous coordination—hells, half the time we'd
been in fights for our lives he'd fought left-handed just to stay in
practice. So why was he so unsure of himself now, just because he'd
lost his hand? It was strange: it wasn't just that his fighting skills were
off, more like he was in pain every time he held a sword. But every
time we tried to talk to him about it he shut us up by saying he "just
needed time."

Valiana turned back to me, her eyes betraying both fear and desperation. "I'm hanging on by my fingernails trying to get the nobles to accept the reinstatement of the King's Laws, Falcio. You've got to stop letting them goad you into chasing symbolic victories; it just makes them want to see us fail even more."

I shrugged, which proved to be a mistake since it made all those little cuts scream at me in protest. "Symbolic victories are important. Men like Kunciet need to learn that they can't—"

"Oh, forget it," she said, and started to walk away. "You win."

I felt horribly uneasy at my apparent victory. "Valiana, the other nobles will think twice now about trying to—"

"No!" she said furiously, spinning back to me, "no, *they won't.* Maybe I can't stop you doing these reckless, foolish things, but I *can* stop you from pretending this had anything to do with the Law. This is just your damned need to show everyone how tough the Greatcoats are."

"He threatened Aline—"

"In fact, he didn't *actually* threaten Aline. He said, 'the safety of a fragile monarch depends on the goodwill of the Gods and the nobility.'"

"Couldn't that be interpreted as a subtle threat?" Kest asked.

"Of course it was a bloody threat," Valiana replied. "It's the same kind of threat that every Duke and Duchess tosses around during every council meeting. It's *politics.* It's what they do."

"Well, then," I said. "Now they can do it a little less."

"How many of the people who don't like Aline do you plan on killing, Falcio?" All the anger was gone from her voice, and I paused a long time before answering. I thought back to all the nobles who had clapped and cheered when the army had come to arrest King Paelis in preparation for his execution.

"All of them," I said. Her jaw tightened and she opened her mouth to speak but then she stopped. "Say what you want to say," I told her.

"Fine. In the four months since the Ducal Concord, those few Greatcoats who have returned have been unable to restore the Rule of Law to the country. People are losing faith, and you—"

A spark of anger lit in my belly, making my wounds hurt. "You think I don't know that? You think I don't spend my nights trying to find a way to put a stop to it?"

Valiana matched me, fire for fire. "I think that's *all* you think about! I think you believe that if you can fight just one more duel, put down just one more Viscount or Margrave or Lord's champion, then maybe, just *maybe* you can prove the Greatcoats are still relevant. You've got Nehra and the Bardatti running all over Tristia singing songs, telling people 'the Greatcoats are coming'—is that what you mean by it? Is that what you want people to think?"

I wasn't sure how to reply, but Valiana was already striding away. This had become something of a pattern between us lately.

"Falcio . . ." Kest began.

I looked at him and then at Brasti. "Go," I said, and the two left to see if there was a way to smooth things over—until the next time I screwed up.

"I must say, First Cantor," Duke Jillard said, walking toward me, "I'm surprised you went to all the trouble of saving the country from civil war if your plan was to start a new one all by yourself."

I sighed, feeling suddenly very tired. "Is there something you would like to say to me, Your Grace?"

I expected another self-satisfied remark from him, but instead his expression turned deadly serious. "The girl is right, Falcio: there are five Dukes left alive, all of whom agreed to your choice of Realm's Protector on condition that you restore the Rule of Law to the country. Did you really expect to do that with just a handful of Greatcoats and the occasional fit of pique?" Before I could reply, he glanced back to the dais. "And now, if you'll excuse me, I believe Duchess Ossia and I have much to discuss."

A wave of nausea threatened to overtake me, and I remembered that it was never a good idea to stand around for too long if you've been bleeding from half a dozen wounds. Ethalia tried to get me to sit back down, but I couldn't: Darriana was still standing there, which meant there was one more part of this ritual left.

She launched straight in with, "If you weren't half-dead already, I think I'd kill you here and now."

Darri's recent protectiveness toward Valiana was something I couldn't pretend to fully understand. Was it simply admiration, or guilt for having betrayed her to the Dashini Unblooded, when Heryn had come perilously close to killing Valiana? Whatever the reason, Darriana appeared to have decided she would repay any real or imagined harm done to her tenfold.

In my case, that meant abusing me publicly until she ran out of synonyms for "idiot" and "coward."

I leaned a hand on the chair, feeling as though a strong breeze would send me flying. "Right, let's get this over with."

"No," Ethalia said, which took me by surprise, and I nearly lost my balance. Ethalia had only slightly more tolerance for bickering than she did for dueling, but it was utterly unlike her to interfere in these matters. She gently but firmly pushed me back down on the chair and began the lengthy process of bandaging my cuts.

Saints, just how bad are my wounds?

"No?" Darriana asked. "Has our precious Sister of Mercy decided at last to become involved in affairs of state?"

"It's enough, Darriana," Ethalia said absently, even as she placed a new length of white fabric over the cut on my belly. "I understand that these are difficult times. I understand that you want to protect Valiana, but Falcio is injured, so I'm going to have to insist that you stop threatening him."

"And if I were to refuse?"

"I would become displeased, Darriana. That should be enough."

Darri gave out a dismissive, almost barking laugh. "Well, now, I wouldn't want to earn the displeasure of a benighted whore of Saint-whoever-the-hell-cares. Perhaps you'd like to go a few rounds in the circle?"

All right, that's too much. "Darriana, shut your—"

Sounding perfectly placid, Ethalia said, "It's probably best not to make idle threats while standing in a dueling court."

Darriana's eyes went wide, no doubt as shocked as I was. "Is that so? Look around you: thousands have died in courtrooms like this one. How many duels do you have to your name?"

"None," Ethalia conceded. She pinned the bandage on my shoulder before turning to face Darriana. "So I suppose I'm due for at least one, don't you think?"

Of everything that had happened that day, nothing had terrified me as much as this. "Could I respectfully ask that neither of you kill the other until my wounds are dressed?" I said, as firmly as I could manage.

"Shush, darling," Ethalia said. "The women are speaking now."

"You'd do it, wouldn't you?" Darriana asked incredulously. "You'd accept a duel from me?" For the first time since I'd met her, she looked genuinely uncomfortable. "You fool—you don't even own a sword!"

"I imagine that will make the outcome all the more embarrassing for you, won't it?"

The two of them stared at each other as I sat there, dizzy and confused, convinced there was something I should be doing and yet utterly baffled by what that might be. I saw Darriana's hand move to the sword at her side and reached down for my own—I'd have to take her quickly, before she drew, otherwise I didn't think I'd last a single exchange with her.

Then Darriana stopped and said, "Some other time, perhaps. Once you've found yourself a weapon."

She waited for a reply but got none, and having lost whatever battle of wills had just taken place, she left the room while Ethalia, as if nothing at all untoward had happened, picked up another length of bandage and began wrapping my other shoulder.

"Well, you're just full of surprises, aren't you?" I said.

She smiled. "I'm inscrutable, Falcio. It goes with being a Sister of Mystery."

"I thought you were a Sister of *Mercy*?"

She kissed me on the cheek. "I can be more than one thing."

It was her way of telling me to leave the matter be, and for a few moments, as she finished dressing my wounds, I did. In the end, though, I couldn't let it rest. "I'm still not . . . since when do you go around challenging former Dashini assassins?"

"I wasn't challenging her," Ethalia replied calmly. "I was setting boundaries for her."

"*Boundaries?* You're talking about her as if she were Aline's age! Darriana's a grown woman—and a *really* dangerous one!"

"She's a grown woman who's spent most of her life as a tool, used first by the King and later by the Dashini. She has no idea how to behave around normal people, how to be close to them, how to disagree with them. She's a grown woman who never had the chance to grow up." She paused. "All of you treat her like she's some kind of deadly weapon, Falcio, so that's how she behaves. She's hurt and she's sad and she's lonely."

I thought about some of the late-night encounters Brasti had bragged about. "She never seems all that lonely to me."

Ethalia frowned. "Brasti treats it like a game with her, so she does the same, but until she learns to respect herself, a game is all there will be between them."

I tried to work my way through the logic of her words, but relationships had never been my strong point. "So you challenged her *for her own benefit*?"

"For her, for you. For everyone." She knelt down in front of me and I could see the discomfort in her eyes. It had genuinely hurt her to force Darriana to back down. "You are all so wounded, Falcio, inside and out, and it's making you all so hard you've become as brittle as glass. Can't you see that? You all fight so hard to protect this country, but there's no one to protect you."

"You think that's your responsibility?" I should probably have seen that ages ago.

"I don't have a sword, Falcio. I can't play at political intrigue with those who would destroy this country for their own gain. All I can do is wait until each battle is fought and then try to heal the wounds before—"

Whatever she was going to say next was lost in a rush of shouts and thumping of boots and clanging of weapons and a sudden clangor as a bell rang out. Two dozen or more Ducal guards raced into the courtroom, and my rapier was in my hand before they'd gotten within twenty feet of us.

"What in hells is going on?" Valiana said, running back with Kest, Brasti, and Darriana close behind.

"Get Valiana out of here!" I shouted to the others, then I told Ethalia, "You have to go with them."

Her face was suddenly very pale. "Falcio . . . something's wrong. Something is . . ." Before she could finish she fell against me, and in my weakened state I started tumbling backward.

Kest caught me, and then took Ethalia from my arms.

"What's happened to her?" I demanded.

"She's breathing normally," he said, laying her down on the dais. "She appears to be in some sort of . . . I don't know, some sort of trance."

Most of the Baern guards took up positions standing between us and the double doors that led to the chaos outside. Antrim Thomas, one of the only Greatcoats who'd returned, now captain of the Aramor Guards, entered the room and pushed through the men of Baern to address Valiana. "This palace's defenses have been breached, Realm's Protector. We have to get you to safety before—"

"The heir," I interrupted, "where is Aline?"

"She's already secure," he replied. His eyes went to Valiana, as though he didn't want to have to be the one to explain how.

"She's in the carriage with her guards and they'll have already fled the palace," Valiana said. "We have protocols in place to both keep her safe and to get her away should we come under attack."

"Why in hells wasn't I part of those discussions?" I asked.

She looked uncomfortable. There was something she wasn't telling me. "Because it's not your damned place to know, Falcio."

"How many men, damn you?" I asked Antrim, then looked at the Ducal guardsmen. "And how in the name of Saint Marta-who-shakes-the-lion did they get through the gates and you not notice until now?"

"That's just it, Falcio," Antrim replied. "I don't think—"

"Just tell us how many men," Kest said.

Antrim Thomas, the King's Memory, hadn't asked to be captain of Aline's guards, but when I'd ordered him to do so he hadn't flinched. He'd been in fights just as hard and deadly as any of us and I'd never seen him back down. That's why I felt a chill in my gut when I saw the confusion and fear in Antrim's eyes as he said, "That's just it. There is only one intruder, but none of us can stop her."

CHAPTER SIX
THE UNINVITED GUEST

We waited inside the courtroom, listening to the shouts of soldiers echoing their way through the halls.

"If it's Trin . . ." Brasti began.

"Shut up, Brasti," Kest said.

"I'm just saying, if this is Trin then I'm quitting the Greatcoats. Three hundred laws in this country, there ought to be one says she can't try to kill us more than once a year."

"Whoever it is, they're coming this way," Kest said.

"Realm's Protector," Antrim hissed, "you must go now—use the door behind the magistrate's throne. We can't ensure your safety if—"

Valiana drew her sword. "I won't protect the realm by running away."

"Now who's going in for reckless symbolic gestures?" I asked. I looked at Brasti, who was already drawing his bow. He hopped up onto the magistrate's throne and balanced with one foot on either wooden arm. From there he could fire over the top of the heads of the guards in front of us if it came to it.

More guards poured into the room, only to be felled before the invading force—I could now clearly make out our foe, but what I saw made no sense to me.

The intruder, who had apparently managed to get around the two dozen scouts patrolling the roads and riverside around Ossia's palace, who must have walked right by the crossbowmen and spearmen who stood at the gates and upon the walls, who was even now knocking down the guards who protected the halls and rooms of the palace, was a thin woman in a filthy, tattered dress with pale, matted hair plastered to her face.

"Is that Trin?" Brasti asked, squinting. "I can't tell."

The woman took a step toward us. She was at least thirty feet away, and even now guards were still rushing in the room behind her, trying to grab at her. Whenever anyone got close, she lifted her hand and with the barest twitch of her fingers sent them sprawling to their knees.

I pushed past the men in front of us and stood before her, maybe twenty feet away. "Who are you," I asked, "and why have you come here?"

As she took a single, small step forward, I said firmly, "You need to stop. You need to stop now and answer my questions before—"

The woman made no reply.

Out of the corner of my eye I saw Antrim signal and two of his men ran past me, their swords drawn, and attempted to cut her down. Before their blades could reach the apex of their motion both men had dropped their blades and fallen to their knees.

"I don't know what kind of magic you're using to prevent the guards from striking you with their swords," I said, "but it's not going to work on arrows." I was *really* hoping it wasn't. "You need to stop. Now."

Still there was no reply. She took another step forward. Now she was less than ten feet away from me.

"Whoever you are, I beg you, *stop*. Brasti doesn't miss, and from this distance he could hit you with both his eyes closed. Do not come any closer."

Kest came to stand next to me. He stared as her and said, his voice low, "Falcio, I think there's something on her face, underneath her hair. It looks like . . . is that iron?"

I peered at her myself and caught a glint of *something* . . . some kind of mask or helm underneath the hair plastered to her face. For an instant I hesitated, remembering the wooden frames Trin had bound to her victims' faces to control them from afar. Was this some new form of that same damnable magic?

Another step closer.

I no longer had time to find out. "Brasti," I said, "the next time she moves, put an arrow through her heart."

"I have her," he said.

The woman raised her foot to take another step, but before it landed on the floor in front of her the whistle of an arrow filled the courtroom, swiftly followed by a second, and a third.

I waited for the intruder to fall, but she didn't.

Brasti had missed.

I turned to Antrim. "Get the Realm's Protector out of here. Now!"

"No—!" Valiana started to protest, but disobeying the Realm's Protector would be easier to live with than letting her be killed. Antrim signaled to his men with an odd gesture of his hand that I didn't recognize—I'd have to investigate that later, I reminded myself—and two of them immediately grabbed Valiana by the arms and began to lead her toward the back of the courtroom, where a single door led into the halls of the palace. Two more walked swiftly alongside them, covering Valiana with their bodies in case anyone intended firing a weapon at her.

"Apparently Antrim's worked out a few new protocols," Kest commented, his blade in his left hand and a look of searing pain in his eyes.

"Oh, now you'll fight," Brasti said from behind us, his voice tighter than usual. He wasn't used to missing his target. I heard the creak of his bow and once again the sound of arrows flying past us one after the other. "Something's wrong, Falcio. I can't hit her. I'm aiming right at her, but—"

"Maybe your aim is just off today," Darriana said, and I saw a blur as she leaped past me, her thin-bladed sword high in the air, point down, coming in for a strike that would drive the tip right through the intruder's skull. At the last instant, all the strength seemed to flee her body and she went sailing past, like a doll flung by an angry child, and crashed against the wall of the courtroom before slumping to the floor.

Antrim shouted, an order I didn't make out, and he and the remaining Ducal guardsmen rushed the intruder—and once again she raised her hand slightly and they fell to the ground.

There were more than three dozen bodies in the room, and only Kest, Brasti and I were still standing.

And the intruder.

"Ossia's guards appear to have decided on a nap," Brasti said.

I looked at the men on the floor and only then realized they weren't unconscious—in fact, they hadn't even fallen, not really. They were on their knees, bowing low before the woman who had just singlehandedly invaded a once-all-but-impregnable Ducal palace.

The woman took another step.

"Falcio, what do we do?" Kest asked as a powerful compulsion to kneel started pushing us to the ground. The impulse to give up, to . . . *accept* . . . was overwhelming. But this woman, whoever or whatever she was, had forgotten one thing about us.

I forced myself to hold my ground, lifted my rapier, and said, "We're the Greatcoats, Lady. We don't fucking bow to anyone."

Stay on your feet, I screamed at my unresponsive body. *Do. Not. Kneel.*

Despite my best efforts, my knees were beginning to buckle. I strained against the force, whatever it was, with every ounce of will, but still I saw the woman growing taller while I, ever so slowly, was bending down. In the periphery of my vision, I could see Brasti and Kest losing the battle too.

I tried to push past the feeling, which was now becoming oddly familiar to me. *I will not bow before you, whoever you are.*

The woman's hand came up a little higher and now I saw a tremble that I didn't think had been there before. I felt the pressure increase, and I lost another inch in the fight. I tried to change from resisting the pressure to kneel to simply throwing myself at her, but that didn't work either, though the shaking in the woman's hand was definitely increasing.

She took another step toward me and the pressure became unbearable. My knees were half bent, and I was slowly losing my balance.

It's too much, I thought, unable even to keep my head up. *If she gets past me, she'll walk right through the palace to wherever they're keeping Aline.*

I heard first one thump and then a second as first Brasti and then Kest fell to their knees.

She'll do whatever it is she's come to do and no one will be able to stop her.

Drops of blood dripped onto the floor in front of me and I realized I was straining so hard that I'd reopened my wounds.

No! I screamed silently. *I swore an oath to protect that girl. You don't get to her without getting past me first.*

With an effort that couldn't have been any harder had my tongue been crushed under the weight of an anvil, I said, "Greatcoats. Don't. Kneel."

The force increased even more and I felt myself beginning to collapse—and then, all at once, the pressure disappeared—it just vanished, not from any surge of will on my part but because something had at last broken in the intruder. She took a stumbling step toward me and I nearly skewered her with my blade before I realized she wasn't trying to attack me—she was falling to the ground herself.

She landed hard on her knees in front of me and then fell sideways and rolled onto her back. Some of the hair slid away from her face and I could now see the gray-black iron mask she was wearing. There were no slots through which I could see her features. I approached her slowly, carefully, my rapier still ready.

"Who are you?" I asked, my voice unusually weak. I leaned over her and swept the rest of her hair back and saw that the mask had been partly broken off, one of the iron bolts attached to a second half that wrapped around the back of her head sheared off.

You don't put on something like this by choice.

Antrim walked unsteadily toward me. "Falcio, you don't look so good."

"Help me get it off," I said, kneeling awkwardly before the woman on the ground. "She wasn't wearing this for protection . . . It's some kind of—" I tried pulling at the straps, but they were held fast. There didn't appear to be any clasps to turn to remove the bolts. I wiped my hands against my shirt so that I could get a better grip but they came away slick and wet and red. *I'm bleeding,* I thought stupidly.

Whatever strength fear and fury had brought me was gone now and I fell onto my side. My face was not far from the woman's and I could see there were small cuts all over her, visible beneath the torn fabric of her tattered dress.

"Someone get that damned doctor back in here!" Brasti shouted.

"The mask," I muttered. "Get the mask off."

I didn't think anyone had heard me, but Kest was raising his heavy warsword in his left hand. He brought it down with stunning force, and for a second I expected to see it driven straight through the mask, but instead, he'd severed the head of one of the iron bolts holding it in place. He did it a second time and I reached out and pulled the mask from her face.

Her face was so tired, so full of pain, that I almost didn't recognize her.

"Who in the name of Saint Shiula-who-bathes-with-beasts is she?" Brasti asked, waiting for the command to fire again.

As gently as I could, I placed my hand upon her cheek. "Not Shiula," I whispered, "Birgid. Birgid-who-weeps-rivers."

At the sound of her name, her eyelids fluttered opened and she reached a trembling hand to cover my own. "We are met once again, man of valor," she said, her voice incongruously beautiful, musical.

Then she coughed, and a trickle of blood escaped her lips. "I have failed, Falcio."

"Failed at what? Who did this to you?"

But her wounds overcame her and her eyes closed. I felt my own injuries begin to steal the last shreds of consciousness from me, but a single question pulled at my thoughts: who had the power—and the *will*—to do this to the Saint of Mercy?

I retrieved my rapiers from the floor and rose to my feet. My vision swam.

"Falcio," Kest said, reaching out to me, "you need to rest. Your wounds . . ."

I didn't hear the rest of what he said. I was too focused on the people rushing frantically about the room and in the halls outside: guards, nobles, merchants. It's odd the way human beings move together, almost like ants. Even in the midst of chaos, there's a kind of flow to the motion of their bodies through space. That's why I noticed one figure, near the far door, who *wasn't* moving like the others. "Protect Birgid," I ordered Kest and Brasti as I took off in pursuit of the man who may have killed a Saint.

As I stumbled through the halls of the Ducal Palace of Baern chasing after my nebulous opponent, I found myself thinking about the style of duelist called a *perseguere*: a fencer who has mastered the art of keeping his blade in contact with his opponent's, so he never feints or retreats, just continually pursues his enemy across the court.

Only it works better if you actually get near him.

I bashed my injured shoulder into the wall as I tried to turn the corner too quickly, then slipped on something wet and sticky. I wasn't terribly familiar with this place and my opponent was moving faster.

As I got closer to the center of the palace, the halls became crowded with people rushing to and fro, either to find out what had happened or to get away from danger. I pressed forward, ignoring them where I could, pushing them out of my way where I had to, but when anyone actually looked at me, I began to notice their expressions quickly changed from irritated to aghast.

I suppose I'm not looking my best right now, I thought, as I reached the main doors, and realized that I'd completely lost my prey. Worse, I was so out of breath and dizzy that it was all I could do to stay standing.

A man stepped in front of me and put a steadying hand on my shoulder. "You don't look well."

I tried to push him aside. "Out of the way. I have to keep looking."

"You won't get far in your condition," he said.

I looked down at my shirt and saw red roses blooming across a white field. *Of course. That's why I'm moving so slowly, why everything is so blurry.*

This also explained what Kest and Brasti had been shouting at me a few minutes earlier: *"Falcio, you're bleeding!"*

The flaw in the perseguere's fighting style is that you can become so perfectly focused on one thing that you miss everything else that's going on around you. For example, I had forgotten just how badly I'd been wounded in the duel with Undriel, just as I had forgotten that I still hadn't fully recovered from the Greatcoat's Lament, or, for that matter, from the neatha poisoning that had nearly taken my life.

Most importantly, as I looked up into the smiling face of the man who'd spoken to me—the man who, unlike everyone else around me, was just standing there, unmoving—I realized that I had forgotten how easy it is to sneak back into a building this size in the middle of a crisis.

"Good," Undriel said, his eyes on mine. "It wouldn't suit me for you to not know."

I almost laughed out loud at the sheer absurdity of the situation. I'd assumed the figure I'd spotted lurking in the shadows must be the man who'd tried to kill a Saint. Instead, this was nothing more than a case of petty revenge over the loss of a duel neither of us ever should have fought.

Undriel drew a thin, straight blade, no more than six inches long, from behind his back.

"You call that a blade?" I said. "Let me show you a proper one."
I reached for my rapier, only to realize I'd dropped it on the floor
several feet back.

"There!" Kest cried from somewhere behind me.

"Get those damned people out of the way, Kest!" Brasti shouted.
"I haven't got a clear shot!"

My eyes locked with Undriel's; we both knew they wouldn't make
it. His hand shot forward, the short blade darting out at me.

Cuffs, I thought; *time to parry with the bone plates in the cuffs of
my coat.* But of course I'd taken my coat off too, so it was only by
some minor miracle that when I slapped Undriel's blade aside it
didn't slice right through the back of my hand. I say "minor miracle"
because a proper one would have sent the knife spinning away.

I grabbed Undriel's collar with my left hand and yanked it forward, smashing his cheek against the corner of the wall, and he
stumbled back away from me.

Two guardsmen finally took some notice and began running
toward us. Undriel immediately stepped back and put his hands up
in the air.

"You seem to have lost your knife," I said, noting his empty hands.

Undriel smiled, and a thought occurred to me then.

I looked down to see the handle of the short knife extending out
of my belly. What had been left of the lovely white field of my shirt
was now subsumed by the red.

"Ha," I said, foolishly. "Hardly hurts at all."

Undriel didn't reply, and when I looked at him to see the reason
for his silence, I noticed that he too had red roses blossoming on his
shirt, where three arrows had buried themselves deep into his chest.

The two of us stood there for hours, although it can't have been
more than half a dozen seconds, both determined not to be the first
to fall. I thought I was doing a fairly good job of it until my legs went
out from underneath me.

"I win," Undriel said, blood spouting from his open mouth.

I guess what people say about me is true, I thought, as I watched
the floor rush up to meet me. *I really do make too many enemies.*

CHAPTER SEVEN

THE RED AND THE WHITE

The world slid beneath me, smooth and sharp, like a tablecloth being yanked from under the dishes, sending us all clanging and crashing to the floor. Even before I hit bottom, the floor softened into a beautiful red river whose currents were pulling me along and under, like a boat taking in too much water. As I drifted along, I gradually left the cacophony of noises behind me until at last only two voices accompanied me on my journey.

"In the name of every Saint who ever lived, Falcio, are you congenitally incapable of actually *winning* a fight anymore?" The voice was male, thin, almost reedy, but it had a mischievous quality that I found oddly charming. "I wonder perhaps, is this some new form of gallantry you've invented? 'Oh, do forgive me, sirrah, for having failed to let you kill me with your blade. Please allow me to stand here and reopen my wounds until I bleed to death'?"

I looked up, or rather, I imagined I looked up to see a man of about thirty years, average height with a bit of a stoop in his posture, keeping pace alongside me as my body listed in the currents. The blood all around me had flowed up from the floor to envelop him in an elegant silk robe too big for his skinny frame. He hadn't bothered to do it up properly, and to my profound horror, I saw that he wasn't wearing any underclothes.

"Haven't I suffered enough of your majesty already?" I groaned.

Paelis, once King of all Tristia, now a corpse these past six years, winked at me. "You speak of the magnificent royal scepter with such disdain? No wonder people keep stabbing you."

"The reason people keep stabbing Falcio is because he insists on pursuing your foolish dream," said a second voice. This one was feminine, and yet its strength blew me further down the river. I looked over to my right and saw my wife, Aline, walking beside me, her simple white gown constructed from the white marble adorning the palace walls.

"This is new," I said conversationally.

A disturbance in the river around me became a family of alligators who swam alongside me and clamped their jaws around my arms and legs before dragging me out of the water and dropping me unceremoniously on a hard, flat rock beneath the hot sun.

A table. I've been moved onto a table of some kind. And the light . . . it's a lantern overhead.

"Good," Aline said. "At least you haven't lost all sense."

I coughed, and felt something wet come out from between my lips. That's never a good sign. Of course, hallucinating two dead people who'd never met in life having an argument over your body probably wasn't a good sign either.

King Paelis took mock offense at my thoughts. "How dare you imply that the royal personage is less than substantial?" He placed his fists on his hips and struck a pose, causing his robe to open further.

"Please don't do that," I begged.

He ignored my complaint. "Have you considered that my presence here might be due to some profound spiritual and supernatural event? Perhaps the Gods themselves, concerned for the state of the world, have returned their finest servant—that's me, by the way—to save it from—"

That next word was something I really wanted to hear, but Aline interrupted. "He's a hallucination," she said, then looked archly at the King. "And not a particularly impressive one, I must say."

"Dear Lady, if, as you claim, I am nothing more than the product of Falcio's fevered brain, then what does that make you?"

Aline turned to me and reached down her hand to touch my cheek. I could almost make myself believe that I could feel the touch of her fingers against my skin. *Almost.*

"I'm his reason, of course. I'm the part of him that realizes he's lost consciousness, along with far too much blood, and that he was dragged along the floor by Kest and Brasti, the only way they could get him to the infirmary."

She paused while four eagles gripped their talons around my wrists and ankles and flew me high up into the air before depositing me into their nest. It was a rather uncomfortable nest.

Aline chuckled then. "You're on a horse-cart, you silly man. It's been several days since you fell. Such an inventive imagination, though. You should have joined the Bardatti instead of the Great-coats." She turned to the King. "I'm the part of him that figures things out when others can't."

I missed that about her—the unshakable confidence in those things she knew to be true.

"You're what makes me believe there's still good in this wretched world," I said.

"No, my darling, that's his job." She pointed at Paelis.

"Ah!" said the King, as if he'd just scored the winning point. "I'm his idealism! His fearless determination to right the world! His keen intellect and—"

"No, that's Aline, too," I said, letting myself feel the warmth of her breath and smelling the haleweed that she used to rub on her face and neck to keep from burning on sunny days. I wanted to live inside that sweet scent forever.

"These are false memories you're making for yourself," Aline warned. "Haleweed stinks of seven different hells, Falcio, remember? We were *farmers.*" She held out the fingertips of one perfect hand. "What farmer ever had hands like these?" Her fingers took hold of a lock of soft hair, a gleaming pale brown, almost blond, and held it up for me to see. "In my entire life my hair never once looked this way."

"Enough!" Paelis bellowed. "Is a man not allowed to love his wife? Is he not allowed to see the beauty that others"—and here he began wagging his finger at her—"even she herself, fail to see?"

That was a mistake. One thing that was absolutely true about Aline was that she never took well to being yelled at. "And what good will he be to the world like this? Clinging to a past painted bright colors by sorrow and need?" She turned back to me. "The enemy's way is deception, Falcio. Yours must be truth, no matter how ugly it might look."

She leaned in closer to me and I could count the freckles on her cheeks now, six on one side, nine on the other. That felt significant somehow.

"Better," she said. "But there's more. You can't beat him unless you learn to see what isn't there."

"How am I supposed to see what isn't—?"

Aline placed her hands in front of her face. Her hair changed color to the pale white-blond of Saint Birgid, and her hands darkened and melted together, forming an iron mask with neither eyes nor mouth.

"Stop," I said, reaching out to try and pull the mask away.

"She can't hear you anymore," Paelis said. "She can't speak. Truth is being buried under deception, faith drowned by fear." Gently, the King lifted Aline by the shoulders and began guiding her backward, away from me.

"Step by step, Falcio, it's all being taken away from us."

A fog the color of ivory began to envelop them, swallowing them whole. "Soon there will be only one step left."

I knew that what I saw and heard was illusion, my mind jumbling memories together as my body struggled against my injuries—and yet I knew there had to be some fact, some essential *truth* to all of this. "What will they do?" I asked. "What is the last step?"

The King was gone now, and I could barely see Aline in the fog. A pair of heavy gloved hands reached out, encircling her masked face. With a vicious jerk they twisted, and the sound of her neck snapping became my entire world.

I didn't recognize the voice that I heard next, but the words were spoken with perfect clarity. "The last step is the same as the first," he said. "I will kill Mercy."

CHAPTER EIGHT

THE MARTYRIUM

I awoke in darkness. This was neither surprising nor particularly unsettling to me until I realized that the air was heavy, almost stifling, the way it gets at the peak of an unseasonably hot summer.

So why am I so cold?

I reached down to grab at my blankets, but my forearm struck against something hard, just a few inches above me. I ran my finger across the surface. It was rough and flat. Something stung as it caught in the skin of my fingertip.

A sliver?

I tried rolling over, only to find my shoulder caught against the wooden boards above me. Panic set in when I reached out to either side and found them blocked as well.

A coffin . . . I'm in a coffin.

The stories told to frighten children and old men, of warriors injured in battle and believed dead by their comrades, only to wake up buried alive six feet beneath the ground, assailed me and I started to breathe too quickly, using too much air. Already I felt as if I were suffocating, trapped underground. Had they thought I'd lost too much blood? Was my heartbeat too soft or slow? Could Kest and Brasti truly have been foolish enough to think that—?

Brasti.

I bellowed, and the sound of my voice echoed over the surface of the wood around me, "I'm going to fucking kill you this time you heartless son of a bitch!"

A distant guffaw was followed by the sound of footsteps running toward me and Brasti calling, "Hang on, hang on, I'm coming . . ."

Blinding candlelight forced me to close my eyes as my prison lifted off of me, and when I opened them again I saw that I hadn't actually been *inside* a coffin at all—Brasti had just removed the lid from one and flipped the rest over top of me.

"It would have come off as soon as you gave it a push," Brasti scolded. "And don't shout, either." He glanced around the room, most of which was cast in shadows. "You'll wake up Kest, and he has no sense of humor lately."

The doors to the room burst open, and Kest strode inside. "I told you not to pull this prank, Brasti. I warned you what would happen if you did—"

It should tell you something about Kest that I was, at that moment, afraid for Brasti.

"Oh, no! I've angered Saint Kest-of-the-deep-brooding-stares!" Brasti mocked. "Whatever shall I do?"

This was always Brasti's idea of how best to deal with trauma: turn it into a joke. I had nearly died, so why not stick a coffin over me to remind me I was alive? Kest had lost his Sainthood along with his hand, so why not make fun of him to show it's not the end of the world?

Kest didn't look as if he was finding any of it particularly funny.

"Fine," Brasti said, grinning as he leaped onto the bed next to mine, "just pass me my bow and then you can draw that great big stick of yours and we'll find out once and for all who deserves to be the Saint of something-or-other!"

Without breaking stride, Kest picked up Brasti's bow, carried it until he was within four feet of the bed and then tossed it high into the air.

Brasti grinned, his right hand already reaching back into his quiver for an arrow while the other went for the bow in midair—but before he could catch it, Kest's left hand was darting out and wrapping around Brasti's fingers in a crushing grip. The bow clattered on the floor. "What makes you think I need a sword to teach you sense?" Kest asked.

Brasti winced in pain, his knees buckling. "Stop it, you fool, you'll break my hand!"

"Apologize to Falcio."

"I was only trying to help!" Brasti said, looking at me pleadingly.

"Trying to help?" I asked. "That's a stretch, even for you."

"Come on, Falcio. You nearly lost a duel to a pompous fop of a swordsman, practically everyone hates you and then you managed to almost die for the hundredth time. Did you really want to wake up to the sight of Kest wiping your brow with a soft cloth while whispering sweet, reassuring words to you?"

"Compared to waking up thinking I'd been buried alive?"

Brasti, obviously born without any sense of self-preservation, chortled for a moment before regaining control of himself. "Come on, admit it! I bet you've never felt more alive than you do right now!"

I sighed, feeling nothing of the kind. "Let him go, Kest."

"Really?" Kest asked, his left hand still firmly in control of Brasti's fingers.

I pushed myself to sit up. "If you break his hand now then how am I going to enjoy the full satisfaction of tearing his fingers off later on?"

"Ah," Kest said, and let go of him. "Good point."

"Now wait a minute, Falcio . . ." Brasti began.

I smiled. "You'll never know when, Brasti. Maybe tomorrow, maybe ten years from now . . ." I paused for a long moment, then said, "No, probably tomorrow."

He hopped off the bed and massaged his hand. "One day there's going to be a God of Humor and he's going to curse the pair of you as apostates."

I rose from the bed, feeling every cut and bruise on my body come to wakefulness. My chest and abdomen were covered in bandages. "How long was I out?"

"Six days," Kest replied.

"Hells, six days . . ."

"Doctor Histus offered to draw you a diagram of the vital organs in your body and the exact distance by which Undriel's smallsword missed them."

"Kind of him," I said. *Histus. That explains the poor bandaging, anyway.* "Why didn't Ethalia tend to my wounds?" Then I remembered the circumstances that had gotten me into this state. "Saints . . . is Birgid—?"

"Still alive, so far as we know," Kest replied. "Ethalia's been working day and night to heal her." He paused for a moment, then admitted, "Falcio, Saint Birgid hasn't woken in all that time. Her injuries aren't healing."

I closed my eyes for a moment, trying to focus and clear the fog from my head so I could concentrate on the matters at hand. Instead, I found myself remembering my first meeting with Birgid—how disturbingly beautiful and youthful she'd appeared, glowing with a power that had filled me with both awe and trepidation. Then the images in my mind shifted to how she'd looked when I'd last seen her, just a few days ago, her hair matted and filthy, trapped behind an iron mask, shoulders and arms covered in tiny cuts that were somehow . . . *precise.* Planned. This was a careful and meticulous kind of cruelty.

"Falcio?" The voice was Kest's, but it sounded very far away so I ignored it.

I stumbled a little, my hand grabbing onto the foot of the bed as my thoughts shifted again. Now it wasn't Birgid I was remembering, but myself, bound to the split tree in the clearing those eight days and nights as the Dashini Unblooded tormented my flesh, my mind, my soul. *Stop,* I told myself. *Breathe. Focus. Think about Birgid.*

I considered the possibility that somehow there were still Dashini out there and that they had captured Birgid and performed the

Lament upon her, but her torture had obviously been different . . . *blunter,* somehow.

"Falcio, you should rest," Kest said. His hand was gripping my arm, and I realized that he was holding me up.

"There's any number of things that Falcio *should* do," Brasti said. "But only one thing he's *going* to do."

For some reason, that brought me back, and I opened my eyes to see Brasti staring at me. I started to speak but he stopped me, placing a hand on my shoulder. "No, please, allow me." He stuck a finger in the air and jutted his chin up and to the right, as though staring at some far-off horizon. "'Though I am grievous injured, I, Falcio val Mond, First Cantor of the Greatcoats and most beloved of the King, must now, in defense of our most sacred ideals, demonstrate my unyielding duty—not to mention, ego—and investigate this most heinous act!'"

"I don't talk anything like that."

Kest looked at me and raised his eyebrows a hair.

"Oh, the hells for the both of you," I said, and surveyed the room to find my clothes, reasoning it probably wouldn't help anyone for me to wander about naked except for my bandages. Near the bed where I'd awoken was an old wooden crate that was serving as a side table. I dressed slowly, careful not to fall over and embarrass myself in front of Kest and Brasti. After the manner in which I'd been woken, though, I felt justified in making them wait.

I finished by slipping my rapiers into their scabbards and took a slow, stiff walk around the dingy room, leaning periodically against the empty beds that emitted the musty smell of disuse. Under each one lay a plain, wooden coffin.

"All right, let's go," I said. Then another question occurred to me. "Where the hells am I?"

"Welcome to the Martyrium of Saint Werta-who-walks-the-waves," Kest said as he led us out through the double doors and into the bright sunlight, "in all her dubious glory."

Broken remnants of single-story buildings gave sad greetings, their crumbling and dirty white sandstone walls overtaken by vines and tall weeds and now listing like weary sentries over the wreckage of roofs long ago caved in.

"Not exactly a palace of the divine, is it?" Brasti asked.

Having seldom taken much interest in the Gods, and even less in their chosen representatives on earth (or at least in Tristia), I'd never spent much time in our holy places, so I didn't have much of a frame of reference to go on. "Where's the sanctuary?" I asked, assuming that's where I'd find Birgid and Ethalia.

Kest pointed to an overgrown path behind me and a larger, six-walled building with a smooth dome about a dozen yards away. It stood on a slight angle, as if the ground on one side was growing tired of supporting its weight. It was ringed by the limbless and headless remains of what once must have been commanding statues of each of Tristia's deities.

"The Gods have seen better days," I said.

Brasti kicked a marble hand holding a hammer that had probably belonged to Craft, or Mestiri, as he's sometimes known here in the south. "Inspiring, isn't it?" he asked, balancing on top of what was left of a carved head that had rolled along the ground and ended its journey against the stump of a dead tree. If the God of Making was troubled by Brasti's blasphemy, he gave no sign.

I turned to Kest. "Why bring Birgid here? Surely she could have received better care at the Ducal Palace?"

"Duchess Ossia's clerics demanded it," he replied. "They said, 'A Saint can only be healed under the protection of the Gods, not in the false comfort and vain opulence of a secular palace.'"

Not that clerics have ever objected to living in that same comfort and opulence . . . "And Valiana went along with that?"

"She needs Duchess Ossia's support, and the Duchess needs the clerics."

"No one much cared about what we thought," Brasti added. "They weren't even going to let Ethalia travel with her unt—"

Kest gave him a sharp look and he went silent.

"What?" I asked.

Kest hesitated, then said, "One of the clerics was insisting Ethalia was . . . *unclean*. He grabbed her wrist rather forcefully." He carefully ignored Brasti. "Someone decided to shoot an arrow about a hair's-breadth from the cleric's hand, and might have followed up with some rather . . . elaborate threats. It triggered something of a diplomatic incident. Neither the clerics nor Duchess Ossia were pleased."

I looked at Brasti, who didn't look even the faintest bit embarrassed. "You were unconscious, and everybody else was useless. So I asked myself, 'What would Falcio do in this situation?' and I thought, 'Well, he'd draw a weapon and make some kind of dramatic pronouncement, wouldn't he?'"

It's hard to know what to say to something like that, so I just said, "Come here."

He looked up at me, eyes narrowed. "What? Why?"

"Just come here."

He did, slowly, warily as if he thought I might hit him. When he got close enough I grabbed him in both arms and hugged him. See, the thing about Brasti's idea of friendship is, it's completely unconstrained by logic or forethought. He doesn't stop to wonder about the consequences of his actions. He just does whatever it is he thinks you'd want him to do for you in that situation. "Some days I love you," I said.

He started patting me awkwardly on the back. "Um . . . all right. Let's not make a thing of it, shall we?"

I found myself laughing for the first time since this latest mess began. I let him go and turned to Kest. "So in the six days I've been unconscious, the Saint of Mercy has slipped into a coma, we've been consigned to some half-deserted martyrium, and Brasti has shot a cleric."

"I barely grazed the skin of his hand," Brasti clarified. "He's still perfectly capable of praying. Maybe even more so, now."

"There's actually one more thing," Kest said, and led the way down a path that went around the side of the sanctuary. Through the sparse growth of trees we could see the main gates of the martyrium, where a great crowd of people covered the grassy field outside. Some were huddling around makeshift tents, others were kneeling by the gates with their hands clasped together, and many just stood there, staring through the gates. None of them looked very happy.

CHAPTER NINE

THE EVIDENCE

"Who in all the hells are they?" I asked, staring at the mass of humanity outside the martyrium.

"Pilgrims, if you can believe it," Brasti replied. "Around a hundred of them."

"Word of the attack on Birgid spread quickly," Kest added. "People from all over the Duchy have been coming here—some are praying for her blessing and some are protesting."

"Protesting what?"

Brasti snorted. "Whatever the nearest cleric is telling them to protest." He pointed at a man in dirty orange robes standing in the center of a particularly large group. "That one appears to think the attack on Birgid is a conspiracy by the Greatcoats to destroy the Saints."

Of course, because when in doubt, blame a Greatcoat.

"You can't really fault them on that, can you?" a voice called out from behind us, and Jillard, Duke of Rijou, resplendent in a purple and silver coat, his black hair freshly oiled and looking entirely out of place, walked through the overgrown vegetation to join us. "After all, by my count you've killed not one but two Saints of Swords now."

I always find it difficult to think of what to say to a man who's tried on multiple occasions to have me killed and who still has no compunction about inserting himself into my affairs. "You look . . . well, Your Grace," I said finally.

"You look much as you always do, Falcio," Jillard replied. "Beaten, bloody, and confused by the world."

Damn—why does he always sound so much cleverer than I do? "While I'm gratified at your concern for my well-being, I'm rather busy at the—"

"I rather thought you might want to have a little chat about this." The Duke took a cloth bundle from inside his coat. He unwrapped it, letting the cloth drift down to the ground, and revealed a rough, curved piece of black and gray metal: the mask that Birgid had worn. "Remarkable the things people leave lying around during a crisis," he said reflectively.

I glared at Kest, who returned what passes for a sheepish expression from him, which is to say, no sign of embarrassment whatsoever. "I was a bit occupied trying to keep you from bleeding out on the courtroom floor at the time."

I would have expected Jillard to take the opportunity to make some further comment on our ineptitude, but instead his stare was deadly serious. "Do you have any idea what I'm holding, First Cantor?"

Why is it that whenever people use my title it sounds like they're impugning my intellect? "Normally I'd say it was stolen evidence, Your Grace."

Jillard ignored my fatuous comment and handed me the mask. He waited in silence as I looked it over. The surface was rough, beaten into shape by the hard strikes of a hammer, lacking any notable signs of artistry or craft. And yet the clasping mechanism on the side was finely and carefully designed.

Someone cared a lot more about how well the mask closed and held than how it looked.

I turned the mask over in my hand. The left side was partially broken off—at first I thought that was where Kest's blade had come down, then I realized the clasps he'd smashed were on the other side. I handed it to him and asked, "How did this happen?"

Kest leaned in to examine the bent and jagged break. "This wasn't from a single blow," he said. "Look at all the dozens of small dents. I suspect she struck her head against some sort of stone surface, repeatedly, trying to get it off."

That image put a knot in my gut, so I focused my attention on the mask itself. On closer examination it wasn't completely without design: the lines carved into its surface made the shape of terrified eyes, though there were no holes there: anyone wearing this would be blind to the world. Similar carvings formed the shape of a mouth, opened wide in a mad, endless scream. Three tiny slits no more than an inch high had been punched through there, and when I examined the back, I saw a small funnel had been welded into it. So anyone wearing the mask would have had that funnel jammed into their mouth. They'd be unable to speak, or to prevent themselves from swallowing anything that was poured into the slits.

I glanced at Jillard. "This looks like something a sadist would devise. Perhaps you could tell me what it is?"

"It's called a mask of infamy," the Duke replied. There was no sign that he had caught my insult.

"A tool for torture?"

This time Jillard hesitated before answering, "Yes and no. Some form of torture is usually involved, but the primary use of the mask is to ensure anonymity."

"You mean, so people don't know who's wearing it?" Brasti asked.

"No," I said, my eyes still on the Duke, "the victim can't see or hear with the mask on—it's designed so that they'd never know who tortured them, isn't it? But why would—?"

"You're asking the wrong question," Jillard said. His voice was full of arrogant annoyance, and yet there was something else not far underneath. Concern. Worry. He didn't like not knowing what was going on any more than I did. "This," he said, pointing to the funnel welded inside the mask. "This isn't part of any mask of infamy I've ever seen."

"Maybe it's there so they can poison the victim?" Brasti suggested. "Or to make sure they can't talk?"

"Putting a blade through the wearer's heart would be surer and require less effort," Kest pointed out. "Why go to the extra trouble?"

I turned the mask over in my hands, looking at the primitive, almost ritualistic carvings, then at the more carefully constructed clasps on the sides. The absence of holes for the eyes meant that Birgid's tormentor thought there might be some chance of her escaping. No doubt a Saint with powers like hers would be hard to keep captive. *So why not just kill her, if that was the desired end?* I thought back to the cuts on her skin. Were they part of the torture? They weren't very deep, nor would they be the best way to inflict pain. Again and again I found myself staring at that obscene iron funnel welded to the inside of the mask. *What had they forced her to drink? And to what end?*

Jillard gave a not-quite-polite cough, making me realize I'd been standing there in silence for some time. "The Ducal Council has asked that I convey to you their outrage at this horrendous crime."

"Well, we can't have the Dukes being outraged, can we?" Brasti mocked.

"In fact, no, you can't," Jillard replied. "You are hereby informed that under the terms of the Council's agreement with the Greatcoats, you will herewith enforce the Laws of Tristia by finding the guilty parties and bringing them to trial without delay."

"Birgid is one of the most powerful Saints in Tristia," Kest said. "We have no idea what kind of person would be capable of this act. How exactly does the Council propose we go about finding the culprits, let alone arresting them?"

The Duke smiled. "Oh, we don't really. In fact, we rather think there's a decent chance that whoever did this will finally be able to put an end to what remains of the Greatcoats."

I sighed, though it felt more like the air was draining out of me. I was tired, and weeks from being fully recovered from my injuries. *I don't want this,* I thought. *My job is to see the King's daughter on the throne, to find the rest of the Greatcoats and bring some semblance of the law back to this damnable country. Gods and Saints are well beyond my jurisdiction.*

I should have handed the mask back to Jillard and told him and the Ducal Council to find some other fool to saddle with this problem, but my dream of Aline and Paelis came back to me. *"Step by step, Falcio, it's all being taken away from us."* Was that simply a hallucination that came with losing too much blood too fast, or had my fevered mind put something more together?

What does it mean, that someone is able to do this to a Saint?

"Terrific," Brasti said, shattering my concentration.

"What?"

I turned to see him strapping his bow over his shoulder. "If you could see your face right now you wouldn't ask." He started off down the path between buildings that led back to the cathedral, then called back, "Let's go and see how merciful Saint Birgid feels when we try to wake her up, shall we?"

CHAPTER TEN

THE SIX DOORS

"Why are there six doors?" I asked, walking the perimeter of the building. I've learned not to make a habit of running into buildings without checking the entrances and exits first.

"Technically, this is a cathedral, not a sanctuary," Kest replied. "Supplicants go through the door dedicated to the deity whose intervention they seek."

Brasti stopped to lean against the stone buttocks of the broken statue dedicated to Purgeize, God of War. Or they might have belonged to Coin. I've never made an extensive study of the subject of Gods' buttocks. "What difference does it make when the doors all go into the same cathedral?" he asked.

I chose the door behind the statue of Love, or Phenia as she's sometimes called in the south. I didn't expect her to be particularly helpful to our cause, but she was by and large the least offensive of the available options for worship.

I passed through the inner arch of the door to find the tiny cathedral in surprisingly good condition, given the crumbling state of the exterior. The domed roof rising some thirty feet above the building was largely intact, and a circular window at the top directed light into the upper chamber, spreading out onto the six colored walls of the hexagonally shaped building.

"What are the bells for?" Brasti asked, pointing to the six-inch-high brass fixtures that were attached to each wall.

"The cleric rings them in preparation for prayer. Each particular God has a different set of bells," Kest replied. He walked over to one of the walls and pointed to a bare oval patch underneath the bell. "There should be a large cameo here, depicting the relevant God."

I glanced around the room. All the cameos had been removed, though I couldn't tell if it'd been theft or vandalism. I turned my attention to the center of the cavernous room and the opening in the floor, ringed by a wooden banister, that led down the winding stone stairs of the *passari deo*: the dark passage that led to the main chapel some twenty feet below.

Why is it that religious people build these grand palaces to the Gods and then feel the need to burrow underground in order to pray to them?

Brasti kicked a broken wooden candleholder, sending it skidding across the floor and into the passari. We heard it clatter down the stairs. "You'd think the clerics would do a better job of keeping their house in order."

"I doubt anyone has lived here in some time," Kest said. He brushed his fingers across the dusty surface of one of the walls. "I came to a place like this during my Saint's Fever, but it felt . . . different."

"Different how?" I asked.

"I'm not sure I can put it into words. I think perhaps this place has been . . . *disturbed* somehow."

"The word you're looking for is 'desecrated,'" said a voice from the shadows at the bottom of the stairs.

"Who's there?" I called down, my hand on the hilt of my rapier.

The three of us waited as a man in his later years, stoop-backed and barefoot, ascended the stone steps. "Probably best not to stab an unarmed member of the faith," he said. "Or if you absolutely must, at least wait until I've emptied this." He lifted up a pail. "If you do decide to kill me, please be so kind as to bring a fresh pail of water to the Lady downstairs so she can continue ministering to our guest."

"You seem a little old to be wearing the gray, *Quaesti*," Kest said politely.

The monk set down the pail and pulled at his plain gray robe as if he'd only just noticed it for the first time. "Alas, none of the Gods have called to me yet. I keep hoping to hear the summons of Coin as I've always looked good in green. 'Obladias,' he'll say, 'get yourself some fine silk robes in seven shades of green and come and live a life of wealth and prosperity in my name.'" The old man shrugged. "Black would be fine, too, though Death seems a harsh master. Really, I'd be happy with anyone except Craft at this point." Obladias winked at us. "Orange robes would look terrible with my complexion. Now blue, there's a fine—"

"You said this cathedral was desecrated?" Kest interrupted.

"Technically it's only the sanctuary that can be desecrated," the monk replied, looking toward the black hole of the passari. "Someone shattered the prayer-stones down there, years ago. The rest of this place is just an old building, really."

"You don't sound upset by all the destruction," I said.

Obladias smiled wearily. "You get used to it, son. I knew a man once—a good man, a *religious* man. Then one day his family gets sick." He shook his head. "Worst thing you ever saw. The children . . . well, I won't grow your sorrows with the details, but this fella, he prayed to the Gods to stop it, over and over. In the end he was praying to Death himself, just to ease his family's suffering."

I held the old man's gaze for a moment, wondering if perhaps the story was his own. "And did the Gods answer?"

The monk shrugged. "Only in the way that they always do—by telling us to find our own answers." He turned and looked around the dusty chapel. "I suppose it's not hard to imagine why people get angry at the Gods. Oh, speaking of which"—he looked up at the sky peeking through the glass in the dome—"ah, hells, I'm late." He walked over to the red wall and gently pulled on the rope attached to the small bell there. It let out a clanging sound like that of two swords striking each other. "All these little rituals we perform, it's hard to imagine the Gods pay attention to them anymore."

I was fairly sure they didn't, but thought it impolite to say so. "Forgive me, *Venerati* Obladias, but we've come to—"

"I'm not a preacher anymore, son. Just Obladias is fine. I assume you intend to go down into the sanctuary and see Saint Birgid. Oh, and your lady friend, too, of course."

The reference to my lady friend struck me. "You know who I am?"

"Of course I do. Can't go within two miles of a tavern without hearing somebody singing a song about you. They're never sure of the name, though. Is it 'Falsio val Mond' or 'Falcio dal Vond'? I've heard both." Before I could answer he turned to Kest. "And you were the Saint of Swords for a little while, weren't you?"

Kest nodded.

Obladias wagged a finger. "You know the Gods don't think highly of apostates, son. Most people would do anything to be more powerful. Why in the world would you throw away a gift like that?"

Kest held up the stump of his right hand. "It was an accident."

The monk looked astonished for a moment, then he broke out laughing. "Well, I suppose that's one way to look at it. Hadn't heard you had a sense of humor."

"And what have you heard about me?" Brasti asked.

"You?" Obladias caught Brasti's painfully obvious yearning. "Um, of course I've heard about you." The monk looked him over, hesitating, then caught sight of the bow strapped across Brasti's back. "Archer, right? No doubt a very fine one. 'He's a great bowman, that . . .' Um, sorry, what was your name, again?"

Brasti turned to me. "I'm really starting to hate this country."

"Come on," I said. "We need to talk to Birgid."

The old monk was still standing in front of the passari. "I'm not sure I can allow that, son. Don't get me wrong, I'm a big admirer of yours, but this is a holy place and the three of you, well, you're not exactly what I'd call men of Faith."

"Do you intend to block our way?" I asked.

Obladias sighed and stepped aside. "Don't see as how I could."

The three of us walked past him and started down the stairs, but we'd only gotten about a third of the way when I heard the sound of several pairs of heavy-heeled boots entering the building.

"Shit," Brasti said, "that's a lot of people."

The last place you want to be if you're about to be attacked is stuck halfway down a stairwell. Being below ground is never a good idea, and on a staircase there's nowhere to move. "Hurry," I said, running back up the stairs, but I was too late: two men in gray robes that did precious little to hide the armor underneath were standing in each of the six entrances. They were all armed, half with pikes, the rest carrying pistols.

"Falcio . . ." Kest warned.

"I know," I said. I don't think any of us had ever seen six pistols all in the same place before. I turned to the old monk. "You summoned them when you rang the bell. All that talk was just to delay us."

"I said that I admired you, *Trattari*," the old man said. "I never said I *liked* you."

As if on cue, a thirteenth man entered the building. He was about my age and height, with short blond hair and a close-trimmed beard. He wore a long leather coat of office that might have been confused for a greatcoat were it not colored a heavy, drab gray like storm clouds waiting to loose thunder and lightning upon an unsuspecting world. The only break in the gray came from six metal disks sewn in a semi-circle around the front of his coat, each one bearing the hue of one of the six Gods of Tristia.

"My name is Quentis Maren," he said, stepping into the center of the room, "First Interrogator of the *Cogneri*."

A cold chill shuddered in my bones. I hadn't intended to speak, but I'm pretty sure I heard myself say, "*Son of a bitch*."

"Someone want to tell me what a 'Cogneri' is before I kill my first one?" Brasti asked, aiming his bow at the man.

"It's the old word for the Order of Ecclesiastical Examiners," I said. "This man is an Inquisitor."

CHAPTER ELEVEN
THE INQUISITORS

In theory, Tristia is governed by two sets of laws: those of its citizens and those of its Gods. The former are established primarily by Kings and Dukes; the latter by—well, people from a very long time ago who claimed to know the Gods' opinions on such matters. Most people live under the King's Laws, which are enforced by the Greatcoats or local constabularies, but the clergy adhere to the rules and precepts of the *Canon Dei*. And who exactly enforces the Gods' Laws, you might ask? That would be the Inquisitors.

"You appear to be out of your jurisdiction, Quentis Maren," I said.

Three against thirteen is terrible odds, but I'm usually pretty good at figuring out ways of improving our chances in situations like this. I just needed a little time. *And maybe a small cannon.*

The Inquisitor narrowed his eyes just a bit, as if he wasn't sure if I was trying to be funny. "Really, First Cantor? A Saint has been attacked, nearly killed. Churches are being desecrated. The faithful fear for their lives. I would say this is very much within our jurisdiction."

"He has a point," Brasti whispered.

"Shut up," I said.

There had never been any love lost between the Inquisitors and the Greatcoats. Neither of us recognized the other's authority, the laws of Gods and those of men being largely incompatible. But for all the stories of zealous tenacity and liberal use of torture in questioning prisoners, the Cogneri had all but disappeared from Tristia. In all my years as a magistrate I'd encountered them only three times, and those men had been aging brutes who did their dirty work with weapons like heavy sticks and rusted crossbows.

Quentis Maren, on the other hand, was young, and he had the look of a careful man. A thin, short-hafted steel mace was attached to a loop on the left side of his coat. On the other sat a holster roughly twelve inches long, with the butt of a pistol sticking out of it.

A sword—a really good sword—costs roughly what you might earn in an entire year working as a farmhand. A shitty matchlock pistol of the kind that rarely hits its target and takes forever to load costs about five times that. Quentis and his men were carrying wheel lock pistols—the ones that didn't require you to prepare them by lighting a match attached to a clamp on top of the weapon; in other words, this was something that you could get ready to fire *before* you came into the building to surprise the nasty Gods-forsaken Greatcoats.

How much did a good wheel lock pistol cost? I wouldn't know. I've never had that much money.

So who pays your bills, Cogneri?

"Falcio . . ." Kest said quietly.

I hate it when he says my name that way. It's almost always followed by a recitation of just how bad our odds are.

"The former Saint of Swords is about to tell you that you can't win this fight," Quentis Maren said, his eyes on Kest. "He'll say that your archer, fast as he is, will take out only two of my men, most likely pistoleers, given his well-known disdain for swords and spears. Then of course my pikemen, who've been instructed to go for the archer first, will kill him. Kest will try to protect you, doing his best to knock aside the pikes while hoping his coat protects him from the pistol balls. However with our greater numbers and the lack of anywhere for you to run to in this room, he'll kill only four of my men before dying himself."

"Three," Kest said.

"Really?" Quentis Maren asked. "I would have thought—"

Kest held up the stump of his right hand.

"Ah, of course you're quite right. Three of mine go to the Gods then."

None of the guards looked much perturbed by the thought.

"What will I do?" I asked, simultaneously repelled and intrigued by the way this man knew so much about us.

"You'll try to kill me, of course. You resent authority. You hate religion. You'll decide that since the fight's over you might as well kill the big bad Inquisitor and go to your death enjoying that small measure of satisfaction."

"It doesn't sound like this works out all that well for you, either," I said.

Quentin Maren shrugged. "My coat isn't *quite* as well designed as yours, I admit. But I think the chain mail vest I'm wearing underneath will compensate against your rapier."

"Not if I fire an arrow through the center of your forehead," Brasti said. "Then you'll be dead *and* embarrassed."

"True," the Inquisitor said. "You're far too fast for me to get out of the way. Of course, my pistoleers are prepared for that eventuality. You'll kill me, but your friends will be dead before I hit the ground."

I worked through the permutations of our present situation in my mind, frustrated as much by the fog and exhaustion caused by my injuries as I was by Quentis having planned this so perfectly. *I could stab him in the neck and pull him to me, use him as a shield while I drew the fire of his pistoleers. Brasti could take out two of the pikemen and we could make for that exit if Kest could . . . No, damn it, the timing is all wrong.*

There's a trick to winning fights like these. Most people try to think about each piece, each fighter and their weapon, and where they are and how fast they can move. That doesn't tend to work; you need to see the *whole* board at once and envision the movements of all the combatants at the same time to find the one path that could lead to victory.

So where is it, damn it? Why can't I think straight?

"I know it isn't your usual approach," Quentis said, "but I'd suggest you consider surrender."

There was a certain logic to that idea. *Except that the last time I surrendered to someone they tortured me until there was almost nothing left of me.* Even if I'd had a hundred years to recuperate from the Lament, I'd still never be able to survive torture like that again. And even if I had a thousand years, I'd still never accept it.

I didn't say anything to Kest and Brasti, I didn't even bother to glance at them. I knew they were watching me and I knew they'd understand what was going to happen next. *There's always luck,* I thought, *and red, bloody rage.*

"Stop!" called a voice from the passari deo.

The fact that I didn't recognize her voice instantly was the first sign that something was terribly wrong. I turned to see Ethalia coming up the stairs behind us, though at first glance I would have sworn she was a stranger.

Everything about Ethalia is in the eyes: the warmth, the calm, that immediate feeling of shared serenity, but all that was gone, replaced by dark rings of exhaustion. Her cheeks were hollow, her forehead lined. "You have to leave, Falcio," she said, in a voice that was neither angry nor sad, merely cold.

"I came to . . ." There was something profound to say here, but for the life of me I couldn't find it. Instead, what I said was, "I have to find out what happened to Birgid."

"She hasn't woken since she collapsed." Ethalia held up her hands. "I'm trying to hold onto her with every salve, every prayer I know, but what little ability I have is dependent on the compassion in my heart." She looked up at me. "Falcio, I can feel your rage all the way into the sanctuary. So can Birgid. You're killing her."

You're killing her.

"Listen, sweetheart," Brasti said, "I'm not sure if you've noticed but the bad men here are pointing weapons at us."

Ethalia came to the top of the stairs and surveyed the men in front of her. Quentis Maren gave a short bow. "Forgive us, My Lady, but we have a responsibility to—"

"If you came to kill Birgid then you must pass through me first."

That took him back a step. "We came to *protect* her."

Ethalia nodded, as if she had taken him at his word. "Then leave, all of you. Her life hangs by the last strand of a spider's web. Let me try and save it with what little strength I have inside me."

Quentis glanced at Obladias, standing there in his plain gray robes with his plain face and plain manners. After a moment, the old man bowed his head.

If you're nothing but an unchosen monk then I'm the Duke of Rijou, I thought, but I didn't have the strength to think that through any further.

"Very well," the Inquisitor said. "The safety of the Saint of Mercy comes first."

I hesitated for a second. Could we have won this fight? Maybe. My head was starting to clear and I noticed now the patch of oil that had spread from the broken lantern that Brasti had kicked when we'd entered the cathedral. One of Quentis's men was standing right in it, the bottom of his long robe practically touching the oil. I had a sliver of amberlight in a tiny pocket on the inside of the right cuff of my coat. If I'd managed to get it out without anyone noticing and threw it hard enough at the patch of oil I might create a distraction that would shift the odds, if only a little.

"Falcio," Ethalia said from behind me. "Please."

I locked eyes with Quentis, wanting him to know that this wouldn't have been a sure thing for him. "Marked," I said.

He gave the smallest hint of a bow. It was a contract, of sorts, with terms and durations and clauses, and it would come to steel soon enough. There would be a victor and a vanquished. There would be blood. Just not today. Whatever it was the Inquisitors wanted from us, it wasn't as important to them as Saint Birgid's life.

Quentis and his men left, followed by Brasti and Kest, leaving me standing there alone with Ethalia at the top of the stairs that led down to the sanctuary below. I felt a momentary spiteful urge to ignore my agreement with the Inquisitor and go down to see if I could wake the Saint and get her to give me something, anything that might help me understand what had happened to her. But one look at Ethalia told me that if I tried to interfere with Birgid's recovery, Quentis would be the least of my problems.

I really need to find a new job. One that doesn't involve swords. Some small part of me wondered whether I should ask her to marry me then, which should tell you just how little I understand the concept of romance. I reached out a hand to touch Ethalia's cheek, but she pulled away. "I'm sorry, Falcio. I can't let you . . . I can only heal her if I remain . . ."

I'm not sure what she was going to say next because Brasti ran back into the building, bringing with him the sound of distant shouts. "Falcio, you've got to come. *Now.*"

"Have the Inquisitors—?"

He shook his head. "It's the pilgrims. One of the guards by the gates said he saw a figure trying to get through the crowds. A cleric got the mob to grab him and they've beaten him senseless and tied him to a post. Falcio, the guard said the man they caught was wearing a Greatcoat."

I started to run after Brasti, then stopped, just for a moment, to say goodbye to Ethalia—but she had already started down the stairs to the sanctuary.

CHAPTER TWELVE
THE MOB

More than two hundred people were now standing outside the gates of the martyrium, although, despite their numbers, the grassy field didn't look nearly as crowded as I'd expected. For the most part, they were milling about in small groups, sticking close to their possessions, their improvised tents, and horse-carts. The road that led to the martyrium was clear, so obviously no blockade was being attempted. No one was throwing stones or shouting slogans; no one was harrying the guards Quentis had brought with him. The pilgrims were simply going about the business of living and listening to whichever cleric or farmboy-turned-mystic had led them here . . . all except for one group on the far side of the field, who appeared to be busily preparing a bonfire.

"I see him over there," Brasti said, pointing out past the gate. "He's right at the edge of the forest. There's a crowd in front of him so I can't make out his face, but I can see his hands tied above his head to the post."

"Well, okay then," I said, and did up the bottom six buttons of my coat, leaving the top six open. I wanted as much protection as I could get, but I still needed to be able to reach inside for my throwing knives.

"Let one of us go," Kest said. "You're exhausted and injured. If the mob attacks—"

"If the mob attacks, it's all over, whoever goes out there."

"Then we all go," Brasti suggested.

"If three Greatcoats go out there and start trouble then it's guaranteed the mob will turn on us. I have a better chance alone."

A couple of Quentis's gray-robed guards laughed. Evidently I didn't look as impressive as I might have hoped. On the other hand, I was oddly reassured that the Inquisitors were not all as calm and perfectly self-assured as Quentis himself, but were in fact just as easily amused and mean-spirited as every other soldier I'd met.

"I don't suppose you'd like to bring your men and help me?" I asked the guard standing next to me.

"Our orders are to protect the martyrium," he replied. "Whatever dispute you and yours have with the pilgrims is your own problem. I'm sure with your grand Trattari ways you can negotiate for his release on your own."

That set his men laughing even harder. You don't reason with mobs for the same reason you don't reason with hordes of fire ants: they're too stupid to understand what you're saying and eventually they'll just swarm over you.

Which isn't to say you don't talk to them. Words are important. Words are, by and large, what got them to become a mob in the first place.

"I still don't see why you have to go," Brasti said. "If it has to be one of us, make Kest go out there."

"There's an art to managing crowds," I replied, "and Kest is terrible at it. Thirty seconds after he gets out there he'll be challenging them to a duel—*all* of them."

"Fine, then I'll go. Just—"

"Brasti, you're even worse. You wouldn't get ten feet without insulting the mob, their cleric, and whatever God they worship.

We'll be lucky if they don't tear down the entire martyrium just to get to you."

He grinned. "I suppose that's fair." He turned and leaned against the gates, and I was modestly reassured that they were sturdy enough not to start listing with that weight against them. "So, what'll it be then? Are you going with the 'Memories Of Ancestors'?"

"Takes too long," I said.

"The 'Child That Might Be Yours'?" he suggested, but I was already shaking my head.

"You think those people are going to look at a Greatcoat and imagine him as one of their own children all grown up?"

Kest peered out at the crowds from inside the gates. "I suggest you consider a 'Your Enemy Is My Enemy,' and then, once you've gotten whoever it is free, make for the road and try to circle back after—"

"No," I said, almost groaning. "I hate 'Your Enemy Is My Enemy.' Besides, whoever they've got bound up out there won't be in much shape to help me in a fight." Before Kest could start up again, I gestured to the guard to open the gate to let me out.

I walked through the narrow opening he made for me, hearing the lock clink shut a moment later.

"Try not to get torn to pieces." Brasti's voice sounded genuinely concerned now. "What are you going to use on the mob?"

I checked the rapiers in my scabbard, making sure I could draw them both at speed. "'Beatti feci forze Deato,'" I replied.

"Are you serious? You're going to try a God's Line on these people? Saints, why not just lie down on the ground and let them crush you beneath their feet?"

"Because that would get my coat dirty." I walked away from the gates and toward the field.

"This is what you do, you know," Brasti called out.

"What's that?"

"When you're tired. When you're scared. You throw yourself into fights you have no real chance of winning."

I searched around for a clever reply but the truth was, Brasti had made a surprisingly insightful observation. "You're right," I said.

"Then why keep doing it?"

I stepped into the crowd. "Because it's the only thing I know how to do that ever works."

It took some time to wade through the men and women, mostly farmers and laborers. They all took note of my passing, but few tried to interfere. The occasional moron with shoulders too big for his brain to manage jostled me, and a couple of children threw rotten fruit. I ignored it all, except for the one tomato I managed to catch that didn't look too bad; I ate it on my way. I hadn't had breakfast.

On the far side of the field I finally saw the man held captive: Allister Ivany, a tall, rangy man we used to call the King's Shadow, was hanging by his wrists from a tall pole that had been mounted into the ground. He looked a little beaten up, but nothing too bad. I couldn't tell from where I stood how many of his bruises were from the people holding him and how many were simply the product of however long he'd been on the road, answering the call I'd sent out for the Greatcoats to return to Castle Aramor.

His captors, a group of about twenty men and women, had the deeply tanned faces and sunburned arms of farm laborers. A few had real weapons, though—spears and old warswords, probably inherited from grandparents who had fought in the wars against Avares. I guessed their leader was the cleric in shabby orange robes that marked him as a disciple of Craft, or Mestiri, as they called him this far south.

It didn't take long for the cleric to notice me, and for the others to start to crowd around.

"Well, hello there, citizens," I said.

When you're about to face off with a crowd, two things are vital: first, you must maintain absolute confidence: for some reason, the thicker people are, the better they become at smelling fear, a scent they find strangely intoxicating. The second thing is to have a plan, and to stick to it. King Paelis had trained all of his Greatcoats in the different ways of dealing with mobs. After all, most days the job meant riding alone into some dirt-poor village or backwater town, declaring ourselves the representatives of the King's Law and thus empowered to hear all cases and render all verdicts—and then, after a few hours, telling people things they mostly didn't want to hear. Far too often their disappointment would be communicated with pitchforks and clubs.

The King had always been fascinated by the workings of the mind, especially the way large groups of people quickly started to share a single consciousness, to become, in effect, one person. And that person tended to be, in my experience, a complete arsehole.

So Paelis developed a variety of strategies for dealing with mobs, and he'd test them out by ordering me to use whatever his latest stratagem was on my next mission. He had a habit of underestimating the potential consequences of his latest theory failing to work.

"You know the motto of the Greatcoats, Falcio," he'd say to me. "'Judge fair, ride fast, fight hard.' If the town should turn against you, I suggest you simply amend the middle part to, 'ride *very* fast.'"

The King could be a bit of an arsehole himself, sometimes.

"Look here," a particularly burly man in his early twenties with hands roughly the size of my head called out, coming toward me. He was holding Allister's iron-shod staff. "Another brown bird for us to roast for supper!"

I pretended to ignore him, but I was taking careful notice nonetheless. I'd just decided he was going to figure prominently in my plans soon—but I wanted him wound up first.

"Hello there, Allister," I said. "Fancy coming inside with Kest, Brasti, and me?"

He lifted his head up to look at me, blowing to part the long black hair that had fallen into his face. "Falcio?" Then he grinned through a split and bleeding lip. "Depends. Have they got anything decent to eat in there?"

The big man who'd spoken earlier stuck out a thick-fingered hand to push my shoulder. I took a step left and forward to evade it while pretending I hadn't noticed.

"Brasti said to tell you that if you carried a proper sword instead of that idiot stick of yours then you wouldn't have been captured."

Allister looked more pissed off by the comment than by the bruises on his face. "Tell Brasti-fucking-Goodbow that it's a *staff*, not a stick, and I will be happy to see him in the dueling circle once this present matter is attended to."

The burly man came back around to stand between me and Allister, and a couple of his friends joined him. "You shouldn't have left the martyrium, Trattari. Now you're going t—"

I raised a finger. "Just a moment, please." I looked over at the cleric in grubby orange robes. "Pardon me, *Venerati*, is this your . . . congregation?"

The cleric said, "The Gods speak through me to these good people."

"Excellent." I pointed to the horse-cart I'd seen him using as a dais on my walk down here. "Could you get up on there, please? I want everyone to be able to hear you."

He spat—I've noticed clerics seem to do that a lot more than regular people—and announced, "If you think I'm going to call off Brell and the others and stop them from giving you the righteous punishment you deserve, Trattari, then you are mistaken."

I sighed. I'm told most clerics are actually perfectly nice people who keep to their own broken-down little churches, confining themselves to offering the occasional words of comfort for travelers and living off whatever meager donations people leave behind. Not that I've ever encountered those sort of clerics, mind.

"I would never ask you to contradict the will of the Gods," I said. "Even if that will is to give me a proper thumping."

"Oh, for the sake of Saint Marta-who-shakes-the-lion," Allister muttered, "tell me you're not going to do a 'God's Line' . . ."

The crowd were all slowly shifting into position around me now, following that strange compulsion that turns normally sane people into a pack of wolves.

The cleric smiled, clearly expecting me to ask him why he was here and what he was doing—to question why the Gods required him to take a Greatcoat prisoner.

Now, here's what you *don't* do with a mob: you don't ask questions. You don't walk up to them with a hearty, "Say there, friend, why exactly have you chosen to tie that nice fellow to a post?" Most of all, you don't *ever* start by demanding that they release him.

The mob, you see, only ever has one reason for beating up a man and tying him to a post, the same reason why they do all the things they do: it's because they're very angry, and they've found someone to take it out on. So you only ever get into a debate with them over the validity of their anger, or their choice of target if you happen to believe arguing with a bear woken too soon from sleep is a good use of your time.

No, engaging the crowd—and most especially their leader—on questions of "why?" will only earn you a spot on the next pole.

Brell, the big man who'd tried to push me earlier, came forward to grab my shoulder, and this time I slid my hand inside my coat. By the time Brell's right foot came back down to earth, the tip of my throwing knife was at his throat.

"Not yet," I said, and let him step back.

I wasn't looking to start a fight with him, nor prevent one; I just wanted everyone to know that I was probably faster than they were. *Saint Forza-who-strikes-a-blow, please let me be faster than them.*

"You do not frighten us, Trattari," declared the orange-robed cleric as he stepped up onto the horse-cart. He might not have liked that it had been my suggestion, but everyone enjoys being a little taller. "These good people do not fear you."

"Told you," Brell said, sharing a look with some of the others, preparing to rush me when the moment came. "You should've stayed cowering inside the martyrium."

"It's funny you should say that, Brell." I glanced back toward the gates that now looked very far away indeed. "You know, I've spent more time inside castles and palaces and, well, pretty much every type of building you can think of in the past few months than I did in all the years King Paelis was alive." I turned back to the crowd. "Greatcoats aren't really meant for hanging around, but it's been a life indoors for me lately. What do you suppose that means?"

"That you're a coward," Brell said, his mouth hanging open, eyes eager.

"You're right. I have been afraid." I shook my head. "I'm not even sure of what, you know? I mean, some days I think I'm scared of everything."

I slid the knife back in my coat and drew the paired rapiers from my scabbard. "That's why I carry these."

Brell and a couple of the people nearest him involuntarily took a step backward.

"You would attack an unarmed man?" the cleric bellowed for the crowd, evidently not noticing the staff in Brell's hand.

"Me? Of course not." The clouds overhead shifted a little, allowing the morning sun to come out. I lifted up the rapiers by their blades, one in each hand, to catch the rays, turning them to shine the reflected light into Brell's eyes, and he started blinking rather a lot.

"Do you happen to know, good Venerati," I said to the cleric on his horse-cart, "from what principle the laws regarding trial by combat are derived?"

Allister looked at me a little aghast . . . apparently he hadn't *really* believed I was going to try the God's Line.

"All laws are derived from the Gods!" the cleric declared, spreading his arms and clenching his fists as if daring me to contradict him.

Nope, not even remotely correct. "Exactly so, good Venerati."

He looked surprised by my admission. So did everyone else.

I turned a little, looking out at the faces in the crowd. "There are sixteen separate laws that mention trial by combat directly, each law governing different situations with different rules and sometimes even specific weapons. But did you know that every one of those laws begins with the same phrase? 'Beatti feci forze Deato.'"

"'*The righteous are made mighty by the Gods,*'" the cleric said in a rapturous voice as I smiled approvingly.

"Exactly. A lovely phrase, and one that makes perfect sense: the only way for trial by combat to be fair is if the Gods themselves are choosing the victor. They will give their righteous strength to the man or woman whose cause is just."

I tossed one of the rapiers to Brell who, having seen me hold it by the blade, caught it the same way. That's a mistake, of course. If you don't catch it just right you'll slice your hand open.

"My cause is—Ow! Hells!" Brell swore, dropping the sword and sucking at the bleeding cut on his palm.

"Careful," I warned. "People might think the Gods don't favor your cause."

Brell looked around at the faces of his compatriots, all staring at him expectantly. To his credit, he knelt down and grabbed the hilt of the rapier and lifted it back up defiantly. "I'm not afraid of you!"

I gave him an encouraging smile. "Nor should you be. The Gods will lend you their might, won't they? Surely I will soon lie dead at your feet, my blood watering the ground and sanctifying your cause." I glanced up at the cleric. "For if our Gods do not love and support those who ambush a man like a cowardly pack of dogs, well then, who really needs that sort of God, anyway?"

I flipped my rapier in the air and caught it neatly by the hilt. "Then again, Brell, if you should lose . . ."

The cleric, like most men of his training, was adaptable in his arguments. He roared to the crowd, "Should a brave man fall, will his fellows flee? Or shall they, like the heroes of old, take his place? For is that not the test the Gods set to us? That we, united, shall never seek to protect our own skin, but shall trade it cheaply, every one of us, until the blasphemers have been slain!"

Crowds always enjoy watching people shout at each other. This one waited eagerly for me to shout out some stupid counter-claim in our ecclesiastical debate. I didn't.

"Well, of course, silly man. *Everyone* knows that." With the tip of my rapier I pointed to individual figures in the crowd, one after another, until I was sure I'd gotten to all of them. "Get in line, if you please."

They looked at me with confused expressions.

"Come on, let's be orderly about this. In about sixty seconds Brell here is going to fall to the ground with a nasty stab wound in his chest. I'll need a couple of you to clear him out of the way so that the next man can take his place. And the next man after that. And so on and so forth." I brought my rapier into guard. "For if the Gods love your cause, then surely one of you will beat me. Eventually."

"You'll tire and falter, Trattari!" the cleric shouted enthusiastically. "You cannot hope to defeat us all!"

I was absolutely going to tire and falter, and probably sooner rather than later. Even now it was taking most of my strength just to keep *pretending* to be hearty and hale. "No doubt you are correct, Venerati," I replied. "And besides, if by some miracle my arm stays strong long enough to get through these twenty righteous warriors, then of course it will be your turn. Surely the Gods will grant you, their chosen representative on earth, the strength to dispatch a blasphemer like me?"

The cleric glanced around the field, possibly in search of a new argument. His followers were all staring at him now.

Brell, who I was, I confess, really starting to admire for his raw nerve, gave a magnificent roar and ran for me, the point of his sword aiming straight for my neck.

There were six smart ways to deflect the blow and three to get out of the way, but none of them would look all that impressive to an impressionable audience, so instead I dropped down low, throwing my left leg back and putting all the weight on my right while extending my blade all the way forward into a long and, I felt, quite elegant reverse lunge.

It took all the strength I had not to be bowled over by the force of Brell impaling himself on my blade as his own sword passed harmlessly over my head.

We stood there, he and I, for a long while, our eyes locked. It wasn't anger or satisfaction that kept me there; Brell's look of surprise and fear as he realized what had just happened made me want to offer what little comfort there was in the face of another as he saw all the things his life could have been slip away. I did my best to convey as much sympathy as I could. I had to believe that deep down, Brell was probably a decent man who'd made the mistake of allowing himself to be subsumed into the madness of crowds. It was out of this small shred of faith in his humanity that I had aimed my blow to avoid his major organs.

He slumped to his knees and I placed my hand on his shoulder, keeping him in position so that I would do as little damage as possible as I withdrew my blade.

"He'll need a healer, if any of you has such skills."

Two men came around and took him away, and a third began seeing to his wound. I didn't fool myself that my aim was so careful that Brell would be sure to live, but I'd given him as much of a chance as the circumstances had allowed.

I knelt down to wipe my blade on the grass. "Come on then," I said, examining my rapier to make sure it was clean. "Let's keep things moving along. Beatti feci forze Deato. If the Gods love you, then surely the next man will beat me."

I rose and faced the crowd. "Who's next?"

CHAPTER THIRTEEN
THE KING'S SHADOW

"That was a remarkably foolish gamble," Allister said, leaning heavily on my shoulder as we trudged back toward the martyrium gates where Kest and Brasti awaited us.

The crowds ignored us, for the most part. I'd had to duel two more men, one of whom had some talent but no training. The other might have had a chance, had he not been using an over-heavy and poorly balanced sword. Even weak as I was, neither had presented any great challenge. It would have been an entirely different situation if they had thought to swarm me en masse, but once I'd put that creeping question in their minds—why, if the Gods loved them so, had they not given any one of the first three men the strength to beat me—gradually stole away any lust for battle. This appeared to be doubly true of the cleric, who'd made his surreptitious exit before the third man had even fallen.

"Lucky bastard is what you are," Allister said.

I hadn't see Allister for more than five years, and I'd just saved him, so it was a bit annoying that he had so quickly fallen back into questioning my tactics. He failed to notice my irritation and went on, "One day, Falcio, you're going to be facing a mob that isn't so mesmerized by your theatrics. What would you've done if that cleric had been better versed in his catechism and simply countered with *Deato publis magni*?"

"'Through the many are the Gods manifest'? That's too complicated for your average roadside cleric." I paused for a moment. "Of course, if you'd like to go back, have them tie you up again and explain to that idiot in orange robes how he could have gotten everyone to jump me at once—"

Allister grinned. "Let's leave it for next time."

We were just about at the gates when Allister stopped me. "No, not here. Around the back."

The weight of him leaning on my shoulder made me question whether I had the energy to make it all the way around the complex myself, let alone half-carrying him. And I wasn't keen on spending any more time out with the pilgrims than was strictly necessary. But Allister's face told me he'd considered both problems, and was still insistent.

"All right," I said. "Just let me tell Kest and Brasti to meet us there."

"No," he grunted, no longer able to hide how much pain he was suffering. "Just you. Something you need to see, going to make your day a whole lot worse."

It took us a lot of slow, heavy steps to work our way around the other side of the martyrium grounds. The tall iron gates ended in a thick stone wall roughly ten feet high. Trees and other vegetation had grown in over the years, so it wasn't entirely impossible to get over the walls if we needed to, but I was really hoping we'd not have to try.

I let go of Allister and let him lean against the wall. He took a few deep breaths before putting two fingers to his lips and letting out a whistle that pierced the air.

"Who in hells are you calling?" I asked.

"My horse. Kicked her away when those men pulled me off her."

"Why in the world would you do that? She might have helped you escape."

"Couldn't take the chance that the mob would catch her."

"I'm sure your horse is gratified by your concern, but—"

"Couldn't let the mob see what she was carrying," he said, then pointed behind me.

I turned to see a pale brown and white mare tear up the ground as she galloped toward us and stopped a few feet away, eyeing me suspiciously. "I'm surprised she came back," I said.

Allister pushed himself away from the wall and walked unsteadily toward her, placing a calming hand against her muzzle and leaning his head onto hers. "Nah, she's a good girl. Practically fearless." He took her reins and led her back toward me, and that's when I saw that she had something heavy, wrapped in black cloth, tied across her back behind the saddle. It didn't smell very good.

"So how long have you been riding around with a corpse strapped to your horse?" I asked, glancing around to see if anyone was watching us, but fortunately the trees were providing substantial cover.

"Longer than I'd like," he replied. "I was coming to find you in Baern when I heard you'd left to come here. Help me get the ropes off, will you? My hands are still too numb; I was tied up for hours."

I unknotted the ropes, leaving the body to hang limp on the horse's back. When I pulled off the cloth covering the head, I found the pallid, lined face of an old man. There was nothing particularly impressive about him. "Who is he?"

Allister looked at the dead man's face with a deep sadness. "That night, back at Aramor, when the Dukes were coming for us? The King called me into the castle library."

My own fatigue disappeared instantly, and I focused my attention on Allister. Every mission I heard about was another possible clue as to the King's great plan. "What did he ask you to do?"

Allister didn't answer, at least, not directly, saying instead, "Did I ever tell you I almost became a cleric?"

That got a laugh out of me. There were any number of words I might have used to describe Allister; pious wasn't one of them.

"It's true," he said. "I studied the *Canon Deo,* the *Canon Sancti,* all the rest of them—I thought maybe I would become a *venerati ignobli,* find myself a nice little peasant church in the countryside, and preach for a living." He broke off and laughed at my expression, then added, "Never saw much point in the *venerati magni* myself. Nobles can all read the holy books themselves if they want." He smiled and looked off into the distance for a moment. "Even thought I heard the Gods' voices once—thought maybe I was meant to be a deator, but, well—"

"Allister, we're both injured and standing *outside* a martyrium, not all that far from the same mob who, not that long ago, planned to set you on fire, not to mention the fact that you've got a dead body on your horse. Perhaps you'd be so kind as to get to the point?"

He glared at me, then said, "Somehow the King knew about my past, asked me that night if I still wanted to be a cleric—it's funny, you know; I don't remember ever telling the King about it. Anyway, I figured he was giving up the castle and just trying to make it easy for me to go and do what I'd always wanted to do." He stared back the way we'd come. "Thing is, by then I'd been a Greatcoat for five years, seen all the shit people do to each other, all the excuses they give, and at least half of it's in the name of some God or some Saint. I just didn't have any faith anymore."

"What did the King say to that?"

Allister rubbed some of the dirt from his face with the sleeve of his coat. "It was the King, Falcio. He did what he always did, didn't he, ignored the thing you'd just said and then changed the subject entirely. Told me he'd met this man living in a cave up Domaris way. My mission, believe it or not, was to go and watch over him."

I looked at the body on the horse. "And that was him."

"Thought it was a shit mission at first," he admitted, looking at his boots. "He lived in this cave by himself, never talked much—just kept asking me to find books for him or sending me out to look for the answers to obscure questions that never made any sense. But you know, it's not as if I had anything else important taking up my time."

"You've been doing this for *five years*?"

He smiled ruefully. "It was peaceful, somehow. Didn't have to fight anyone or kill or even judge anything. I learned a lot from reading his books, listening to him mutter to himself." He looked at the old face lying on the black cloth. "Felt like I was just starting to understand the crazy old fool." Allister let out a long breath and I thought I saw an unexpected softness in his eyes. "Few weeks ago I came back from a long trip—he'd asked me to find him a copy of an old map; I did—but by the time I got back to the cave, he was dead."

I was about to ask how his charge had died, but Allister was already hauling the corpse off the horse, nearly falling over in the process. I steadied him, then the two of us laid the body on the ground, and Allister began unwrapping the black cloth until the old man's face and upper body were revealed.

Covering the man's arms and chest were tiny shallow cuts, just like those I'd seen on Birgid.

"Found something else in that cave," Allister said, reaching into one of the saddlebags and pulling out a smaller bundle wrapped in the same black cloth. He unwound it to reveal an iron mask. "This was bolted to his face when I found him."

"Son of a bitch," I swore.

Allister gave a sad, weary smile. "He was, in fact, a son of a bitch." He lifted the black linens to cover the old man back up in a strangely gentle gesture. "Wondered for a long time why the King had sent me to guard this rude, snoring, farting hermit, how this was supposed to renew my faith. And yet, somehow, those years watching over him did just that." He looked me in the eye as he said, "I'm almost positive that this man was Anlas-who-remembers-the-world. The King wanted me to protect the Saint of Memory." He let out a single, racking sob. "I failed him, Falcio."

"You guarded him for five years," I said, as gently as I could. "King Paelis couldn't have expected more."

Allister turned to look at me, his face as angry and tortured as the one etched into the iron mask I held in my hands. "*Really*, Falcio? You think you know his mind so well? Because I swear, I'll retake my oath right here and now and support you as First Cantor from now until the Gods tell me otherwise if you can tell me what the King's plan was."

We'd never been friends, Allister and me. We had nothing in common, for one. And I had long suspected that he thought I was an arrogant, moralizing show-off who spent my life trying to prove to everyone else I was better than they were. My suspicions about this came from the number of times he'd said these very words, or some variation, loudly and forcefully to my face.

I wasn't overly fond of Allister, either. He reminded me too much of the boys who'd pushed me around when I was young, jeering about my father leaving my mother and me and coming up with an endless variety of unpleasant reasons why. So we didn't like each other very much.

But we were Greatcoats, and in the end, that's all that mattered.

"I don't know what the King's plan was," I admitted, "but right now I don't care." I held up the iron mask Allister had given me. The carvings on its face had the same rough, almost haphazard quality as the one Saint Birgid had been wearing, though I thought perhaps the eyes and mouth were portraying a slightly different variation of terror and madness. It had the same clasping mechanism on the sides to hold it in place, and the same iron funnel fused to the inside.

"The plan I care about right now is the one that belongs to the man forcing these onto the faces of the Saints."

CHAPTER FOURTEEN

THE FIRST DECEPTION

We brought Saint Anlas's body back into the martyrium with us. Some of the pilgrims took a few tentative steps in our direction, maybe having some spiritual intuition as to what we carried, perhaps just curious as to why we were walking so boldly back into their midst. Kest and Brasti stood on the other side of the gates, weapons in hand, eyes on the crowd, ready to take on anyone who might make a move on us. But I wasn't the least bit concerned. As soon as we'd come in sight of the entrance I'd spotted Quentis Maren and his Inquisitors, and it was clear he'd noticed that we were carrying a body with us. He opened the gates immediately and some of his men rushed to assist us, confirming what I'd already suspected.

"How many?" I asked, as we passed into the martyrium and the gates closed behind us.

The Inquisitor looked as if he was considering feigning ignorance.

"How many what?" Brasti asked. "And who is that?"

I waited until we had moved out of view of the pilgrims before taking the dead Saint off the horse and setting the body gently on the ground. I motioned for Quentis to examine him, and he knelt and carefully unfolded the cloth, just as I had done.

"Saint Anlas, I believe," the Inquisitor said after a moment. He hesitated. "Though I'd never met him personally."

Obladias, the old man who was still doing his best impression—not that it was very good—of an uneducated country monk, confirmed it. "That's him. I knew him well enough."

"Really?" Allister asked. "He never mentioned you."

The monk responded with a brief chuckle. Maybe he knew the Saint hadn't been one for conversation; maybe he didn't care if we believed him. I didn't particularly care, either.

"How many, Cogneri Quentis Maren?" I demanded, making the name of his order into an insult. *It feels good. No wonder people do it to us so often.*

The Inquisitor remained silent for a long time.

"You might as well answer him," Duke Jillard said, walking down the path toward us. "Falcio has likely figured out a great deal of what you've been hiding. He's a little slow sometimes, but he usually gets there in the end."

"Do any of you work for him?" Brasti asked of the gray-robed Inquisitors standing around us, and when none of them responded he looked at me and asked, "Any reason I can't shoot Jillard, then?"

I kept my attention on Quentis. "*How many?*"

Finally, the Inquisitor spoke. "Twelve."

Twelve . . . I was struggling to grasp what it would take to . . .

"Twelve *what?*" Brasti asked. "Would someone *please* tell me what we're talking about so I can decide if I care?"

Obladias snorted and said to Duke Jillard. "Hard to imagine how that Ducal Council of yours thought to restore order to the country with geniuses like this on your side."

Brasti shrugged. "I leave the details to these two," he said. "Mine is a more infallible intellect."

"He means ineffable," Kest remarked.

"Which one's ineffable?"

"Shut up," I said to them both, then to Quentis, "Twelve dead Saints and you didn't think to inform the Realm's Protector?"

"Or the Ducal Council," Jillard added.

"I don't report to her," Quentis replied. "Nor, Your Grace, to you. The Order of Inquisitors—"

I cut him off. "The last time I checked, the 'Order of Inquisitors' had been reduced to a handful of angry old men sitting in their little dungeons staring at rusted implements of torture and trying to remember which one to brush their teeth with." I motioned to Quentis's men. "I see newly trained guardsmen here, in newly made coats and armor and carrying weapons that must have cost your churches half their reserves. So tell me, *Lord Inquisitor,* when did you first discover that someone was murdering Saints?"

It was, I felt, an impressive interrogation. I don't know why, but Inquisitors really piss me off. And Quentis actually bristled, which pleased me more.

"We found the first body a year ago," he said at last. "The second, six months later. After that, a month, and then . . ."

My temporary sense of self-satisfaction faded as the full force of his words began to take hold of me. A year ago, someone had found a way to murder a Saint. No doubt, when it was one Saint, Quentis and his Inquisitors had thought this was something they could manage—an aberration that could be kept secret. But now more dead bodies were turning up, and soon everyone, noble and peasant alike, would find out that the beings they prayed to for safety were no safer than they were. I looked at the gates, and out at the pilgrims on the other side. *Hells. They already know something is wrong.*

"The pace of the killings is increasing," Jillard said, "but why?"

My exhaustion returned and my wounds stung as if they were fresh. I glanced at Quentis and then at Obladias, wondering if they had already figured it out. I knew the answer because, as Jillard had already pointed out, I might be a little slow, but I get there in the end. I knelt down and picked up the body of Saint Anlas. Cradling him in my arms, I started toward the cathedral.

"The answer is simple, Your Grace," I said. "Whoever is behind this is getting better at killing Saints."

* * *

I found Ethalia waiting outside the cathedral for me. Barely an hour had passed since I last saw her, and yet she looked as if a week had passed. Her hair was disheveled, her arms hung limp at her sides and her cheeks were streaked with tears.

"Birgid?" I asked quietly.

"She's awake," Ethalia said, which surprised me, then she murmured, "but . . . it won't be long."

I felt a fool standing there with the rotting body of one Saint already lying dead in my arms while the woman I loved was breaking into a thousand pieces, already mourning the next one. Kest came and took the body from me, and I took Ethalia in my arms. She let me hold her, though only for a moment, then she stepped backward, away from me. "Birgid wants to see you," she said.

"Not alone," Quentis said, coming up the path toward us with Obladias close behind.

"She has asked to speak with Falcio," Ethalia said. "Not you."

The old monk showed not the slightest deference to either Birgid's wishes or Ethalia's grief. "The Saints, little girl, are the province of the church," he started. "Now step out of the way and—"

His words were cut off by the sound of wood creaking as Brasti bent his bow. The arrow nocked to the string didn't move an inch. "I really don't care how many pistols your men have, Quentis," he said conversationally. "They won't be fast enough to keep me from sending the old man to whatever hell most deserves him. And while I might not be a progeny at deception—"

"He means *prodigy*," Kest pointed out.

"Which one means I'm clever enough to figure out that the old bastard isn't just a monk and they probably don't want him dead?"

Quentis Maren's look of concern confirmed Brasti's suspicions, but the Inquisitor kept his eyes fixed on me. "Falcio, you know how serious this is. You can't expect us to—"

"You'll come with me," I said. I turned to Ethalia. "Did Birgid specifically say I was to come alone?"

"No, but . . ."

I took her hands in mine. "I'm sorry, but Quentis is right. If our situation was reversed I would never allow him to speak to the only witness . . ." I cringed at the use of the word. *This is the woman she looks up to more than any other person in the world.* "He needs to hear what Birgid has to say."

Ethalia acquiesced reluctantly, but let go of my hands.

"I'll be coming along as well," Obladias announced.

Damn right you will. I looked from him to Quentis and gestured at the pistol hanging at his side. "How fast are you at drawing that weapon?"

His eyes narrowed. "Fairly fast. Why?"

I opened the door to the cathedral—the one behind the statue of Death. "Because if Birgid recognizes either of you as the man who hurt her, you're going to find out you aren't nearly fast enough."

CHAPTER FIFTEEN

THE LAST BREATH

Walking down the stone stairs of the passari deo and into the shadows below reminded me that my primary aversion to religion was the practice of praying below ground. I mean, what sort of God thinks it's a good idea for their followers to entomb themselves, and *then* ask for health and long life?

"The sanctuary is not far," Ethalia said, steering me along the trail of candles that began at the bottom of the stairs and led into the darkness.

"They go first," I said, and stood aside to let Quentis and Obladias pass in front of us. If Birgid recognized one of them, I didn't want him behind me. I reached inside my coat and loosened the first of the six throwing knives in my leather bracer. For all my threats to Quentis, I was pretty sure I'd have a devil of a time drawing my rapiers inside the confined space of the sanctuary.

"Does it help?" Ethalia asked, her voice flat. She didn't turn to look at me and kept her eyes to the front as we entered the passage.

"Does what help?"

"Making yourself angry. Making yourself hungry for violence. Does it make you faster or stronger?"

"I . . . No, not especially."

She still wasn't looking at me. "Does it make you more cunning in battle, or shield you from pain? Or is it the pain itself that makes you—?"

"What? No, why are you saying this?" I started to take her by the arm, but stopped when she flinched. "Ethalia, what's wrong?"

She finally stopped and turned to face me. "I spent half my life cultivating peace inside myself, learning compassion, so that I might master the healing ways of my order. All those years . . . and now, when I need those skills the most—when *she* needs me the most—I find that I lack the strength because I have compromised my spirit with violence."

I looked for words of comfort and reassurance, for some clear, logical argument why Ethalia shouldn't blame herself, but none came, because I realized that she *wasn't* blaming herself. "You mean me," I said. "You think that being with me, with my . . . *violence* . . . that it's weakened your abilities?"

Ethalia wiped a hand across her eyes. She looked like she hadn't slept in far too long. She stepped aside and gestured for me to enter the sanctuary chamber. "Go to Birgid. She wants to speak with you, and that is the only gift left that either of us can give her now."

The sanctuary was a large chamber dug out of the dirt and rock, looking more like the abandoned den of some massive burrowing creature that had long ago left for more promising territory than somewhere to feel a God's touch. I dragged my boot heel against the floor for a moment, and then stopped myself. I didn't need to test whether the surface might be slippery; it wasn't going to come to a fight, not here. I did it by reflex, because there's nothing quite so embarrassing as falling on your ass when you're trying to draw your weapon with speed. Having done that, unintentionally, I could feel the ground was smoother than the walls, no doubt worn over time by the knees of however many thousands had come here over the years to pray. The only decorations were the silks in the six colors of the Gods of Tristia, hanging loose around the walls and shifting lazily in the faint breeze caused by our movements; I felt like I was entering a tent. Scattered candles had been lit around the chamber, but they provided little illumination and my eyes hadn't yet adjusted to the darkness.

"We pray in the shadows that we may summon the light," a voice said from the far side of the room. I recognized the voice as Birgid's, though only barely.

A brief flash of white light filled the room and then just as quickly disappeared, leaving me twice as blind as I'd been before. I was half-way to drawing a knife when I realized what had caused it. "You would think that if the Gods intended Saints to be candles in the dark, they might have made them a little more reliable."

"Had the Gods made the Saints," Birgid replied, "then I'm sure they would have done a more thorough job." I saw the blurry outline of an arm reaching up from a sleeping pallet at the far end of the room. "Come then, man of valor. I have little enough time left to me without you standing there like a tree waiting for the woodsman."

With the room blanketed in darkness once again, I picked up one of the little candles on the floor and walked over to where Birgid was stretched out on a pallet. "You know, if you keep talking like an old granny, people are going to think you're . . ."

The words left me as I reached the bed and saw what had become of the Saint of Mercy. I'd known she was dying, and I knew well what dying looked like. But I hadn't expected this.

When I'd met Birgid-who-weeps-rivers for the first time, just a few months ago, she had looked to be no older than twenty, with hair so blond it cascaded over her shoulders like white gold, resting against skin of a pure, pale honey lit from within by the morning sun. Even a week ago, when she'd turned up at the Palace of Baern, her face and body covered in filth and wounds, some of that ethereal beauty had remained. The woman on the sleeping pallet was not the Birgid I knew.

"I'm old," she said, narrowing her eyes and turning a hundred wrinkles into a thousand. "Get over it." She coughed into a piece of white cloth held between bent, stiff fingers and examined the results.

"Can we skip the part where I spend hours trying to explain to you how the youth I retained while I held onto my Sainthood now flees my body?" She coughed again. "Along with other things."

I glanced back at Ethalia, but she stood outside the door, out of view. Had this happened all at once, or had Ethalia been watching, day after day, struggling to save this woman so dear to her as she ever so slowly faded? "Well," I said, turning back to Birgid, "I'd sort of had my heart set on an extended discussion of just how terrible you look, but if you insist, we can move straight on to how bad you smell."

I heard a sharp intake of breath a few feet behind me, but she laughed then, and a little bit of the woman I'd first met on the road came back. Apparently Quentis or Obladias had taken offense at my jibe, but Birgid hadn't. "Ah, now I remember why I liked you, Falcio val Mond. So very, very belligerent in the face of those whose very nature demands you revere them."

I looked around until I found a small but sturdy oak box which I assumed housed the sanctuary's religious texts. I dragged it over to Birgid's bed and sat on it. "Belligerence comes with the coat, I'm afraid."

She reached out and ran the tips of her fingers across the cuff of my sleeve. "A slave to your ideals," she murmured. "And therein lies our one hope."

"All hope is given by the Gods, and all glory owed to them," Obladias said from behind me. "You of all people should know that, madam."

There was a brief flash of light again, a sudden glow around Birgid that came and went in an instant. "I assume, Venerati," she said coldly, "that there is some reason why Falcio brought you with him. Knowing him as I do, I doubt it was so that you could quote verses from the *Canon Dei* at me."

"You've got that right," I muttered, then turned to what I really needed to know. "Birgid, can you tell me who did this to you?"

"Did you know that the first Tristians came here as slaves?" she asked, ignoring my question. "That's why our churches are almost all underground—because our ancestors were brought here in chains to work the mines. They spent their nights on their knees, passing around whatever little lump of ore they had managed to hide and smuggle out, taking turns smoothing it in their hands, rubbing their skin raw as they prayed to any God who would listen to come and destroy those who oppressed us." She glanced over to where Obladias and Quentis were standing by the door of the sanctuary. "But you won't read that little fact in the *Canon Dei,* will you, Venerati?"

"Nor will you find any reference to the Saints," the old monk replied. "Shall we debate the relevance of that 'little fact' too?"

I felt my jaw tighten, along with a profound urge to deliver my thoughts on the subject forcefully to the bridge of Obladias's nose. *Focus,* I told myself sternly. *You have a job to do, and Quentis has a loaded pistol at his side.* "Birgid," I said gently, "have you seen either of these two men before?"

She looked up at me for a moment as if she hadn't understood the question, then gave a little chortle. "You mean, is the man who captured me, bound me in an iron mask, forced horrible liquids down my throat and cut my flesh here in this room? Is the murderer of my fellow Saints standing a few feet away so you can challenge him to a duel to the death and save us all a great deal of time?"

"See, when you put it that way I don't sound very clever."

Birgid lifted a hand and motioned me with her finger to lean in. When I did, she whispered quietly into my ear, "I don't know."

As she pushed me away, without much force, I could see tears of frustration in her eyes. "The mask . . . it bound more than just my body," she said. "It denied me the abilities of my Sainthood."

I really wanted to ask her what those were—I really hadn't the barest idea of what being a Saint really meant—but I could feel time slipping away from us. *Deal with the things you know,* I reminded myself. *Deal with the crime.* So instead I asked, "How did you get free? How did you manage to get to the Palace of Baern?"

There was silence for a little while, then she started, "They had me chained to a wall. When nothing else worked, I began smashing my head against it, over and over, until, finally, a piece of the mask shattered. There was a man there, a servant, who tried to stop me.

His will was weak, and I found that with the mask partially broken I could set my Awe upon him. I forced him to free me and then . . . and then I walked. I was in a daze, a fog so thick that the days and the miles meant nothing to me. I walked so long and so far that I couldn't mark the weeks or the miles. My need drove me, directed my steps, even when I couldn't see or hear or think."

"Your *need*?" I interrupted, but she dismissed the question.

"I cannot guide you to the man who did this to me, Falcio." She glanced at Quentis and Obladias. "He could be one of these two, Falcio, or he could be you, for all I know. That damned mask . . ." She drifted off for a moment, her eyes closing.

"Birgid?" Though I hated it, I needed to bring her back to the subject at hand.

"There is a weight to him," she said, slowly, as if searching for words to encompass the nature of the enemy. "A great and terrible intellect. A mind that would see this world shaped to his liking." She opened her eyes then. "Falcio, his desires cannot abide Mercy. He will destroy it unless you stop him."

Quentis Maren spoke for the first time. "Why the others, then, Saint Birgid? He may despise Mercy this much, but why kill the others?"

"I suspect he despises a great many things." She shifted on the pallet. "Do you know why the Saints came into being, Inquisitor? We had a purpose once, and it wasn't wandering around giving blessings at weddings and harvests and being worshipped."

Quentis came a little closer and I started to reach into my coat, but Birgid touched my arm, stopping my hand. The Inquisitor spoke carefully, respectfully. "I know what I have been taught, My Lady, but I have the sense that you would disagree."

"Trust that sense, then, Inquisitor. For it is rare in a man who chooses your rather idiotic profession. Tell me, how many so-called heretics have your men tortured today? How many senile old codgers or silly children have your men put to the knife for misquoting the canons?"

"That was a different time, My Lady," Quentis replied, "when those of my order misunderstood the calling of the Gods."

Birgid gave a soft snort. "The only thing the Gods ever call any of us is fools, Inquisitor."

To his credit, Quentis took the jibe with good grace and merely bowed. "We all play our roles, My Lady."

"What then is the actual role of the Saints?" I asked, not wanting to waste time on a theological debate.

Birgid opened her mouth and for an instant, for the smallest fraction of a second, I thought she would answer me. Instead, she pursed her lips. "No. This is a thing which each Saint must learn for themselves; it has never been shared with those not called, and I will not be the first to break that Law."

She started coughing then, a great, wracking cough that shook her so hard I thought it might be her last. When it was finally over, she said, "Damn it all! Ethalia! Are you too busy sleeping with men for money to bring me some tea?"

"It wasn't I who bedded Caveil-whose-blade-cuts-water," Ethalia said archly as she leaned over me to pass a mug to Birgid. The smell of lemon and ginger-root rose in the air. "Remind me again, who was it who got pregnant with Caveil's child and gave birth to Shuran, the man who nearly destroyed our country? I wonder, oh wise and terrible Saint, if perhaps we should withhold judgment about the value of our respective professions?"

Birgid's laugh was strained and cracked and beautiful. It would have been utterly infectious, were it not so clearly coming to its end. She handed the mug back to Ethalia and touched her hand as she did. "You above all others," she said. "Always do I hold that angry little girl in my arms and in my heart."

Something wet touched my face and I realized that Ethalia was crying; she had leaned over me to hold hands with Birgid, tears slipping from her cheek to mine. A life that had once been measured in centuries had ground down to weeks and days and now, finally, minutes.

I still had questions, dozens of them, but I could tell Birgid was done answering them. She had said all that she wanted to say to me and now it was time for me to leave her and Ethalia to spend these final moments together.

But Birgid surprised me, letting go of Ethalia's hand and grabbing weakly at mine. "Will you do something for me, man of valor?"

"I will," I replied.

She held out both hands. "Lift me in your arms," she said. "Carry me from this dark, empty place up and outside so that I may take one last breath in the light of day to carry with me on my journey."

As carefully and as gently as I could, I slid my hands under her frail body and lifted her from the bed. She weighed so little I wondered if perhaps she were already a ghost and I was merely imagining that I held her.

I walked slowly out of the dark chamber of the sanctuary. The Saint of Mercy felt so fragile in my arms that I feared any sudden motion might cause her bones to break. Obladias and Quentis stood aside, casting their eyes down to the ground, perhaps out of respect, or maybe because they were religious men and it was too hard to see a Saint come to this. Ethalia didn't look away but took Birgid's hand and held her gaze every step of the way.

When we reached the top of the stairs I looked around the colored walls of the sanctuary. I was oddly unsure of which door to choose, which God to follow. In the end, I went to the pale purple wall and the door that would be guarded outside, however poorly, by the statue of the Goddess of Love.

"There are still things worth saving," Birgid said as we exited into the warm sun. A light breeze lifted the thin white strands of hair from her face. It was, I supposed, as close to a parting gift from the Gods as we were likely to get. Birgid looked pleased, though, wearing the big toothy grin of a card player who has just laid down her last hand to win the final round. Her Sainthood gave another little flash, a soft glow barely noticeable against the afternoon sunlight.

Ethalia stood close by, smiling down at Birgid, trying to fill the old woman's last vision of the world with love.

And in the midst of this, I felt a desperate desire for this to be over. Ethalia was breaking inside and it should have been my job to hold her, to help her grieve and mourn, and then to lead her on those first fumbling steps toward healing.

But I needed to hunt down the man who had brought this upon us and end him.

Birgid's description of him came back to me: *A great and terrible intellect. A mind that would see this world shaped to his liking.*

I was so sick to death of those who kept wanting to twist and destroy what my King had tried so hard to build, what so many Greatcoats had died to protect.

Birgid shifted in my arms and I looked down. She reached up and placed a hand on my neck, pulling me closer to her.

"Are you . . . ? Is there—? Can I do anything for you?" I asked.

She didn't answer, but I felt her take in a breath so deep I feared her ribs might shatter from the effort. She held it a long time, and then kissed me on the cheek and whispered, "Forgive me, Falcio. I would have spared you this if I could."

Shame burned in my gut. While I stood there letting my frustrations roil, she was breathing her last. I put on my best wry grin and prepared something clever to say, something that might bring one last stutter of laughter to the Saint of Mercy, but when I looked down at her, the life had already fled her body. I waited, wondering if perhaps some last flash of light might come, or there'd be some great parting of the skies above us and thunder and rain would be unleashed to mark her passing. Even after Quentis approached and the old monk, Obladias, started muttering whatever useless prayer his Gods demanded be uttered at this moment, still I waited. Someone said my name, but I ignored them. Moments before I had wanted to be done with Birgid, and now I couldn't let her go.

Only when I felt someone trying to take her from me did I finally kneel and ease her body down on the soft grass that lined the path. I gazed at her face, willing it to look peaceful or serene or whatever words we use when recounting such events to others, though it would have been a lie. I've seen a great many dead people in my life. They just look dead.

"Falcio?" Ethalia said. I didn't think it was the first time she had spoken.

"Why did she say that?" I asked. "Why did she ask me to forgive her?"

When she didn't answer, I tried to turn, and only then did I feel that heaviness upon me, that distinctive sluggishness. I couldn't seem to get to my feet. For a moment I wondered if perhaps I'd been struck on the back of the head, or if Quentis had shot me in the back—sometimes it takes a few seconds to feel a wound when you're hit. But I didn't recall hearing pistol fire, or feeling anything hit me. I simply couldn't rise.

The grass beneath me became brighter for a moment, as if the sun had come out from behind the clouds. *That can't be right. There weren't any clouds in the sky.* The answer came to me then, even before I drew on every ounce of will inside me to force my body to respond, to demand that my hands push me to my feet and my legs straighten themselves. And as I stood, before I turned, I understood why Birgid's final words had been to beg my forgiveness. I knew what need had driven her to smash her head against the walls of her prison over and over until she could escape, and I knew that she had not, in fact, come to the Palace of Baern in search of me.

I knew all of this even before I found myself staring at the source of the light coming from the new Saint of Mercy.

His desires cannot abide Mercy. He will destroy it, unless you stop him.

CHAPTER SIXTEEN

THE SAINT OF MERCY

I reached out to her, of course. It's what you do when the woman you love is scared and in pain. It's what you do when she has just become the next target of a man who murders with impunity those whom others revere.

Move, I thought. *Ethalia needs you.*

She was standing six feet away from me, illuminated by the soft glow of the Sainthood that had once belonged to Birgid-who-weeps-rivers. She stood with her arms at her sides, staring down at the ground as though it was very far away, as if she had awakened to find herself standing at the edge of a cliff, hundreds of feet up, looking down at the village where she'd grown up, trying without success to find her family home because everything had suddenly become too small.

I'm not normally very poetic, so I suppose the whole thing with the cliff and the village was my first piece of evidence that something was *very* wrong.

Come on, I commanded my mind and body, *go to Ethalia.*

We're working on it, they replied in unison.

The glow faded from her and I was able to take a first slow step toward her. I could hear the sound of wind passing through the trees, of insects clicking, and people off in the distance shouting, so I knew time hadn't actually stopped. It was just me. *Just a couple more feet,* I told myself, *and then you hold her in your arms, you tell her this is going to be all right, that you're going to solve this problem together. You promise to keep her safe. Then, if she doesn't look like she thinks you're an idiot, you ask her to marry you.*

I heard the sounds of Kest and Brasti running toward me, shouting at me, neither realizing I couldn't possibly hear what they were saying over the sound of blood rushing in my ears.

I took my second step. *Close enough,* I thought, and reached out my hand, my fingers stretching to touch her, to pull her close to me. That would solve everything. We would talk, I would joke, she would pretend I was funny. We would figure it all out. Together.

My fingertips felt the first, light brush of the skin of her arm and the smile I'd started seconds ago finally reached my face. Then she turned and saw me reaching for her.

Everything about Ethalia is in the eyes.

Fear. Confusion. Loathing.

"Get away from me!" she screamed.

"Ethalia, it's me . . . It's—"

"Do not touch me with those hands," she said, her voice full of sorrow and yet utterly unyielding. "Those hands of violence—hands meant only for holding swords and for shedding blood . . ."

And as she ran away from me, through the door and into the cathedral, an old dueling phrase came to mind.

Deato mendea valus febletta.

The Gods give every man a weakness.

"We have a problem," Kest said, running toward me, Brasti hot on his heels.

"We have a problem." Really? Is it a big problem or a small problem? Is it something on the order of finding even more dead Saints lying

around, or something simpler, like the woman I love fleeing from me in utter disgust?

"Give me a minute," I said.

Kest grabbed me by the shoulder and shook me. He hardly ever does that without a good reason. "Minutes are all we have, Falcio. Listen, can you hear them? The pilgrims are rushing the gates."

"Duke Jillard's already left," Brasti said. "He took one look at the mob and rode out of here, closely followed by his personal guards."

The first shouts reached us from off in the distance, and Kest renewed shaking my shoulder. "The gates won't hold long, Falcio. Allister's found a back exit out of the martyrium but if the pilgrims find it before we leave we'll be trapped."

That certainly *sounded* serious. Pilgrims. Gates. Trapped. All very serious words, said in a serious voice by a very serious man. *So why can't I make sense of any of it?* I needed to clear my head somehow. I felt a profound urge to stab someone with my rapier. *No, that hasn't been working out lately.*

"What in the name of Saint Laina's left tit is wrong with him?" Brasti asked.

"I believe he's suffering the aftereffects of the Saint's Awe," Quentin Maren replied. "It's the spiritual influence they wield over us— each Saint's Awe is different, attuned to their nature."

The "Saint's Awe." That sounded like a perfectly sensible explanation. On the other hand, he might be making it up. *Stop. Focus. What's happening right now?*

"Whatever the cause," Kest said, "we need to get Ethalia out of here before this place is overrun."

The sounds of shouting grew louder. "You can run off any time you like," Obladias said, "but the Saint of Mercy stays with us. Only the church can guide and protect her as she comes into her Sainthood. This is a matter far outside your understanding and even further outside your jurisdiction."

"Very logical," I said. "Sensible, practical thinking, Venerati." I had no intention of following it. I turned to Kest. "Go and get Ethalia from the cathedral. She'll . . . I think she'll be more comfortable if you talk to her."

"Assuming I can get the new Saint of the Mercy to listen to me, then what?" Kest asked.

"Take her to Allister and the horses. Brasti and I will meet you there in a minute and then we'll go to Aramor."

"Falcio, you realize that's *not* what Obladias is suggesting?"

"Yes, I'm aware of the distinction. He has laid out his very clear, sensible thoughts on the matter and now we're going to do the exact opposite."

"You'll do nothing of the kind, Trattari," Obladias said.

"Go on," I told Kest. "Brasti and I will meet you when we're done."

"Done what?"

Obladias had had enough of me by then. "Inquisitor Maren, by order of the Church and under the command of the Gods, draw your weapon and fire on this man."

I wasn't looking for a fight. At least part of me recognized that making an enemy of the Church could cost us, later on. That part of me was very, very small.

"Falcio . . ." Quentis warned. He hadn't yet reached for his pistol, which told me several very important things.

"Quentis, if you think I'm letting you take the woman I love into custody so that you and your fellow Inquisitors can turn her into your own personal pet Saint, then you're even crazier than your friend here. And judging from the sneer on his lips, I'd say he's so crazy that he's about to say something he'll regret."

Come on, you arsehole. Just give me an excuse.

The monk—and now I definitely knew there was no way in any hell he was simply a monk—practically growled, "Listen to me, Trattari. I don't give a damn what relationship you think you had with this woman before, but she's a Saint now and is the property of the Church."

Property of the Church. Okay, that'll do.

The slight whisper of steel sliding across leather filled the air as my rapier fairly flew from its sheath. Its point floated an inch from Quentis Maren's neck before his hand had even reached his weapon.

"I warned you I was fast when I set my mind to it."

"You're taking quite a gamble," he said. "How do you know I don't have my men ready to fire on you?"

"Oh, I'm pretty sure you had several of them ready to take me once we'd left the cathedral. But I'm hearing two hundred crazed zealots trying to knock down the front gates and I'm thinking that those men went to help the others." I locked eyes with him to see what reaction he'd have to what I said next. "Those pilgrims out there didn't just up and decide to storm the martyrium. Someone told them that the body of Saint Anlas was here. Someone whipped them up into a frenzy. Who do you suppose gave them that little nugget of information? Because I think you have a spy among your men."

To his credit, Quentis Maren didn't so much as blink. "If there is someone disloyal among my Inquisitors, I'll soon find them. In the meantime—"

"In the meantime," Brasti said, an arrow nocked and ready, "I'd say you should probably get ready to give a truly inspiring speech to those pilgrims, because that gate is coming down now and Kest and I took care of a little business just before we came here."

"And what business was that?" the Inquisitor asked.

"We set all your horses free. Judging from how fast they ran, I'm guessing they don't much care for crowds of slightly insane, screaming people."

"You know I could kiss you right now, don't you?" I said to Brasti.

"Always the sentimental one."

Brasti kept his arrow aimed at Quentis as the two of us started backing away, heading for the path leading toward escape. Obladias began cursing me—the Tristian religion has some very nasty curses that doom a man to every kind of hellish torment imaginable.

Oh well. I've been cursed plenty of times in my life and nothing too bad's happened yet, right?

"Tell me how this ends, Falcio," Quentis said as he watched us backing away. "Saints are dying, the people are terrified, and soon they will all know that their lives are even less safe than they thought. Whatever force is behind this is more deadly than any of us have seen, deadlier than anything that has existed since the Gods themselves walked the earth. What exactly is it you think you can do, you with your bare handful of Greatcoats?"

"That's simple," I said. "We're going to find the son of a bitch who killed Birgid, and then I'm going to arrest him."

CHAPTER SEVENTEEN
THE SHATTERED STONES

It's remarkably hard to sustain the image one has of oneself when riding into danger, sword held aloft, sitting astride a fine black warhorse, when it's pissing rain down on your head. First of all, riding about with a rapier extended just gets you funny looks to go with your sore arm and rusted blade. Second, if you push a horse to run great distances at speed in a downpour you generally just end up with a dead horse. By the sixth day since our departure from the Martyrium, however, I was no longer entirely opposed to that outcome.

"Stop leaping over everything, you damned fool," I said to my horse for the hundredth time, but the damn thing ignored me. As usual.

I've never had a very good relationship with horses. It's not that I dislike them—I mean, who *doesn't* like horses? They just don't reciprocate the sentiment in my case.

My current mount, a copper-colored Tivanieze, was bred for traveling through rough, mountainous terrain, and insisted on staying in practice by jumping wildly across every puddle, bump, or pothole on our otherwise smooth road. I was slowly, mile by mile, being driven mad by his choppy, stuttering gait. It didn't help that I was spending most of that time watching Ethalia riding a few dozen yards ahead, slowly succumbing to the Saint's Fever. *So much faster than it had taken Kest,* I thought.

I'd tried to stay close to her, to reassure the woman I loved, but my proximity only made matters worse.

"Maybe you should try talking," Brasti suggested.

"I've tried," I said. "All she says back to me is, 'I can abide.'"

"No, no, I meant *talk to the horse.* Be nice to the poor fellow— maybe give him a name."

The sight of a broken tree branch lying in our path—no, not even a *branch,* a *twig,* no more than two inches high, sent the Tivanieze leaping several feet in the air, and I was very nearly jolted from the saddle. "Stop it, you arsehole!" I shouted.

"'Arsehole' is a terrible name for any beast," Brasti chided.

Kest looked back from a few yards ahead. "He did call the last one 'Monster.'"

"She had fangs," I countered. "It was a perfectly reasonable name."

A few seconds later a squirrel skittered across the road in front of us, and my damned horse veered playfully toward it as if he were contemplating chasing after it. I pulled hard on his reins to get him going in the right direction again. "I'm definitely sticking with 'Arsehole,'" I informed him.

"Church up ahead," Allister called out.

"Joy of joys," Brasti said, standing in his stirrups to look down the road. "Maybe the seventh time's the charm."

It was going to have to be. We'd stopped at every roadside church and backwoods shrine on the road from Baern in hopes of finding a working sanctuary. We weren't quite sure what we were looking for, but we were quite sure we hadn't found it.

"I can abide," Ethalia said each time we failed to find a place with whatever invisible spiritual characteristics were required to ease her suffering, and each time I'd wait until she'd ridden ahead, out of earshot, before I turned to Kest and asked, "How long until it over-comes her?"

Not that he ever gave me an answer that was any use. It had taken him longer to feel the effects of the Saint's Fever during his brief tenure as the Saint of Swords, but that might have simply been because Kest is so damned disciplined that he forgets to acknowledge agony, even when he has a pistol bullet lodged in his shoulder. *Or even a hand severed from his arm by his best friend's blade,* I reminded myself.

"This one's no good, either," Allister called back. He and Ethalia were already off their horses and had made it into the church grounds ahead of us. Kest, Brasti, and I followed.

"Most of the damage is old," Allister said, surveying the broken walls and crumbling ceilings. He knelt down and examined a piece of wood, part of a shattered wooden pulpit. "Some of this is newer, though, maybe six or seven weeks."

That troubled me: the destruction might be too recent to be coincidental, but it was too old for us to be able to track whoever was responsible.

"Looks like a war-ax took out that pulpit," Kest observed.

"Maybe," Allister said, "but I see blunter work done on the door." He lifted a sheared-off wooden railing out of the way so he could peer down the stairs that led underground. "It's all just dirt and rubble down there. The stones look like they've been shattered methodically with hammers."

Kest turned to me. "Those stones are the markers for the sanctuary. It's within them that new Saints binds themselves until the Fever passes."

"How does it work? What . . . mechanism takes away the fever?"

He shrugged. "Who can say? I wasn't the Saint of Swords long enough to learn how any of it worked."

"Maybe that's why you never quite got the hang of it," Brasti suggested. "Maybe they should hand out little pamphlets for new Saints, you know, a guide to get you past the first few months."

I ignored him. It had begun to drizzle again. "We should go," I said. "Maybe the next sanctuary will be intact."

"You know," Brasti pointed, pulling up the collar of his coat, "if one of these clerics had had the sense to build his little sanctuary inside a tavern, it'd be the best maintained and most visited religious site in the country."

As I walked back outside I saw Ethalia standing there in front of her horse, hair tangled from the rain and wind, her pale skin somehow made paler by the gray clouds overhead.

I began walking to her. "Are you—?"

"I will abide," she replied. She put a foot in the stirrup and wearily hoisted herself onto the saddle before kicking her horse into a slow walk.

I looked after her. This had become the pattern with us, as if even my concern was somehow painful to her.

I felt a hand on my shoulder. "She doesn't mean it," Kest said. When I didn't reply, he added, "There is always the sanctuary of Saint Forza-who-strikes-a-blow on the border near Aramor. That's where I found my reprieve from the fever. It's not more than three days away from here."

"And if it's been desecrated, too?" I asked, and mounted my own horse. What was happening wasn't happenstance. It wasn't just the long and steady decline of religious observance in Tristia. Someone had a plan, and I was far too many steps behind them.

We trudged on like that, day after day, watching the miles pass, and villages large and small pass by with them. The people who lived nearby claimed to have no knowledge of what was going on, and showed little sign of being concerned, though they were quick to blame us for failing to protect the churches. I got an earful from Allister when I brought it up.

"The country didn't stop falling apart the day you took up residence in Castle Aramor," he said, giving me his trademark glower. "For every Knight who no longer comes to beat on their door demanding taxes a second and third time each season, there's a bandit leader or band of brigands equally happy to tear things apart. These people are poor and they're scared, and you sending people to shout *The Greatcoats are coming! The Greatcoats are coming!* in every tavern and inn really isn't helping."

"That wasn't the entirety of the message," I said.

"Oh?" Allister asked. "So the Bardatti just forgot to mention what circuit courts each of us is assigned to, or who replaces the gold coins we use for the juries? Ran out of my supplies years ago—no hard candy left, no amberlight, no black fog." He ran a hand down the front of his coat. "Three of the bone plates shattered a while back. Do any of you know how to replace them? Can't even figure out what kind of animal *has* bones this thin and strong."

"You know, Allister," Brasti said, reaching into the pocket of his coat and pulling out an apple, "your nervous griping is taking all the fun out of this trip." He took a bite and grinned. "Maybe if we found you a proper weapon you wouldn't feel quite so scared all the time."

From atop his horse, Allister casually reached back and loosed the iron-shod staff attached to his back. He let it slide down into his palm and spun it around before flicking his wrist. Suddenly the staff was fully extended and Brasti's apple had gone flying into the ditch.

"Feel free to let me know when you want a bout, Goodbow. Kest says you're even worse with a sword now than you were the last time I knocked you off your feet."

A good deal of nonsense followed. Brasti, Kest, and I had spent so much time together over the past few years that I'd forgotten how competitive Greatcoats could be when they got around each other. At least the vigorous debate over weapons and tactics improved Allister's mood. Normally I'd have been happy to join in (especially since the rapier is, obviously, the finest weapon ever devised) but my thoughts were occupied with visions of heavy iron masks, of desecrated churches, and of the shallow cuts on Birgid's skin. How in the world were a handful of Greatcoats supposed to protect however many dozens of Saints and hundreds of churches when we didn't even know what we were facing?

No wonder the fucking clerics brought out the Inquisitors.

"We should stop for the night," Kest said, startling me out of my reverie. "The sun's getting low and the chances of one of the horses taking a stumble will only increase once it's dark."

"Been down this road before," Allister said, "back when I used to ride the King's Seventh Circuit. There used to be a tavern, quite a large one, couple of rooms to rent, about five miles ahead."

"Perhaps we should make camp instead," Kest said, doing his best not to look right at Brasti. "Less risk of running into trouble that way."

Brasti groaned. "Of course you'd rather sleep out in the cold, Kest. It's perfect for men like you and Falcio. You two are only happy when you've got some cause for misery." He stood up on his stirrups and looked down the road ahead. "But I hear the call of music, a soft bed, women and, most importantly, beer."

"You can *hear* the beer?" Kest asked incredulously.

Brasti ignored him and pointed ahead. "Those are *my* Gods, Falcio. That's *my* sanctuary. Refusing me the chance to pray at my righteous altar is nothing short of religious persecution."

I was about to tell him to shut up, that the last thing we needed was the risk of conflict with the local bully-boys, but Ethalia gave a weak smile. "I don't think even I could stand to witness Brasti's equivalent of the Saint's Fever."

That smile, the flicker of ease, however temporary, in her eyes, was enough for me.

Brasti grinned. "Ethalia, you're my new favorite Saint." He kicked his horse into a trot and set forth down the road.

"All right," I said, "let's go and visit Brasti's Gods and see what they have to tell us."

CHAPTER EIGHTEEN
THE TAVERN

The Bone Maiden's Tavern proved to have all the things Allister had promised and Brasti required. There were beds for rent, and food aplenty. The price was cheap enough, and the rooms small enough that we could afford to each have our own, a rare luxury on the road. I didn't really notice the noise coming up from the common room downstairs as I lay back on my bed, still clothed, enjoying the relative peace and quiet for as long as it would last.

That didn't turn out to be very long.

Banging on my door was swiftly followed by Brasti's head as he pushed it open and peered in. "There you are! What in the name of Saint Zaghev's balls are you doing hiding in here?"

"Trying for peace and quiet. Unsuccessfully, apparently."

He hauled Kest in behind him and the two of them stood awkwardly in the narrow gap between the door and my bed. "Well, this is just pathetic," Brasti said.

"Why are the two of you here when you're supposed to be guarding Ethalia?" I demanded, pushing myself up.

Kest put a warning hand on Brasti's shoulder. "I told you this was a bad idea."

Brasti was having none of it. "Oh, don't worry about Ethalia. Allister's keeping a *very* close eye on her. In point of fact, that's why we're here. Kest and I are on a vital mission of friendship and loyalty."

"And here I thought you were on a mission to get drunk and bed the local schoolteacher."

He folded his arms across his chest. "I can do more than one thing at a time. I'm ambidextrous."

Kest began to speak. "That's not what—"

I sighed. "All right. Get on with it."

"I just thought you should be aware, oh First Cantor, that our esteemed colleague Allister is, even as we speak, downstairs and setting lustful eyes upon your woman."

I stiffened. "He's taken her down to the common room? Has he lost his mind? What if—"

"She's unharmed," Kest said. "It was her idea. She said the music was helping to soothe the fever."

"Did it do that for you when you had it?"

"No, but then, Ethalia and I aren't exactly alike."

Thank the Gods for that, at least.

"The point is," Brasti said, jabbing a finger at me, "that it shouldn't be Allister down there with her. It should be you."

"She doesn't want me," I replied, too quickly to maintain anything that sounded even remotely like personal dignity. I tried to recover with, "Her Sainthood makes my presence painful to her."

Brasti leaned back against the wall and put the heel of one boot on the edge of my bed. "Well, it just so happens I have a suggestion that might soothe the spiritual troubles between you. How about, instead of pining here in your little room, you go down there and be a fucking man for a change?"

"All right," Kest said, grabbing Brasti by the arm, "that's enough for—"

"No," Brasti said, shaking him off, "it's not. You want to know what the real problem is with you, Falcio?"

"Yes," I said. I'd pretty much already decided that this conversation was going to end with me punching Brasti in the mouth so any additional fuel he wanted to add to the fire was fine with me. "Go ahead and tell me what's wrong with me."

"You buy into all this shit about Gods and Saints and magic and curses."

Even Kest was surprised by that. "You don't believe in Saints and magic? After all the things we've seen?"

Brasti waved a hand in the air. "Of course some of it's real. I mean, it's a giant pain in the ass, so it has to be real. But that doesn't mean you have to take *everything* as if it's a commandment from the fucking universe to get down on your knees and beg for forgiveness."

He took his foot off the bed, which I knew was because he was about to say something he knew I didn't want to hear and he needed to keep all his limbs free to deal with my reaction. "The thing that's keeping you and Ethalia apart isn't her Sainthood, Falcio. You can pretend all you want that everything was perfect with you both before, but there's a reason you didn't ask her to marry you when you had the chance."

"You stupid son of a bitch, I was trying to recover from the damned—"

"No, Falcio, don't use the Lament as your excuse for everything. The problem started long before that."

I started working through the distance between my fist and his face and the sequence of movements required to bridge that gap. "Is that so?"

"I'm fairly certain that you should stop talking now," Kest said.

Brasti ignored the counsel. "It's Aline."

"You think that because I'm trying to help the King's daughter I can't—"

"Not *that* Aline. Aline-your-wife, you idiot. You know, the woman whose memory weighs so heavily on you that before Ethalia you hadn't gone near anything female for *years*? The woman—and I can't believe I'm saying this out loud—whose name you invoke every time you have to fight for your life?"

I leaned back against the head of the bed, suddenly too weary even for the temporary pleasure of giving Brasti a split lip. "You don't understand."

"Of course I don't. So explain it to me." He waited barely a second before going on, "You can't, though, because it's all horseshit." He sat down on the corner of the bed, apparently now confident that I wasn't going to beat him senseless. "Think about it, Falcio. You're a young, beautiful woman. Smart, caring, sensuous—"

"Focus," Kest said.

"Right. Anyway, so you find this man you think you're destined to be with and—well, despite obvious physical defects, apparently some women do find you attractive, go figure. And here *you* are, spending every day of your life with the memory of your dead wife hanging over your head: *Aline*, the perfect woman. *Aline*, the noblest sacrifice. *Aline*, the purest—"

He must have noticed my fist clenching because he stopped for just a moment. Then he said, "But it's not just you, Falcio. Ethalia buys into all of it too. So she finds you, a man she barely knows but has sworn she loves and who claims he loves her, and then Birgid, the woman who mentored her, the woman she idealized and adored, dies, and suddenly there's this damned Sainthood hanging over her. How do you suppose she feels?"

"Unmoored," Kest said, before I could answer.

"Exactly. So *of course* everything feels fated or cursed or whatever. *Of course* it feels like some sign the two of you can't be together. Imagine the relief for both of you to finally have an excuse why you'll never have to get to know each other properly, never have to deal with each other's annoying faults. Never have to figure out that love is *hard*."

I wanted to disagree, to tell him to shove off or, better yet, just ignore him, bury my head under the pillow until his annoying whining voice shut up, but somehow I couldn't. I looked at Kest, who'd always been my measure of what was true in the world.

"This is . . . out of my area," he said.

Terrific.

"Listen," Brasti said, putting a hand on my shoulder, "go down to the common room. Walk in like a man, mind you, not some shade of the long dead. Go up to Ethalia, take her hand, and lead her out onto the dance floor."

I suddenly found myself laughing out loud. "Dancing? You want me to *dance* with Ethalia?"

"Why not? If you're both so fucking cursed then I'm sure lightning will strike you down. But maybe you'll find that it's not some momentous curse, nor a mystical cure. Maybe it'll just be dancing. Maybe you're just a man and she's just a woman and every once in a while it's okay to just be human together."

I stared at him for a long while. I have witnessed some terrifying things in my life, horrible things that made me question the very foundations of my own sanity, but none of them were quite as discomforting as Brasti Goodbow sounding as if he might be making sense.

Dancing, I thought. *Well, there's a tactic that never occurred to me.*

CHAPTER NINETEEN

THE DANCE

The common room was packed with townsfolk—men and women of all ages, and even a few children chasing each other around, though long past any decent bedtime. The music was loud and fast and infectious. Three musicians sat on stools on a small stage at the far end of the room, the sound from their guitars and flutes amplified by the wooden walls around them. Below the stage a well-worn dance floor extended out about ten feet, terminating in a wide semicircle barely large enough to contain the dozens of dancers happily spinning and bouncing each other around.

It took me a while to work my way through the crowds until I could finally make out Allister and Ethalia sitting at a small table not far from the door. She had changed from her plain traveling clothes to a simple country dress of white and blue layers. The last time she'd worn it was the night we'd arrived at the Ducal Palace in Baern, when we'd walked through the Duchess's garden maze together. She'd plaited her long dark hair into a single loose braid that hung over her left shoulder, just like the other women in the tavern.

Despite her attempts to fit in with the crowd, to me she might as well have been glowing like the sun, and if the other patrons didn't share my awe of her, Allister certainly did. He leaned in and said something to her, and she returned a small smile of acknowledgment. The sight gave me a mean twinge of jealousy for a moment. I tried to shake it without success.

At least Brasti would approve.

I was about to head toward them when one of the musicians caught my eye. He was a tall, thin man with black hair that hung just above his shoulders. He had a large silver hoop in one ear which I suspected meant something to troubadours but nothing to me. He nodded toward the other side of the room and when I followed the line of his gaze, I saw another musician, a blond-haired woman stringing a guitar, at the side of the stage.

I hadn't had much experience with the Bardatti other than Nehra, but she'd assured me they were spreading the word and on the lookout for Greatcoats. Perhaps this woman had information for me.

"I'm Falcio val Mond, First Cantor of the Greatcoats," I said, once I was close enough to her that I could speak my name without too many others overhearing.

"A fellow tried to use that line on me yesterday," she said, still stringing her guitar.

"I—"

"Besides, if you're going to try and pick up a woman using another man's name, you might as well get it right. Everyone knows that *Falsio dal Vond* is the First Cantor of the Greatcoats."

"Oh for the damnation of Saint—"

She turned and grinned. "Got you."

"Got me?" *This is why I prefer to spend my time dealing with people who want to kill me.*

"Sorry," she said. "Nehra made me promise to use that on you when I saw you." She stuck out a hand. "I'm Rhyleis."

I shook hands with her and felt the odd sensation of the calluses on her palms rubbing against mine. It made sense, I supposed, though our respective instruments were very different.

Rhyleis had a performer's face, all sharp angles, her every expression magnified as if the Gods wanted to make sure even those in the cheap seats would catch her meaning. I could imagine her playing the role of a mythical princess or a starving crone. Was she beautiful? Probably to most, but not to me.

Then why are you even thinking about her looks, you idiot?

Rhyleis caught my scrutiny and gave me a wink that unsettled me. I covered it as best I could. "How did Nehra know I'd be here?"

She tilted her head. "Well, let's see. You were in Baern and had to head back north eventually, which meant you'd likely be on this road, and"—she gestured toward the far door that led to the rooms upstairs; I turned and saw Brasti there, giving me a thumbs-up, possibly assuming I'd decided to give up on Ethalia and seek comfort elsewhere—"can you imagine him *not* making you stop at a place like this? It's the busiest tavern in the region."

I wasn't sure I was entirely convinced about her logic, but I let it go. Nehra was also annoyingly glib about the power of the Bardatti. I supposed that wandering troubadours probably didn't want common folk to be overly concerned about any possible esoteric abilities the people playing in their villages might have.

"I take it you have information for me?"

Rhyleis reached out and ran a finger against my cheek, looked into my eyes and sighed. "Is that all you think I'm good for, Falcio? Information?"

"I . . . we only just—"

Again she smirked and let go. "Relax, First Cantor, I'm playing with you."

I was beginning to lose my affection for the Bardatti sense of humor, but suddenly Rhyleis was all business. "We've spread word to those Greatcoats we could find. There aren't many of us to do the job, though, and, frankly, even less of you around."

"How many?" I asked.

"Last I'd heard we'd made contact with eleven Trattari."

It always irritates me when Nehra and the other troubadours call us "Trattari," though I had larger concerns at that moment.

"*Eleven?* That's all?"

"It's only been a few months," she replied, "and it's a big country. Well, actually, it's a small country as these things go, but there's still a lot of ground to cover."

"Which ones have you met?"

"Antrim Thomas and Allister Ivany, although I see you already know that. I saw Talia, the King's Spear about a hundred miles north of here a few weeks ago. She said she'd be on her way back soon."

Eleven. Eleven out of what should be a hundred and forty-four counting Kest, Brasti, and me. Where did we all go?

"There's something else," Rhyleis said, drawing my attention back.

"What is it?"

"This thing with the Saints. It's worse than you've heard. I'm hearing lines in the songs about a cult of some sort."

"'Lines in the songs'?"

She put a hand on my arm again and pointed to the other musicians. "Listen . . . *here.*"

They were playing a rousing chorus of "Any Rose In Spring," the words familiar to anyone in the southern half of Tristia. It's about a foolish young man trying to choose between the seven girls he meets, not realizing that none of them actually want him.

"I don't get it," I said. "The lyrics are the same as they always are."

"Listen to the notes of the countermelody," she said.

I did, but though I had some passing familiarity with music, that was pretty much limited to knowing roughly which end of a flute to blow in. "I'm not—"

"Sorry," Rhyleis said, "I just assumed . . . the Trattari used to use the same language in some of their songs."

"Pretend I'm not from two hundred years ago when the Greatcoats all wrote symphonies for every verdict, will you?"

"Fine. The countermelody is like a code, used against the primary melody to delineate which words . . . no, you know what, let me just tell you what it says."

Thank the Gods.

"A long time ago there was a cult who called themselves the God's Needles. Rumor has it that they used a set of esoteric rituals intended to turn their members into Saints themselves. That's all we know."

"Well, I'd never even heard of them before now, if that makes you feel any—"

She shook her head to cut me off. "You don't understand, First Cantor. We're the *Bardatti*. Keeping track of these things is what we do." She hugged herself. "I'm not sure I like the idea of something that's kept itself hidden from us this long suddenly appearing."

I didn't like the idea either. *God's Needles.* Why dredge up something old and long forgotten; why *now*?

"I need to get back on the stage," Rhyleis said. "Emeryn is butchering the harmony up there." She ran the backs of her fingernails over the strings and then adjusted two of the tuning heads minutely before picking it up and heading toward the stage. She stopped after a step, though, and told me, "Oh, and you should probably pay more attention to your woman. Your friend there has eyes for her."

"Saint Zaghev . . . is there no one in this country with anything better to do than concern themselves with my love life?"

Rhyleis grinned, though there was something else in her eyes. Sympathy, maybe? "A noble hero, filled with valor and pain? A beautiful woman of wisdom and compassion? Two lovers torn apart by Sainthood to boot?" She ran back to me and kissed me on the cheek. "Why, Falcio, it's a song so tragic it would turn any girl's head."

She left me there, troubled by the information she'd brought me and confused by her demeanor. I couldn't forget that it was Bal Armidor, a Bardatti himself, who'd in some way set me on the path I'd taken in this life.

I suppose there's a reason why sane men keep their distance from musicians.

My first instinct was to head back up to my room, but seeing Brasti smirking at the back of the tavern soured me on that idea. Then it occurred to me that it was entirely possible the whole affair with Rhyleis had been engineered by him, though she didn't strike me as someone easily brought into another's scheme. Eventually I let all of it go and walked over to the table where Ethalia and Allister sat. I ignored the quizzical look from him and simply extended my hand to her.

"Are we leaving?" she asked. "Is there some kind of danger or—?"

"Just dancing," I said.

She sat there for rather a long time, staring at me. I knew I looked like an idiot standing with my hand out like a beggar pleading for pennies, but I have my own stubborn streak at times.

Let her tell me to go away. Let it be because she doesn't want me near, not for the excuse of some vague spiritual forces.

At last she reached out her own hand and placed it in mine. Her touch was light, tentative, as if she feared my skin might set hers aflame. It very nearly broke my heart then and there.

The hells for hearts, I decided. *I'm done apologizing.*

I led her out to the increasingly crowded dance floor. The musicians had been playing a raucous jig but the moment we set foot on the floor they shifted into a slower cantadia, the playing so seamless I could almost have believed it was simply the natural progression of their set. At least, I might have believed it had Rhyleis not winked at me. Within moments, only a few dancers remained on the floor.

I held Ethalia neither near nor far from me, but kept the elbow of my right arm at the perfect half-bend that was, though technically correct, perhaps a bit too formal for a place like this. I had left my coat in my room so I could feel the warmth of her arm resting on mine, the bunching of my linen sleeve pressing against my own skin. Everything felt alive again, the different parts of my body all chattering noisily at me, for once not simply to remind me of my various poorly healing cuts and bruises. *You're alive,* they said. *Safe, healthy, happy.*

I wondered whether this might be some effect of Ethalia's Sainthood, but when I looked at her I saw a similar look of confusion and curiosity to the one I suspected I was wearing.

That, or you've lost the rhythm again.

Whatever the answer, neither Ethalia nor I spoke at first, but simply submitted ourselves to the melody, our feet following the steps of the cantadia's slow, swirling journey around the floor. Few of the inn's other patrons joined us. It's not a common dance in the country.

Which only proves this is Rhyleis playing with me.

"I am surprised," Ethalia said as the song was ending.

Before either of us could pull away, the musicians transitioned into another slow song, this one an embrazia, so called because the form requires the dancers to hold each other close. A second wink from Rhyleis affirmed my conviction that the Bardatti were a menace.

"Surprised by what?" I asked, trying to keep my attention on the steps.

"You're a good dancer."

That almost made me laugh. I could still recall the dozens, no, *hundreds* of times I'd tromped all over Aline's feet as she taught me to dance. "And again," she'd say, determined to make me a passable partner. I swear I'd sweated more over those lessons than all my years learning to fence.

"I can tell when you're remembering her," Ethalia said, shaking me from my thoughts.

Surprised, I stared into her eyes, searching for some clue as to her feelings on the subject. I saw no rebuke there, nor resentment. I pondered what to say next, finally settling on what was foremost in my mind. "Brasti thinks the trouble between you and me is that I can't let go of Aline."

I expected Ethalia to shake her head or deny it or, as she often did at the things Brasti said, maybe give a little smile and say, "Such is the wisdom of Brasti Goodbow." But she did none of those things, just looked past me, past the other patrons and the walls and, it seemed, the very world itself. The musicians, finally recognizing the rest of the tavern wasn't pleased at the sudden absence of fast drinking songs, kicked into a blistering version of "All's the More," to great cheers. Ethalia said something, but I couldn't hear over the din.

"What did you say?" I asked, my hands still on her arms though we weren't dancing anymore.

"It's not important. We should—"

"No, tell me."

She looked up into my eyes. "I can't be Aline, Falcio. Not even for you."

"I never asked you to. I would *never*—"

"I thought it was a sign, at first, that I shared some of her memories of you."

I was going to ask her what she meant but then I remembered my very first encounter with her, in Rijou during the Ganath Kalila, Jillard's infamous Blood Week, when she'd known Aline's exact final words to me.

"But Aline is always with you, Falcio. She's always there—I can feel her pushing at me, demanding that I fight for you, protect you, love you as she would." Ethalia looked away. "I can't bear the weight of her. I thought it was natural, something that would fade, but it doesn't. Sometimes she—"

I shook my head, cutting her off. This too smacked of excuses. "She's not a ghost. She isn't haunting you. This isn't some curse you're under."

"I don't know what it is. In some way, we are connected through her—but no woman could ever fight for you as she did. No woman could ever be *who* she was. But when the Saint's Fever is upon me it's as if she's there beside me, mocking me, telling me to get up and fight. I never even *met* her, Falcio, so why is it I feel her presence so?"

There were a hundred things I should have said then—the kinds of things Brasti would say; hells, the kinds of things any sensible man would have said. But my guts were twisted in knots and I felt bitter and angry, and I couldn't tell if it was at Ethalia or myself or Aline, or maybe the whole damned world.

Ethalia pulled away suddenly.

"What is it?" I asked, already glancing around the room for whatever threat might be coming for us, thinking it was a mistake to have come down here without my coat and my rapiers.

"It's nothing," she said, reaching out for me again, but the skin around her eyes had tightened, as if she were about to reach into a fire.

I stepped back, just a hair, and even that small distance made the tension in her face lessen. Whatever illusions I'd allowed myself, the thought that perhaps this was just a problem between two people, two lovers, who could work together to solve it, shattered. My very presence was causing her intense pain, and I could see she knew what I was thinking.

"It's not . . . it's only when you become . . . there's a rage inside you, Falcio, it—"

The music was so cacophonous now that I couldn't think. And the other dancers filling the floor around us were pushing past me, against me, grabbing at me. *Be calm*, I told myself, but even thinking those words brought pictures to my mind: Saint Birgid, her face battered and bruised, her skin pale from loss of blood; an iron mask, shaped so that the wearer was blind, unable to cry out for help, so that they could be beaten and tortured without fear of being caught.

Be calm? What the fuck is there to be calm about?

I looked around at the people in the tavern. Had someone here been part of it? Were they laughing even now at the memory of it? Of Birgid being tied to the split branches of the tree as they shoved needles into her—

No! Birgid didn't undergo the Lament, I did . . .

I forced my breathing to slow down, not by letting go of my anger but by channeling it as if preparing for a duel.

"Falcio?" Ethalia's voice sounded very distant, but even through the haziness of my vision I could tell how much it was hurting her to be this close to me.

"I'm sorry," I said, turning away.

She grabbed at my arm, her fingers feeling cold and lifeless, like iron shackles closing around me.

"You should get some rest," I said, shrugging off her grip. "We need to make for the Sanctuary of Saint Forza at first light."

CHAPTER TWENTY

THE SANCTUARY

We traveled past the border of Baern and into Luth the next day, arriving at the Sanctuary of Saint Forza in the late afternoon. I'd fully expected to find it destroyed—it wasn't, but that didn't help us at all.

"I don't understand," I said for the third time.

The sanctuary was above ground, a small stone edifice made up primarily of columns arranged in a circle with the remains of its roof partly blocking out the sun, though much of it had tumbled to the ground. Ethalia sat cross-legged at its center, eyes closed in concentration, beads of sweat dripping from her forehead and marking tracks down her face.

"It's been destroyed," Kest said. "I'm not a Saint anymore but even I can feel something's very wrong here."

Brasti walked over and inspected the columns. "It looks fine to me. Is it because of the roof or something?"

"No. The structure itself was no different when I came here."

"Then what's changed?" I asked.

Allister walked around the perimeter of the small building and finally said, "Lady Ethalia, may I enter?"

She nodded without opening her eyes. Allister stepped between two columns and walked around the room. "Here," he said.

The rest of us joined him. "What do you see?" I asked.

He kicked aside some pieces of broken stone and plaster from around one of the bases of the column. "Someone placed these here to cover the marks."

I knelt down and saw a smear of reddish-brown against the base of the column: blood.

"There's more here, too," Kest said, from the other side.

"Well, clean it off," Brasti said, rubbing at one of the marks until it started to disappear.

"Is it making a difference?" I asked Ethalia.

She opened her eyes. "No. It's . . ." She rose to her feet and came over to where I was kneeling. She reached down and started to press her fingers against the bloodstain, but her hand shot back as if she'd been bitten by a snake. "It's the blood of a Saint," she said. "I'm sure of it."

Brasti was still busy rubbing it away from one of the columns. "Well, let's just get rid of it. Problem solved."

Not having any better ideas, we spent the next hour doing as Brasti had suggested, but it achieved nothing. So that was one more thing we'd learned: apparently the blood of a Saint could be used to permanently desecrate a sanctuary.

"We'd better head out," Kest said to me, looking at Ethalia. "This isn't going to work. Our best bet now is to try the chapel inside Castle Aramor. It was rumored to be a sanctuary once, long ago."

"*Rumored?*" I said. "How is that going to help Ethalia?" I hated this. All of it. Where was an enemy I could fight? Where were the conspirators we could hunt down? This passive form of assault wasn't something I knew how to deal with. "All right," I agreed at last, "let's go. We can make Aramor by week's end if we don't lose too much time along the way."

As I was readying my horse, Allister approached me. "Falcio? I'm sorry if I've been . . . uncouth . . . as regards the Lady Ethalia."

"Uncouth?"

"I was woken in the middle of the night by a rather strident visitor."

It took me a moment to puzzle out what he was talking about but then I almost smiled. "Brasti decided to have a little chat with you, did he?"

Allister grimaced. "He made certain things clear to me. I had no idea that you and she—"

I waved him off, not because I believed him, because I didn't—he'd known; anyone would have known. But Allister and I had never been all that close and I guessed he'd reasoned that since she obviously couldn't bear to be near me, whatever had been between us must be over—so why should he not seek her out? Part of me wished I'd been there when Brasti had come for him. Another part of me recognized that as hypocrisy. I had no claim to Ethalia. She wasn't property, and this sort of brotherly code was nothing more than us making decisions for her.

"She's a free woman," I said at last. "She has the right to whatever comfort is available to her now."

That answer appeared to trouble him more than if I'd reiterated Brasti's threat. "If you don't mind my asking, Falcio, are you all right? You sound . . ."

"He's fine," Brasti said, coming over and slapping a hand on Allister's shoulder. I saw how hard he gripped him; the clear message was to ignore everything I'd just said and remember that he and Kest were nearby.

I sighed. A better man than me would have said something.

"Falcio's just twisting his guts in a knot like he always does," Brasti went on. "It's somewhere between a hobby and a lifelong vocation with him. Soon enough someone will come along and try to kill us and Falcio will be back to normal."

The clatter of iron-shod horseshoes against the rocky surface of the road interrupted him. Kest and I drew our swords, Allister retrieved his staff, and Brasti pulled his horse-bow Insult from the clasps that held it against the back of his saddlebags. He quickly bent it back and strung it before grabbing one of his shorter maple arrows and aiming down the road. "Ah, see?" he said. "Here comes someone to lift our spirits now."

A lone rider raced up the road toward us, coming from the same direction we had. I squinted to see better, but the distance was still too great and the rider was kicking up a good deal of dust. I always envied Brasti at times like this.

"It's a woman," he said, his tone excessively optimistic. "Perhaps she saw me at the tavern last night and is now so lovestruck that she's left her husband and family behind, just to come and declare her love for me."

"No," Ethalia said, "she carries great fear inside her. I can feel it from here."

"She *is* riding rather quickly," Kest noted. "Wait . . . What is she wearing?"

Brasti's eyes narrowed. "Falcio, that's a greatcoat."

She was getting closer now and I too could see the stiff brown leather of her coat. Then I noticed Brasti was still aiming for her. "Brasti? Why are you still—?"

"Because I can make out her face now." He pulled back harder on the string. "And I've never seen her before."

None of us knew the woman who was pulling hard on the horse's reins and very nearly throwing herself to the ground in her rush to kneel in front of us, but we all recognized her coat. The leather was a dark, rich brown, like all those the Tailor had made for the first Greatcoats, but this one was tempered with a hint of green and bore on the right breast the subtle inlay of a long wooden shaft ending in a sharp diamond-head point. The first time I had seen it was the day its owner had received it from King Paelis himself. She'd spoken her oath in a strong, clear voice, despite the tears in her eyes, and her oath had ended with, "My name is Talia Venire, and I am the King's Spear."

"Where is Talia?" Brasti asked, his arrow pointed squarely at the woman's chest. At this distance Insult would send the maple shaft flying straight through her heart, regardless of the thickness of the coat's bone plates.

"Please—!" she begged, her voice muffled by the long tangles of black hair covering her face, "Please! My name is Evi—I'm not a Greatcoat—"

"We know that," I said sternly. "Now tell us why you are wearing one." None of us had seen Talia for years; even back in the day I'd barely spoken to her. But though we'd shared no more than a few passing conversations, I remembered her eyes: bright, sharp, darting around at everyone in the room as she walked in, quickly followed by a mischievous smile, as if she'd gotten us all figured out.

"I . . ." Evi's face became pinched and her eyes filled with tears. "I stole it." she whispered. "I'm sorry—it was cold and my father had thrown me out of the house and I—"

"You're lying," Brasti said, his voice tight. "Talia would never let her coat out of her sight, and I doubt you're strong enough or stealthy enough to take it from her."

"Terrorizing her isn't going to help," Ethalia said. She knelt down and reached out a hand, but the woman bent over her knees and covered her head, repeating, "I'm sorry . . . I'm so sorry . . ."

"Sorry for what?" I asked. "You sound unnaturally repentant if all you did was steal a coat when you were in need."

She moaned, a brief string of incomprehensible words, and Allister, losing patience, grabbed the back of her coat and hauled her to her feet, a little roughly for my taste.

"Gently," I told him. "We need answers."

The woman—more of a girl, really, now that I could better see her face through the mess of hair, pulled away from Allister and grabbed hold of my arm. "I'll tell you whatever you want to know, I swear, but we *must* get away from here. There are men chasing me."

"You stole one of their horses," Kest said. It wasn't a question; none of us had needed more than a glance at the big, well-groomed gelding to recognize that this was not the sort of animal a young woman of obviously meager means could afford.

"I . . . I did." Evi gripped my arm more tightly. "But I swear it was only to escape—they saw me taking the coat and it was clear that they didn't care about why—they started pushing me, forcing me further down the alley, away from the eyes of others in the village . . . I could see they were getting ready to attack me, all of them." She looked back the way she'd come and said urgently, "Please, let me go, sirs, lady—they'll be here soon. They were going to—"

"Who were these men?" Kest asked. "How many are there?"

The words tumbled out in a hurry as she was pulling on my arm, as if to drag me with her. "Four, I think, no, five—there was someone in the store buying supplies. One of the men made a joke and the others laughed and I saw that one of the horses hadn't been properly tethered so I took my chance—I pushed the one in front of me, really hard, and he stumbled into one of the others, and then I ran as fast as I could and I grabbed the reins and took the horse and rode as fast as I could—"

Kest's eyes narrowed as they do when he's working through the odds of a tactical maneuver. "Your story doesn't make sense. You wouldn't have been able to evade them, not unless they were either very fat and slow or . . ." He stopped and his gaze went to me. "Unless they wore armor."

"They were Knights," Evi said, "but not proper Knights, hiding their colors so you couldn't see what Duke or Lord they served, only the cold, hard steel of their armor." She looked up at me, her face a map of all the grief in the wide world. "I beg you, sir, help me. I don't want to die at the hands of those men for taking a coat."

"I'm hearing riders in the distance, Falcio." Brasti said, his arrow still aimed at Evi, even as she held onto me for dear life. "They're not moving as fast as she was but they'll be here in a minute."

She pulled at me again. "Please, we must go. They'll run us down if we stand here." She pointed up the road. "I know this road—there's a bend, just about fifty yards ahead. We can find cover and—"

"Stay calm," Ethalia said, again reaching out to the girl, but she clung to me.

Allister, Kest, and I exchanged glances. "We can outride them if we leave now," Allister said. "Bring the girl with us and leave her in safer hands, in the next village, perhaps?"

Brasti bristled at that. "I'm not Gods-damned running if these bastards have—"

I thought about it. "No, they've seen a woman in a greatcoat and they know she stole one of their horses. I doubt they'll leave it alone. Besides," I said, pushing Evi off me as gently as I could, "I imagine Talia will want her coat back."

Kest and Allister started leading our horses up the road, but Brasti wasn't done. "Speak," he snarled at her, the arrow still aimed at her heart. "Your story has a hole in it bigger than the one I'm going to put in you if I don't get a truthful answer. Where is the woman who wore that coat?"

Evi's crying turned to wails. "Dead," she moaned, "she was dead when I took the coat from her body. That's why those men are after me. I saw them kill her."

The *clack-clack* of the horses' hooves against the hard ground was getting closer and closer.

CHAPTER TWENTY-ONE
THE WOMAN IN THE COAT

The sharp bend in the road that Evi had mentioned was indeed a more defensible position: the path narrowed here, and the ground became uneven. The forest on either side would provide a quick way of evading the Knights' charge if it came to fighting. Horses wouldn't be able to maneuver in the dense brush and fallen trees, and plate-armor would make them clumsy over such troubled ground.

"This is an excellent position from which to launch an ambush," Kest said approvingly.

Allister loosely tethered our own horses to a branch of one of the trees. "Perhaps we should give up on all this rubbish about enforcing the laws and take up new careers as bandits."

"Finally the man with the stick has a useful suggestion," Brasti said.

Swordsmen who've spent most of their adult lives contending with just about every form of conflict, from individuals in one-on-one duels to facing off against massive armies, tend to like to show each other how calm and reasonable they are in those moments just before the next bloody onslaught threatens to crash over them like a wave. Even Ethalia, who had always abhorred violence even before she became a Saint knew such talk for what it was: a way to dissipate the tension and fear that might otherwise get us killed once the fighting actually began. Of course, no one had bothered to communicate this to the rather frantic woman in the stolen greatcoat, who cried, "Why are you all acting like this?" She started pulling at my coat sleeve again. "Come on—we need to get into the forest! Those Knights will run us down—!"

"Not with Brasti firing two-foot-long ironwood arrows into their throats," I said soothingly, gesturing to where he stood a few yards behind us. She ran to him and took up position behind him, and Brasti grinned at me as if this was final confirmation of the bow's superiority over the sword.

"What should I do?" Ethalia asked.

"Can you do that thing you do where everybody we don't like falls to the ground?" Brasti suggested.

She closed her eyes for a moment, then swayed and had to steady herself against one of the trees lining the road. "No . . . no, I'm sorry. I'm weaker now than I was at the martyrium."

"In that case just stay out of the way of my arrows."

The sound of the horses' hooves against the hard ground became loud and crisp. It wouldn't be long now.

Kest joined me in the center of the road. "Are you planning on delivering a speech to the Knights prior to the fight? And if so, could you give me some sense of how long you're going to—"

"Shut up, Kest." *Saints! Everyone's on my back these days.* "Let's just see what these men are really after to start with. There might still be a chance to avoid bloodshed."

The clack of the horses told me they'd slowed to a walk. They turned the bend and came into view.

They made for an odd quartet. Usually Knights all belong to a single Lord or Marquis or Duke, so their armor and weapons all come from the same craftsmen. The four men in front of us wore a mishmash of plate and chain, and each helm was a different shape. They looked rather shabby to my eyes.

They halted and I waited silently for the usual grave pronouncement or poorly veiled threat, only to find the moments ticking by as they just sat there on their horses, staring at us from behind their metal masks.

"Can we help you?" I asked at last.

Still no one spoke for another long while, then one of the Knights at the back finally asked, "What could we possibly want from Trattari?" He wore a helm that covered his entire face, with the front extending out to a point—the sort I've heard Knights call a "pigface bascinet" (which doesn't sound very Knightly to me).

"Oh, I don't know," Brasti replied. "Directions? Recommendations for a good tavern? Fashion advice?"

"Heretic," he growled, and drew his sword.

"Bide, Sir Uden," the Knight in front said. His helmet bore steel horns like those of a bull. I took him for the leader even though neither he nor his three companions wore the usual tabards over their armor that would have signified their position and Ducal affiliation. Evidently Knights without Lords didn't have the same fascination for displaying their rank and privilege that so characterizes their more servile brethren.

"They're Trattari, Sir Belastrian. The Gods want their blood. They *demand*—" Pigface started, but Bullhead held up a gauntleted hand to stop him.

"I said bide, Sir Uden. The moment will come soon enough."

So, no little stars on your tabards but still a chain of command.

"If you're waiting for us to offer up the woman then you'll be sitting there a good long time, Sir Knight," I said.

"These roads and all who travel them belong to the Church of Duestre," Sir Belastrian said. "And we, his Knights, will administer his justice."

"Which one's Duestre again?" I asked.

"God of Craft," Allister replied from his side of the road, his staff in hand. "That's what they call him in Hervor, anyway. Didn't know they called him that in Luth now."

"Such earthly distinctions are meaningless to us," Sir Belastrian pronounced grandly.

Pigface had a more pragmatic view of the world. "Stop wasting words on these Trattari, Belastrian. I'm tired of waiting."

I had a bit of a diatribe prepared for a moment such as this: a nice, long speech about how those who once droned on about honor and loyalty to their Lords could so quickly and easily become pious martyrs for a religious doctrine I doubted even one of these men understood. I had a funny bit at the end, about swallows trying to fly in two directions at once and ending up crashing into trees, and I was looking forward to trying it out, but Kest interrupted me before I'd even had a chance to begin. I suspect that was intentional.

"This is going to be tricky," he said.

I turned to glance at him. "Is it your hand?" I whispered. Since I'd taken off his right hand, Kest had been suffering from phantom pains that were as crippling as any blow. This really wouldn't be an opportune time for such a reoccurrence.

"No," Kest replied, "it's just that I'm not used to fighting so few opponents. I'll have to work against my own reflexes to avoid killing more than my share."

"Well, you're not killing mine," Brasti said, sighting along his arrow at the man in charge. "Allister, you're new to our little family. You don't mind if Kest takes your man, do you? He's gotten rather sloppy since losing his Sainthood and we're trying to boost his confidence."

Allister kept very still, his hands unmoving on his heavy staff. "Saint Ebron-who-steals-breath! I'd forgotten how much you three jabber when you should be fighting."

"I've made the same observation to Falcio," Kest said. "He never seems to—"

"You're doing it too."

"Ah. Right."

"You would sully these roads with blood?" Sir Belastrian's voice was full of pious outrage.

For some reason I found that funny. Who ever heard of a Knight who wasn't looking for an excuse to kill a Greatcoat? Maybe they finally got tired of having us beat them senseless from one end of the country to the other; perhaps they had finally developed some sense of self-preservation while discovering piety.

Something struck me as implausible about that thought, and not just because most of my encounters with the truly religious usually involved murderous violence. Despite not being able to see the men's faces very well through their mismatched helmets, I could tell they were itching for a fight, and yet we'd been goading them plenty already, and still they just sat there on their horses. Were they really waiting for us to attack?

No, I realized, *they're not waiting for us at all.*

"Into the forest!" I shouted.

"Wait, what?" Brasti asked.

"It's a trap—they've just been stalling u—"

But I was too late; the sounds of thick ropes being severed preceded several heavy logs slamming down from the forest like trees felled by thunder, crashing onto the road behind us. Their massive trunks had foot-long iron spikes sticking out of them that would surely stick any man trying to get over them quickly. The road north was barred to us.

One of the Knights pulled a loaded crossbow from behind his saddle and raised it, his finger on the iron lever that served as its trigger.

"Brasti!" I called out.

"I wouldn't try it," Brasti said, aiming his arrow at the man with the crossbow. "At best you'll get one shot away, and while you're fumbling with your next bolt I'll have had time to shoot you, your fellow Knights and both your grandparents on your mother's side."

"Well," Sir Belastrian said, looking past me, "we can't have that, can we?"

And all at once I realized several things, the first being that these men hadn't been *chasing* the girl in the stolen greatcoat—they were working with her.

"Brasti, look out!" I shouted, but I was too late; she'd thrown herself against him, jarring his right arm and sending his arrow into the ground.

I raced for the crossbowman, trying to draw his fire to me, but I was too slow. He shot, and I turned just in time to see his bolt hit Brasti in the leg.

He stumbled, struggling to keep his balance while drawing another arrow from his quiver, but behind him, the woman in the stolen greatcoat was smiling as she drew a long dagger from inside her sleeve. Its blade was so thin I could barely see it, even from this distance.

"Brasti, the girl!" I yelled, and he spun awkwardly, throwing up his left arm to protect himself, bow still in hand, as Evi jabbed the blade down with furious speed. I expected to see it blocked by the bone plates but its point must have been wickedly sharp, for it pierced straight through and Brasti screamed, dropping his bow to the ground.

"I am the God's Needle!" Evi cried with ecstatic fervor, raising the knife for another strike, but before she could stab again, Ethalia had grabbed her arm and was holding it back. Brasti struck out at her, trying to jab the arrow in his hand into her shoulder, but it failed to get through her coat.

I was moving toward them to help Brasti when I felt something heavy strike me in the side: one of the Knights—the pig-faced one—had swung a broadsword at me; luckily for me, the plates in my coat had successfully blocked the blow. Hurt like the hells, though, but I resisted the urge to fall back and instead stepped in close, cutting off the distance he needed to bring his sword back for another swing. He tried to push me away with his other hand but I deflected it even as I jammed the pommel of my left-hand rapier hard against the rectangular slit in his helmet that allowed him to see. The steel around it bent inwards—not quite enough to cut off his vision but more than sufficient to give him a good scare. He stumbled backward and I helped him to the ground with a hefty kick to his groin.

Normally there's nothing quite as entertaining as watching a Knight on his back trying to get back up, but I was too worried about Ethalia and Brasti to properly enjoy it. Instead, I sought them out again, in time to see both of them struggling to keep out of the way of Evi's lethal dagger. Brasti was still standing, but he was horribly unsteady on his feet and using Ethalia to steady himself.

"With this act my Sainthood is assured!" the woman screamed, now sounding completely crazed as she raised her blade again, but at the last instant, just as she was about to lash out, Brasti jammed his arrow into the only part of her that was exposed: the side of her skull. Even over the din I could hear the sickening sound of the iron head punching through bone.

Brasti looked pale, and not just because of his wounds. In less gruesome circumstances I might have made a joke about archers not being used to getting their hands dirty, but I was feeling rather nauseous myself—

"Falcio, *focus!*" Kest said, his warsword coming within a hair's breadth of my head as he blocked a blow that had definitely been intended for me. His voice was so full of pain I thought he must have been hit, but I saw no sign of any injury. The loss of his hand was once again causing him some kind of agony I couldn't understand.

"We need to get into the forest!" Allister shouted.

"No," Kest said, pushing off the Knight who'd been attacking me. "There are only four of them."

I drew my second rapier as the Knights started coming at us in formation. They still didn't charge, though, instead moving together, blocking the road behind them and pushing us backward. The only way out was the forest.

Which is exactly what they want, I realized, too late.

"Don't go into the woods!" I shouted, but my voice was drowned out by the shouts of a dozen or more men coming from the dense undergrowth. They had no helms nor armor. Most were carrying spears or shortswords, but I counted three with bows getting into position on the other side of the massive spiked logs, obviously intending to use the barricade as protection while they fired upon us.

So this was why the Knights had delayed their attack, and why the girl had led us to this position. Her little story about a dead Great-coat and the men responsible had inflamed our anger and used it to ambush us. The Inquisitor had warned me that we weren't strong enough to protect Ethalia, and here I had dragged her straight into a trap. *I hate it when other people are right.*

CHAPTER TWENTY-TWO

THE SMILE

Four Knights, three archers, and nine men brandishing assorted spears and swords surrounded the five of us. We had no place to run, no way to maneuver, and no plan. We'd faced similar odds in the past—hells, we'd faced much worse at times—but we'd had more opportunities, places to move to, ways to sow confusion among our enemies. As it was, I reckoned we were going to have to get *very* lucky, very fast. It was a shame luck was an infrequent companion of ours.

"You've got to hold off the Knights," I said to Kest.

"All four by myself?" he asked, which worried me; it wasn't like Kest to undersell his own abilities.

I glanced at Brasti who was now struggling to get the crossbow bolt out of his leg, using his one good arm and with Ethalia helping, without passing out. "If you wouldn't mind."

"I can give you two minutes," Kest said. "After that one of them will outflank me on my weaker right side to—"

"Just do it." He needed to keep them off us long enough for Allister and me to get around the spiked logs and deal with the archers, which would give us a decent chance of surviving the next two minutes. "Allister, take out the—"

"Don't tell me how to fight, Falcio," he said, using his long staff as a pole and vaulting neatly over the logs. He landed surefooted as a cat on the other side and shifted his grip on the staff before swinging it around in a heavy arc and smashing the iron-shod end into the face of one of the archers. The man went down hard, and Allister went for the next bowman, who was already backing away, trying to get enough distance to take aim without running into the third.

"Interesting," Kest said even as his warsword swept in a wide arc to knock away two opponents' blades with one blow. "Slower than a sword, but I can see the—"

"Focus," I said, pointing at the two unarmored men rushing us with long two-handed swords. *What's the world coming to when I'm the one telling people to shut up and fight?*

Brasti gave a scream as the bolt finally came out of his leg. For a second I thought he might pass out—but then his eyes went wide. "Falcio look out!"

Too late I saw the fourth archer hidden in the forest aiming for me. I swore and as he fired I dropped my rapier and brought the arms of my coat up to protect my head. I felt the stunning force of the arrow strike me in the side, sending a shock through my ribs, but the plates in my coat held. Few bows can match the force of Brasti's longbow, and I thanked whatever Gods weren't already arrayed against me for that. Pulling a throwing knife from the bracer clipped inside my coat, I breathed through the pain and threw it at the archer. The knife buried itself in his shoulder.

"That was a nice shot, Falcio, given you've just been hit by an arrow," Kest said.

"I was aiming for his belly," I grunted, glancing at Kest, only to catch sight of another man coming for me from the forest, his ax swinging in a horizontal arc intended, I had no doubt, to separate my head from my shoulders. I dropped to my knees, the ax blade slicing the air above me and whistling past, and grabbed my rapier from the ground.

I rose quickly, hoping to stab the man before he could attack me again, but he'd used the thwarted momentum of his swing to try and take Kest's head instead. It was an awkward maneuver, which Kest easily ducked, then used the force of his own spin to bring his warsword slicing just a few inches above the ground, at ankle height. There was a terrible crunch as the blade first shattered our opponent's bones, then cut right through. The man screamed as he tumbled to the ground, four inches shorter than he'd been when he started his attack. I was simultaneously reassured and unnerved by the strength and precision Kest displayed with just one hand.

"You know," Kest said, rising and preparing to take on his next opponent, a great bull of a man wielding a heavy spear, "I really am more comfortable when we're outnumbered."

As absurd as it sounded, he had a point.

You might think a large group of men would simply rush at their opponents and overwhelm them—but have you ever tried to strike a target while ten other people are running headlong beside you, jostling your arm and getting in the way of your swing? In a confined space, somewhere like the martyrium's preparation room, and properly arrayed, the way Quentis had prepared his men, the fight might have played out very differently. But these people weren't at all organized, which made me think they were more likely brigands bribed or pressed into service by Sir Belastrian and his fellow Knights. And that suggested that none of the four were high-ranking, and so were more used to following orders than giving them.

We'd probably been outnumbered four to one when the fight started, but like I said, winning on numbers alone isn't as easy as people think; now only two Knights remained and maybe five of the unarmored men. Besides, Kest, Brasti, and I are very good at fighting ridiculous odds, which is probably why, despite the chaos and blood and burning anger over having been tricked and ambushed, I was smiling for the first time in weeks.

"You see, Allister?" Brasti shouted around the arrow held between his teeth as he knelt on the ground reaching for his bow with his right hand, "Falcio's back."

But Allister was having his own problems now: the archers on the other side of the logs were all dead, but two men with heavy clubs were pressing him back and I could see Allister's left arm was hanging uselessly at his side.

"Brasti, shoot one of those bastards," I called.

"I've got it," Kest said, and hurled his warsword through the air, pommel first.

Throwing a sword is, by and large, one of the dumbest things you can do. They're really not designed as projectiles, and the odds of hitting your target aren't good. That's why I was especially annoyed when the pommel struck one of Allister's attackers squarely on the side of his head.

"What?" he said to me, looking a trifle miffed at my expression. "You're not the only one allowed to throw a blade, you know."

"No!" Allister shouted, and Kest and I turned to see him stumbling back against the logs—the second club-man had managed to trip him, and though his coat had protected his back, now he was trapped between the spikes and his attacker was lifting his weapon, preparing for a heavy blow. I reached into my coat for another knife as Kest took off at a run for the logs, but I knew neither of us would get there in time.

"I've got it," Brasti shouted.

I turned just in time to see Brasti, sitting on the ground using both feet to push against his bow as he held an arrow between two fingers. He nocked and released and the sharp *twang* of the bowstring was followed by the *whoosh* of the arrow as it flew through the air. An instant later its journey ended in a soft *thunk* as the point buried itself in the neck of the man with the club.

Kest and I watched in awe as he slid first to his knees and then fell to the road.

Allister twisted out from between the spikes and then clambered to his feet. He looked utterly baffled, then he caught sight of Brasti, still on his ass, and worked out what must have happened. "Saint Merhan-who-rides-the-arrow . . ."

"For now," Brasti said, grinning despite the obvious pain he was in as he started getting to his feet.

But Allister hadn't been praising Brasti's skill, brilliant though he was. As I moved closer I saw what he'd seen: the woman in the stolen greatcoat had risen from the forest floor—with Brasti's iron-wood arrow still buried in the side of her skull—and was walking toward us.

She was smiling.

CHAPTER TWENTY-THREE
THE KING'S SPEAR

"I am the God's Needle," the woman said, and the feathered end of the arrow bobbed up and down as she walked slowly toward us.

"Which God would that be?" I asked, reaching down to pick up both my rapiers from the ground. "Because if he were here, he'd probably tell you that you don't have long to live."

She laughed, and under normal circumstances I would have appreciated that from an enemy, but not with the blood dripping down the side of her head from a fatal wound. Then, because apparently that wasn't disturbing enough, she turned to Ethalia and said, "Hello, sister."

Ethalia recoiled, though I couldn't tell whether it was from the madwoman's greeting or because of some other influence I couldn't see. She folded at the waist as though she were about to vomit. "You . . . are . . . no sister of mine."

The God's Needle spread her hands beatifically. "Do you not sense my Awe, sister? Do you not feel it slip and slither inside you?"

Ethalia forced herself upright, raising one hand in front of her. The first touch of her Awe pushed at all of us—it was weaker than before, but still enough to make Kest, Brasti, Allister, and me begin to stumble. It didn't have any such effect on the woman with the arrow through her skull. "Ah, ah, ah. I'm sorry, sister, but I'm beyond *your* Awe." She took a step toward her. "How do you enjoy mine?"

Whatever she was doing, she did more of it, and Ethalia began to convulse, teetering like an uprooted tree. I couldn't imagine what sickly sensation was worming through her. *Wait—why can't I imagine it?* "Ethalia, stop using your Awe."

Her mouth was open, her jaw slack, and I wasn't even sure she could understand me. "Sweetheart, please, stop now."

I don't know whether Ethalia heard me or whether she just couldn't keep fighting, but she fell to the ground and instantly the pressure on us disappeared.

"Clever," the God's Needle said. "You figured out that—"

She didn't finish that thought, because I'd thrown myself at her and used every ounce of my strength and momentum to drive the pointy end of my rapier deep into her chest, shattering the bone plate inside the stolen greatcoat and piercing her lung. My left blade was embedded in her belly—but to my everlasting revulsion, she began giggling as she grabbed at both blades, ignoring the great gashes they opened on her hands and instead holding them in place, preventing me from withdrawing them.

Laugh all you want, I thought, *I'm not done with you.* A long time ago, I'd paid far, far too much money to have my rapiers custom-made for me, with the blades held against a coiled spring that could be released with a press of a lever near the top of the grip under the guard. It was a great idea; unfortunately, the physics hadn't been quite worked out and instead of flying through the air when released, which is what I'd intended, instead they flopped unceremoniously to the ground. In this event I didn't care: I pressed the levers, releasing the blades, and with my fingers still clutching the heavy steel guards, I punched the God's Needle so hard her jaw shattered.

She still wouldn't drop.

"We . . . aren't like you, Trattari," she said, her jaw hanging off, her voice almost unintelligible. "We fear neither pain nor death."

"Good for you," I said, and drove my left fist into her shoulder. Something broke there, so at least she wouldn't be able to grab me. "I imagine we'll have lots to talk about once we get you tied up and haul you back to Aramor. Then you can tell us all about how powerful and beloved of the Gods you are. And you can tell us who you work for."

For the first time, I saw something akin to concern in her eyes. Her voice was almost a growl when she said, "He who forges our destiny is far beyond any man. You will never know his name."

She struck out with her other arm—even off balance and half dead she had impressive strength, and I staggered back a few steps until Kest caught me.

The woman smiled. "It is true, I cannot defeat all of you, so I leave you with a message from the Gods, Trattari." She reached up a hand and gripped the shaft of the arrow lodged in her skull. It made a sickening sound as she pushed it in harder, then twisted it and finally pulled it from her head. The laugh she gave sent my guts into knots. "We will hunt down every Greatcoat who seeks to put the laws of men above those of the Gods. And we will slay the heretic Queen, for her life is an abomination."

Brasti stumbled toward me and leaned against my shoulder. "I really don't think you should be calling other people 'abominations,' you know," he pointed out.

She ignored Brasti and turned her gaze back to me. "You above all others will suffer, Falcio val Mond, for you would make your blasphemous ideals into a God of your very own. I hope you are there to witness the glorious moment when one of us buries our Needle deep inside the false Queen's mouth."

The woman looked down at the arrow in her hand and for a second I thought she might try to hurl it at us. Instead she opened the front of her greatcoat, tearing it against my blades, then she slammed the point of the arrow deep into her own belly. She looked up at me and her smile widened. "It feels so *good*," she said, though her voice was now barely a whisper, and she ripped it out—only to drive it straight into her chest.

"Stop!" Ethalia screamed, visibly sickened by the sight, but the madwoman ignored her.

Again and again the Needle stabbed herself, each time letting out a moan that was half agony and half some mad ecstasy, until finally she fell to the ground. Kest, Brasti, Allister, and I stood over her, and her eyes went to each of us in turn. "Each of us needs kill only one Saint," she said, "and for that, eternal pleasures are promised to us." She opened her mouth and showed me her tongue, which was the blue of the pertine. "The Greatcoats we kill for free."

I felt so sick that I couldn't speak, but Ethalia rose to her feet and said suddenly, "She's lying."

The woman's eyes went wide, and so did mine. "What do you mean?" I asked.

She ignored me and knelt down to lean over her. "I was next to you when you stabbed Brasti. You could have taken him in the throat or the chest, but you went for his arm."

"Ethalia's right," Kest added, "You could have ordered your archers to fire at us from the forest, or given more of your men bows, but you didn't. I think whoever commands you has ordered that you capture Greatcoats if you can, not kill them."

The woman's mouth spilled blood as she spoke through her broken jaw. "You deceive yourself, apostate—"

"No," Kest said, "I don't think so." He looked at me. "Think about it, Falcio."

Allister shook his head. "This is wishful thinking, Kest."

"No," I said, letting the patterns and possibilities tumble around in my head, "he's right. Alive, they can interrogate us for what we know, or use us as hostages, or for whatever damnable rituals they think their Gods might want them to inflict."

"There's a disturbing thought," Allister said.

The light, broken sound of the woman's laughter brought our attention back to her. "It matters not, Trattari. My work is done, and my reward awaits." Her eyes began to flicker shut.

Kest grabbed what was left of her jaw with his hand. "I don't think so," he said. "I don't think you were expecting us to be here—you saw us pass through the village and rounded up your men to come after us."

"So what?" Allister asked, sounding mystified.

"It means she didn't know that there would be more Greatcoats she might kill or capture," I said, as I finally understood what Kest had been driving at. "It means they wouldn't have killed the one they did capture unless they had to. It means Talia might still be alive."

With the last ounce of strength granted to her by the poison in her veins, the woman on the ground screamed in outrage and despair before she finally left this world.

"I don't understand," Brasti said, holding his bandaged arm as we followed the tracks into the forest. "Why search here and not the village? That's where she spotted us; that's where the Knights came from."

"She wouldn't keep Talia in a place where there were people who might see them holding a woman against her will," I replied, sliding the blade of my right rapier back into its guard and pushing against the inner spring until I felt the click of the retaining lever snapping back into place. "They must have a camp here in the forest; I'll bet the others lie in wait there until they get the signal to attack."

"Which is a good reason to keep your mouths shut," Allister said, his own voice quiet. "We don't know how many might be waiting for us."

Chastened, we followed him along the winding forest path. He was an even better tracker than Brasti, who nonetheless felt the need to point out every broken twig and bent piece of foliage to ensure we knew that he too could have found the camp, and just as quickly.

Allister insisted we move slowly and quietly, being careful not to raise the alarm too soon, in case there were a lot of people guarding the camp, but even before we reached the place I'd known what we would find. These traps were designed to take down a single Greatcoat, two at most. With four Greatcoats, there was too much chance of one or more of us escaping: so they would have sent every able-bodied man they could muster to ensure they succeeded in overpowering us. And that meant there wouldn't be many left guarding the camp.

Out of the corner of my eye, I saw Ethalia stumble, and I reached out an arm for her to grab onto. "Are you all right?" I whispered. "Is it the fever?"

She shook her head. "No, the . . . the violence. I know you had no choice, Falcio. It's just . . . the nature of my Sainthood makes it hard for me."

There wasn't much I could do about that, so I tried instead just to provide support for her as we made our way into the forest.

It took us less than an hour to find the cultists' lair. It wasn't much of an encampment, to be honest, and looking at the number of tents, I was convinced I was right, that almost all the men had come for us on the road.

"Stay back!" someone called out from behind one of the thick trees. His voice was deep, thick—so, a big man: that made sense if you had only one person to guard a captive. The slight quiver that accompanied his words served to confirm to me that he was alone.

"We're not here to hurt you," I said. "We want the woman you're holding hostage."

A tall, stocky young Knight stepped out from behind a tree, his armor mostly obscured by the woman in tattered rags he was holding against his chest. One meaty hand was clamped over her mouth, while the other held a knife to her throat. "I'll kill her long before I let you have her, Trattari."

"Talia . . ." Brasti said.

It was her all right. I would have recognized her by her hair even if I couldn't see her face. Talia had the brownest hair you'd ever seen—not the mix of shades of auburn and mahogany and chestnut and all the shades of tree and soil that most people have. Hers was the color an artist might use to paint a single sliver of oak.

I signaled the others to stay back and walked toward the pair, my hands outstretched, my rapiers still in their sheaths. "There's been plenty of blood today, my young friend. Let's not add to Death's tally. He's not a rewarding God, I promise you."

The young Knight pressed his point to Talia's throat. "The good God Purgeize will bless my blade!"

Talia was barely managing to stand on her own feet. Her gaze was confused, unfocused, but I still found a fierce anger there, and a desire to act. I caught her eyes and gave the tiniest shake of my head, hoping she would understand that I needed her to stay still. "War is an even greedier God than Death," I said.

"I do not fear you, Trattari!"

Why does everyone *always* feel the need to tell us that they aren't afraid of us? I took a final step and said sadly, "Of course you don't. All that matters to you is doing this one service for your Gods and then you'll go happily to the grave, is that right?"

"He who dies in service of the God will be returned as a Saint," the man said, repeating someone else's words in that stilted way.

So was this how the madwoman on the road had gotten these men to follow her commands? She must have shown them her strength and then promised them Sainthood in exchange for killing Greatcoats . . . Hells. All she'd needed were men who were strong, stupid, and desperate for purpose—in other words, Knights.

Ethalia stepped forward and said gently, "You've been lied to."

"How would you know, woman?"

"She's a Saint," Brasti explained, "so, you know, she's kind of the expert here."

The young Knight's jaw tightened. "Then when I've dealt with these men I'll kill you next. The time of false Saints is past."

"Well, then, that's where you have a little problem, friend," I said, placing my hand on the hilt of my rapier.

His eyes darted around at the others. "If anyone tries to draw an arrow on me I'll slit her throat!"

I stared him in the eyes, long and hard. Anyone could make threats; not everyone would follow through with them. The problem here was that I could clearly see the mixture of fear and religious fervor shining in his eyes. I knew he'd follow through. A good part of him believed that the act of killing Talia would find him favor with the Gods.

I don't know if that's true, Sir Knight, but none of us are going to find out today.

"Do you know what a vinceret is, Sir Knight?" I didn't bother to wait for an answer. "It's a type of duelist who specializes in what we call 'the quick draw.' The vinceret's strategy is to wait until the magistrate calls for the duel to begin, and then pull his blade and strike so fast that the battle is over less than a second after it's begun."

"You're too far away, Trattari," the Knight said. "You're at least nine feet away, and that rapier at your side isn't long enough to reach me even if you could draw it fast enough."

"Well, I can see why you would think that. But in fact my rapier is three feet and two inches long. And my lunge when fully extended is . . . Kest, how long is my lunge again?"

"Last time I looked, at full extension it was six feet, Falcio."

"Six feet," I said. "Now if you add those two numbers together you get something that's just long enough to bury the point of my sword two full inches into your throat."

The man holding Talia swallowed. "You can't—"

"I know, I know. Even if I had studied the ways of the vincereti—which I have, by the way—what are the odds of me being able to reach across my body, draw my rapier, bring it into line, and lunge with the perfect accuracy needed to stab you in the neck when all you have to do is pull that little knife of yours across Talia's throat?"

"You'll never make it in time. It's impossible," he said, more as if he were trying to reassure himself than threaten me.

"It's not impossible," I said, "just *very* hard. But, you know what? I'm actually pretty damned fast when I want to be. Then there's your other problem—your reflexes. See, it's actually a lot harder to stand there and slit someone's throat at the expense of your own life. Once you see me coming at you, your body's going to try and take over. It's going to tense up, even as it tries to get away. So Talia's going to get a nasty cut—but probably not a fatal one—and you're going to die for nothing."

The Knight began mumbling words, prayers to his God, I imagined.

"That's right, son: the Gods guide you. Sure, you can smell your own piss right about now, and every muscle in your body is starting to freeze, slowing you down. And that taste in your mouth? Not pleasant, is it? So while you're praying to the Gods for help, ask yourself one simple question."

"Wh . . . what?"

"Do those Gods of yours *really* love you?"

I saw the fear in the quivering of his mouth but it wasn't as strong as his faith. "Purgeize take me in your—"

His last word was cut off by two inches of steel in his neck.

I stayed exactly as I was, my rapier extended into a lunge that had been quite possibly the fastest of my entire life. Talia's eyes were wide, and focused on the blade that rested against her right cheek.

The Knight began to gurgle and blood poured from his throat onto her hair. His left hand, the one holding the knife, twitched as he struggled to command the muscles to commit one last act of blind faith. They wouldn't, though, and Talia reached up and pulled his hand away from her throat with a slow, careful motion that was almost gentle. She stepped out from his grasp and turned to watch him sink to the ground.

Brasti came forward and awkwardly, painfully, removed his coat and placed it over Talia's shoulders, though she didn't appear to notice. "Falcio tricked you," she said to the Knight, now on his knees. His hands were trying to stop the blood coming out of his throat. "He made you think about your muscles to get you to tense up, and he kept talking about the Gods so you'd start praying." She knelt down in front of him. "Both those things slowed you down. You could have gone to your Gods with a sacrifice worthy of their gift. You could have killed a Greatcoat."

The Knight's eyes were wide with terror as Talia's words washed over him. But she wasn't done. "Your blessed Purgeize will be very angry when you meet him," she continued, "so give him this message for me. Tell him that Talia Venire is coming for him. Make sure the God of War knows that he's next."

The Knight's body slumped down to the ground. I found myself oddly uncomfortable about the way Talia had spoken, but as I had no idea what they might have done to her while she'd been their captive, I kept my mouth shut.

Ethalia didn't. "That was unnecessarily cruel," she said.

Talia looked neither hurt nor offended by her words. "That isn't cruelty," she said.

She left us and ducked into one of the tents. When she returned she was carrying a long spear with a diamond-headed blade at the end. Her name had been earned by her deadly skill with that weapon. "Come with me," she said, and motioned for us to follow her. "I'll show you what cruelty looks like," she added as we followed her into the forest.

"Wait," I called out. "Where are we—?"

"I wasn't alone when they caught me."

CHAPTER TWENTY-FOUR
THE BLOOD MOTHS

The first body was hanging naked from the tree, the flesh filthy and covered in tracks of blood that had dripped from wounds to his chest and neck. His arms had been bound to two branches that split off at odd angles from the trunk of the tree. I've seen plenty of dead people before, men who had met their ends in just about every way imaginable. I'd never seen one quite so white. Below his body was a pile of leaves, sopping and soaked through with blood.

"It's Harden," Kest said as soon as we were close enough to make out his features. "The King's Whisper."

"I knew him, back in the day," Allister said. "He and I both served under Quillata."

"He was my brother," Talia said. "Did he ever tell you that?"

"No," Allister replied, "he never mentioned anything about his family."

She nodded absently. "There weren't any other siblings in the Greatcoats. Harden was always worried that meant there might be some unspoken policy against it. He always was a little naïve." She closed Brasti's coat around herself as if she'd only then realized she was cold. "I suppose that's why he fell for the woman's ruse and made us rush headlong into a trap."

"What was Harden doing?" I asked. "What was his mission?"

Talia didn't answer but instead pointed. We'd all been so focused on the first body that we hadn't even noticed the second.

This man was bound to a post, his arms forced to full extension by ropes that were looped around the branches of nearby trees. Unlike Harden, he was clothed in some kind of heavy robe stained a dark red. Sunlight broke through the leaves of the trees above and died on the gray-black iron surface of the mask clamped to his face.

"Harden said his name was Gan," Talia said. "I didn't believe him at first."

"Why?" Brasti asked. "It's not as if Gan is an uncom—"

"Gan-who-laughs-with-dice," she said.

All of us stared at the dead man. He was a little shorter than average height, and thin, but with the signs of a belly beneath the dark red rags. "Apparently the Saint of Gambling drew a terrible hand," Allister said.

I didn't think the joke was very funny. "We should cut him down," I said, and reached into my coat for a knife.

"Stop," Talia said, grabbing my arm, "they move quickly once awakened." She gestured for the rest of us to move back a few feet, then she knelt and picked up a small stick.

"What do you mean, 'they move quickly'?" Kest asked. His eyes narrowed. "And what are those clothes he's wearing? They almost look like they—"

"He's not wearing any clothes," she said, and threw the stick.

There was no sound, but the instant the stick struck the body, the dark red fabric of his robes exploded into hundreds of tiny scraps as they left behind the pale, dead flesh. Then something even stranger happened: instead of falling to the ground, the red scraps twitched and flew in the air, swirling together in a floating cloud of crimson.

"Saint Shiulla-who-bathes-with-beasts," Brasti swore. "Are those . . . *butterflies*?"

"Blood moths," Talia replied. "That's what the woman who took my coat called them."

The swarm slowly flittered up into the sky. I followed as Talia approached the corpse of Saint Gan. With the moths gone, I could now see the dozens of tiny shallow cuts on the flesh of his arms, his chest, his legs.

"The moths did this?" Kest asked.

"No," Talia replied, "the woman . . . There was some sort of ritual to all of this. She forced liquid through the opening in the mask—I don't know what it was—and then took a knife and made those small incisions you can see all over his body. She was methodical about it—patient, I'd say. She had this box—a plain thing, really, made of something like sandalwood, and the blood moths were inside. They start out white as snow, but after she placed them on the wounds . . . they just sort of turned red. Not just the bodies, but the wings too."

"But why?" I asked. "What's the point?"

She didn't reply, but went back to reciting her story as though she had to get it out all at once or risk being unable to speak of it. "The moths just sit there, unmoving—I thought maybe they'd died from gorging themselves on the blood. But they aren't dead. After a while, that crazy bitch would reach over and very carefully pick one off the body." Talia shuddered visibly. "Then she ate it."

Ethalia, who had been silent for a very long time, said quietly, "This is what they did to Birgid."

The way she said it transformed the words from an observation to a vow. She locked eyes with me, I think because she wanted me to see that the pale blue ocean that had once been there had hardened into its own kind of iron. Ethalia would do whatever was required to fulfill her role as the Saint of Mercy now. Everything else was in the past.

My thoughts were pulled back by the sound of Kest shattering the clasps on the mask of infamy covering Saint Gan's face.

"He looks . . . *ordinary*," Brasti said. "He could be any country drunk betting black pennies in the tavern."

"I suppose you're right," I said, but I was lying. I had no idea what the man tied to the tree looked like because I couldn't see his face.

"Falcio? What's wrong?" Ethalia asked.

"I'm fine," I said.

"You aren't fine. You're shaking . . ." She reached out a hand to touch my face and her fingertips felt like burning embers. She stumbled back, breaking contact, gasping for breath. "The terror . . . it's . . ."

"It's nothing," I said. It wasn't true, of course, but that was all I could manage just then.

"You're white as a corpse, Falcio," Kest said. "I think you should . . ."

His words sounded further and further away, and I felt myself drifting closer to the body tied to the tree. When I stared into the man's face I didn't see Brasti's country bumpkin; I saw my own face, staring in frozen agony at the cold, empty world. It was my broken body hanging from the tree.

Stop this, I told myself. *That's not you*. But I could feel the ropes binding me, so tight my arms and legs were numb. There was nothing but darkness. There was no land, no roads, no people, only the tree. Only the needles and the pain and the endless torment.

They've come to give me the Lament again.

"What the hells is wrong with him?" Allister's voice was calling out.

Thin branches full of leaves were swatting at my face.

Odd. I don't remember seeing any leaves on the tree.

The words of Heryn, the Dashini Unblooded who had overseen the Lament, repeated themselves over and over in my ears: "*Shall we begin?*"

Breathe, I told myself, willing my heart to slow. *Heryn is dead. Darriana killed him. The Lament is over.*

Over? What a foolish thing to say . . .

"What's going on?" Talia asked.

"It's the Lament—the torture he experienced months ago," Ethalia said.

"But he's recovered," Brasti said.

"No. He hides it, he holds it in, but the Lament is always with him."

Distantly, I felt something inside her reach out to me, something that tried to ease the fear, and for a moment, I felt myself coming back—then Ethalia fell to her knees and again I was drawn back into it.

"I'm not strong enough," she cried. "I can't help him."

It's not the Lament, I told myself. *You're in a forest hundreds of miles from the place they held you. The Lament is over. It's over. It's over.*

Someone slapped me hard across the face and only then did I realize it wasn't the first time. I opened my eyes to see Kest, his face impassive, but behind his eyes I could see concern and sadness and guilt mixed together.

"I'm fine," I said, pushing him away.

"You're anything but fine," Allister shouted. He turned to the others. "What in name of Saint Zaghev-who-sings-for-tears is going on with him?"

"Leave it," Kest said. Even I could hear the warning in his voice now.

"Well, the First Cantor can stand here until winter comes," Talia said, removing Brasti's coat and handing it back to him, "but I've got work to do and I don't feel like waiting around for Falcio to get his courage back."

Though she didn't elaborate on that work, I knew exactly what she meant. And I also knew the way she was speaking to me was intentional; it was the same way Allister spoke to me, testing boundaries. I reached down to help Ethalia up, but she shook her head, and I knew it was because she wasn't strong enough at that moment to endure my touch.

"Falcio?" Kest said, and we exchanged glances.

What was I supposed to do now, let Talia go off and start looking for revenge against anyone she could find? Did I even have the right to refuse her?

Of course you don't have the right, you fool, I cursed. *You have a Gods-damned* duty *to refuse her.*

I looked at her and at Allister both. There was precious little admiration in the way they looked back at me, and I couldn't blame them. The Greatcoats had been disbanded for years, and we'd all been apart ever since the King had died. Why should they listen to me now?

Because there's a reason why the King named the Cantors, and, no matter how stupid and slow you are now, there's a reason he made you the First.

"Brasti, go back to the road and get Talia's coat. Kest, help Ethalia, then go with him."

Kest seemed to sense what was happening. "Falcio, I'm not sure that's—"

"Just do it," I said. "Consider it an order."

Without further complaint, Kest gently lifted Ethalia by her shoulders and helped her make her way back to the road.

"I'm not leaving her here," Brasti said.

Talia gave him a wan smile. "Why, Brasti Goodbow—have you decided that you love me after all this time?"

He looked at her awkwardly for a moment, then turned and went toward the road.

Talia shook her head. "Who would've thought . . ." She looked up at me and any affection that had been in her voice disappeared. "Well, you might as well ask whatever it is you were too uncomfortable asking in front of Brasti. They didn't rape or torture me, if that's what you're wondering. The woman burned my clothes. She kept saying I was *unclean*—which, given how long it's been since I had a ba—"

"I need to know if you're a still a Greatcoat."

Even before the words had finished leaving my mouth, Talia had let the tip of her spear drift down toward my chest. "I don't know if you're genuinely stupid, Falcio, or just tired of life."

"Both." I didn't bother to push away the spearhead. "But I'm also the First Cantor of the King's Greatcoats, so get your weapon out of my face and answer the damned question."

The command struck her like a blow. For the first time since we'd found her, I saw tears in her eyes. "My name is Talia Venire," she said. "I am the King's Spear and yes, you fucking sack of dirt, I am a Greatcoat."

"And you?" I said to Allister.

He snorted. "Sorry, Falcio, but you don't get to talk to me that way anymore. From what I can see you've pretty much screwed up the whole—"

"Either answer my question or take off the damned coat so I can give it to someone who can."

Allister's hand gripped his staff a fraction tighter and the iron-shod end twitched toward me a fraction.

Damn, but he's quick.

"You really think you're fast enough to draw that rapier of yours on me the way you did with that idiot Knight? Who in all the hells do you think you are to tell the rest of us—"

"I'm Falcio val Mond," I said, "called the King's Heart, and, in case you've forgotten, I *am* the fucking First Cantor of the Greatcoats. So either answer my question or make your move and find out just how fast I can be."

Allister's jaw was so tight I could hear his teeth grinding.

He'll go with the back of the staff first, I thought. *He'll feint with the top and then—*

Whatever move he was planning, he let it go and set the bottom of his staff against the ground. "My name is Allister Ivany. I was named the King's Shadow, and yes, I'm still a Greatcoat."

I let out the breath I'd been holding in for a long while. What replaced it was more guilt than relief. How long had the other Greatcoats spent on the road, reviled by one half of the country and hunted by the other half? Was dressing Talia and Allister down like this really the best way to remind them of who they were? Talia had been captured, beaten and forced to watch her brother tortured to death. Was I bringing her back, or breaking her spirit?

"Well, you ass," Talia said, "we answered your damned question. Now what? Are you waiting for us to kneel down for you, too?"

Okay, not much danger of breaking her *spirit.*

"Greatcoats don't kneel," I said. "Kest, Brasti, and I are going to find a sanctuary for Ethalia and then get to Aramor so we can put Aline on the throne before the whole country goes mad."

Allister shook his head. "Do you really think a fourteen-year-old girl is going to—?" He stopped abruptly. "All right. Tell us what you want us to do."

"If Greatcoats are being hunted, then we need to get the word out. Find the Bardatti—start with the ones from the inn if you have to, then go north. Tell them what's happening, and find a way to gather the rest of the Greatcoats safely and bring them back to Aramor alive."

"How are we supposed to do that?" Talia asked. "I'm not even sure that's possible."

"It may not be," I admitted, "but you're Greatcoats. Doing the impossible comes with the coat."

While I waited for Kest and Brasti to return with Ethalia, I forced myself to look up at the dead Saint, wondering how long it would take until the features of his face stopped looking like my own, how long until I stopped feeling the ropes tight against my skin.

I glanced back over at Harden, who also wore my face. *It's possible that you've been beaten, poisoned, and tortured one too many times to ever hope to stay sane.*

For some reason it bothered me that they'd stripped him naked. I wasn't sure why, since it had likely been the least of Harden's worries at the time. But something was gnawing at my thoughts.

"Well, you're not dead, so that's something," Brasti said, approaching me with Kest and Ethalia alongside. "Though from the look on Talia and Allister's faces you might want to sleep with your rapier next to you."

Why not? I thought, trying not to look at Ethalia. *No one else wants that spot anymore.*

It was a petty, small-minded thought. There were vastly worse things happening in the world than my love life. I could almost feel someone turning the screws, as if Heryn was still driving his little needles into my flesh.

Heryn's dead. Stop conjuring him up. Leave the Lament behind. Focus on the next problem.

My vision of Aline came back to me, her words ringing loud in my ears. "You can't beat him unless you see what isn't there."

So what isn't here?

"Falcio?" Kest asked.

"What?"

"You're drifting off again."

"I'm not . . . I . . . Something's wrong. I'm missing something important."

My eyes went back up to Harden's naked corpse, wondering again what perverse satisfaction his killers had taken in stripping him bare, in taking his—

"Hells!" I shouted, "Harden's greatcoat—where is it?"

"Why? What does it matter now?" Brasti asked, but Kest was already moving through the tents, knocking them over and rummaging through their contents.

"I'm not finding anything but rags and bits of food," Kest said.

"Maybe they burned it?" Brasti suggested.

"Check the fire pit," I said, running to the center of camp.

Brasti, Ethalia, and I knelt down in front of the fire pit and the three of us started running our hands through the ashes looking for any sign of Harden's coat.

"Falcio, there's nothing here," Brasti said, showing me his blackened hands. "Even if they did burn Harden's coat we're not going to find anything."

"The buttons are gold, assuming Harden hadn't already used them," Kest said, joining us.

Brasti stopped. "Even if he had them, the killers would've taken the gold, wouldn't they?"

"The buckles," I said, "the rivets—there's metal all over our coats. Find *something*!"

"There's nothing here, Falcio. Saint Felsan-who-weighs-the-world, what's wrong with you?"

"Where was Aline headed after she left Baern?" I asked Kest. *Please, tell me it's Aramor. Tell me she went back to—*

"The Ducal Palace of Luth," Kest replied. "She insisted on going ahead with the plan to visit each of the Duchies, to show everyone she'll have their interests at heart when she rules."

I was already on my feet before he finished his sentence and running back toward the road.

"Falcio, what—?"

"They took Harden's coat," I shouted back.

"So you think they're laying more ambushes?" Brasti asked, chasing after me. "Isn't that what you sent Talia and Allister to deal with?"

"The woman who ambushed us," I said, still running, trying not to stumble on the rough ground. "Before she died, she said something. 'I hope you are there to witness the glorious moment when one of us buries our Needle deep inside the false Queen's mouth.'"

I made it back to the road, thanking what Saints were left when I saw that our horses were still there. "Come on," I cried, "we have to get to Luth, now!"

The way the woman had said those words. I hadn't understood at the time but they weren't an idle threat. She hadn't been speaking with the mad conviction of a zealot but the certainty of someone whose plan was already in motion.

"I don't understand," Ethalia said, mounting her horse as I kicked mine into a gallop. "What does this have to do with Harden's coat?"

"I told Valiana I wanted Greatcoats standing guard over Aline, but she's never met the others. That's why the killers took Harden's coat. That's how they're going to get to Aline."

CHAPTER TWENTY-FIVE

THE THRONE ROOM

Five days of hard riding, spending sleepless nights trying not to fall off our mounts and stopping only to let them rest while we debated our plans and blamed each other and everyone we knew, and none of it, in the end, made any difference.

The Ducal Palace of Luth came into view, looming over the massive arch that led into the capital city: a reminder to its visitors that all trade passes beneath the Duke's watchful eyes. The sight had probably been more imposing when there was an actual Duke on the throne, but with Roset dead, Luth was now governed by a timid and very temporary Ducal Protector.

"Left or right?" Kest asked.

The main road went under the arch and up to the palace, so horses and wagons had to creak up one of the paved paths that went up a gentle incline on either side to reach the narrow courtyard above.

"Right," I said, thinking it didn't matter which one we chose. It turned out I was right.

"What in the name of Saint Iphilia-who-cuts-her-own-heart are they doing?" Brasti asked, peering at the crowds ahead of us, massed outside the courtyard.

"They're praying," Ethalia said. "Like the ones at the martyrium."

"Let them pray," I said, and kicked Arsehole's copper-colored sides to induce him to greater speed. Ahead of me several of the pilgrims suddenly rose and locked arms across the roadway.

"I don't think they're going to let us through," Kest pointed out.

I leaned forward on my horse's neck and said, "All right, Arsehole. You've been hopping your way through half the South. Show me what you can really do."

Jumping over obstacles is tricky at the best of times. It's worse when it's people, because the horse tends to get scared and wants to turn. So jumping over a dozen religious fanatics while riding uphill?

"Come on," I urged, and Arsehole raced forward toward the crowd. For a second I was afraid he'd hesitate, but then I felt the muscles of his powerful, mountain-bred hindquarters launch us into the air. *This must be what it feels like to fly,* I thought for that brief moment as we sailed over the heads of the shocked pilgrims.

Arsehole landed perfectly on the other side and took off at once, not slowing for even a moment. I glanced back and saw a few of the pilgrims break ranks and start chasing after us, which was a mistake, since it created a gap for the others to ride through.

"You are a damned good horse," I said. Arsehole didn't reply, no doubt because he really wasn't an especially bright horse.

The path ended inside the courtyard where guardsmen armed with spears and crossbows awaited. "Dismount," the gate captain shouted to me. I reined in the horse but stayed mounted. "I'm Falcio val Mond, First Cantor of the Greatcoats."

"I know a Trattari when I see one," he replied. "Now get off your horse before we shoot you down."

"Listen to my words very carefully, Captain," I said. "The life of the heir to the throne of Tristia is in danger, in this palace and on your watch. Now let me pass."

His eyes narrowed but he considered me carefully and finally signaled his men to stand down. "Fine, but I need you to report the situation so that I can—"

"I'll report later," I said, but before I could I kick Arsehole into motion, a crossbow bolt flew at me, fired by one of the guards standing next to the captain. It missed my thigh but caught the saddle and glanced off the horse's flank. The beast reared up in shock and the only thing that stopped me from flying to the ground was flinging my arms tightly around his neck.

"Down, boy," I said, as soothingly as one can while being shaken mercilessly by a horse in terror. "Come on, Arsehole," I added for good measure, "the wound's not so bad as that."

Arsehole, quite reasonably, didn't listen, but I nonetheless managed to slide off him before he went charging into the center of the courtyard.

"Damn fool!" the captain shouted, ramming his fist into the side of the man who'd fired at me. "The Ducal Protector would have my head for seeing a Greatcoat harmed, not to mention what the *Realm's* Protector would do!"

"Falcio—" Kest began.

"Go," I said, looking at the sky above me. It was close to midday. "The three of you get to the throne room—if the Ducal Protector is holding court, Valiana and Aline will be there. I'll follow. Kest, if you find him—"

"We'll find him, Falcio," Brasti said.

I watched the three of them ride straight through the courtyard and into the front entrance to the main hall before turning back to the gate captain. "There's an assassin coming for the heir. He'll be dressed like us."

"A Greatcoat? But—?"

I cut him off. "It doesn't matter how." But, of course, it did matter. We were supposed to be smarter than this, *better* than this. *Damn you, Harden, for letting yourself get taken,* I thought irrationally. I pointed to the other guards. "Take your men and get as many more as you can find. Tell them to bring crossbows to the upper gallery of the throne room." When he nodded his assent I added, "And Captain? Find some men who can bloody well aim."

The young guard who'd fired at me was still bowing repeatedly. When I looked at him he started gabbling, "I'm sorry, sir, I . . . I thought you were about to attack the captain—"

I grabbed him by the front of his jerkin and shook him. "Go and take care of my damned horse." I took off at a run toward the main entrance and immediately felt a twisting pain lance through my ankle. I'd not even noticed landing awkwardly after sliding off Arsehole's back.

"I can send more men with you," the gate captain called after me.

"Just the crossbowmen in the gallery," I shouted back, begging my ankle to hold out just a little while longer.

I don't know who you are, I cursed my nameless opponent, *but I know why you've come. You don't get to touch* her. *Do you understand that? You don't get to touch my King's daughter.*

Inside the palace, men and women crowded around marble pillars and shuffled like cattle toward the interior hallways, sometimes pausing to talk or smile or sneer at one another. Luth was one of four Duchies that now stood without a Duke or Duchess on the throne; instead, they had to rely on the tenuous leadership of hastily appointed Ducal Protectors whose primary qualifications appeared to be timidity and a distinct lack of ambition.

I hobbled my way through the crowds, ignoring the variety of salutations, none very friendly, until I caught sight of Kest, Brasti, and Ethalia's horses in the care of two rather confused-looking pages. The horses were not terribly happy, surrounded by such a press of people, and the boys were having some trouble trying to keep control of them. But I went straight past them and into the wide corridor leading to the throne room.

"Saint Laina-who-whores-for-Gods," I mumbled to myself, "how the hells do I get through that?"

The throne room of Luth is one of the largest rooms you'll ever see. It's over a hundred feet wide and nearly three hundred feet long—a fitting tribute to the self-aggrandizement of the Ducal throne's past occupants. Brasti used to joke that the servant tasked with bringing food from one end of the room to the other needed a fast horse just to make sure the soup wasn't stone-cold when it arrived.

Surveying the room, I could see what must have been three hundred people milling about between me and the throne. The six guardsmen standing at the entrance were looking overwhelmed, so I took advantage of the situation to push past them and disappear into the crowd before they could think to stop me.

I couldn't even see if Aline was there from this distance, nor could I spot Kest or Brasti, or Ethalia. Fortunately, I didn't really need to: Kest would be making his way toward the throne, moving with that eerie efficiency of his, while Brasti would be seeking a vantage point from which he could use his bow to take out the assassin once we spotted him. Ethalia would be working her way to Valiana, so she could let her know what was happening without the assassin picking up on it.

I glanced up at the galleries. The gate captain's crossbowmen were nowhere in sight and not for the first time I cursed how ill-prepared we were to protect our future Queen. The Dukes kept those few Knights and soldiers they still trusted in their own Duchies, which left Aramor no choice but to start recruiting and training guards from the local populace. They were looking to be decent folk, all in all, but they were too few, and there was no way they were ready to withstand any real kind of threat, not yet—and who knew what we'd be facing over the years to come?

"First Cantor." The voice came from behind me and I didn't need to glance back to identify him as I kept moving toward the main dais. Tommer, wearing his own black leather attempt at a greatcoat, was walking close behind me. "Are you well, First Cantor? I saw you come into the palace, but—"

"Not now, Tommer," I said.

Tommer might be young, but he wasn't stupid. He caught the concern in my voice and asked quickly, "Is the Lady Aline in danger?"

"Not for long," I said.

"I can see Brasti," Tommer said, and started to raise his arm.

"Stop," I said. "Don't draw attention to him."

We were halfway to the dais, but the throngs were thicker here and I couldn't even make out the elaborate oak and silver throne of Luth at the end of the room. I wound my way around a group of merchants and froze as I saw a man in a Greatcoat several feet away from me. I started to draw a knife when I felt Tommer's hand gripping my arm. "That's Senneth, the King's Thread," he said. "Captain Antrim introduced me to him last week. They served under Winnow together."

Hells. The beard was new, but I recognized him now. I did my best to loosen the grip on my knife. I was so full of fearful tension that I wasn't sure I'd have been able to throw the damned thing at this point.

Tommer pointed to one of the guards standing by the columns lining the room. "Shouldn't we alert the guards? They could—"

"No," I said, "if we alert the guards the assassin will realize we've caught on. Besides, he might have accomplices among them."

"Is there no one we can trust, First Cantor?"

I pushed past another group of men on my way toward the throne. *I trust Kest and I trust Brasti,* I thought. *I trust Valiana, Aline, and Ethalia. The rest of the world can go—*

"Hey!" a man said, grabbing my shoulder as I tried to push forward so I could actually see the dais. "Wait your turn, Trattari!"

I turned to remonstrate with him, but Tommer stepped between us. "I will deal with this, First Cantor."

I nodded, grateful now for Tommer's intervention and ignoring the fact that I'd been annoyed with him just moments before. I was finally within sight of the throne. It was empty, but a slim figure in the yellow and silver coat of office of the Duchy of Luth stood in front of the dais. He looked young, perhaps twenty-five, with fashionably cut reddish-blond hair grazing his shoulders. He might have been good-looking, but all I could see was his stooped posture and flinching demeanor as he cowered under a barrage of complaints being fired at him by a pair of merchants. I noticed their clothes looked considerably more expensive than his. The young Ducal Protector—I'd been introduced, but couldn't remember his name—kept glancing over at Valiana, who stood a few feet away. She was listening intently, but apparently unperturbed by the merchants' litany of complaints. Perhaps the young man was hoping that as Realm's Protector, she might step in at some point and save him.

Then I finally caught sight of Aline, sitting in a chair at the side. She might be King Paelis's heir, but her status was still somewhat nebulous, at least until the Ducal Council got off of its collective ass and properly elevated her to the throne. A quick motion to my right made me turn in time to see Kest standing behind one of the columns, pretending to prop up a clearly unconscious man as if he were helping a drunk cross the street. I worked my way a little closer.

"Is that him?" The man had a short mustache and beard, recently trimmed, and smooth skin; along with his expensive clothes that suggested noble birth.

"I'm not sure," Kest replied. "He had a knife hidden in the sleeve of his shirt."

"How in hells did you spot that?"

He shrugged. Kest never bothers to brag. It's not that he isn't as egotistical as the rest of us, it's just that he thinks bluster and braggadocio is a waste of energy.

"All right, let's get him out of the way and . . ." I'd been turning back toward the throne again when I saw Aline smiling at me, her hands pressed against the arms of her chair as if she was about to get up to run and greet me. Behind her, in the shadows of the long red velvet curtains that dressed the curved wall of the dais, two men in greatcoats were moving very slowly toward her.

CHAPTER TWENTY-SIX
THE TWO GREATCOATS

I felt rather than heard the scream that came from my throat for my ears were filled with the rush of my own blood, pumping furiously, desperately trying to give my muscles the strength they needed. There was a painful crunch in my ankle as I pushed off of it, using all the force my legs could muster to begin the longest run of my life. I was thirty feet from Aline; she stood far closer to the men who were about to kill her. She couldn't see them. She was still smiling at me.

A slight whisper followed by the vibration of a blade slicing through the air told me I'd drawn my right-hand rapier. I'd sliced the fold of a man's sleeve as I'd pulled the sword into line in front of me. The men in greatcoats behind Aline were moving so slowly; it was as if the whole world was grinding to a halt—but I wasn't moving any faster. I willed myself to be stronger, praying for Brasti, wherever he was, to see the assassins, to let me hear an arrow sing as it flew through the air. He'd have to get them in the face, otherwise their coats would protect them. *Do it,* I thought. *Show us all you can aim true, even with a wounded arm, Brasti. I swear I'll agree every time you tell us the hundred reasons why the bow is superior to the blade.*

But no arrow came. The two men were still in the shadows and likely Brasti hadn't noticed them yet. I called out his name, but I wasn't sure if anyone could hear me above the din that had erupted as those nearby saw me running and screaming like a madman toward the dais where Aline, even now, was smiling innocently at me.

How could she not *know*? How could she not sense that someone was about to push the point of a blade into her heart? *Don't you understand, you stupid,* stupid *girl? They've come to kill you!*

I knocked an old woman to the ground as I ran past her, nearly catching her walking stick between my legs but overbalancing her. I ignored my hurt ankle to leap over the stick as it clattered to the floor beneath my feet.

Aline's expression didn't change, even to laugh at my awkward rush toward her. *She knows,* I realized. Men and women close to the dais were now pointing behind her and she could see them doing so. *She knows she's about to be attacked and she thinks I'm going to save her.*

The two men in greatcoats were hesitating, having caught sight of each other. *They aren't together,* I realized thankfully. *So only one's a traitor . . . but who . . . ?* Both of them looked at me as I screamed, "Step back!" My foot hit the first of the three steps to the dais and slid off the edge, forcing me to scramble inelegantly to keep my balance.

One of the two men nodded at me as though we were old friends and took a quick step back, but his hands were drifting to his pockets. The other, noticing those movements, drew a falchion from inside his coat. Its subtly curved blade the length of a shortsword gleamed in the light.

"Brasti, now!" I shouted.

"You're in my damn line," he shouted back at me, and I dropped to my knees, the hard marble floor sending a painful shock all the way up my legs.

"Take the shot!"

An arrow flew barely an inch over my head, slamming into the coat of the man holding the falchion. By some magic it pierced his coat and went into his shoulder, unleashing a scream followed by a string of curses as he stumbled backward.

"The next one goes in your throat," Brasti called out. His voice sounded light and airy, as if this were all a game, but I could hear the razor-edged tension hidden beneath.

"Falcio, what is going on?" Valiana asked from behind me, her hand reaching to her side for a sword that she no longer carried; the head of state obviously wasn't expected to defend herself. The young Ducal Protector of Luth was standing over her protectively.

I could see guardsmen coming up behind her as I pushed myself up. "Assassin," I said, my voice barely a whisper, then I added, "a Greatcoat." Aline's eyes were still fixed on mine. As I moved toward her, the other man, the one who had nodded at me and backed off, suddenly grinned as a long, wickedly curved knife slid down from the sleeve of his coat.

"The Gods command me!" he shouted and raised his arm.

Saints, no, we shot the wrong man—"Brasti!"

"Fucking guards are in the way!"

I threw myself forward, knowing all I had to do was put myself in the way of that knife, and knowing I was too far away. The assassin's smile grew wider as his eyes met mine; he too knew I couldn't get to him. Even then, even in that moment, Aline's eyes remained on me, waiting for me to come to her, waiting for me to save her.

I can't reach you, sweetheart!

The assassin's dagger had just begun its downward trajectory when a hand reached out and grabbed it awkwardly by the sharp blade, stopping it inches above Aline's head. It was the man Brasti had hit and he was grimacing in pain. The arrow was buried deep in his shoulder, but still he gripped the knife, stopping the assassin's hand.

"I can't hold this much longer . . ." he groaned. "Somebody shoot this bastard!"

An arrow shot through the air and into the assassin, hitting him square in the right side of his chest, but he didn't fall. As though entirely incapable of feeling pain, he grinned and pushed down harder against the unknown Greatcoat's hand.

"I am the God's Needle!" the assassin screamed, his voice full of rapturous madness. "He commands the girl to die! He says . . ."

The assassin's expression changed and he looked down to see the point of a falchion driven deep into his chest just below his neck. "I am Mateo Tiller," the Greatcoat said, his face contorted in pain, sweat dripping from his forehead. He twisted the blade hard and the assassin's knife slid from fingers no longer under their owner's control. "I am the King's Tongue. He says go to hell."

For a moment no one moved and everything was still, except for the blood oozing from the assassin's chest and along Mateo's blade before it dripped onto Aline's face. Even then she sat calmly, looking only at me, ignoring the would-be killer's blood staining her cheeks. I ran to her and grabbed her out of the chair, holding her in my arms, the leather coat wrapping around the two of us. I could hear Kest and Brasti shouting at people to stay back and summoning people we knew in the crowd to form a perimeter around us.

The would-be assassin was still spewing his religious madness at the world around him, but several of the guards were now holding him down.

"I'm all right," Aline said in my ear. "Don't squeeze so hard, Falcio."

"I'm going to choose to ignore that command," I said, listening instead to the beating of her heart and hoping I could slow my own down to match it.

"I wasn't afraid," she insisted.

"Well, I damned well was."

"I need to . . ." She started wriggling, trying to get her arm out from under mine, so I let her go and she reached up and wiped some of the blood off her face.

For a moment the two of us just looked at each other.

"Don't stare at me like that, Falcio," she said. "I know I look stupid with blood on my face."

"You look like a clown getting ready to put on a children's show."

"Well you smell like the backside of a horse."

"That's perfume," I said. "I brought it for you as a gift. Don't you like it?"

"*You* must. I smell it on you all the time."

Behind us people were shouting; Valiana was asking questions, and Brasti was doing his best to answer them. For Aline and me, this was a place we'd been to before, death only a hair's breadth away, too many times. I reached out and hugged her again. "We have to stop meeting like this," I said.

She started to say something but stopped.

"What is it?"

"Nothing," Aline replied, pushing away from me. "Valiana needs you."

I turned and saw the woman I'd named my daughter standing before me, waiting to speak to me. Despite the chaos around us, the look of determination on her face made me want to hug her too. Unfortunately, someone else got in the way.

"First Cantor," the young man said, giving a slight bow that made a lock of red-blond hair fall over his face, "I am Pastien, Ducal Protector of Luth. I've long looked forward to talking to you."

I was about to tell him that he was going to be waiting a while longer but Valiana gave a slight shake of her head. I glanced around and realized the nobles and merchants of the court were all watching us intently. *She doesn't want me to weaken him in front of his court,* I realized. "My Lord Ducal Protector," I began, then hesitated. *What the hells do I say to the man? I've barely even heard of him.* "My pleasure in meeting you carries with it that of all the Greatcoats. Never have I heard an ill word spoken of you." *There. That's all I've got.*

Apparently it was enough: Pastien looked like he'd just escaped execution, and Valiana gave me a slight wink that said I hadn't just destroyed the country. "My Lord Ducal Protector," she interrupted, "I know you will forgive us, but we must get Aline away from here. There could be a backup plan in place and this room is too crowded for us to protect the heir properly."

"Of course," Pastien said. "Forgive my foolishness in delaying you."

He wasn't the only fool. I'd so desperately wanted to know that Aline was all right, to *feel* that she was all right, that I'd failed to consider that other assassins could still be hiding among the crowd. "I'll go with her," I said.

"You won't." Valiana's tone brooked no dissent. "We need you here. The assassin is dying and I have no idea what in all the hells is going on."

"Aline stays—"

"I will care for her."

One look at Ethalia, and the rush of danger burning through me calmed, if only for a moment, and all I wanted was reach out to her, to connect to that sense of the world being perfectly safe and sane that I felt only when we were together. But everything about Ethalia is in the eyes, and those eyes no longer looked at me the way they used to.

You're getting maudlin in your old age. "Thank you," I said, and looked around. Spotting Kest, I said, "Go with them. Kill anyone who tries to touch them. *Anyone.*"

Kest squeezed my shoulder and said quietly, so that only I could hear him, "It's what I do best. Now you need to do what you do best."

As I returned my attention to the dais and the assassin, any feelings of love or pain drained out of me, leaving a burning rage that threatened to feed on itself. I so badly wanted to put my hands around the throat of the impostor wearing the stolen greatcoat that I had to squeeze them until my knuckles went white.

"Breathe, First Cantor," Mateo Tiller said, holding his bleeding shoulder and leaning rather unceremoniously against the throne of Luth. "You're making me nervous."

"We need a healer!" I shouted, then I saw someone was already heading toward us, her silver case at the ready. "Take care of this man," I said, pointing to Mateo, but he was shaking his head.

"Don't be stupid," he grunted. "Help the assassin—we need him alive so we can interrogate him."

Reluctantly, I nodded to the healer and as she set about her business I said thoughtfully, "I think I remember you now. You joined the Greatcoats not long before—"

"Yup," Mateo said, "barely got a year in before everything went to seven hells. This job isn't what I was promised—and I do believe I'm owed some back pay."

"Aren't we all," I said, and extended a hand to shake Mateo's. "That was damned good work."

He pushed himself off to a fully standing position and accepted my hand. "It was damned, anyway." He was a little taller than me, thick hair brushing his shoulders and a beard that reminded me of Brasti's, though Mateo's was a deep brown rather than red.

"'The King's Tongue.' What does that mean?" I asked. I didn't really care, but I was still shaking and I needed to try and slow my heart down before it burst in my chest.

He gave a smile that was more grimace than grin. "I suppose you wouldn't remember, but I used to be a page. I always knew I wanted to join the Greatcoats and I used to follow King Paelis around asking questions about the law all the time, hoping he'd let me join the order. Then he'd get annoyed and threaten to have my tongue cut out for him to wear as a necklace. I said that would make me the King's Tongue and then he'd *have* to make me a Greatcoat."

"That's a nice story," I said, "but you're lying."

"True, but I'm in a lot of pain, so it's possible that I forgot the real reason."

The sound of a scream made us both turn.

The healer was pressing a red cloth against the assassin's chest. "I can't save him," she said. "The sword went through his lung. Saints know why his heart's still beating."

I glanced at Mateo. "You should have hit him in the stomach. He'd have lasted longer that way."

"I was aiming for his stomach, but you had Brasti-fucking-Goodbow shoot me in the shoulder. Bastard managed to hit the exact spot where the bone plates in my coat were broken from a spear last year. So I'm sorry if my aim was off, but kindly go fuck yourself, First Cantor."

"Sorry," I said, and actually meant it. If only I'd recognized him sooner, this might have gone differently. "How did he even get so close to Aline?" I wondered aloud.

"Apparently whenever a new Greatcoat arrives, she and Valiana insist on greeting them personally," Mateo replied. "I got here yesterday, and the Realm's Protector asked that I stay close by. This fellow," he said, kicking the assassin's foot, "arrived a couple of days before me. Said his name was Harden something."

"Harden Venire, but that's not him. Harden is dead."

The healer called to me, "I've got this man as stable as I can make him. Not sure what's been keeping him going but it won't last. He's got minutes, no more."

I went to walk over, and nearly passed out when I put all my weight on my ankle. Now that the immediate danger had been dealt with, my body was obviously intending to have a few words with me.

"Here, sir, I found this for you." I turned to see a guardsman holding out a walking stick. "If you hand me your rapiers I can hold onto them for you."

"I'm fine," I said, taking the cane from him, but I'd barely taken a step before the damned thing got caught up in my scabbard and nearly sent me flying. "Hells, take it," I said, unbelting the damned thing.

"That's the wrong side, sir; the doctor said you should use the stick on the opposite side to the injured leg."

"Hells, fine." I handed him the other one and walked gingerly over to the assassin. While I'd been fumbling about, Valiana had gotten there first.

"Give me the name of the man who sent you," she said. The rage, barely contained in her voice, was enough to make me hold my breath.

The assassin tried to speak, but all I heard was the gurgling of his throat as his body struggled to hang onto what life remained in him. "Who sent you?" Valiana repeated, kneeling down beside him.

"I am a Needle of the Gods. It is their will that commands me."

"I already met one of your Needles," I said. "She didn't impress me, either. Who sent you? Why now? How many others are there besides you?"

"Everyone," he rasped, blood bubbling up from his mouth. "The whole world is commanded to see the girl dead and you destroyed by despair."

The gurgling got worse for a moment and I feared he could no longer speak, but he opened his mouth and I realized he was laughing.

"Give me a name," Valiana said. "Give me a name and we can ease your suffering."

"You . . ." His eyes focused on her. "You are the little bitch who calls herself the Realm's Protector, aren't you? You have come to me, just as the God said you would."

"Then name your God," she said. "Or is he so full of fear he hides even his name behind the man he sent to kill a child?"

"There is only one God," the assassin said. "Let me give you his true name." He opened his mouth wider and I thought he was trying to speak, but instead he stuck his tongue out and bit down hard on it. Blood gushed from the wound, though it was not enough to make a difference to a man already dying.

Valiana turned to me. "Why would he—?"

The assassin's head shot up and as Valiana turned back to see what he was doing, his mouth was on hers. She pulled away instantly, a look of utter revulsion on her face as blood from the man's tongue dripped down her mouth. I dropped down to my knees and drove my fist into his face, though the force of my blow caused more pain to my knuckles than I suspected it did to him.

He laughed, the sickening, distorted sound coming out in guttural exhalations.

I punched him a second time, then a third, all the while repeating my questions, over and over, shouting at him, "Speak, damn you to all the hells! Who sent you? Who is your God?" but all he gave in return was more blood and spit and laughter.

When this didn't work I leaned in to him and whispered, "I don't care if you do think the Gods sent you, you bastard. There are seven hells for those who would kill children and I will make sure that you find yourself in the worst of them."

The assassin let out one last, long breath, all that his torn lungs and slowing heart could provide. The air leaving his body came out as a sigh of satisfaction, the whisper of a man answering a lover's kiss.

The gurgling stopped, though blood still seeped from his mouth. I felt a hand on my shoulder and turned to see Valiana wiping the sickening red smear from her face. Despite the horror we had just witnessed, she spoke gently and clearly. "Come, First Cantor. His filthy work is finished. Ours is just beginning."

I stood up and spared one last look for the assassin. He was as ordinary a man as any—young, maybe Mateo's age, with fine facial hair on smooth, barely tanned skin. He didn't look as if he'd ever so much as done a hard day's work, never mind trained to be a killer.

"Falcio," Valiana repeated, pulling at me. "We need to go."

But I stayed where I was, paralyzed by the figure laying at my feet. The expression on the assassin's face, with the blood still leaking from his mouth and the last light gone from his eyes, was the most peaceful and contented I had ever seen.

CHAPTER TWENTY-SEVEN

THE BEDROOM

It took me an hour to free myself from the guards and noblemen and every other Saints-cursed bastard demanding to know what had just happened, and were they safe?

"The Dukes will want a report," Valiana told me as we walked along the upstairs hall toward Aline's rooms.

"The hells for the Dukes," I said. My ankle was screaming every time I stepped on it. *A lifetime practicing with swords and yet somehow walking with a stick escapes you.*

"I'll take care of the report." Valiana's voice was flat, tired, resigned.

I let my steps slow to a halt. "No, I'm sorry. I should do it. I'm just a little . . ."

"Used up?" she offered, giving me a weary smile—too weary for a young woman of twenty. "It's becoming a common affliction. You should see poor Pastien when he doesn't have to put on his brave face for the court."

There was very little I cared about less than the well-being of the young Ducal Protector of Luth, but I wasn't entirely stupid; Valiana obviously wanted me to ask.

"So what's he like?"

There was a note of affection in her voice when she answered, "Pastien is . . . well, he's very decent, I think. He keeps trying to find ways to keep the Duchy stable until a new Ducal line is selected, but he's young and out of his depth."

That almost made me laugh. "You're younger than him."

"True, but I suppose I . . ." She hesitated, looking for the right words. "In some ways living with Patriana taught me a great many things that are helping me to do this job. Pastien doesn't have that experience—and he's surrounded by some of the most avaricious noblemen I've ever met."

"Can he hold the Duchy together?"

"Not as things stand. He's under pressure to grant more autonomy to the Margraves and Viscounts over their respective lands." She gestured toward one of the windows that faced the courtyard. "More and more pilgrims are showing up every day, and Pastien doesn't have nearly enough troops to protect the palace. I sent for a hundred Aramor soldiers to help bolster his own guardsmen."

"A hundred? You realize we have precious few of our own?"

"I know that, Falcio." All the weariness returned to Valiana's voice. "But unless we can stabilize the smaller Duchies like Luth, the rest of the country will never be governable." She put a hand on my arm. "We have to give Aline a strong throne, Falcio. Without that . . ."

She let the words hang there for a while. I wished I had something to say that might comfort her, but my thoughts were filled with visions of crazed religious zealots who didn't even have the decency to die when you stuck a blade through their hearts. Weighed down by our respective concerns, we started walking again, and soon reached the door to Aline's bedroom. Kest was waiting outside, with Tommer in his black leather greatcoat standing next to him. He was holding a shortsword in his two hands, point to the ground.

"What is he doing here?" I asked Kest.

The dispassionate shrug I got in reply managed to eloquently convey both that Kest had had no say in the matter of Tommer's presence and that I should leave it be.

"I should have been there to protect her, First Cantor," Tommer said, his voice still a little high-pitched for such earnest declarations.

"You're not a—" I was about to say, "You're not a Greatcoat," but then I remembered how the boy had stood in front of the nobleman who'd tried to stop me in the throne room, how he'd stood between Aline and the Knights in black tabards when they'd come to kill her the year before, how he'd stood up for justice in Rijou. "Just make sure Kest doesn't fall asleep on the job," I said finally.

The boy nodded very seriously.

"How is Aline?" I asked Kest.

"Ethalia's taking care of her," he said, which wasn't much of a reply to my actual question. Kest isn't much use when it comes to discussions of feelings so he shifted to something more practical. "A number of nobles, including two members of the Ducal Council, have demanded to see the heir. I sent them away, but I suspect they might return. If they do, should I—?"

"If anyone you don't trust with your own life tries to walk through that door, Kest, teach them the first rule of the sword."

"Well, about that . . ." He paused and glanced at Valiana.

"I haven't told him," she said.

"Haven't told me what?" I asked, and when neither of them spoke, said firmly, "I may only be carrying a stick but I swear I'll see the next person to give me a vague half-answer in the dueling court."

Valiana took a deep breath. "The Tailor is here, Falcio." She cut me off before I could begin to reply. "We *needed* her. With every-thing that's been going on, we had to have someone who knows about the more esoteric aspects of the country's history. I decided to have her brought to Luth."

I'm not sure what was on my face but it was enough to make both Tommer and Kest flinch. Valiana held her ground. "Say what you want to say, First Cantor."

I wasn't even sure where to begin. "You *decided* to bring the Tailor here? Did you happen to forget that she's a convicted—?"

"No longer. The Ducal Council issued a pardon for her."

"Why in the name of Saint Zaghev-who-sings-for-tears would those bloody fools give her *a pardon*? Do they *like* it when people try to have them killed? Because I'd be more than willing to grant them their wish at this point!"

Somewhere around the middle of my little speech my voice had turned into a bellow that was reverberating throughout the hallway. The door to Aline's room opened and Ethalia stepped out, looking stronger than she had on the road. I hoped that meant that the Saint's Fever had passed for now.

"Lady Ethalia," Valiana began, "if you could persuade Falcio to calm down, I would—"

"Realm's Protector," Ethalia interrupted, her voice quiet but carrying an edge, "rest assured that if there were one person in this world who would induce me to violence, it is the woman currently sitting at Aline's bedside." She turned back to me. "But we are where we are right now, and you, Falcio, need to get yourself under control before I let you go into that room."

Before I let you go into that room? "I'm perfectly controlled," I said, trying to control myself.

Ethalia reached out and took my wrists. She winced, as if holding plates left too long in the oven. "Look at your hands, Falcio: they're still shaking. And don't pretend it's just nerves. You're scared and you're frustrated and you're so full of rage you can't even feel it anymore."

"I'm fine," I said, and tried to pull my hand away to reach for the door, but Ethalia didn't let go, even though I could see it was hurting her.

"That look in your eyes will terrify Aline far more than a hundred assassins," she said softly. "Is that what you want for her?"

I looked at Kest for support but he just shrugged. "You always look like you want to kill someone to me so it's hard to see the difference."

Thanks a lot. "All right," I said, "I promise to behave and not try to kill the Tailor, all right?"

Ethalia held onto my wrists for a few seconds longer, making me feel like an errant child needing to be calmed. "Very well," she said at last, letting me go and stepping away from the door. "Try to remember the life Aline has lived, and the one she has yet to live."

I found Aline sitting up in bed with the Tailor sitting on a chair next to the bed. Oddly, she was forgoing her usual practice of continually sewing something or other and instead holding Aline's hand, which both surprised me and on some very deep level offended me.

"Ladies," I said, by way of greeting.

The Tailor grinned up at me. "Why, is that the great *Falsio dal Vond*, come to save us from all the nasty people of the world?"

"Not *all* the nasty people, apparently," I replied, then I remembered Ethalia's caution and tried to laugh as though this were just a joke between old friends. The Tailor, apparently as aware as I was of the nervousness in Aline's expression, made her own attempt at a friendly chortle. *Well, it turns out we're both terrible actors, so we have that in common.*

"Well, sweetling," the Tailor said, rising from her chair, "I'm sure you want to catch up with Falcio here, so I'll say goodnight." She leaned over and kissed Aline on the top of her head before joining me at the door. "You and I will see each other soon, won't we, Falcio?"

Through a rather massive act of will, I forced my mouth into a semblance of a smile. "It's a promise."

That sent the Tailor into her more customary cackle and she patted me on the shoulder as she walked through the door. Valiana and Ethalia entered after she left and sat on the edge of the bed. Aline smiled at them; for a moment I felt the heavy iron weight around my heart ease, just a little. *Let me protect these three*, I prayed to whatever Gods were listening. *Destroy the rest of the country if you must, but let me hold these three close to me, always.* But my mind went back to the assassin's face as he lay there dying on the ground, smug with the self-satisfaction of a zealot who believed he had the right to kill the girl who I had sworn to keep safe from harm.

"Falcio?" Aline was still looking at me, but her expression had changed. There was fear in her eyes that I hadn't seen before and it took me a moment to realize it was *me* who was making her that way. Ethalia caught the look on my face and then whispered into Aline's ear, causing her to start giggling.

I went to Aline's bedside. "Well, your Majesty, it appears you still haven't won over all your subjects."

"Do we know who the man was?"

"Not yet," Valiana replied, "but we'll find the people who sent him."

Aline looked down at her hands. "It was my fault. He came like the others before and presented himself at court. He said his name was Harden and he was the King's Whisper. I looked him up and he was there in the records. I know how happy it makes you when they return and so—"

"It's not your fault," I said. "You did nothing wrong. I should ha—"

"Stop it!" she said, her voice so loud and high-pitched that I thought Kest might burst through the door. I reached out to her, but she pushed my hands away. "Stop taking the blame for *everything*. People want to kill me—it's not all your fault every time one gets close."

"All right," I said. She was wrong, of course. She didn't understand yet how these things worked, that with the right strategy and more care and more time I could—

"But we have to change things now, Falcio. *I* have to change things." She looked at Valiana and Ethalia. "Forgive me, Realm's Protector, Lady Ethalia," she said, using her "official" voice, "but I would speak with the First Cantor in private for a little while."

The two of them rose simultaneously and gave me warning looks before leaving the room. Aline waited until the click of the door signaled that we were alone. "I'm the one who demanded that the Tailor be brought here," she said.

"Valiana already told me that she—"

"Valiana lied," Aline said, then gave a confused little smile. "She keeps thinking she has to protect me from everything and everyone as well."

I kept silent for a moment. Aline had just been through a terrifying experience that would have left *anyone* feeling helpless. I couldn't take away whatever sense of control she thought she had. Nonetheless, when I finally spoke, I said, "I can't allow the Tailor to go free."

"We need her, Falcio. She knows all the Greatcoats—*all* of them. If she had been down there with me she would have—"

I rose from the bed and turned away. I really didn't want her to see my face as I said, "She tried to destroy the country. She put assassins into greatcoats and sent them to do murder to get her way."

"*My* way," Aline pointed out. "I knew what was happening—I went along with it."

"You didn't know. You were just—"

"Look at me!" Aline said. "I'm not some little girl in pigtails. I was thirteen when the Tailor came to me with her plan and I'm fourteen now. How much wiser do you think one year has made me?" She rose from the bed and came over to me. "I know what we did was wrong, Falcio."

"Then why did you do it?" I tried to keep the disappointment out of my voice.

"Because I was scared. I'm always scared. I wake up every morning—*every* morning, Falcio—and I swear it takes every ounce of will I have just to rise from my bed." She looked up at me. "Some days the only reason I do is because I don't want to disappoint you."

"Aline . . . the Tailor is too dangerous."

"But we *need* dangerous right now, Falcio. We need someone who knows all the dirty secrets of the world."

"You don't think I can protect you," I said. It wasn't a question.

It felt like she waited a long time before, "No, Falcio, you can't. You're the bravest man anyone's ever met—"

I laughed then, but it was an ugly thing. *She didn't see me nearly shit myself when I saw Harden's body hanging from the tree. Brave? I would run screaming from the room right now if I thought the Dashini might come for me again.*

If she saw the fear in me, she gave no sign. "The Tailor knows the politics of Tristia. She knows the ways of war. She's got a hundred tactics that might help us."

I thought about those "tricks and tactics": she'd been using them to try and bury the noble families not so long ago. "I can't believe Jillard hasn't had her killed yet." *What's happened to the world when you can't even count on rapacious murderers anymore?*

"Duke Jillard consults with her regularly, Falcio. He might not like her, but he respects her intellect. He would very much like to know what she knows about the world."

I held my tongue, waiting for my sense of betrayal to pass; I couldn't believe she'd gone to the Dukes without speaking to me first. *She's right, though. You can't help her govern the country. The Greatcoats weren't meant for that.* "It sounds like you've gotten it all worked out."

She gave that quirky little smile that I recognized. "I do." Then she hugged me hard enough to take the edge off the pain. "I love you, Falcio. You're fast and you're clever—but you'd make a lousy politician."

I laughed, this time unexpectedly without bitterness. "Gods, you remind me of him sometimes."

"Who?"

"The King. Your father." I felt her tense up and realized how stupid I'd been to say that. "I'm sorry, Aline, I don't—"

"No, it's all right," she said, but let go nonetheless. "It's just . . . I wish I could have known him." She walked over to her night table and picked up a thin leather-bound book. "I found some of his journals—I read them at night, and I try to picture his face, as if he were reading to me. But I know I'm just making it up in my head."

There was nothing to say: I had known Paelis as well as any man alive and I missed him every day. If I were a better storyteller I could help her feel a connection with him through my own recollections, but somehow, whether because I'm just not that articulate or because I felt too jealous of those memories to share them, I was never able to do it.

"Did you know that he's buried up in Pulnam?" Aline said. "Near the village of Phan, where we hid from Trin's forces?"

"I didn't," I replied. What an odd thing. I'd left Castle Aramor before Paelis had been buried and had never in all these years thought to find his grave.

"Isn't that strange?" Aline went on. "We were right there, sitting on that little hill and looking up at the stars together, and he was buried not thirty feet from where we sat. I think that's why the Tailor spent so much time in Phan after he died."

That made sense. It was a place where Dukes and Knights would be unlikely to ever venture, where she could set herself up and visit her dead son without fear that anyone would find the grave and unearth the body for Saints-know what nefarious purpose. I thought back to sitting on that hill, trying to imagine where precisely he might be buried. Should I have felt it, somehow, when we were there? For all the times I imagined the King talking to me, cajoling me, making fun of me, I hadn't ever had the slightest glimmer of his presence there.

"Falcio?"

"Hmm?" I said, pulled from my thoughts.

"I have a favor to ask." She paused as if trying to choose just the right words. "If . . . if I do die sometime soon—"

"You're not going to die."

"I am," she said, her voice firm, "and so will you, one day. But if I die before you, would you take me back to Phan? Would you bury me up on that hill near my father?"

"Aline, I'm not . . ." It wasn't an unreasonable thing to ask. Why shouldn't she lie next to her father when the time came? Life had kept them apart; maybe death could bring them together. And yet I didn't want to say the words.

"I want to hear you say it," she said.

"All right," I said, "but only because you're going to be Queen one day and I plan on being a terribly unruly subject."

She didn't laugh, but my answer seemed to satisfy her nonetheless. "Good." She held a hand to her mouth and yawned. "I'm very tired now, Falcio. I think I'll go to sleep, if that's all right."

I hugged her one last time. "Of course. We can talk again in the morning." I watched her step back to her bed and sit down on top of the covers. She leaned back until her hair touched the pillows and closed her eyes, looking as fragile and vulnerable as a piece of crystal that would shatter if you gripped it too hard.

I would have to push the Dukes now, get them to move up her ascension. The sooner Aline took the throne as Queen the sooner the country would get that the issue was settled, and those voices whispering dissension would realize the game was over. There is a deep and long-standing fear of shedding royal blood in Tristia; even among the lunatics.

Aline was so still that I wanted to reach out and make sure her heart was still beating. Kest must have slipped into the room because I felt his hand on my shoulder. "She's alive, Falcio. Trust in that and stop imagining her death."

He was right; it did no good to fret. I should just be glad that Aline was safe for now. But how could I do that while staring down at the pale skin of the young girl who even now looked as if she might already be dead?

CHAPTER TWENTY-EIGHT

THE ALLY

I left Aline's room and headed off in search of the two things I needed most at that moment: food and solitude. As though the Gods themselves had once and for all decided to declare war upon me, I hadn't even made it to the grand staircase leading to the main body of the palace before the next attack on my sanity, if not my life.

"My Lord First Cantor!" a voice called out from behind me, and I spun around to see who was accosting me now, twisting my ankle in the process.

"Son of a bitch," I swore.

The young, handsome, irritating face of Pastien, Ducal Protector of Luth, looked as if I'd just smacked him across the nose with a book. "Forgive me, my Lord First—"

"Not 'Lord,'" I said. "Just 'First Cantor' or 'Falcio' or 'Bastard Trattari' is fine."

He stared at me aghast. "I would never call you—" Finally that small part of his mind which would hopefully grow into a sense of humor one day told his mouth to smile. "Ah, yes. I'm sorry . . . Falcio . . ." He said the word tentatively, waiting for an approving nod from me before continuing, "It's just that, around here, people are rather sensitive about titles and such things. Yesterday I made the mistake of referring to the Margrave of Talthier's lands as a Demesne instead of a March. I thought he was going to summon a scribe and write up the declaration of war then and there."

"The nobility don't have to work for a living," I said. "They need a way to pass the time, and being offended is their favorite hobby. Just listen to their complaints with care and patience and when they're done, nod your head sagely, make a great show of reading the biggest, oldest tome of court protocol you can find, and then, after a few minutes, look up and very seriously tell them to go fuck themselves."

His laugh was a little more relaxed this time, and a little more genuine. "I think, First Cantor, that I will need a great deal more fencing practice before I attempt your strategy."

Against my better judgment I found myself rather liking this earnest, affable man. His was an unenviable role; he would never please anyone and it was unlikely to bring him much in the way of reward, worldly or otherwise. I wanted to help him, if I could. "Follow Valiana's lead," I suggested. "She has a way of seeing the whole board and knowing which piece can be moved and which should be left alone."

"She's *amazing*," Pastien said, and his eyes took on that faraway look that country boys get the first time they see the majesty of a castle off in the distance. "I've never met anyone so clever, so . . ." He paused and said, "That's actually what I wanted to talk to you about."

"Valiana?"

He nodded. "I . . . I realize that you aren't actually her father, but she chooses to be called Valiana val Mond, so . . ." He pulled at the front of his coat to straighten it. "Sir, would you grant me your permission to court Valiana?"

I stared at the boy: privileged, presumptuous, no doubt born to a wealthy family who had, however mistakenly, bought him his current position. And now it was entirely possible I was going to have to kill him. "Let me see if I have this straight: Saints are being murdered, half-crazed pilgrims are massing outside this very palace, and the heir to the throne of Tristia was almost assassinated a few hours ago. But you want my permission to *court* Valiana?"

Pastien looked so stricken I might as well have clubbed him across the face with the brass tip of my walking stick. "I'm sorry . . . you're right. It was foolish of me to—"

That small part of me that wasn't a complete ass managed to gain temporary control of my mouth. "No, it's . . ." *It's what? People aren't allowed to fall in love anymore just because you screwed up your own life?* "Look, Valiana is the Realm's Protector of Tristia. She—"

"Of course," Pastien interrupted, "her duties are too great for any—"

"Please don't make this harder than it needs to be."

"Right, sorry."

"What I meant to say is that Valiana is quite possibly the wisest and most determined person I've ever known. It's not for me to say whether you can or can't court her. Just try to . . ." *No. I'm drawing the line at giving him advice.* "You don't need my permission to court her. You need hers."

Pastien grinned, rather stupidly, I thought, then words came tumbling out of his mouth—a recitation of every usage of every word of positive or complimentary meaning ever devised. On the other hand, my ankle was killing me and I was distracted, so it's possible he just announced his plans to murder us all in our sleep. After what felt like far too long, he gave a dignified bow and took his leave.

Why is life so much easier when people are trying to take it from you than when you're forced to actually live it?

"And thus is a troubled nation protected from its enemies," came a mocking voice from behind me, and Jillard, Duke of Rijou, pushed himself away from the wall a few feet away. His supercilious drawl complemented the carefully groomed black hair, freshly oiled and slicked, and the gleaming red and gold Ducal robes.

"Given that you have been one of this troubled nation's most nefarious enemies, Your Grace, I suppose you would know."

Jillard gave me the slightest tilt of his head by way of acknowledgment. "Ah, but that was yesterday, Falcio. Today, we are the best of friends."

I descended the staircase, careful not to trip over my unwieldy stick in the process. *After all, I might need it to brain Jillard with.* "What is it I can do for you, Your Grace?"

He looked surprised at that, a perfectly false impression of a man with hurt feelings to go with his next words. "You? Do for me? Why, the thought of *you* doing something for *me* hadn't even occurred to me. In fact it is I who've come to do you a favor."

I paused, because my ankle hurt, but also for effect. "As you can see, Your Grace, I'm tired, beaten, and injured. I'm not sure I could survive the kind of favors you provide."

Jillard nodded smugly, apparently feeling the time for pleasantries had passed. "I'm a valuable friend to have, Falcio, and you are a man especially in need of friends like me." He held up a hand and began counting off on his fingers. "You need to keep Aline alive. You need to defend Valiana from the Ducal Council. No doubt you're even at this moment worried about the fate of your little Sister of Mercy—although now that Ethalia's a Saint I imagine she must find your company less . . . appealing."

I briefly considered bashing his head in with my stick and smiled. "Your Grace treads in dangerous waters."

Jillard let his hands drop, unconcerned. "You know, I just realized something for the first time. Has it ever occurred to you that those you're so driven to protect are always women?"

"Perhaps it's because men like you are so determined to destroy them, Your Grace."

"No, I don't think so, Falcio. That's the lazy answer, the one that lets you pretend to be a man of justice." He cocked his head and stared at me. "My, my . . . is it possible that the death of your wife left you with such a terribly narrow sense of duty? I wonder, Falcio, when you see a man being beaten on the street, do you think, 'A-ha! A victim of evil-doers! I must save him with elegance and flair!' or do you sigh and mutter to yourself, 'Well, I suppose I should do something. The wretch might have a wife, after all, and I wouldn't want her to be upset over his death.'"

"No, Your Grace," I replied wearily, "when I see someone being beaten and tormented, man, woman or child, I always think the same thing: here is Tristia, the land of my birth, a place where corruption and violence always have a home."

"Careful, Falcio. You almost sound as if you hate your own country."

"I do," I said, before I could stop myself, and realized, maybe for the first time, that it was true: I hated Tristia. I hated it as much as I hated Jillard and Trin and Patriana and all the others that would see it destroyed—or worse, in fact, because it was this wretched nation that had given them birth.

It was a dangerous and foolish thing to say to Jillard, however; he could have used the admission against me. Instead, he looked at me with an expression that almost approached sympathy. "Why then?" he asked gently, "do you fight so hard to save it?"

I hesitated to answer, partly because I knew everything I revealed was another knife he could one day put in my back. But my thoughts turned to Aline, sitting there on her bed, trying so hard to be brave even though she was certain that one day soon she would die at the hands of an unseen enemy. "For her," I said.

"Good," Jillard said, as though I had just conceded the argument. I suppose in a way I had. "The heir to the throne nearly died today at the hands of a madman, Falcio. She was ill-protected, and that is your fault. So let's stop acting as if we're equals, and instead you can come with me so that I can teach you how to better serve her."

He turned and began walking down the hall at a pace that made it clear he expected me to follow.

"You do realize that most of the attempts on Aline's life came from you, don't you?" I called out as I tried, to the great complaint of my ankle, to hurry down the rest of the stairs.

"That was yesterday, Falcio," Jillard called back. "Times have changed. Best try to keep up."

The Duke of Rijou led me all the way across the palace, past a pair of guards and down a set of stairs to a basement that, by my estimation, shouldn't even have existed. "We're actually inside the left side of the arch itself," he told me when he saw me looking around, calculating where we were. "The architecture is really rather fascinating."

He led me into a long, poorly lit room with a flagged floor. The walls were bricks and mortar, but one long side was set with cabinets and shelves filled with small jars and boxes and books. On the other side the wall was lined with a dozen or so wooden drawers, each one about three feet square. I knew even before the smell hit me what was inside those drawers. "You brought me to the death house?"

Those who died in the palace were brought here for temporary storage before being assigned appropriate burial, depending on their house and rank.

Jillard sounded amused. "You look uncomfortable, Falcio. Are you quite all right?"

"That would be my ankle, Your Grace, and if you just made me walk all this way as part of some elaborate, theatrical threat, I promise you there will be one less empty coffin in that wall tonight."

He didn't even do me the courtesy of looking nervous. "Don't be silly—why would I bother threatening you when all it does is make you smug and self-righteous?" He went over to one of the shelves and retrieved a brass lantern that turned out to have its own sparking mechanism to light the wick. The room brightened, and I could now see the tables at the far end of the room, and the body on the one closest.

"It's the assassin," I said, staring at the man who'd tried to murder my King's daughter. His body was still clothed, though thankfully someone had taken off Harden's greatcoat. It bothered me the way the corpse lay in such quiet repose. There was a tray of sharp metal instruments next to the table, and I picked up one of the knives between my thumb and forefinger, enjoying the blade's balance and feeling a powerful compulsion to use it to cut the assassin into pieces, to remove whatever humanity was left in him, to make him suffer in death, if not in life.

"A terrible thing, isn't it?" Jillard said, "Having to resist the righteous impulse to commit atrocities against one's enemies." He sounded genuinely sympathetic.

"What did you want to show me, Your Grace?"

"I want you to look at his face, then his hands and then his feet."

"You want me to *what*?"

The Duke just gestured toward the body, and then walked over and leaned against one of the cabinets. "Just tell me what you see."

I'd already spent more than enough time in the throne room staring at the man's face. The ruin he'd made of his mouth by biting off his own tongue was now obscenely accentuated by the swelling of his face. "He used to be better-looking," I said flippantly.

"He did indeed," Jillard replied. "I must say, you were rather amateurish in the throne room, Falcio. If you're going to interrogate a man, always make sure you have control of his jaw so he can't bite off his own tongue. A truly committed spy will always do that first to keep from blurting out secrets under torture."

"He was bleeding out rather quickly. I'm not sure how much torture he needed to worry about."

"Not all men know how to resist torture, Falcio. That should be your first clue."

Except that most assassins and spies *are* trained to deal with pain—so this man wasn't a professional. He was fairly young, which didn't tell me much. In life his face would have been smooth and clear, neither tanned nor overly pale. His hair was reasonably short and well kept.

"Now his hands," Jillard said.

I picked up first his left then his right. Neither showed the calluses I'd associate with a soldier or a swordsman. His skin was soft.

"Now the feet, Falcio."

Irritated as I was by Jillard's tone, I nonetheless complied, because a picture was starting to form, and sure enough, once I'd removed his boots I found that the soles of his feet were also smooth. Most people can't afford the kind of footwear that fits well enough to keep from getting various ailments ranging from fungus to malformed toes. This man was wellborn.

The thing about spies and assassins is that, contrary to romantic songs and stories, they're usually poor. Pretending to be a noble is harder than one would imagine, since most noble families actually know each other. So when a man comes to listen to your secrets or slit your throat in the night, he's usually disguised as either a servant or a soldier. *Besides, rich people don't need to risk their lives for money.*

"Do you know who he is?" I asked.

Jillard joined me at the table. "No, but I suspect he comes from a minor noble family, possibly the third or fourth son of a Lord." He turned to me. "This wasn't your first encounter with these so-called 'God's Needles,' was it?"

"Your spies keep you well informed, Your Grace, since I only just informed Valiana of that incident some two hours ago. Does the Realm's Protector know that you've got—?"

He waved a hand absently as though the issue was irrelevant. "The one who attacked you. What do you remember about her?"

I thought back to the woman who'd ambushed us on the road. Had she been the daughter of a noble family as well? She'd played the part of a commoner at first, but her voice, her diction once she revealed herself as a God's Needle, had changed, become more refined. I hadn't thought anything of it at the time, but now it seemed too much of a coincidence.

Jillard caught my expression; evidently I'd confirmed his suspicions. "I read about a peasant cult, hundreds of years ago, who believed they could gain power for themselves by drinking the blood of Saints. Of course, they died out so one would assume it wasn't very effective."

"So someone has recreated the cult of Saints, only now they're recruiting from noble families?"

Jillard said, "Although that doesn't appear to be the only thing that's changed." He gestured to the body of the man who'd stood there laughing even as the blade dug deep into his heart. "It appears that drinking a Saint's blood really does give you unnatural abilities now."

"I can't help but wonder, Your Grace," I said, struggling to keep up with Jillard as he strode back up the stairs, "this sudden concern for Aline's well-being. Is it perhaps because, once we get down to considering those most likely to—and capable of—engineering something like this, your name is certain to be high on the list?"

The Duke favored me with a hint of a smirk. "A grand conspiracy, Falcio? Religious fanatics masquerading as Greatcoats? Such things were always more to Patriana's taste; I prefer less grandiose methods to achieve my ends. Besides, having to spend time listening to such religious nonsense, their fantasy of being some kind of agent of the Gods?" He shivered dramatically. "I think I'd rather stab myself."

Although there was no act too vile for me to readily attribute to Jillard, Duke of Rijou, I had to admit this was precisely the wrong time for him to act. His own position within the country was still precarious; people hadn't forgotten his part in Tristia's most recent agonies.

"This sort of thing would suit your daughter well enough," I said. On these occasions where circumstances forced me to spend more than a few seconds in Jillard's presence, I found it helpful to remind him that Trin was the fruit of his loins.

"She does have a taste for the theatrical," Jillard admitted, "but she has never been one to repeat herself."

"So, the clerics?" I said, more to myself than to him. I'd never thought about it before but there was a decidedly old-fashioned bent to the churchmen of Tristia: perhaps they weren't too keen on a woman taking the throne?

The Duke actually laughed out loud. "Those fools? They couldn't conspire together to write a decent sermon, never mind orchestrate something like this. No, Falcio, I fear we have a new enemy now."

I'm not sure which I found more terrifying, the idea that there might be a new player on the board, or Jillard's use of the word "we."

He must have read my mind. "You might as well accept it, Falcio"—he placed his hand on my shoulder and I had to restrain myself from shrugging it off; I really needed to hear what he had to say—"it's you and me against the forces of darkness: two dashing heroes preparing to risk all to put that darling little girl on the throne."

I knew I was repeating myself, but I couldn't help it. "That's the same 'darling little girl' you tried to have killed, you understand?"

The Duke of Rijou looked singularly disappointed. "You know, you really are a bitter, vengeful creature at heart, aren't you, Falcio?"

"And you, Your Grace, are a spiteful snake who slithers his way into power on the strength of his ability to deceive and manipulate others."

"I believe you're thinking of Shiballe, my servant."

It was a fair point.

Beyond his arrogance and corruption, the Duke of Rijou was in every conceivable way a despicable human being; he'd tried to have me killed on more than one occasion. On the other hand, by that standard I suppose he was no better or worse than any other Duke in Tristia, which was hardly a reassuring thought. But I badly needed an ally, and he was at least highly intelligent. I removed his hand from my shoulder. "I'm going to find a reason to kill you one day. You know that, don't you?"

"Of course," Jillard replied amiably. "Although that won't be until after I've watched you rot away in one of my dungeons, moaning on in endless agony about the King's Laws. I imagine that after a few decades even that immense pleasure will fade, at which point I shall gladly give you the honor of killing me. All in all, a fair arrangement." He stopped walking, turned and extended his hand to me. "Marked?"

"Marked," I said, and shook his hand. I must have been feeling rather suicidal at that point. As we continued through the great hall I noted that someone had hung up the old tapestries once again. The one that caught my eye featured a circle of heroically rendered noblemen assembled around a rather humble King. You'll find similar in every palace in the country.

"Now that we've cleared that up," Jillard said, "let's get to business," and he ushered me into the castle's infirmary, a huge room with many smaller chambers off it where the wounded could recuperate in some comfort.

"You're not planning on treating my wounds, are you, Your Grace? Because while I recognize your significant expertise in the causing of all manner of wounds, I have some doubt as to your ability to heal them."

He looked at me as if I'd just suggested marriage. "*Treat your wounds?* Don't be silly, Falcio. I'm here to give you something far more valuable—and necessary, given our present circumstances."

"And what would that be, Your Grace?" I responded politely.

"A lesson in politics." And he led me through the infirmary to a small room at the end where a woman in her later years was propped up in bed, her left leg splinted and raised. A younger man, burly, but dressed in fine clothing, looking enough like her to be a son or a nephew, perhaps, sat by her bed. His eyes narrowed when he caught sight of me and he started clenching his fists.

"Your Grace!" the old woman shouted happily, and began rustling at her bedding, as if straightening it might improve the room's appearance.

"Please, Lady Ingetha, do not trouble yourself for me."

"Two visits in one day, Your Grace! You do me such great kindness!"

Jillard smiled and reached over to hold one of her hands. "My Lady, the pleasure is mine." He paused theatrically and announced, "I must confess, however, that it isn't by my design that I return to you this evening."

Lady Ingetha looked at me, then back at Jillard, and the Duke reached out his other hand and laid it on my arm. "Falcio here insisted we come—he's been absolutely beside himself with worry since the events of this afternoon. 'How is she, Jillard?' he's been demanding, over and over. 'I must see her!'"

The old woman's eyes widened, and she reached out her other hand for mine. Even her son looked a little less homicidal, though

I imagine I just looked confused. I neither recognized the Lady Ingetha's name, nor did I remember ever having met her. "I'm sorry, My Lady, but I—"

"He had no choice, you see?" Jillard broke in. "The life of the heir to the throne was at stake. 'If only I could have leaped sooner, Jillard,' he kept telling me, 'I might have saved that poor woman from being injured.'"

Only then did I make the connection. "I hit you," I said, stupidly.

Lady Ingetha squeezed my hand. "It wasn't your fault, dear. You had to protect the heir." She gave a sidelong glance at her son. "I could never blame you for that."

The man appeared to reach a decision; he rose to his feet and extended a hand to me. "I said some wrong-headed things about you, First Cantor, and about the Greatcoats. I was wrong."

We shook, and he nodded as if we'd just settled a trade agreement. *This is why Jillard brought me here—not to visit the woman I'd injured, but to placate her son's outrage.* How close had I come to creating yet another enemy of the Crown for Valiana to contend with?

I glanced over at Jillard. His expression was studiously neutral, but even with all his skill he couldn't keep the delight from his eyes. He'd taught me my lesson: I needed a political ally. I needed *him.*

"Oh, Love bless all of you," Lady Ingetha said, her eyes glistening. "To think such great and powerful men are so concerned over the well-being of an old woman!"

Jillard smiled and reached down a hand to stroke her cheek. "And what else should great and powerful men concern themselves with, My Lady?"

She batted his hand away affectionately. "You are an outrageous flirt, Your Grace, always have been: a veritable demon in the guise of a man."

Well, I thought, as Jillard and I left the woman and her son, *at least one true thing was said tonight.*

CHAPTER TWENTY-NINE
THE BOX

I wandered the Palace of Luth for the next several hours, propelled by the need to puzzle through the insanity of recent events, not to mention a perverse desire to master the use of the damned cane. When you've spent most of your life learning to wield a sword with some degree of facility, it feels odd to be overwhelmed by a wooden stick.

However, all I really accomplished was to make my ankle and my head equally sore. Bleary-eyed, I accepted defeat and set out in search of a bed.

The palace halls were almost empty by then, but eventually I found a young woman in a page's doublet who appeared to know what she was doing and, more importantly, where I was supposed to be. "The Ducal Protector set aside rooms for you," the page informed me, and proceeded to recite directions so complicated they should by rights have led to buried treasure.

"Thanks," I said, after having her repeat them for the third time.

"That Lady Ethalia is remarkable," the girl said, wistfully. "She moves with such perfect grace, doesn't she?"

"Um . . . I suppose so," I mumbled, a bit taken aback; generally speaking, pages don't express opinions to guests. But Ducal pages came from noble families, of course, so to her a Greatcoat was probably little better than a common tradesman.

I left the girl and headed up the stairs and down the successive hallways, following the route she had assured me would lead to my rooms. It wasn't until I turned the corner into a narrower passageway lined with elaborately carved wooden doors that I realized why the page had mentioned Ethalia.

The damned Ducal Protector put us in the same room, I realized. *He doesn't know we're not together anymore.*

With all the insanity that had been whirling around us, there had never quite been a moment in which to discuss something as banal as sleeping arrangements. Now two guards stood in front of the door that led to what I had no doubt would be a wonderfully comfortable private apartment with a wonderfully comfortable bed that I would *not* be sleeping in tonight.

I turned to leave. Even as full as the Palace of Luth was, there must be a spare room somewhere—and if I couldn't find a bed anywhere else I could always find Kest or Brasti and bunk with them.

"*You know your problem, Falcio,*" I imagined Brasti declaring, ghostly finger wagging at me in the empty air of the corridor. "*Your problem is that you allow life to be complicated.*"

I knew Brasti's advice would be to walk straight down the corridor to my room, give the two guards a wink, and knock on the door.

"*Now, when she opens the door,*" my ethereal adviser went on, "*forget all this shit about Saints and fevers and devilry. Kiss her full on the lips and count to sixty. When you're done, take her by the hand and lead her to bed.*"

Although it would defy all natural laws, I wondered if Brasti might just be right for once. Why was I accepting the premise that magic and intrigue and—Gods-help-me!—religion should dictate the terms of our existence? When had I become so willing to let the darkness of an hour fill the entirety of my day? Even during the worst of the years since King Paelis died, when Kest and

Brasti and I spent every day fighting just to stay alive, we'd shared the same world view: that we would laugh in the face of death and stare down the worst of life's tragedies.

You've fought pikemen with a crossbow bolt in your thigh, taken on three duels an hour later with the wounds still fresh. Hells, you've beaten Knights and Dashini assassins and Shuran himself in worse condition than you are now. Stop being such a milksop.

I held up the walking stick and stared at it. I'd only been carrying this thing around with me for a few hours and already I felt like an old man. I leaned it against the wall and left it there.

A true swordsman likes a little pain—it focuses the mind.

I strode up to the guards without allowing myself to limp. "Good evening, gentlemen. Nice night, don't you think?"

One of the guards looked as though he might say something, but caught a glance from the other and contented himself with, "A fine night, First Cantor."

I was gratified by his use of my title. Ducal guardsmen usually just call us "Trattari scum" or "tatter-cloaked coward."

I raised my hand to knock on the door when I noticed something sitting against the floor—a wooden box about a foot square and perhaps eight inches tall. "What's that?"

"Oh, hells," said the guard. "I almost forgot. That's for you."

"Someone left me a box?"

"I believe so, sir." The guard reached down at his feet and lifted up the worn oak case. "There's no note on it so we just assumed—"

"Who brought it here?" I asked.

"It was here when we arrived, First Cantor," the second guard said.

I examined the card; finding nothing other than my name on it, I turned my attention to the box itself. It was entirely possible that it was a trap of some kind, but most of the time it's vastly easier and more reliable to send someone to stick a knife in the back of your neck. Nonetheless, I worked my way carefully around every edge, looking for anything that might trigger once I opened the lid. Finding nothing, I handed the box to the shorter of the guards.

"What's your name, guardsman?"

"Sedge, sir. Lord Meretier sent our company to join the palace guards after Duke—"

I cut him off. "Save your life history for the tavern, Sedge. Just hold the box out so the front faces the opposite wall."

He did so without hesitation and I took up position next to him and carefully opened the lid. When no magical fire appeared or exploding darts shot out, I looked inside.

The other guard saw it first. "Saints . . ." he swore.

Inside the box was an iron mask.

Like the one Birgid had worn, it was roughly fashioned to look like a face full of madness and fear. There were no holes for the eyes, just the same three thin vertical slits like those of a Knight's visor where the mouth should be. The same strange iron funnel had been welded to the inside, designed to be forced into the mouth of the wearer, preventing them from speaking.

Keeping them from doing anything but screaming.

"Where is the man who gave you this?" I asked, expecting my voice to be cold with rage, and yet to my ears I sounded more like a child walking into a dark room full of imagined terrors.

"It's as we said, sir," the tall one replied. "It was here when we arrived."

"What's your name?" I demanded.

His voice trembled. "I'm Beltran, sir. I'm one of—"

"Who gave you orders to guard this door?"

"The Ducal Protector himself, sir. He said the lady needed complete silence and solitude on account of some sort of condition she—"

"There's something underneath," the other guard, Sedge, said suddenly. "In the box."

I looked back inside. Sticking out from under the back half of the mask with its cruel-looking clamps to hold the two pieces together was the corner of a note. I removed it gingerly. It had been written in plain, almost merry handwriting.

It said, *You Will Make Her Wear It.*

"Who put this here?" I asked, my hands shaking so hard I nearly dropped the mask.

"We told you, sir, it was—"

I grabbed Sedge by the neck with my left hand. Even through his leather collar I could feel his throat contracting. "Are you lying to me? Did someone bribe you to bring this here?"

Beltran drew his blade, looking uncertain what to do. "Sir, it's as we said, the box—"

The man I was choking grabbed at my arm. "Please, sir, I swear—"

"Falcio?"

The blood rushing in my ears was so loud I hadn't heard the door open. Ethalia stood only inches away from me, dressed in the pale blue nightgown that Aline had gifted her.

I released the guard and held the mask at my side, out of view.

"Falcio, what's wrong?" Ethalia asked.

I tried to speak, but words wouldn't come and she looked at me with concern and pity in her eyes. She stretched out a hand. "Come inside. We can talk."

"Forgive me," I tried to say to the guard, to her, to the world around me. "I took a wrong turn on my way to bed."

"Nothing to forgive, sir," Sedge said.

I looked to the other guard, Beltran. He nodded. "Perfectly understandable, First Cantor. We should have searched for the messenger when we found the box here. We apologize." He started to bow.

I'd been about to turn and head back down the hall, but his deference stopped me cold. "You *apologize*?" I asked.

Ethalia's eyes were on me. "Falcio? I can feel your anger. You're burning up inside. Whatever is wrong—?"

With my free hand I shoved her backward, sending her tumbling into the room, and before either of the guards could react, I swung the iron mask and caught Sedge on the ear, knocking him back into Beltran.

Ethalia was back on her feet. "Falcio, why are you—?"

"Bar the door," I shouted, "for the love of Saint Birgid!"

My choice of Saint was enough to make her comply instantly; the heavy door swung shut and the click of the latch was followed by the sound of the bar dropping in place, echoing in the empty hallway. Sedge was holding his face with one hand and his sword with the other. Beltran stood next to him, his own shortsword at the ready. "Sir, please, calm yourself. Let one of us get the captain, and we can sort this out before—"

"I've been a Greatcoat for fifteen years," I said. "Ten of those years were spent going back and forth to palaces like this one. I've been dealing with guardsmen and soldiers from every part of the country. Let me tell you: in all those years, never once have I met a Ducal guard who's ever *apologized* to a Greatcoat, especially not one who'd just been accused of taking a bribe. And I've never met one who would even *think* of bowing to me."

For a long time the two guardsmen just stared at me, looking as innocent and confused as children who'd been struck without reason. Then the shorter one, Sedge, his face red and already swelling, broke. It started as a twitch at the side of his mouth, then twisted into a wide grin.

"Who'd've thought that politeness could get you into so much trouble?" His voice and diction were clearer now, no longer a rough-born soldier but someone of wealthier stock.

Beltran, also recognizing the game was done, said, "Not as much trouble as attacking two men when you can barely stand, and you without even a sword in hand."

"You can scream for help if you like," Beltran added politely. "But we cleared the wing an hour ago."

Sedge winked. "'First Cantor's orders,' we told them." He'd taken on his fake guardsman's voice. "'Wants to reconcile with his Lady.'"

It annoyed me no end to realize it had been that easy. For the first time I took more careful stock of them both. Sedge was a little shorter than me, but his shoulders were broader. If he got his arms around me I'd have a difficult time getting free. Beltran was a few inches taller than either of us, with a long reach that would serve him well, even with a guardsman's shortsword. He walked a little heavier on his right foot, though, which likely meant he had a problem with his left. That would shorten his lunge.

I took a step back and the pain in my ankle jagged up my leg, helpfully reminding me that I was the most vulnerable one of the three of us.

"Looks like he didn't appreciate your gift of the stick, Sedge," Beltran said.

"You?" I said, my eyes on the shorter of the two guards. My memory of the moments after the attempt on Aline's life were vague, but it might well have been this man who'd handed me the walking stick—and so handily taken my rapiers from me.

Sedge giggled. "Who would have thought it would be so easy to disarm a Trattari?" He mimed the gesture of offering me the cane. "Here you are, sir. Better stay off that ankle, sir. Oh, here, let me take those heavy swords from you and put them somewhere safe, sir."

"Who sent you here?" I asked, taking another step back, ignoring my ankle, which really was complaining bitterly. *So much for pain focusing the mind.*

"The Gods themselves," Sedge answered.

"Any particular God? Just in case I want to lodge a complaint."

Without warning Beltran thrust his blade at me and I had to jump back out of the way. Even then, the tip caught me on the right side of my chest and only the bone plate in my coat kept me from taking a stab wound that would have ended the fight then and there.

I've never been fond of shortswords. They don't have the reach or finesse required for dueling. But a guardsman mostly deals with the closed-in spaces of a castle or palace, the halls and corridors and small rooms to which a shorter sword is perfectly suited.

Sedge tried for a heavy cut on my left side, swinging the whole of his body into the blow. I raised up my arm to take the force against my bicep and forearm; the heavy leather held, but the impact was still brutal. This man was stronger than he had any right to be.

"You should have done what you'd come to do, Trattari," he said. "We had so many fun games planned once you and the whore were in the room together."

I'm really getting tired of people calling Ethalia a whore. I was still holding the mask, and now I threw it as hard as I could at Sedge's face, hoping the recent memory of being struck by it would make him flinch—it didn't, but I was still able to use the distraction to reach into my coat to pull out one of my two remaining throwing knives. *Damn me, I haven't replenished any of my weapons in weeks.*

I threw the knife at Beltran's face and it dug deep into his right cheek, piercing flesh and cracking teeth. It hung from the side of his face for a moment before sliding out and falling to the floor. The look of pain that crossed Beltran's face was too quickly dismissed for my liking.

"We've tasted the blood of Saints, Trattari. We feel neither pain nor fear anymore." His words were slurred and blood flowed from the wound, but he didn't appear overly troubled by it.

"We are the God's Needles," Sedge added, and the two men stepped forward as one, obviously preparing to outflank me.

Sedge leapt forward, his sword extended—not a swordsman's practiced maneuver, more like a boy who'd just been handed a blade for the first time, and I swerved and let it go past me, then struck out with the heel of my palm. I caught him square on the chin, but I swear I hurt my hand more than his jaw.

I drew my second throwing knife, knowing I'd have to keep this one in hand if I was to have any chance at all. For the next several seconds my opponents came closer, backing me up as they stabbed at me with their shortswords. A good half the blows hit, despite my best efforts to parry with my throwing knife.

"You look tired, Trattari," Beltran said. "Would you like a moment to rest?"

He stepped toward me at an angle, forcing me closer to the wall, and my back foot caught on something, and I dropped my knife as I tripped backward. I flung my hand out to support myself against the wall, only to have my fingers find the object that had tripped me. It was the bloody walking stick.

Sedge smiled. "Look here, an old codger's going to shake his stick at us."

I held the cane in my hand, taking note of its heft and balance for the first time. "There's something you should know," I said.

"What's that, Trattari?"

I extended the cane, letting the weight of it guide my grip. "This stick is thirty-two inches long. It weighs an ounce or so under three pounds. Now, that's heavy for a cane, so I'd guess it was made for a big man." I rotated the shaft in my hand. "The decorative knob on the end of the curved handle is made of brass and weighs a good six ounces on its own." I flipped the cane around. "They've weighted the bottom end with this brass band near the base—here, see?—to balance out the weight."

"Wouldn't want the old codgers tipping over," Beltran said, but his eyes were narrowed, revealing a trace of uncertainty. *Good.*

"The best part is that by my estimation, at full extension these weighted ends carry a striking force roughly comparable to that of hitting someone with the pommel of your shortswords. I say that just in case you'd like to bash yourselves in the heads with your own weapons and save me the trouble."

"Why are you telling us all this, Trattari?" Sedge said, smiling despite the first hint of sweat on his forehead. "Is it maybe because you think you can stall until someone comes to help you? You really can go ahead and scream—no one will reach you in time."

"Oh, I won't be calling for help," I said, backing up another step. The ankle still hurt like the devil every time I stepped down, but it didn't bother me so much anymore. "I mention all this because I thought you should know that the reason I can describe the weight of this cane, its balance and striking force, is that, well, whether it's a sword or a stick or a busted broom handle, when it comes to fighting, I know how to use it."

I held the bottom end out and wiggled it in the air. Sedge, apparently tired of hearing me boast, made a grab for it with his free hand. I spun the end in a tight circle, and his hand got nothing but empty air until I brought the end back down and struck him hard on the wrist.

"I wanted you to know so that once this is over, you don't feel too badly that you got beaten senseless by a man holding a walking stick."

CHAPTER THIRTY
THE WALKING STICK

Next to sanguinists, my least favorite opponents in a duel are *ludators*. The ludator's strategy is to look for ways of knocking his opponent over, removing any advantage of greater reach or skill, and finishing the fight on the ground. It's a dangerous business, for it requires getting in very close, but you'd be surprised how many duels end up with two opponents grappling around on the floor. Few duelists expect to find themselves in such a position, so when they do, it's generally too late to find a way out of it.

Sedge and Beltran, though neither of them were duelists by my estimation, would definitely fall into the category of ludators. Sedge, who was shorter and wider, was especially keen to grab me. His sword was barely a factor in his thinking as he tried to rush me and bowl me over. It was the move of an angry amateur—although it also happened to be the perfect strategy for this situation.

"All those bloody stories," Sedge said, "all those times I watched Greatcoats ride into my father's demesne and look down on us, as if we were no different from the commoners in the streets. And yet, here you are, weak as a—"

He made a snatch for my empty hand. Normally I'd have let him take it and simply stabbed him through the throat, but the end of my stick wasn't pointy enough to do the job neatly, and the thick leather of his jerkin came up to just below his jaw, so instead I flipped the stick around and used the handle to hook Sedge's arm and yank him off balance. I made a fist of the hand he'd tried to seize and slammed it against his temple, helping him on his way. His skull struck the wall with enough force to give me hope that I might have knocked him unconscious.

"Heh," he said, shaking his head and readying himself for another try. "Tickles."

Of course, I thought, *because life isn't challenging enough without crazed zealots who don't feel pain and can't be knocked out.* "Guards!" I shouted at the top of my lungs. "*Guards!*"

Beltran smiled. "Thought you were going to fight us honorably?"

"Sure," I said, "just me and a fucking stick against two men with swords? *Guards!*"

Beltran thrust at my face with his shortsword, but I fully extended my stick now and he couldn't come close enough to connect. The brass-banded end jabbed into his neck, stopping his forward momentum, leaving the point of his sword still two inches away from my face. I had to work hard not to flinch, though. There's nothing quite so unnerving as seeing the steel tip of a blade that close to your eyes.

"Damned cane," Beltran growled. He tried to reduce the distance between us by swinging his shorter blade hard toward my sides, goading me into parrying; had the blow collided, the walking stick would have broken in half and the fight would be done. Instead, I let the tip of my cane drop, Beltran's blade sliced at empty air and I returned the favor by popping him in the nose with the brass end.

"Get out of my way," Sedge complained. The corridor was too narrow for both men to attack at once, especially while Beltran was swinging wildly.

"Not yet," Beltran said. "Gonna cut him down first."

"Take your time," I said. "I've got all night."

Unfortunately for me, Beltran's plan was a perfectly sensible one. My left ankle was slowing down my retreat and I couldn't hope to keep dodging his swings for long. Parrying them would soon shatter the stick, so I had no choice but to catch Beltran's blade on the brass-reinforced end, and even as I struggled to keep my grip, I felt the metal beginning to give way, telling me the brass wasn't going to hold up to the damage Beltran would eventually inflict.

"Guards!" I shouted one last time, wondering, *Why is it that when I'm trying to sneak into a Ducal palace I practically drown in guardsmen, yet the one time I actually need one, they're nowhere to be found?*

My walking stick, despite my laudatory recitation of its virtues, was not a great weapon. I wasn't going to end the fight by stabbing them, so as long as they were willing to endure a little pain, it was only a matter of time before one of them bore me to the ground. Then I'd be done.

Had Kest been there, he could no doubt have provided a lengthy discourse on the tactics of stick-fighting, its application to my current predicament and some detailed history of its origins. No doubt these would include wise old shepherds, denied the right to carry steel but still needing to protect their flocks from wolves and thieves, or perhaps a slave culture of centuries ago, once daring warriors taken captive and needing to make sure their children and their children's children kept up the old fighting ways for the day when freedom could be reclaimed.

None of which is going to help you beat the shit out of these two arseholes. Time to switch tactics.

When Beltran readied his next swing, I kept my cane low, exposing my head, and the guardsman gave a growling laugh and swung for my neck. I ducked down, letting the blade pass harmlessly overhead, and then swung out with the brass-weighted end of the handle against his knee. The shattering sound was music to my ears. I'd broken his kneecap.

Unfortunately, Beltran didn't seem to care.

I've had my knee broken once in my life and even months after the event, the pain of standing on it was almost unbearable. So it should tell you something that Beltran just grinned and kept coming at me, even as the bones crunched in his damaged leg with every step.

And people ask me why I hate magic so much. "You could at least try to look hurt," I said, annoyance momentarily overcoming the panic that was starting to set in.

Beltran grinned. "We are but novices in the path of the God's Needle, Trattari. We've only drunk the blood of two Saints—wait until we've had our third." He lunged toward me, which was a foolish move; even if his broken knee didn't cause him pain, it was still throwing him off balance. He fell to the side and hit the ground.

Sedge moved in to take his place. "Once we've killed you, Trattari, we'll be allowed to drink our fill from your woman. I wonder if she'll taste the same." He licked his lips.

I backed up a bit further; I was near the end of the corridor now, not far from the gallery above the palace foyer. I had to stall. "Taste the same as whom?" I asked.

"Birgid," Sedge said.

Beltran had gotten back to his feet. "She cried so much you could see the tears dripping from under the mask. Who'd've thought Birgid-who-weeps-rivers was so aptly named?"

Sedge grinned. "Those tears tasted almost as sweet as the blood. Can you picture it, Trattari?"

"I can," I replied, and things changed for me then—not the way they'd done in the old days of madness, where I would lose control and forget who I was and what I'd done. Instead, the world became sharper, clearer; what mattered now was not the pain in my ankle or the anger in my heart. It wasn't even about what these bastards had done or why, or how'd they'd become the way they were. This was no longer a matter of winning, or even surviving. This was a matter of *practicalities*. This was *physics*. I couldn't hurt them, so I had to break them. They weren't men trying to fight me, they were objects moving through space, boulders rolling inexorably toward me. I would either find a way to smash them or I would be crushed under their weight.

The gallery above the grand foyer had a staircase at one end going down, and at the other was a sort of wide interior bridge between the two wings of the palace—a relic of some ancient architect's desire for a grand high domed ceiling in the center of the grand foyer, and the subsequent realization that guests might not find it convenient to go from their bedchamber down the stairs, along a cold corridor and then up another flight just to get to the privy.

Sedge made a rush for me as he'd done before, arms spread so he could use his heavy shoulders to knock me down and get on top of me. There wasn't the room or the time to dodge so what had to happen next had to be all about timing and fluid motion. *You don't beat the ludator by running away.* The instant before Sedge slammed into me, I slapped both my free hand and the one holding the cane down against his shoulders and pushed off as hard as I could. My feet left the ground and as the momentum of his charge drove us back a full ten feet, I went over the top of him; I came down on my knees onto his shoulders and sent him face-first to the floor. I felt him try to push himself back up, like a wild horse bucking off an unwanted rider, and then his hands reached around as he tried to grab hold of my legs. When he bucked a second time, I used the momentum to launch myself forward. I landed reasonably well on both feet—I was proud of that—though I heard something crack in my ankle. I ignored it.

Beltran's shattered knee was making him move like a man drunk beyond measure, but he had worked his way close to us now and his sword was coming in a heavy swing, aimed at my head. I leaned back, letting it pass by, and as I swayed forward again I jammed the end of the cane into his left eye. There was a sickening squishing sound as the soft orb was crushed against the inside of his skull, but I didn't have time to check if that was enough to stop him because I had other problems to deal with: Sedge was coming for me again. *Gods, that man is unstoppable!* But I hooked his wrist with the crook of the cane and lifted it high overhead, keeping his hand from reaching me even as his body passed by me. As he turned to face me again, I yanked hard on the walking stick, pulling him off balance, and this time as he stumbled to me I rammed the heel of my left hand into the bridge of his nose.

A cracking sound filled the air as the tiny bones broke and a blossom of blood spilled out of his nose, filling the air around my hand as if I'd summoned it by magic. Before the first drop had hit the floor, I had leaned my back against the gallery railing and kicked out with my good right foot. The heel of my boot broke Sedge's jaw and smashed his front teeth. I saw his eyes become unfocused, just for a moment, and whirled the cane around to strike the side of his head.

Maybe I can't make you feel pain, you bastard, but I can keep hitting you until your brain turns to soup in your skull.

"Halt! What's going on here?"

The stick stopped in midswing as the owner of the voice behind me caught my weapon in a firm grip and I glanced around to see a man of my height in a guardsman's uniform carrying a mace in his free hand. He pulled hard on the cane, yanking me away from Sedge.

"Hold him!" Sedge called out, already rising to his feet. "He's an assassin dressed as a Greatcoat come to kill the Ducal Protector!"

I felt the guardsman's shift in weight even before he raised up his mace.

"You idiot," I shouted at the man, "do you really think an assassin would come to commit murder armed with a damned *walking stick*?"

He looked at me, then the cane. "No one move until I can determine who—"

Whatever he was going to say next was cut off by Beltran's blade passing through his back and out of his belly; the steel tip kept coming toward me, as if Beltran thought he could finish two problems in one thrust. The guard who'd gotten between us stared at me, his eyes wide with shock and fear. "I'm . . . sorry," he said. Then, with greater courage and will than I would have thought possible, this man of no more than twenty years took hold of the end of the sword that had ended his life and raised his other arm, holding the mace out for me. Beltran figured out what was happening and tried to pull his blade back, but the young guard kept his grip on it, ignoring the blade cutting deep into his hand and adding to the blood already spilling out onto the floor.

I took the mace in my free hand and brought it up high. Beltran gave up on his sword and let go in a bid to escape the blow, but the young guard fell back into him and I brought the mace down on Beltran's head with every ounce of strength and fury I had in me. The left side of his skull broke apart, he teetered for just a moment, the muscles in his jaw tightening as if he were about to smile, then finally he fell to the floor.

The cost of that victory was too high: Sedge had regained his senses and, lacking whatever human decency would have demanded he pause, even for an instant, at the mortal wounding of his comrade, he barreled into me, grasping me around the waist and pushing me hard against the gallery's railing.

I tried bringing the mace back up for a strike but he was ready for it; he took hold of my left wrist and slammed it down against the top of the railing. I screamed from the sudden pain and felt the mace slip from my grip. A moment later I heard the crash as it struck the marble floor below.

"Long way down," Sedge said, grunting as he started lifting me up.

He was hunched over, his head buried into my side, making it impossible for me to hit him with my elbow anywhere that might have made a difference. I struck him on the back as hard as I could anyway, but he showed no sign of feeling the impact. If I could have hit the back of his neck I might have done more good but I couldn't get to it.

I felt my feet starting to lift off the carpeted floor.

"Goodbye, Trattari," he said, "Don't worry about the whore. I'll put the mask on her myself."

Again and again I struck him with my elbow and the stick, but I couldn't get any leverage. I felt the top of the railing biting into my back as Sedge began to tip me over it. Like an idiot, I looked down and saw the hard marble floor thirty feet below me. I tried to hook my foot between the bars of the railings, but it was too late now; my weight was coming over the top. Within seconds I'd be all the way over. I was left with precisely one option.

Let's see just how well made you are, I told the walking stick, *because otherwise this is a stupid way to die.*

I flipped the cane over so the curved end was extended. I'd briefly considered trying to hook it to the wooden rail but I wasn't at all confident the railing would hold. Instead, I hitched it to the next best thing: my opponent's neck. As I started to fall, I brought the curved handle down behind Sedge's head and my sudden weight forced it in place with a grip he couldn't hope to break. I was now hanging in the air, clinging to the bottom of the stick, while Sedge stared down at me, mightily confused by his predicament. He tried to pull himself back up so he could get the handle off his neck, but my weight was too great. We were stuck in a strange sort of impasse, though not one that could last.

I'd expected him to just stand there and wait for me to slip down—my grip wasn't very secure, after all; try hanging from a stick for a while and you'll see what I mean. But Sedge apparently wasn't content with waiting. "Let's go and greet the God together," he said, and started leaning over the edge, obviously preparing to tumble us both to our deaths.

"You give your God my regards," I grunted, and pulled as hard as I could on the walking stick, the way you might if you were trying to use it as a handhold from which to leap up higher in the air. I didn't, though; instead, I kept my grip and let my weight come back down hard with its full force on Sedge's neck.

I caught the confused look in his eyes an instant before I heard the loud snap of his skull separating from his spinal column. He let out a soft sigh as his legs gave out and his body slumped down, transformed in an instant from my would-be killer to the anchor that tethered me to life. I swung there for a moment, hanging from the broken neck of a man whose eyes were still blinking in incredulity at what had just happened.

Drawing on the final dregs of my strength, fueled by the absolute determination not to have gone through all that only to slip and fall to my death, I hauled myself up the length of the walking stick an inch at a time until I could grab Sedge's jerkin and with a final grunt I pulled myself up and over the railing.

Falling to my hands and knees on the floor, I croaked, "I win."

Then I glanced up and saw Ethalia standing in the hallway, her eyes filled with horror and revulsion. She was looking at me.

CHAPTER THIRTY-ONE
THE REMNANTS

For a little while the only sound was that of my lungs, pumping like a bellows, punctuated by growls that I tried to pretend were just pain and exhaustion demanding to be given voice. *Calm down,* I urged myself, *you're pushing her away.*

Ethalia tried to step closer, to come and see to my injuries, but she couldn't; the violence in me was pushing her back as hard as any gale. I was making her sick, quite literally: her lips formed the syllables of my name, but I couldn't hear her over the sound of my own breathing.

Distant calls began to echo through the halls, followed by the sounds of heavy footsteps thumping along the floors below. Ethalia and I looked at each other then, both feeling the same relief: someone else would come and help me. She didn't have to touch me. Ethalia said my name again, and all the sorrow in the world was written in wet tracks down her cheeks.

"Go," I said, instantly regretting the harshness in my voice. I managed to get the next words out more softly. "I'll be fine."

She hesitated, still unwilling to abandon me, but she was the Saint of Mercy now, and I had just killed two men without remorse. Had

I hesitated, even for an instant, when I'd taken up the dying guards-man's mace and used it to cave in half of Beltran's skull? Had there been an ounce of mercy in my heart for Sedge when I'd felt the crack of his neck breaking travel down the wooden shaft of the cane to my hand? *Not bloody likely.*

My vision blurred and Ethalia's form split apart for just a moment, becoming two people. In my dazed state I imagined the other was my wife, Aline, wearing a greatcoat and standing protectively by Ethalia with a sword in each hand, as though promising to guard her for me. I chuckled a little. I don't think Aline had ever held a sword in her life. But my wife had always been a protector, even young as she was, finding ways to keep the people she loved safe and sound. I had let her protect me, and it had cost us everything.

For the next few seconds of my life that thought brought me a strange kind of peace. I was a man of the sword now—not the best fencer, perhaps, but good enough when the moment called for blades. I fought, I bled, and I did what I had to do without hesitation in order to protect the people I loved. The way Aline had done for me.

So if the price of keeping Ethalia safe was that I must lose her heart? *Well, then, all you damned Gods and Saints, you chose the right man for the job.*

My vision started to shift from blurry to black. *She's safe,* I thought. *You can pass out now.* I had just begun to let my eyes close when I caught sight of the sudden movement of a thick, meaty hand rising up from the floor to grab Ethalia's ankle. She screamed as if she were being burned and began to stumble.

Beltran, blood and viscera still dripping from the side of his head, pulled her toward him as he rose to his knees. "Not . . . done . . . yet . . . little . . . Saintling," he said, his shattered jaw filling each word with a ragged glee.

The God's Needle had one hand on Ethalia's ankle and the other on her leg as he dragged her inch by inch to the ground. His knee crunched and crackled where I'd shattered it; his limbs twitched erratically even as he pulled her toward him. A small piece of his skull hung loosely from a flap of skin. *He ought to be dead.*

Why are you still alive, you thrice-damned monstrosity?

I summoned my final reserve of strength and hurled myself at him, but the result barely got me to my hands and knees. Instead I had to crawl toward him, reaching out and failing to grab his foot—I was not impressed that not only was he not dead, he was moving better than I was.

"You should have stabbed him through the heart after you killed Sedge," I imagined Kest scolding me. "A man who doesn't feel pain can keep fighting long after others have fallen." In my defense, when you cave in someone's skull they usually go into shock and die. Beltran was just taking a little longer.

The sounds of boots and shouts grew louder, but not loud enough. *They're still too far away,* I thought helplessly, scrambling after the madman's leg. *They won't make it in time.*

Ethalia was trying to push Beltran away, but to no avail. Whatever last thread tethered the madman to this life made him unconcerned about injury or capture.

I sucked in air, trying to find some fuel for my limbs, and I clambered toward Beltran. My hands brushed the floor, looking for a weapon but finding none. *Fine,* I thought, grabbing the collar of his jerkin and hauling him back, *I'll tear your head from your neck with my bare hands if that's what it takes.*

He threw an elbow behind that managed to hit me squarely between the eyes, filling my vision with black patches.

Don't pass out, damn it!

I dug my fingers into his hair and pulled, forcing his head back, but he tore away from me and I fell against the railing next to Sedge's body. I shook off the clumps of Beltran's hair and skin. The madman still had hold of Ethalia and now he spun her around and set his hands around her throat and began to squeeze. I grabbed the walking stick that was still hanging from Sedge's neck and swung three times at Beltran's back, striking his shoulder, his kidney, and finally the back of his head, and at last Beltran's body spasmed. He was dying quickly now—but still he wouldn't let go of Ethalia.

Her eyes had widened as lack of breath forced her mouth open in a desperate attempt to suck air into her lungs. She reached up and dug her fingers into his hands, trying to pry them off her, but Beltran just kept laughing as he squeezed the life from her. Again and again I smashed the end of the cane against his body, but my blows were growing weaker by the second. Both my enemy and I were losing what little strength had remained to us, but I was losing faster.

He turned to me and grinned sickeningly, then stuck out his tongue and bit down hard, severing it from his mouth in a great splatter of blood. "A kiss goodbye," he mumbled, his words as mangled as his tongue, and he pulled Ethalia to him in an obscene lover's embrace.

I stopped trying to hit him and in desperation brought the stick down as hard as I could against the gallery railing. The end broke off, leaving me with a shortened, jagged shaft about two feet long, and I drove it into Beltran's side, feeling ribs part as the edge passed through his flesh. A shudder ran through his entire body and his hands around Ethalia's neck no longer held their grip. She pulled them off her and stumbled back, sucking in a long, ragged gasp of air.

I kept both hands around the shaft of the stick and used it like a handle, spinning Beltran around to face me. I was sure I'd torn through at least one vital organ, but I was still determined to make sure he was good and dead this time. But he kept blinking at me, his eyes fluttering like the wings of a butterfly struggling to take flight against a strong wind.

"Who . . . are you?" he mouthed, his gaze soft and confused, as if he had forgotten who I was, who he was, what he had done.

"My name is Falcio val Mond," I replied. "I am First Cantor of the Greatcoats. When you get to hell, tell your God who sent you."

For a moment Beltran looked as if he were about to spit at me, then a thunderous crack sounded in my right ear and a puff of gray-black smoke filled the air between us. Beltran fell forward, his weight driving me down to the floor beneath him. There was a large hole in what was left of his face.

I lay there, the dead man's body on top of me, the smell of him stifling me. My ears were ringing, my throat choking on the smoke. People were moving around us.

None of it made sense to me.

"Are you all right?" a voice asked from very far away, but I didn't answer. My eyes were still fixed on Beltran. Then several hands lifted his body off of me and carried it a few feet away down the hall. The men carrying him were wearing sturdy gray coats.

"Falcio, can you hear me?" I recognized the voice, but I couldn't put a name to it until I turned my head to see Quentis Maren standing over me. The Inquisitor's long wheel lock pistol was still in his hand and thin wisps of smoke were seeping from what I now saw were two separate barrels. *He could have shot me first if he'd wanted,* I thought absently. *He could have said I got in the way and no one would have questioned it.*

He knelt down and reached out a gloved hand to grab me by the shoulder and haul me to my knees. "The Church will keep Saint Ethalia safe now," he said.

I looked into his eyes to see if I believed him.

He looked angry. "I *warned* you, First Cantor. You knew these madmen were out there. You knew they were hunting Saints, but you took her from our protection. The Greatcoats are too few and too weak to fight this, Falcio. The Saint of Mercy nearly died because of your arrogance."

I think I would have preferred it if he'd shot me.

CHAPTER THIRTY-TWO
THE TONGUE

It's never a good sign when people debate whether they should move you or not after a fight.

"I could use your body as a medical textbook," the small, bespectacled doctor who'd introduced herself as Pasquine informed me. I found her derision and lack of sympathy mildly reassuring. Doctors are usually nicer to you if they think you're about to die.

Long gray coats swirled around us on the second-floor gallery as Quentis set his men to securing the hallways while he focused his attentions on convincing Ethalia to accept the protection of the Church. Whether out of loyalty to me or distrust of Quentis, she refused.

I wondered if I was about to find myself facing off against a dozen Inquisitors without so much as a broken cane for a weapon, but the Ducal Protector's own palace guards arrived and I was able to lie back and enjoy the unusual and rewarding experience of watching two different groups of people who generally antagonized me beyond reason threatening each other over questions of jurisdiction.

Quentis left his subordinates to deal with the guardsmen while he bombarded Ethalia with questions of a largely supernatural nature regarding the God's Needles. I took some small measure of satisfaction at his annoyed look when she explained exactly how I'd figured out they were only masquerading palace guards. "But could you not *sense* them?" Quentis asked. "Is there no way to detect their presence?"

"I noticed nothing," Ethalia replied, "until the larger man"—she gestured to Beltran's body on the floor—"grabbed my ankle, and I was overwhelmed by a sense of . . . *wrongness,* of . . . the only word I can think of is desecration."

Well, I thought, feeling a little punch-drunk on pain and exhaustion, *at least there are some people out there she finds more disgusting than me.*

"Forgive me, *Sancti,*" Quentis began, possibly hoping his use of the archaic title would sway her, "but I would feel better if you would allow us to—"

"I'll be fine," Ethalia said, closing off the discussion. She glanced over at me, looking more than a little concerned for my current state of health, and I gave her what passed for a smile in my current condition by way of telling her that it was all right to leave me. Ethalia tried to give me her own reassuring smile before heading back down the hall to her rooms. Of the two of us, I felt I was the better actor.

Quentis turned his attention to the doctor. "What is his condition?" he asked Doctor Pasquine.

"None of your business, Cogneri," she replied pleasantly. I was starting to like her more and more.

"Am I going to live?" I asked, then added, "I will consider it no reflection on your talents if the answer is no, I promise you."

She opened my coat and looked less than thrilled by what she saw. "Bruises on top of bruises and fresh cuts on top of those barely healed." She tore open the front of my one decent shirt. *Well, it used to be a decent shirt,* I reflected, looking down on the grit, dirt, and blood embedded in it.

You never think about things like clean clothes when you're going from one life-threatening crisis to another. Once the fight's done, though, you really do start to wish you didn't have to smell your own stench on top of that of the men you've just killed. Fortunately, once exhaustion takes over you stop caring quite as much.

Boots on the stairs alerted me to Brasti coming to my rescue, with Kest alongside him.

"It's a little late," I said, though I doubt they heard me. I was having rather a difficult time staying focused.

Brasti's right arm was in a sling, but he was still trying—rather clumsily, as far as I could see—to nock an arrow as he approached. Kest's face was contorted with that mysterious pain that washed over him every time he drew his sword now, ever since the day he'd lost his hand, along with his Sainthood. A strange sadness swept over me as I watched the two of them trying so hard to be the men they once were. *Look at us,* I thought, feeling myself drifting in and out of consciousness, *three broken men trying to pretend we can continue living in the past . . .*

"Step aside," Brasti said cheerily to the Inquisitors who had moved to bar his path. "We wouldn't want to dirty the floor with more blood than necessary." He glanced over at me. "Though Falcio seems to have done a pretty good job of it already."

. . . blustering our way through one crisis after another, trying in vain to bring back a world nobody wants . . .

Quentis Maren signaled his men to let them pass, and Kest paused to look at me, no doubt wanting to make sure I was still breathing before he went to examine the bodies of the two God's Needles on the floor.

. . . all the while struggling to make sense of things far outside our understanding.

I watched Kest with no little amusement as he went over the wounds on their bodies one after another, working out exactly how many moves it had taken me to defeat them, no doubt preparing to scold me with a recitation of the ways I could have ended the fight quicker, had I only been more efficient in my use of the walking stick I'd picked up for the first time a couple of hours ago.

Brasti stood over him. "You have to admire their dedication, what with biting off their own tongues rather than risk being interrogated."

The doctor smoothed a thick white ointment across my chest and neck which sent cold chills through me even as it burned my skin. "Ow," I said.

She smiled at me even as she continued to rub the ointment into my bruised flesh. "'Ow'? You survive all this bloodshed and it's the medication that makes you moan like a child getting his first toothache?"

"You wouldn't understand," I said, too tired to explain. I reached into my pocket for the last piece of the hard candy that Kest had given to me months ago. I'd been saving it for a special occasion.

"Hold it," Doctor Pasquine said, grabbing my wrist.

"It's fine," I said. "It's just the King's hard candy. We use it to—"

"I know what it is." She sniffed at it and then let go of me. "'Hard candy.' Makes it sound like something you give to children rather than a deadly toxin."

"It's saved our lives on a number of occasions," Kest observed, still inspecting the bodies, apparently oblivious to the rather intense scrutiny of Quentis's Inquisitors standing behind him.

The doctor looked up from her painstaking work cleaning a wound on my upper shoulder. "I don't doubt the toxin is effective. I'm simply saying that someday you're going to take it one too many times and wonder why your heart has just burst out of your chest. There are costs to these things, you know."

I looked down at the tiny piece in my hand. How many times had I relied on the hard candy to keep my sword arm strong, to keep me awake, to keep me from just lying down in a ditch and giving up?

"What costs?" I asked her.

"What do you mean? I told you, it can kill you if—"

"Yes, but you said 'costs,' plural. What other costs?"

She wrapped a loop of bandage around me. "I don't know the exact formula King Paelis's apothecaries devised, but I do know that these kinds of concoctions play havoc with the vital fluids of the body, and those in turn can put a terrible strain on the mind."

Brasti chimed in, "Oh, don't worry about Falcio. He knows all about insanity—he used to go berserk all the time." He peered down at the ruin of Beltran's body. "Apparently he still does. Saint Laina's tits, Falcio, how long did you keep hitting this guy after he was dead?"

"I didn't," I replied. "The bastard just wouldn't die."

I was still staring at the hard candy held between my index finger and thumb. *What if it's as simple as this? What if these God's Needles don't really gain supernatural abilities from drinking the blood of Saints? Maybe they've just got something like the hard candy, only much, much stronger?* "Kest, could a human being—I mean, not a Saint or whatever—have survived all those injuries and still kept fighting?"

"I . . . suppose it's possible," he replied.

"But highly improbable," Quentis said, taking a sudden interest in our conversation. "Look at the wounds on this man's body. Who could—?"

Kest cut him off. "Many of the wounds are fatal, but none of them would necessarily kill a man instantly. It's just a matter of ignoring the pain and not going into shock."

"'Just ignore the pain and don't go into shock,'" Doctor Pasquine repeated as she wrapped an endless roll of bandages around my torso. "You make it sound so easy."

"But it's possible, isn't it?" I persisted.

"In theory," she replied. "But I suspect any compound capable of producing such an effect would destroy the internal organs, and no doubt the mind as well." She ran the last loop of bandages around me before sealing them with a clear, sticky substance. "Now, on the subject of madmen determined to kill themselves, if you could see your way clear to avoiding any strenuous activity for the next few days, there's a possibility you might live. Get some rest."

"He can't," Brasti said, reaching down a hand to help me up. "Falcio has a very important meeting of the Greatcoats to attend. Vital matters of law and justice and—"

"Brasti heard about a tavern in town that stays open all night," Kest said.

"Not just *any* tavern," Brasti corrected, his eyes gleaming with anticipation. "Apparently it's chock-full of ladies-in-waiting, lonely to the point of desolation with nothing to do while their mistresses amuse themselves in the palace." He straightened the shoulders of my coat. "Now look, Falcio, I know you'd rather find someone else to try and kill, but Ethalia's safe, Aline's got half the guards in the palace around her, and Valiana is busy meeting with the Dukes, who, by the way, have the rest of the guards. As magistrates we must now turn our attention to saving a small but potentially very open-minded portion of the country from a fate worse than death."

"Which fate is that?" I asked.

"Never knowing the joy of kissing a Greatcoat." He gave me an appraising look. "Best take the hard candy first, though. Nobody wants to dance with a corpse."

The doctor threw up her hands. "I give up." She started to walk away. "Do whatever pleases you, Trattari. Go and fight duels or bed noblewomen to salve your self-worth. Just don't go kissing girls with weak hearts or very old people."

I had no intention of kissing anyone, young or old, but the comment struck me. "Why not?"

Doctor Pasquine stopped and pointed to the fragment of hard candy in my hand. "Those sorts of compounds pool in the tongue. You go slithering your tongue in some poor girl's mouth who's never been exposed to the stuff, and she's liable to have a heart attack then and there."

"What happens to a healthy one?" Brasti asked, looking interested.

She grimaced up at him. "Likely she'll be fooled into thinking your kiss sends her all aflutter."

"Why, that would be just terrible," Brasti said. He reached out a hand to me, palm up. "Can I have the rest of your hard candy, Falcio?"

Kest said something then, but I didn't hear it, for my eyes were fixed on Beltran. His mouth was still hanging open, displaying the ruin of his tongue, encased in dried blood and spit. We'd all assumed the assassin who'd gone after Aline had been trying to make sure we couldn't torture any answers out of him, but Beltran had already known he was dying.

"Falcio?" Kest asked, and I realized then that he was holding me upright.

What was it the doctor had said about the cost of using these compounds?

They put a terrible strain on the mind.

I lifted my hand to my mouth and swallowed the small fragment of hard candy. The familiar metallic taste hit me first, followed a second later by the sensation of my heart beating faster, my blood going hot in my veins. Within seconds I felt strong and focused. *But not as strong as Sedge and Beltran were.* So whatever they had in their veins was much more powerful than the hard candy, which meant the adverse effects would also be stronger. *They knew it too. That's why they bit off their tongues.*

Somebody called my name again, but by then I was already stumbling to the stairs, my feet barely touching the steps as I struggled to remember where the meeting rooms on the first floor of the palace were. Brasti and Kest chased after me.

"Tell the doctor to follow us," I shouted as I ran.

"Why?" Brasti asked. "Who's—?"

"Those men couldn't feel pain. They didn't care about being interrogated. They just wanted to do as much damage as they could before they died."

The memory of the assassin in the throne room played over and over again in my mind: his mouth full of blood, his hand reaching up to grab Valiana behind the neck, pressing his lips against hers.

The toxins pool in the tongue, Doctor Pasquine had said.

CHAPTER THIRTY-THREE
THE RELEASE

The Diplomatic Chamber, a modestly sized room off the massive hall housing the throne, provided a more discreet and comfortable venue for important negotiations. The décor was elegant but not ostentatious, creating a feeling of calm and safety. Or at least it would have, had Kest, Brasti, and I not just kicked in the door.

"Um, Falcio?" Brasti whispered, "Are you sure about that theory of yours?"

"What in hells is this?" bellowed Hadiermo, so-called "Iron Duke" of Domaris, a man of considerable bulk who always had a pair of retainers standing next to him holding his massive two-handed sword, just in case he suddenly needed to show everyone how dangerous he was. Hadiermo's most notable feat by my reckoning was the way he'd lasted barely two weeks in the war against Trin before he'd sued for peace. Iron is sometimes quite bendable, it appears.

Next to him slouched Erris, Duke of Pulnam. He was very nearly as old as his Duchy, and as devoted to his religion as any man who thought it best to get on the Gods' good side while he still could; Erris also had the distinction of having waited a full two weeks longer than Hadiermo before betraying Aline.

"Treason! Betrayal! Duplicity!" he shouted, in between bouts of coughing, evidently unaware that each word meant pretty much the same thing.

Also seated at the great oval table were Duke Jillard, who looked mildly amused at our entrance, Pastien, Ducal Protector of Luth, who looked as if he knew he should probably say something but wasn't sure what exactly, and Valiana.

"Falcio?" she asked carefully.

Beside the council, more than a dozen guardsmen and retainers were seated at the back of the room, and I found myself both annoyed and curious about why I was counting two Inquisitors and a cleric among them.

Nothing seemed amiss. *Valiana looks fine,* I thought. But I wasn't about to take chances. "You have to come with me," I said, reaching out a hand to her.

"How dare you disrupt the business of this council?" Hadiermo demanded.

"Forgive me, Your Grace," I replied, not wasting any effort on sounding convincing.

Valiana stared at me for what felt like a long time and I expected her at any moment to command me to leave, or at the very least ask me to explain why I'd just broken up a meeting of the Ducal Council. As she did none of those things, I examined her face, and started to notice the signs of strain: the wrinkles at the corners of her eyes, as if she were trying to ignore a headache, the paleness of her cheeks, the soft sheen of moisture on her forehead.

"Oh—" she said, as if in that instant she had worked out everything that had taken me so long to understand. She rose to her feet, slowly, supporting herself on the table. She was shaking. "I've been feeling so . . ."

"It's going to be all right," I said, my hand still extended toward her. "The doctor will be here soon."

"It was the blood from his tongue, wasn't it?" Valiana shivered, just for a second, and at first I took it for revulsion at the memory, but then it happened again—

"I've had enough of this." Duke Erris creaked to his feet. "Bad enough I should waste my time with a girl playing at being Realm's Protector, but—"

"I didn't even know anything was wrong at first," Valiana said, talking to me as if we were the only two people in the room. She brought her fingers up to her face and very softly ran her nails down her cheek. "Then it started to . . . it just keeps whispering to me." Her eyes filled with tears that spoke of a terrible struggle, of terror and frustration and, now, finally, of resignation. "I fought so *hard*, Falcio. I swear I did." The fingers ran down the cheek again, but this time they bent inwards like claws and the nails left bloody tracks down her face.

"No!" I cried, bridging the distance between us, completely ignoring the guardsmen's swords and the Inquisitors' pistols, all aimed squarely at my chest. I could see that Valiana was about to let go completely.

"Hold on, sweetheart. You've got to hold on." She hated it when I called her "sweetheart," but I meant it as a kind of reassurance; a promise that we would fix whatever was wrong with her.

She gave me the tiniest of smiles in response, a last valiant effort before the battle was lost. "I'm glad you're here," she said, and then Valiana val Mond, Realm's Protector of Tristia and the bravest person I'd ever known, went completely, undeniably mad.

CHAPTER THIRTY-FOUR
THE MADNESS

Sometimes, in the dark hours of night when I can't sleep, when I'm convinced that someone is coming for me and my hands reach of their own accord for my rapiers, I wonder what I must have looked like during the Lament. As the Dashini Unblooded tortured me, taking me step by step toward the ninth death, I wonder what madness and despair etched on my face? Would I even have recognized myself?

I stood there watching Valiana writhing and screaming uncontrollably as she tried to tear the flesh from her bones in that elegant chamber, surrounded by finely dressed Dukes with all their retainers and guardsmen, and I thought I knew what I must have looked like at the very end of the Lament. Whatever poison was in the Needle's tongue, it was dragging Valiana shrieking to her own ninth death.

"Someone help me, damn it!" I shouted, grabbing hold of her wrists and struggling to hang on to them. I hauled her hands away, sickened at the sight of her flesh caught in her nails, but with mad strength, she tore them back from me and again tried to claw at her own face.

"Don't try to hold her with your hands," Kest warned, wrapping his entire left arm around hers and twisting away from her, using the leverage of his whole body to keep her immobile. I followed his lead and for a moment it looked like we had control of her—but then she screamed, so loudly I thought my eardrums would shatter. Her eyes were so wide and confused that I knew she had no idea where—or who—she was. She kept pulling against my grip, almost dragging me off balance, and when that failed, she started kicking, hitting me first on the shin and then on the knee. I stumbled, horribly aware of my injuries, even with the hard candy, and tried to wrap my own leg around hers to stop her. Brasti tried to hold her ankles and got her heel in his face for his troubles.

"Someone help, for Saint's sake!" he shouted, but no one else moved, not the Dukes, not their retainers or guardsmen.

"See here!" Duke Erris said, his wheezing old voice practically cackling with glee, "See what happens when you give a woman power? It breaks her mind like glass. And look at these feeble Trattari, barely able to hold her!"

Speak again and I will see you dead, I swore as I struggled to hang onto Valiana.

"What ails her?" Pastien finally asked. He went so far as to rise to his feet, but he wasn't actually coming to help.

"She's been poisoned," Brasti said, trying to hold her ankles again. "Now go and find out why that damned doctor isn't here yet!"

The sound of light footsteps from the hall reached me, followed a moment later by the sight of Aline running into the room, Tommer close behind her. I shouted, "Don't come in here!," but I was too late: Aline was staring in horror at what remained of the woman who had saved her life so many times. I saw more fear in Aline's face then than in all the times her own life had been in danger. "Oh, no—" she whispered, then she turned and fled the room.

It's not her fault, I told myself firmly, tying to ignore the profound sense of disappointment that was washing over me. *Of course she'd run—she's seen too many of the people she cares about hurt.*

"Tommer, you leave as well," Duke Jillard said, rising to his feet.

"What ails my sister?" Tommer asked.

"The woman is clearly mad," Duke Hadiermo said, coming around the table to face Valiana, "and I call a vote of this council to remove her as Realm's Protector."

"Get the hells away from her, you fool," I warned, barely able to cling on to Valiana's arm.

"Perhaps this is not the time, Hadiermo," Jillard suggested laconically, which made me wonder exactly what he was planning. The Duke of Rijou *always* had a plan.

The Iron Duke of Domaris reached out a thick, meaty hand and attempted to clamp it around Valiana's jaw—only to pull it away bloody and missing a chunk of flesh from the heel of his palm where her teeth had ripped into him. "Take this madwoman into custody!" Hadiermo commanded his guards. "A night in a cell will sort her out."

"She's losing her mind, you fat ass," Brasti said. Then Valiana's wild flailing caught him in the side of the head, and he fell to the floor. She kicked out again and her heel caught Hadiermo on the hip. She was spitting and foaming at the mouth, her eyes looking everywhere and nowhere at once.

"My blade!" Duke Hadiermo called to his retainers and instantly they hefted the two-handed greatsword and started toward him. "I will save us all a great deal of—"

He stopped speaking as he noted the tip of a short, thin sword at his cheek. The room fell silent, except for Valiana's mad shrieking, as all eyes turned to the small hand holding that blade. There was not even the slightest suggestion of a tremor.

"The next man to lay hands on my sister faces me in the circle," Tommer of Rijou, standing a full two feet shorter and a good two hundred pounds lighter than the Iron Duke, said, his young voice clear as a bell.

It has long been a puzzle to me how the Dukes of Tristia manage to keep their family lines intact when they seldom show any signs of caring for anything beyond their own power and sense of entitlement. In this one respect, Duke Jillard was different: he very clearly loved his son.

"Back away, Hadiermo," he said now. He hadn't raised his voice, but his intent was clear.

The Iron Duke didn't bother to hide his disdain. "See what has become of this nation? You would let your boy issue threats against his betters?"

"He isn't threatening his betters," Jillard replied. "He's threatening you. Now step away from the Realm's Protector and be very, very careful that you don't inadvertently touch my son as you do so."

It says something rather terrible about our world, that as I stood there trying desperately to hang onto Valiana, whose crazed thrashing was losing none of its force, I found myself admitting to some small shred of respect for Jillard.

"The hells for all of you," Hadiermo said at last. He signaled to his retainers and turned to leave the room, nearly running over the doctor, who was finally rushing in, her healer's case clutched in both arms. He pushed the small woman out of the way, not caring that he'd nearly knocked her to the floor, then turned and yelled, "Better to have summoned the veterinarian to deal with this creature!"

Doctor Pasquine's composure was remarkable as she set her case on the table and opened it. "Keep her steady, if you can." She removed something small and shiny and then opened a small vial and carefully poured some of its contents onto the object.

"What in hells is that?" Brasti asked. "And what took you so damned long?"

The doctor carefully held up what looked like a three-inch long very narrow knife. The contents of the vial could be seen sitting in a groove that ran the length of the blade. "I had to get an inunction blade," she replied. "It's the only way to get the fluid into her vein."

"You're going to cut her?" I asked, my mind spinning back to the Dashini Unblooded and their long, thin needles. *This isn't the time for reminiscences,* I told myself. *Focus.*

"We need to calm her and this is the fastest way. Now keep her steady or I'll end up slicing her vein open."

We did our best, while the rest of the room watched. *Always fascinating to watch someone else suffer, isn't it, Your Graces?* I thought bitterly.

The doctor gripped the inunction blade tightly, like a knifefighter about to face her opponent, and with a single, precise thrust she drove it into Valiana's arm.

"How long?" Kest asked, grunting from the effort of keeping Valiana still.

The doctor didn't answer; she was peering at her patient, looking concerned. "Something's wrong. The amount I gave her would put a pony to sleep—she should already be unconscious."

"Give her more," Kest said, a growing urgency in his voice.

Doctor Pasquine shook her head. "I can't—too much could kill her."

"She's going to die if you don't," Kest said. He turned his head to me. "Falcio, she's not weakening."

At first I didn't understand. "So? Just hold her. If you're tired—"

"No, *look* at her, Falcio: Valiana's barely half our size and it's all we can do to hang onto her. Her muscles and joints can't take this kind of strain—she's going to tear her arms from their sockets."

"What can you do?" I pleaded with the doctor, and without a word she refilled the groove in the tiny blade and drove it into the vein. This time I could feel something happening to Valiana but whatever it was, it wasn't affecting the madness that was driving her.

"It's not working," Doctor Pasquine said. "It's as if there's something more than poison doing this, something almost—"

"Spiritual," said Ethalia from the door, her face pained as if she were standing too close to a fire. She was leaning a hand on Aline for support. She looked down at my girl. "You were right to bring me, My Lady," Ethalia said. "This is an enemy that all of us must face together."

Ethalia walked over and stood behind Valiana, then reached out her hands and placed them on either side of Valiana's face—only to fall back against the table, moaning.

Tommer rushed over to help her stand. "Lady, are you—?"

"Wait," Ethalia said, her breath coming in and out in quick gasps, almost as if someone had punched her in the stomach. I watched helplessly as she steeled herself and again stepped forward and once again placed her hands on Valiana's cheeks.

At first, Valiana bucked all the more, and I was afraid that Kest was right, that she'd simply tear her arms from their sockets, but a few moments later I felt the strain against my grip lessen and the spasms fade a little.

"It's working," Brasti said, clutching Valiana's legs. "Whatever you're doing, keep doing it."

"I don't *know* what I'm doing," Ethalia said, breathing in ragged gasps. "I'm just . . . trying . . . to—"

Suddenly Valiana shook again, not as badly as before but enough that I nearly lost my grip on her arm. Sweat was dripping from Ethalia's jaw. "I'm . . . It's like I'm trying to grab onto water. She keeps slipping from me. *I'm losing her!*"

"Falcio," Brasti said, his face bruised from Valiana's kicks, "look at Ethalia—she can't take much more of whatever it is she's doing."

"Someone needs to take my position," Kest said. "I can't grip Valiana properly without my right hand—I'm losing hold of her."

"You," Jillard said to one of his guards, "do as he says."

The guard hesitated, but not for long; you don't survive in Rijou by disobeying the Duke. Kest ducked down a little to let him seize Valiana's arm. "Steady," he warned, "she's stronger than she appears."

The guard looked irritated as he took his position. "I think I know how to hold a—"

He fell back abruptly, blood flowing from his nose where Valiana's wild swing had struck it. "Saint Forza's bloody—"

"Hold your position, damn you," I shouted.

The guard piled back in again and finally managed to get a grip on her. She'd started snapping her teeth at him like a wild dog—we'd need to gag her if this went on much longer, or else risk that she would tear someone apart. I forced myself to look at her, hating myself for wishing I could cover her snarling face.

Gods help me, I thought, as a terrible little seed that had been growing in my mind finally blossomed into the blackest of all flowers.

I turned to Kest, gagging even before I could get the words out. The mere thought of what I was about to say was forcing the bile to rise up in my throat. "Kest, I need you to—"

"I can't hold on," Ethalia screamed. "Oh sweet one, I'm so sorry, I can't hold on to you!"

"What do you want me to do?" Kest asked me.

Valiana screamed again, a horrible hissing sound, and this time I could tell her throat was giving out from all the abuse it was taking. Ethalia's face was streaming with tears as she lost the fight to hold onto Valiana's mind. Everyone else was looking at me.

You will make her wear it, the note had read.

"Bring me the iron mask," I said.

As I held the foul thing in my hands, the cold iron froze my blood and the rough edges bit into my palms, a sharp contrast to the finely crafted brass clasping mechanisms on the sides which signified finesse, precision, intent. This was a thing made only for torment and despair.

Damn all you Gods to every hell there is. Don't make me do this.

"Pull her away from the table," I said, my own voice as cold and hard as the metal mask.

Brasti and Jillard's guardsmen hauled her forward, although she was pulling away hard, the joints in her arms straining so badly I expected to hear them tear apart at any moment.

Think of another way, damn you! There has to be some other—

"I need you to hold her head," I told Pastien, Ducal Protector of Luth, but he didn't move.

"Kest only has one hand, damn you! He can't hold her head—get behind her and do it!"

Still he didn't move. His mouth was frozen in horror at what I was asking him to do. His words from hours earlier—*Sir, would you grant your assent for me to court Valiana?*—rang hollow to me now.

"Get out of the way, you fool," Jillard said, pushing him aside. He gritted his teeth and held out his hands, then pressed them against Valiana's head, keeping it still. I was about to turn to Kest, but of course I didn't need to say a word; he already knew what had to happen next. He took the back side of the mask and took up position next to Jillard.

Valiana's mouth was open wide, though no sounds came out anymore, for she had pushed her throat well past its limits. I held up the mask in front of her face, erasing her eyes, her mouth. She wouldn't be able to see once I put it on her, wouldn't be able to speak . . .

There might be some medicine, my mind screamed at me. *The doctor could be wrong about this! You might be—*

"Now," I said, and Kest and I simultaneously closed the mask over Valiana's face. A sickening thunk announced to the room that the two pieces had mated together. I heard another faint clack: Valiana had tried to bite through the shallow metal cone that now kept her from closing her mouth.

I have taken away her ability to speak.

I turned the clasps, first on the right side, then on the left, and just as Kest had predicted, each one broke off as soon as the bolt had tightened, locking Valiana inside. The mad bucking stopped abruptly. Valiana fell forward into my arms and the iron mask struck me square in the mouth. I tasted blood.

I didn't care.

Kest put two fingers to her neck. "Her heart's beating almost normally." His eyes narrowed. "But how could an iron mask counteract a poison? There must be some sort of mystical aspect to—"

"You did it," Pastien said, edging closer to us. "Her madness has passed. She is . . . . calm."

"I did it," I repeated, but the words meant something very different to me. I had just sealed the girl who was as close as I would ever come to a daughter, the girl to whom I had given my name, inside a mask of infamy.

I was a torturer now. *Her* torturer.

A hand touched my shoulder and I knew immediately it was Ethalia's. "Falcio," she said gently, "you did what had to be done."

Before she'd been a Saint, Ethalia had always known exactly what I was feeling without me having to say it, what words would bring me to my senses. Apparently she had lost that ability.

I let my eyes drift over to Pastien, then to Duke Erris and his retainers, and the guardsmen in the room. "Get out," I said.

"Now see here, *boy*," the Duke of Pulnam grumbled, still determined in his dotage to prove he didn't fear anyone but the Gods, "you will not address—"

It was Jillard who cut him off. "Best we do as the First Cantor says, Erris." He began leading the old Duke out of the room, but paused as he passed me, glancing first at Valiana's still form in my arms, then at me. A brief flash of something akin to sympathy passed between us: the look of a man who knew what it was to fear for his child. Then the Duke of Rijou gave a slight shake of his head, which, along with the words that came next, told me that our brief alliance was at an end. "Besides, my dear Duke of Pulnam," he added, "there are matters of great importance that we must now discuss."

With Valiana trapped behind a mask of infamy, the politics of Tristia had turned once again.

CHAPTER THIRTY-FIVE

THE CURTAIN

"The problem with you, darling husband, is that you will insist on drawing your blade before you even know who you're supposed to be fighting."

The soft voice jolted me awake. I lifted my head from where it lay buried in Valiana's shoulder and saw that I was hanging onto her like a sailor believing he could keep the mast of his ship from being torn away by the storm. Someone had installed the two of us on a small purple and silver sofa set against the back wall of the Diplomatic Chamber. I felt slow and sluggish, as if I were stuck in time—a leaf held by the breeze, neither rising nor falling—while the world turned around me.

Brasti paced down the center of the room, gesturing wildly as he and Kest argued over our next move. In contrast, Tommer stood calmly in front of the locked door of the chamber, his blade drawn, ready to challenge anyone who tried to demand entry. Aline watched him from a chair at the council table. Ethalia leaned against the wall in the shadows in the far corner of the room, facing away from us. She looked . . . *thinned*, somehow, lessened by the unbearable effort she'd expended trying—and failing—to save Valiana.

I don't expect I look much better, I thought. My arms were leaden, my legs numb from sitting too long. *How long have I been like this?* I needed to shake myself out of this lethargy and help the others decide our next course of action—but that would have required letting go of Valiana and I couldn't do that, not yet.

"You've never been able to let go of people, though, have you?" The familiar voice, a little stern, a little teasing, drew my gaze toward the tall curtained windows that opened onto the palace courtyard. There I found my wife, in front of the long curtains, gowned in their purple velvet folds, her hair fashionably tied back with their silver tasseled cords.

"If only you'd composed such poetry for me when I was alive," Aline said, looking down at her garments. "Honestly, husband, can you remember a single time when I wore clothes of such frippery?" She stroked her blonde ringlets. "And what sensible woman would style her hair in such an impractical fashion?"

"Falcio has always been a poet, silly woman," King Paelis countered, and I turned my head to find him leaning against the council table, armored in glistening oak that flowed up from the polished surface. "His blade carves epics of valor across the canvas of this troubled nation."

Aline's eyes narrowed. "Really, Falcio? And how exactly is conjuring up that skinny wreck of a man in such glorious fashion going to help unmask the enemy? How will you be able to break the iron shackles binding the future if you insist on making such a fool's paradise of the past?"

It struck me as odd, and more than a little unfair, that my hallucinations were so much more well-spoken than I was. "A dream doesn't have to be real to be worth fighting for, does it?" *Not bad,* I thought, *Not exactly Bardatti standard, but not bad either.*

Aline threw up her hands, sending ripples along the curtains. "So be it. Keep your illusions." She walked toward me, the thick fabric of the curtains following behind. "But you must see past the distractions your opponent places in front of you. While you fence with shadows, he shapes the world to his own perverse design."

"A name, woman!" King Paelis bellowed, giving voice to the question foremost in my mind, though he was sounding a bit like a petulant youth. "Tell us the enemy's name! Is it Quentis? Jillard? One of the other Dukes?"

"Perhaps he needs no mask of his own," Aline replied. She sat next to me on the arm of the sofa, the bottom of her dress matching its purples and silvers. She was looking at Valiana. "He fits his masks to others, and in so doing hides his own face. This is his genius, Falcio. You can't beat him at this game."

"Ah, she has us there, First Cantor," King Paelis said. He lay back against the tabletop, his hands resting across his chest. The browns of his armor melted into the oak of the table, and slowly he sank inside it, as if the hard surface were merely a reflection in a pool of shallow water. "To strike the enemy you must first pierce his deceptions."

I knew he and Aline were only delusions, apparitions born from exhaustion and injury—and yet still I pleaded with them as I held Valiana ever tighter. "Tell me how! How am I to find my opponent when I can't even protect the people closest to me?"

"Silly man," Aline said. She rose and placed two fingers to her lips then gently pressed them against the crude mouth carved into Valiana's mask. "That is exactly why he attacks them." A breeze from the window rustled the curtains, blinding me with silver light, and when the curtains had settled again, Aline was gone.

"Why is who attacking what, now?"

I raised my head groggily to see Brasti smirking down at me. The faint wetness just below my lower lip told me I'd drooled in my sleep again and I tried to wipe it away surreptitiously, only to find my hand tightly clasped in Valiana's. *She's conscious,* I realized, and only then noticed the way her other hand was traveling across the rough iron surface of the mask. Her fingers were trembling as they sought out some means of escape, doing so carefully, methodically.

"She appears to be lucid again," Kest said gently.

The relief I felt at the easing of her madness was overshadowed by the appalling irony of its cure. Thought the mask of infamy had restored Valiana's sanity, it held her captive, locked away from us and from the world.

Ethalia knelt down and carefully took Valiana's hand away from the mask and pressed it between her palms. There was no shimmering light or flickering fire—not that I knew what Saint's magic was supposed to look like, but it was a fair guess—but after a moment, the tension in Valiana's shoulders eased. Lines of pain and weariness appeared on Ethalia's forehead.

"You can't help her if you keep exhausting yourself," I said.

"Then what use is the pitiful strength I do have?" she replied, with more anger and frustration than I'd ever heard in her voice before.

This is destroying her, I thought. I was aching to reach out and comfort her, and acutely aware my touch would only make it worse. She had never asked to be made Saint of Mercy, but now she was driving herself mercilessly to fulfill the role given to her. I wondered if it was some unstoppable spiritual imperative, or misplaced guilt over Birgid's death.

She rose to her feet. Catching me staring at her, she gave me a small shake of her head, plainly telling me to focus my concern elsewhere. "Talk to her, Falcio. It will help her to hear your voice."

The mask had no openings for Valiana's ears or eyes; the gray landscape of its surface was broken only by three thin slits, each about an inch long; they had been cut into a wretched grin. "Keep squeezing my hand," I said. I kept my mouth close to those slits, hoping my voice would reach her, and almost immediately her fingers crushed mine. I ignored the pain and held on.

"Could we not cut more holes into the mask?" Tommer asked.

Kest shook his head. "Not without risking injury—and if we damage the mask, it might not curb the madness. We don't yet know how it works . . ."

Ethalia reached out a hand toward the mask and her fingers began to twitch. "Kest is right. There is more than iron at work in this mask."

Hells, but I hate magic.

"Fine," Brasti said, "then let's go and find whichever blacksmith made the damned thing and hang him from his toenails until he tells us who paid him to do it!"

"There are likely more than a thousand blacksmiths spread across Tristia," Kest pointed out. "We could spend a decade looking, and even then, it's entirely possible none of them made these masks—they could be artifacts from an older age."

Aline rose from her chair and came to sit on Valiana's other side. "How long can she stay like this?"

Kest, Brasti, and I looked at each other, united by the foul memories of our early days in the Greatcoats, when the King sent us to cities and towns that had seen no real justice in decades. In the deepest cells of the Ducal prisons we had found men and women encased in devices not so very different to these masks. Their jailers trickled water and thin soup into their mouths each day, keeping them alive for years. And every time one of us had borne witness to such depravity, we'd forced promises from each other for a clean death rather than a life entombed that way.

How long can she stay like this? Far too long.

Valiana's hand felt very hot against the sudden cold of my own as I wondered how many days—or even hours—it would be before she was begging me to make that same promise to her. Could she survive a week like this before she was pleading with me to end her suffering?

The silence enveloping the room was broken by a distant grunt, followed by a heavy thump just outside the curtained windows. I let go of Valiana's hand and got to my feet. Kest drew his warsword, grimacing in pain as he did. Brasti, his arm still bandaged from the wound he'd taken from the God's Needle on the road, lifted his bow and awkwardly nocked an arrow.

Of course I'd been too distracted and too stupid to search for my rapiers, so I went to the table and grabbed the closest thing to a weapon that I could find, which turned out to be a small brass statuette of Roset, the deceased Duke of Luth. His arm was outstretched as if he were in the midst of delivering a magnificent speech.

Let's hope you're more eloquent in death than you were in life, Your Grace.

One of the windows creaked open, but the heavy curtains muffled the voice that called out, "If Brasti's in there, tell him not to shoot."

"Mateo?" Brasti asked, easing his pull on the bowstring.

The purple and silver velvet parted to reveal Mateo Tiller, still dressed in his road-worn, dusty greatcoat, the scabbard of his curved falchion strapped to his back. He dropped down from the windowsill to the floor. "Well, well," he said, rising to his feet and wiping sweat-soaked hair from his forehead, "if it isn't the Blade, the Arrow, and the—" He stopped and peered at me. "Should I call you the King's Ugly Little Statue now, Falcio? Because I have to say, I think the old name worked better."

I set the brass statuette back down on the table. "I have to ask, Mateo: what in hells are you doing climbing up the side of the Ducal Palace of Luth in broad daylight?"

"And how did you manage it with an injured shoulder?" Kest added.

"Rather painfully, thanks to the arrow wound courtesy of the world's most annoying archer." Slowly Mateo removed his coat, grunting in the process. "And to answer your question, First Cantor, I was climbing *down* from the roof, not up."

"You look like hell," Brasti said.

"Yeah? You should see yourselves." Mateo grinned. "I've seen rotted corpses with more—" He froze when his eyes landed on Valiana. "Saint Unas-who-makes-tears-burn," he swore, and then turned to me. "Where is the son of a bitch who did this to her and why haven't you killed him yet?"

Kest tried to intervene. "She was driven mad by poison. It was the only—"

I cut him off. "It was me. I put the mask on her."

I'm not sure what Mateo saw in my expression, but after a few seconds he let out a long breath. "I'm sorry. I just assumed—"

Ethalia strode to the table and picked up a jug of water. "This man's shoulder is bleeding through his bandages." She pulled out a chair and motioned for him to sit.

"I'm just glad that the famed Brasti Goodbow missed my heart by half a mile."

"Those weren't my usual arrows," Brasti insisted. "I'd had to grab the first ones I could find. I was just testing the range."

"That's fine, you missed," Mateo said. "It happens, especially when you're getting a little long in years."

Ethalia began removing his shirt, revealing his lean, muscular frame, and the bloodstained bandages that covered one shoulder. "The stitches held, for the most part," she said after a moment, "but your acrobatics have stretched them and part of the wound has reopened."

Brasti whispered to Kest and me, "We should consider the possibility that Mateo reopened his wounds on purpose."

"Why would he do that?" Kest asked.

He gestured at the Greatcoat, who was smiling up at Ethalia. "So that he could show off his chest."

"Beautiful *and* commanding," Mateo said. "You are undoubtedly my favorite Saint, My Lady."

"I doubt that," she replied. "I'm the Saint of Mercy, not Gullibility." Despite the jibe, she smiled as she went about treating his wound, and I found myself absurdly jealous that touching him didn't appear to produce the same pain that she experienced with me.

Maybe he's just less bloodthirsty than you are.

"I've cleaned the wound and tightened the stitches," she informed us after a few minutes, "but it needs a fresh bandage to keep out infection."

"Alas, I ran out of mine ages ago," he said.

Neither Kest nor I had ours, but finally Brasti unbuttoned his coat and reached inside. "Fine, use mine—but just so you know, Mateo, I was saving these for someone vastly more important."

As Ethalia went about bandaging the wound, Aline said something into the slits in Valiana's mask, and then came over to greet Mateo properly. "I never had the chance to thank you yesterday for helping to save my life."

He gently pushed Ethalia's hands aside and stood, managing as much dignity as a man can when he's shirtless and dripping with his own blood. Looking at Aline this close set him to stammering, "I . . . I only just realized how much you look like the King."

She smiled back at him, entranced.

"We tried to find a less silly-looking monarch," I said, "but she was the best we could do on short notice."

At first Mateo was aghast at my comment, then he caught Aline's grin, and shared a look with the rest of us, filled with that same mixture of hope and grief that Aline brought to every Greatcoat: the joy of seeing our King in her, tempered by a bitter reminder of the man we'd lost.

Mateo tried to tilt his body forward in a bow, wincing as a grunt of pain escaped his lips.

"Sir," Aline said, "that isn't necessary! You needn't—"

"A Greatcoat doesn't bow," Tommer interjected, his voice almost scolding, "not even to a King or Queen."

"This would be Tommer, son of the Duke of Rijou," Brasti said.

At the mention of Jillard, Mateo's eyes grew suspicious, but he saw the look of raw admiration on Tommer's face and grinned. "You are correct, of course. A Greatcoat needn't kneel, even to a monarch." With substantial effort, Mateo bent at the waist before Aline. "But a gentleman *always* bows before great beauty."

Brasti jostled Kest. "That's a good line. Remind me to use that one when we go to the tavern later."

Aline gave a curtsy that almost but not quite hid the blushing of her cheeks; it only faded as she moved back to sit with Valiana.

Tommer's lips were moving silently and I realized suddenly that he too was intent on memorizing Mateo's slick turn of phrase. He saw us watching him and flushed red from embarrassment.

Mateo saved him, extending a hand. "It is a pleasure to meet you, Tommer of Rijou. I'm Mateo Tiller."

Tommer shook hands with him excitedly, the grim sentry giving way to a teenage boy no longer able to contain himself. "I've seen your name in the Greatcoats' Register—you're the King's Tongue!"

Mateo gave a rueful smile. "Not a name I chose for myself, I assure you." He looked at the boy and I saw him hesitate for a moment. "I . . . wonder if you might do me a small favor, Tommer."

The boy stood arrow-straight. "I'd be honored, sir."

"There is an important message I need delivered, something I can't trust to just—"

"Don't," I said. "Tommer may be Jillard's son but he's risked his life for Aline in the past and he considers Valiana his sister. Don't use tricks to get him out of the room."

Mateo glanced from me to the boy, then sighed. "Forgive me, Tommer, that was unworthy of me." He rose and put his bloodied shirt back on before addressing the rest of us. "I'm snuck down because I was wandering around the palace a little while ago when I spotted three members of the Ducal Council secreting themselves into the small library on the top floor."

"Why there?" Kest asked. "There are surely more secure locations to meet in the palace."

"That's what I thought," Mateo said, "so, having nothing better to do, I decided a little judicious spying was in order. I found a staircase that led onto the roof and climbed down to an overhang outside the library window. I've spent the last two hours listening to them." He turned to me. "Falcio, they were in the library because that's where the books of law are kept. The Dukes were writing up a decree to replace the Greatcoats."

"Replace us?" Brasti asked. "With what?"

"With whom," Kest corrected absently, his eyes fixed on Mateo, but the moment Brasti had asked the question, I knew the answer. Saints were being murdered, churches desecrated, pilgrims massed outside palace doors, and we had failed to do anything about it.

"The Cogneri," I said. "The Dukes are going to replace us with the Order of Inquisitors."

CHAPTER THIRTY-SIX

THE MESSAGE

There was a lot of shouting in the discussion that followed, most of it directed at the Dukes for betraying us, and a fair bit more at the Inquisitors, who we knew were indifferent to enforcing any laws save those that let them hunt down and punish heretics. A few times we even railed at the Gods themselves, for ever having created such a cesspool of a country. By unspoken consent, one particular group was left out of our recriminations: ourselves.

None of us wanted to admit the simple truth: in the past six months we had utterly failed to bring back anything resembling the rule of law to Tristia. What gains the country had made were due entirely to Valiana's careful administration and her uncanny skill at navigating the politics of the nobility.

And what has the First Cantor of the Greatcoats accomplished? I run around the countryside chasing my shadow, always two steps behind, while the enemy destroys sanctuaries and kills the Saints.

"I have a suggestion that I believe will solve all our problems," Brasti said. He slung his quiver over his shoulder and picked up his bow. "How about I go and put an arrow through Quentis Maren's heart?"

"Do you have any actual evidence against this man?" Mateo asked.

"Absolutely!" Brasti held out a hand and started tapping each finger in turn. "First, he's a damned Inquisitor, so that should be enough of a reason. Second, he keeps trying to get control of Ethalia, supposedly for her own safety, but I think we can toss out that notion. Third, he and his men are too well armed for religious zealots. Fourth, he's cleverer than Falcio, so he has the mind for it, and fifth . . ." He paused, apparently having run out of reasons.

"You do realize that Quentis has handled himself honorably until this point," Kest said.

Brasti jumped on that, tapping on his little finger. "Ah, exactly! I knew I'd forgotten one."

Tommer stared up at him. "So behaving innocently is evidence of guilt?"

"Of course it is," he replied. When no one spoke, he looked around at the rest of us as if we were idiots. "Am I really the only person who remembers Shuran? Strong? Smart? Capable?" Brasti looked at Kest and me. "And so righteous the two of you were ready to duel over who got to marry him first."

Aline, who'd been sitting quietly for some time, rose from the sofa. "So your proposed strategy, Brasti Goodbow, is that we should go out and kill anyone in a position of power who *isn't* obviously corrupt?"

"*Exactly.* Any man with power in this country who shows a shred of integrity is almost certainly a violent lunatic." He bowed theatrically. "Thus ends the only lesson in Tristian politics you'll ever need as Queen."

Aline looked over to me. "Why exactly did my father choose him to be a Greatcoat?"

"Every village needs an idiot," I replied.

"Fine," Brasti said, "mock me—ignore me. But when it turns out that the Inquisitor is secretly bedding Trin and that the two of them hatched this whole plot during a particularly rousing session of lovemaking, don't expect me to save the day."

The sound of Valiana banging her fist on the arm of the sofa caused us all to turn. "It's all right," I said, going to her and trying to take hold of her arm. At first I feared the madness might be returning, but then she began gesturing with her hand, her thumb and two fingers pinched together.

"I think she wants something to write with," Kest said after a moment, and started looking around the room for writing implements. Mateo eventually found what we needed inside an elaborate silver box that I suspected had been intended only for use during the signing of highly important treaties.

I dipped the pen in the small bottle of ink and then placed it in Valiana's hand and guided it toward the sheaf of paper I'd balanced on the arm of the sofa. Immediately she began to write, the words coming out as a tangle of scrawled lines.

"It's unreadable," Brasti said. "I think you have to be able to see in order to write."

Aline took the paper and studied it. "No, I think I can make it out. It's . . . There, you see? That part says 'Realm's Protector overrides decree.'"

The rest of us peered down at it. "It looks more to me like she was trying to draw a drunken snake being eaten by fleas," Brasti said. "Even if you're right, though, what does that mean?"

"It's a legal interpretation," Kest replied, "and a rather dangerous one."

Tristia has a hornet's nest of laws, ancient and modern, secular and clerical, overlapping jurisdictions and incompatible dictates. Apart from King Paelis, no one had spent as much time trying to unravel their disparate meanings as Kest had.

"You have to understand," he went on, "a *Realm's* Protector isn't like a Ducal one. They can't simply be voted out by a council. The position has no legal limits on its authority. The Dukes might have chosen to put Valiana in power, but once they did that, their own roles reverted to that of advisers. They can write all the decrees they want but in theory, she can override them all."

None of us bothered mentioning the obvious: that such broad powers had the effect of making the Realm's Protector irremovable if she chose not to step down. *The hells for it,* I thought. *She may be a dictator, but she's our dictator.*

"If all that's true," Brasti asked, "then why does she keep letting them make her life hell?"

"Because Valiana knows the history of those who frustrated the Dukes' desires one too many times," Aline replied. "She knows what they did to my father."

Once again Valiana began scrawling on the paper. We'd all been speaking so loudly—practically shouting at each other—that she must have heard what we'd said. She wrote something short and then scratched two sharp lines underneath. I went to her and took up the piece of paper. It said, *Not Afraid.*

Of course you aren't, I thought. *That's why I need to be afraid for you.*

Kest walked over to me and spoke quietly. "Falcio, no matter what laws we invoke, if Valiana stays locked behind this mask, the Dukes will argue that she is incapable of fulfilling her duties. They will claim that Tristia has no Realm's Protector anymore."

Everything we'd worked for, everything Valiana had accomplished these last months, would unravel.

"We may not know who the enemy is," Kest said, "but we can be sure that removing the Realm's Protector is a key part of his plan."

"We need a cure for her," I said.

He looked doubtful. "We don't even know what poison runs through her veins. How can w—?"

I cut him off, both because I was tired of my failures being given voice and because I had an idea—not a particularly good one, I confess, but it was all I had. The enemy kept shaping the world to his liking because I couldn't work out his methods. I was a man of laws and swords, and this was poison and torture and conspiracy.

Who do I know who happens to be an expert in those things?

I turned to Tommer. "I need a favor," I said.

He looked back at me with that unbreakable admiration of his. "Command me, First Cantor."

I was keenly aware of the irony of my words when I replied, "I need a message delivered, Tommer. Something I can't trust to anyone else."

CHAPTER THIRTY-SEVEN

THE BODIES

For the second time in as many days, I found myself inside the palace's death house, the well-dressed figure of Jillard, Duke of Rijou, leaning casually against one of the examining tables. He'd placed a goblet of wine on Sedge's chest. "I confess I was surprised to hear from you so soon, Falcio. If you were a better man I'd almost say it was an honor."

"If you were a better man, it might be."

He stared at me quizzically for a moment. "You know, I have no idea what that meant."

Neither did I. I'd just thought it sounded clever at the time.

The Duke gestured to the rapiers that were now sheathed at my side. "Found your old friends, I see. I do hope you didn't ask for this meeting just so you could murder me. That would be terribly gauche for a magistrate."

I wondered briefly whether the jibe was a test to see if I already knew about the Ducal decree handing authority over to the Inquisitors. Not wanting to give him the satisfaction, I kept my expression neutral and joined him at the examining tables. "Actually, Your Grace, I was hoping you could tell me how these men died."

Jillard reached over and picked up the goblet sitting atop Sedge's chest. "I'm fairly sure this one died from you breaking his neck." He gestured with the goblet at Beltran. "This one . . . well, you made quite a sculpture out of his skull."

"That part I already knew, Your Grace."

He narrowed his eyes and the corners of his mouth crept up. I'd piqued his curiosity. "Then what is your real question?"

Tell me how Valiana was poisoned. Tell me how to save her and then tell me where I can find the man who arranged it all.

I couldn't ask him what I wanted, not directly, anyway. If he knew the suspicions I was harboring about how the God's Needles got their abilities, it might prejudice his examination of the body. *Also, I don't discount the possibility that Jillard himself is behind all of this.* "I was wondering if there might be something else that contributed to these men's deaths. Something attuned to your family's more . . . toxic interests."

Jillard stared at me, then raised an eyebrow. "I swear, Falcio, I'm considered to have a reasonably serpentine mind but even I can't discern what you're saying."

I pointed to the corpses on the tables. "Just . . . pretend these men had no wounds. What could you tell me about their deaths?"

Jillard's eyes narrowed, but he nonetheless reached past me for a thin, flat metal instrument sitting on the wooden tray. He lifted one of Sedge's hands and began probing at his fingernails. After a moment, he put down the hand and then pried open the dead man's mouth, pressing the instrument against the tongue. "Ah . . ."

"Could you elaborate?"

Jillard pressed the instrument down, forcing the jaw open wider, and used his other hand to tilt the hanging lantern overhead to illuminate the inside of the assassin's mouth. "There. You see that?"

The man's tongue was a mixture of every shade of black and red. "It looks like a dead man's tongue."

"Almost. But it's actually a little *too* red. Given the manner of his death, it should be more gray by now. How well do you know your poisons, Falcio?"

"A little better than I'd like, thanks to Duchess Patriana." I leaned down to get a better look, but I still couldn't see what Jillard was seeing. "Not well enough to know what you're talking about."

"There are three toxins that leave the inside of a man's tongue with this sort of reddish residue. All of them are fatal." Jillard put down the instrument and left the table to go and search through the large wooden cabinets on the wall behind us. He rummaged through them all, paying no mind to the chaos he was creating. After a minute he returned with a small package wrapped in plain white cloth. "Most poorly organized death house I've ever seen," he muttered, and removed the cloth to reveal a rough, rectangular block that could have been carved from soap or chalk. "Halcite," he said, waving the lump beneath my nostrils.

I nearly gagged from the scent. "Hells, that smells worse than death itself."

Jillard picked up another instrument from the wooden tray, this one a thin metal stick with a tiny flat spoon at the end. He dug at the surface of the halcite and then scraped the white powder it yielded onto Sedge's tongue, leaving a white stain against the red and black.

"And?" I asked, after a moment.

"Patience," Jillard said.

The white patch began to smolder and hiss and I half-expected smoke to start roiling from the man's mouth. "It's changing color," I said.

Jillard held up a hand. "A few seconds more . . . ah, there it is . . ."

I leaned in to see that the white residue had now taken on a glistening, coppery color. "It looks almost metallic."

"That's the halcite reacting with the toxins. *Adoracia fidelis* would be my guess."

"Adoracia?" I asked. The name wasn't among the rather long list of things I'd been poisoned with thus far in my life.

Jillard carefully tapped the tiny spoon against the edge of the table and placed it back on the tray. "Comes from the plant of the same name. You grind it up into a brown powder and then inhale. It's said to numb pain, keep you awake, lend strength to your muscles." He smiled at me. "Oh, and it tends to give one rather pronounced religious hallucinations."

I was careful not to react to this confirmation of my suspicions. *Terrific,* I thought, *because what was really missing from Tristia was droves of psychotic zealots who ignore fatal wounds while imagining the Gods are speaking to them.* "And where might one find this Adoracia fidelis?"

"Where do you think? Churches, mostly in the middle lands of Domaris. In the old days, before Adoracia was banned, less scrupulous clerics would cultivate it in their herb gardens." Jillard mimed dropping grains of powder onto his palm. "They'd rub a little on their hands and when the congregants lined up to kiss the palm they'd get just enough Adoracia in them to feel a touch of that old-time religious devotion. I believe it also helped to liberate the gullible from their coins."

The implications of Jillard's words were more than troublesome. Could the clerics, fearful and angry over the murder of their Saints and the desecration of their holy places, have turned to this poison to—*to what? Turn their congregants into assassins?*

"I can see the wheels turning in your mind, Falcio," Jillard said, leaning back against the table and crossing his arms over his chest, "but these men couldn't have gotten their abilities by inhaling Adoracia."

"But you just said—"

"Oh, for Saints' sake, man! If it was that easy to make nigh-on unkillable warriors, don't you think I'd already have an army of them? It's as I told you: Adoracia is a poison. The adverse effects on a man's mind are a dozen times more powerful than the physical benefits." He pointed at Sedge's corpse. "The quantity of Adoracia required for what this man did would have shattered his mind instantly."

Damn it all. My believable explanation had just turned into another dead end. "Then we're back to this being"—*I can't believe I'm saying this*—"magic that comes from drinking a Saint's blood."

"Don't be a fool!" Jillard snapped.

I stared at the Duke, and noticed lines on his forehead, a slight pinching at the corners of his eyes. "You know something you aren't telling me," I said. "This isn't the first time you've encountered Adoracia."

He hesitated a moment, and when he did speak, his voice was hushed, as if he were suddenly afraid someone else might hear. "Patriana had a certain passion for . . . I suppose you might call it improving on the human condition."

"*I make things useful,*" she had told me in the dungeons of Rijou. The memory of her smile, of the clear-eyed determination and her utter conviction that what she was doing was right and just had made me shudder; now I discovered time hadn't dulled my reaction. "She was insane," I said.

"That would depend on your perspective, I suppose, but you can't deny she was a rigorous investigator into these matters."

She had killed twenty Greathorses trying to create one obedient warhorse. I wondered whether Monster resented me for having killed Patriana before she could get to the Duchess herself.

"She uncovered a treatise on an esoteric mode of torture," Jillard explained. "I thought it was rubbish, just supernatural claptrap, but Patriana always did have a keen scientific mind and she thought there might be some use in distilling the ritual down to its more fundamental, chemical procedures." He picked up his goblet and swirled the wine within, then breathed in the aroma before sipping. "The problem with substances such as Adoracia," he continued after he'd swallowed, "is that you can't simply drink them in any significant quantity. Patriana uncovered a rather unusual delivery mechanism." He held the goblet over Sedge's mouth and allowed a slow drip of wine down his throat. "She forced the poison into one subject." He set down the goblet back down and lifted Sedge's arm. "Then she cut him open to let another drink the blood."

Images of Birgid and Saint Anlas, the shallow cuts on their bodies, filled my head. "That's . . . How can that even work?"

Jillard let go of Sedge's arm and it fell lifelessly to the table. "It's a depth of biology that goes beyond my understanding. Somehow by circulating it in the bloodstream of one victim and then using their blood as the serum for another, you could manage to impart the necessary properties without killing the recipient."

"But if Patriana found a way to deliver the drug, then—?"

He cut me off. "It didn't work, at least, not in any usable way. The victims' minds were destroyed so quickly—the terrors were *so* profound—that every one of them died within minutes. The blood-serum only appeared to work when it was fresh, sucked up in careful doses over time." He looked away as he admitted, "It's really quite disgusting to watch."

Apparently we've finally found a depth of depravity that bothers even the man who brought the Blood Week to Rijou. The memory of Saint Gan-who-laughs-with-dice, his body covered in bloated red fluttering insects, took away any smug satisfaction I might have found in Jillard's reaction. *Why the moths? They must serve as some sort of . . . storage vessel for the blood, keeping it usable so it could be parceled out in precise doses . . .*

"Of course," Jillard said, "none of it would help unless you had a mind so strong it could resist the insanity from the Adoracia long enough for it to circulate into the bloodstream." He reached inside his coat and pulled out a partially broken iron mask—the one Birgid had been wearing. He held it so the inside was facing me, that metal funnel sticking out. "Ingenious, don't you think? To use the only beings we know of whose focus is so perfect, whose minds are so disciplined by . . . whatever spiritual nonsense drives such people . . . that they can withstand the madness the poison inflicts."

"Except most of the Saints have some form of Awe that would make it difficult to hold them," I said.

Jillard flipped the mask around and set it down on Sedge's face. "It would appear the mask's magical properties include preventing the Saints from using their Awe. I suspect it also holds back the effects of the madness somewhat."

"But Birgid was wearing the mask when she came into the court-room at Baern, and her Awe nearly dropped all of us—"

"*Nearly,*" Jillard said. He pointed to the broken side of the mask. "This was quite damaged by the time you took it off her, was it not?"

I didn't bother to answer; I was too busy fitting all the pieces together in my head. Someone was capturing Saints, locking them inside the masks so they couldn't escape, and then feeding them the Adoracia so that their followers could drink from the blood and turn into "God's Needles": perfect, fearless, devoted killers, unable to feel pain, and just crazy enough to do exactly what you commanded them to do. I whispered, "But how could anyone—?"

Jillard gave a dismissive snort. "How could anyone *what*, Falcio? Participate in such an obscene venture? After all this time are you really so blind to the lengths people will go in search of power?"

I stared at Sedge and Beltran and thought back to the woman on the road and the assassin in the throne room. They'd all been convinced they were being granted greatness. *They thought they were becoming Saints themselves.* "Son of a bitch," I said aloud.

"Quite," Jillard agreed.

I tried to shake off my disgust; that didn't matter, not right now. "So what treatments are there for Adoracia poisoning?" I asked.

Something not unlike sympathy passed over the Duke's face. "There are none, Falcio. None, save the one you have already found."

An iron mask, and a life entombed within it.

I was about to leave when the Duke gripped my arm. I turned, a little surprised. I don't think he'd ever deigned to touch me before. "They will destroy Valiana if they can," he said. "Not just my fellow Dukes, but the minor nobles—the Margraves and Viscounts and Lords. They thought they could manipulate and threaten her, but she's outwitted them at every turn. She's . . . surprised all of us."

"Careful, Your Grace. You almost sound as if you admire her."

He looked oddly disappointed at my jibe. He let go of my arm and sat back against the edge of the table. "The Gods play strange tricks on us, don't they? For years I thought she was my daughter and never spared a thought for her. Now I know she isn't, and I find myself . . ."

"Regretful?" I suggested.

He shook his head as if to banish the thought, then walked past me to the door of the death house. "In all likelihood she's the daughter of a peasant farmhand, pushed out by some gap-toothed slattern in the hay next to the pigs. But Tommer . . . No matter what I say to him, he insists she is his sister. He would trade his life for hers in an instant." He stopped, hand on the door handle, but didn't look back as he said, "If my son dies, Falcio, I'll make you pay for it."

CHAPTER THIRTY-EIGHT
THE FAVOR

I made my way up the long winding stairs from the death house and along the back hallway to the grand foyer of the Palace of Luth. Bright marble floors clacked under the heels of noblemen and commoners busily striding to their respective destinations. I counted a dozen soldiers in yellow and gold livery guarding the huge double doors that opened out into the courtyard. Anyone seeking entry was briefly interrogated and their papers checked to confirm they had business in the palace.

A dozen more guards stood just outside the doors, keeping watchful eyes on the two hundred pilgrims who were milling about and muttering prayers to their Gods. I wondered what they were praying for.

I was on my way back to the diplomatic chamber and Valiana when I was—very politely—accosted by Pastien, Ducal Protector of Luth, who was doing a fair impersonation of a more majestic figure in his long gold coat trimmed in black. Three guardsmen accompanied him, along with Quentis Maren. *Already weaseling your way into power, Inquisitor?*

"First Cantor," Pastien said, grabbing my shoulder earnestly. "I'm so glad to find you here."

I didn't share the sentiment. "My Lord," I said, and sidestepped him before pushing past his men.

"Falcio, please."

People rarely say *please* to me. I stopped and turned.

"I . . ." Pastien stumbled over his own tongue for a few seconds, then he managed, "How is the Realm's Protector?"

I suppressed the urge to give him directions to the diplomatic chamber and tell him to ask her himself. *If you did, my Lord, you'd find her trapped in an iron mask, unable to see or speak.* I might have said as much, but I was keeping an eye on Quentis Maren. "The Realm's Protector is well, my Lord," I replied. "I'll be sure to tell her you asked."

Pastien nodded, and it was as if his shoulders sagged under an invisible weight. "In the chamber, when it happened, I was . . . unhelpful." He was taller than me, and yet it felt like he were gazing up at me like a scolded puppy. "It's just that . . . Valiana is so strong, so commanding . . ."

He let the words hang there, but I didn't reply. *If you're looking for absolution, pray to a Saint. If you can find any left.*

After a few seconds, Pastien straightened himself. "I realize this is a difficult time, First Cantor, but I wish to ask a favor of you."

A favor. Absurdly, I found myself glancing at the guardsmen's swords and the holster at Quentis's right side where he kept his wheel lock pistol. *It'll be tricky,* I thought, *but I swear, if Pastien asks my permission to court Valiana again I'm going to kill him.* "How can I be of service, my Lord?"

"A delegation of clerics from around the Duchy is arriving in the morning." He glanced back briefly at Quentis Maren. "I believe they are coming to demand that I present to them my plan for protecting our churches."

"How *do* you plan to protect them?" I asked.

He looked distinctly uncomfortable at the question. "We have few soldiers left in Luth, I'm afraid. Most of our Knights were part of Shuran's secret army and those who weren't . . . well, Knights prefer to serve Ducal lines, you understand, not . . . temporary figures such as I. Valiana sent for a contingent from Aramor, and it should arrive in two days."

"Then it appears your problem is solved," I said. "Now, if you don't mind—"

"My nobles want me to step down," Pastien said, glancing at the men and women who walked past us, and they, in turn, looked upon their current ruler with expressions that ranged from mild disapproval to outright disdain. "They think I'm weak, ineffective," he went on. "In truth, I think it was only seeing Valiana standing beside me, supporting me, that kept them from trying to push me out sooner."

That last note of self-pity in his voice set me on edge. What *had* Valiana seen in this overdressed mop of a man? "I'm afraid the Realm's Protector is indisposed, my Lord. You'll have to find some other prop to lean on tomorrow."

The guardsmen looked as if they were very keen to get me into a dark room and discuss my attitude. Quentis Maren just looked bored.

"I deserved that," Pastien said, without any equivocation, and it made me hate him just a tiny bit less. When he spoke again there was a little more steel in his voice. "The problem, First Cantor, is that there are farmers in my Duchy who need help to survive this poor growing season. We have roads that caravans can't travel because they are in such disrepair; those that aren't are patrolled by brigands who consider any traveler their lawful prey." The young man's eyes caught mine. "I know I'm not very good at this, Falcio, but if I'm forced out, who is going to look out for my people?"

My mind turned back to the walk up the staircase with Valiana two days ago, the smile on her face as she'd said, "He's very decent, I think. He keeps trying to find ways to keep the Duchy stable."

I sighed. "What can I do to help, my Lord?"

"If you could persuade Aline . . . I mean, the heir . . . if she were to stand with me when we greet the delegation tomorrow, show her confidence in me, then the clerics might be predisposed to deal with me directly. My nobles are religious men and I believe the support of the clerics would go a long way to secure my position, for a little while at least."

"You think a fourteen-year-old girl is going to impress a group of crotchety old priests?"

That actually took him aback, but he rallied quickly. "She has a keen intellect, First Cantor. Her knowledge of the political and economic landscape of the country is excellent, and Valiana has consulted with her on every decision."

This was news to me. I knew Valiana had been training Aline, preparing her to one day take the throne, but somehow I always envisioned that day being a long way away. *This,* I thought, *this right here is why I'm so bad at politics. I keep seeing the world as it was and not as it is.*

"Besides," Pastien went on, "Aline is King Paelis's child, heir to the throne of Tristia. The clerics will respect that above all else."

I found myself moved by the way he spoke, such an odd combination of faith in Aline and doubt in himself. I might have relented then, had I not seen his guardsmen's eyes turn suddenly to the palace entrance and heard shouts coming from the courtyard. I followed the sounds, but couldn't see past the crowds of gawking nobles standing behind their personal guards and retainers. I pushed past them, careful to keep track of anyone nearby holding a weapon who might think this an opportune time to kill a Greatcoat, but no one was paying any attention to me.

When I finally got close to the open doors, I saw the sea of dirty white-robed pilgrims rushing about madly, all tripping over each other as they tried to escape the enclosed space; some even ran onto the spears of the guardsmen keeping them from entering the castle. Billows of thick gray fog rose up from the ground in the center of the courtyard, expanding so rapidly it was as if it were chasing the fleeing pilgrims.

Nightmist, I thought crossly. *Will I* never *be rid of fucking magic in my life?*

Suddenly, in the midst of the swirling gray chaos, a flash of silver rose up and then down just as quickly, and a bright red splatter painted itself briefly against the gray canvas as the shouts turned to screams. For a brief moment, the sun split the fog and I saw a single man, black-haired and clothed in chain mail, swinging a two-handed warsword like a scythe. His blade whirled in the air, and again blood followed in its wake.

"Gods, what's happening?" Pastien asked, and I turned to answer but already his guards were pulling him back to safety.

The screams rose in volume, and when I looked back outside, I caught a glimpse of the attacker's face: he was grinning at me with unbridled excitement, his eyes wet with tears of joy as his blade came down again and again, killing the panicked men and women caught inside the courtyard and obscured by the nightmist. None of the pilgrims, not one of them, tried to fight back; they just trampled each other to death trying to escape.

A fox among the chickens, I thought, a knot twisting my stomach. *Look how easily he feeds.*

The last of the guards backed into the palace as others began closing the heavy doors. I grabbed one of them by the collar. "What in hells are you doing? Those people—"

The man shook me off. "Have you seen what's out there? We're not damned well going out there to be cut down by that animal or trampled over by the mob!"

I shouted for Pastien, telling him to order his soldiers to put a stop to the butchering outside, but his men had already hustled him away to safety. Valiana would have been the first to go out there.

I turned back to the doors, the gap between them shrinking, now five feet, then four feet . . . three.

Saint Marta-who-shakes-the-lion, I swore silently, *if you happen to still be alive, now would be a fine time to lend me a little strength.*

I leaped through the gap.

CHAPTER THIRTY-NINE

THE FOX AND THE CHICKENS

Of the many things I hate about nightmist, foremost is the way it plays with sound. The pilgrims' screams echoed as if they were coming from everywhere and nowhere at the same time. Their pitch sometimes lowered into howls or rose into squeals that threatened to make my ears bleed. It was maddening and terrifying all at once. Had the damned pilgrims simply tried running toward their attacker rather than away, they might have stampeded over him. *Tristian courage at work,* I thought bitterly. *It's a miracle we don't get invaded every second Thursday.*

It was an ignoble thought, and unfair. These men and women were tired, cold from sleeping outside, hungry from lack of food, and the nightmist created its own kind of chaos that would disorient and confuse even trained soldiers.

I drew both my rapiers, taking reassurance from the solidity of their leather-bound grips. *No more cane-fighting for me.*

"What's the plan?" asked a voice close behind me, and I was surprised to find Quentis Maren at my shoulder. "What's the matter?" he added. "Aren't you pleased to see me?"

"Just a little curious which side you're on." I started trying to push through the crowd in front of us.

"I've told you before, Falcio," the Inquisitor said, shoving aside a man who was blocking our way, "I serve the Gods."

"Yeah?" I pointed toward the gray mist in front of us, and the figure of the God's Needle some forty feet away, his thick chain mail catching the occasional stray beam of sunlight, his laughter coming at us in waves as his blade sliced into defenseless flesh and bone. "So does he, apparently."

The Inquisitor drew his twin-barreled wheel lock pistol in one hand and hefted his mace in the other. "Not any God I know."

The two of us were buffeted around by the crowd as people rushed around searching for a nonexistent safe place.

Quentis lifted his pistol in the air, then said, "I can't get a clean shot."

I glanced at the weapon. "Can that thing go through chain mail?"

"On a good day, up close. Not from this distance."

More screams. More blood. And still we couldn't get through.

"Then shoot him in the head, damn it!"

"I can't—the weapon's not accurate at this distance, and especially not in this fog. I'll just end up hitting one of the pilgrims."

"Come one, come all!" shouted the madman in the center of the courtyard. "Don't be shy, little piggies!" He swung his sword in a blistering horizontal arc, taking a man's head clean off. "You've so little blood among you, and I am a thirsty man!"

Everything he did was helping to worsen the panic in the crowd. They were out of their minds with fear now, running wildly, getting in each other's way and, worse, ours. I kept having to drop the points of my rapiers just to avoid skewering people running into me.

"Here," Quentis said, "let's try this." He raised his pistol in the air and squeezed the trigger, and the air shattered around us as the mist turned the crack of the weapon into something closer to the explosion from a cannon.

Men and women scattered and the path before us finally cleared enough to force a way through.

"Not bad," I conceded.

"That gives me one shot for our friend."

"Can't you reload?"

"Yes," he replied, "I just need two minutes or so uninterrupted with no one jostling me. How likely do you think I am to get that?"

Brasti will be pleased to hear pistols have a weakness. I glanced ahead and could now see the God's Needle more clearly. He was, I reminded myself, just a normal man. *Just very, very big, and wearing the thickest chain mail I've ever seen, and in all likelihood he's much stronger than me and completely unable to feel pain or exhaustion.*

"Don't miss," I said, and started off at a run for our enemy.

The Needle kicked the body of a dying woman off the end of his blade and I could see he was slowing now—but not from any tiredness, just because there were now so many corpses in his way. How many had he killed already, fifteen? Twenty? His grin widened when he saw us. "Trattari and Cogneri," he said. "What an odd pair of birds have fluttered inside my little cage." He took a step toward us.

"Now would be an excellent time to shoot," I said.

Quentis moved in front of me, raised his pistol and tried to fire the second barrel, but nothing happened. He quickly twisted a cog on the side of the weapon and squeezed the trigger again. Silence. "It won't spark," he said.

"Nightmist," the God's Needle explained pleasantly, standing there as if he were politely giving us our chance. "Makes things rather wet."

I found myself suddenly acutely aware of the dampness glistening all around us, of the strands of hair sticking to my forehead. "Any chance you can dry that thing out?" I asked Quentis.

The Inquisitor holstered the weapon. "You really don't know anything about firearms, do you?" He hefted his mace and began walking in a slow, careful arc as he attempted to flank our enemy. His mace wouldn't have the reach of our opponent's two-handed sword, which meant I was going to have to provide a distraction if Quentis were to make good use of it.

"Have you tasted fear, little bird?" the God's Needle asked, swinging his warsword over his head with incredible speed before bringing it crashing down against the back of a disoriented man trying to flee, just like a forester felling a tree. "Do you taste it now?"

"You know, I would," I said casually as I raised my blades into a forward guard to give me the greatest reach, "but there are so many of you God's . . . is it 'God's Pins'? I forget. Anyway, I'm actually having trouble keeping track of the ones I've killed, so I thought perhaps I should name you after flowers. How would you like to be called 'Dandelion'?"

The man's grin was intact, but his eyes narrowed. He reached down to the ground and lifted a dying man up by his throat. "I have drunk the blood of Saint Ebron-who-steals-breath," he said, and squeezed, almost effortlessly snapping the man's neck. "Three nights ago I drank the blood of Saint Forza-who-strikes-a-blow," he went on, flipping his sword in his hands to hold it by the end of the blade and swinging it like a hammer behind him where the crossbar crushed the skull of another pilgrim. "And last night"—he kissed the fingertips of his left hand like a patron praising his meal—"I tasted the blood of Saint Marta-who-shakes-the-lion."

I suppose it's doubtful that my last prayer was heard, then.

Without warning, the God's Needle flipped his weapon in the air again, grabbing it by the hilt and then swinging the blade out behind him. Quentis Maren's head would have come separated from his shoulders had he not ducked down low. Dandelion had apparently expected that, though, and he kicked the Inquisitor in the chest, knocking him flat on his back. The nightmist made echoes of Quentis's hoarse gasps for breath as he scrambled backward, trying desperately to stay out of range. Dandelion, looking only mildly interested, stamped toward him and raised his heel, preparing to crush Quentis underneath.

A thought came to me unbidden. *Two seconds: just hesitate for one moment longer and the leader of the Inquisitors will die, leaving us one less problem to deal with. One less person who could threaten the people I care about.*

I took two steps into a run and jumped as high as I could. *I'm absolutely going to regret this later,* I thought as I kicked out with both feet against Dandelion's ribs, and he went toppling sideways. He fell onto one of the dead bodies on the ground—a softer landing than the one I got, for my shoulders hit the courtyard stones, sending a shockwave lancing down my arm.

Quentis managed to get his feet under him and swung his mace at the madman's head, but Dandelion got his arm up in time and blocked the blow. The thick chain mail of his sleeve denied us even a broken bone that might have slowed him down.

If Sedge and Beltran had been wearing mail like that, I realized, more than a little horrified, *I'd be dead right now.*

Dandelion reached out a hand and grabbed Quentis by the ankle, yanking him off balance and sending him crashing to the ground again.

This isn't working. He's going to outlast us.

I got myself off the ground and thrust my right rapier as hard as I could into what looked like a weaker point in Dandelion's chain mail, and by some miracle I managed to break through one of the links and the blade went into his side. He turned and looked down as if he'd just been bitten by an insect. Without even a trace of fear, he raised his hand in the air and closed it into a fist. *Hells,* I realized, *he's going to smash my blade with his bare hand.*

I withdrew the blade and immediately thrust for his eye—a tricky target on the best of days—and I was right; the Needle was too quick, weaving to the side and sweeping his heavy sword up diagonally. I lunged off my right leg, dropping my arm to my side and felt the gust of wind as Dandelion's sword passed by. I used the opening to stab him in the thigh, but once again, it made not the slightest difference.

Quentis swung his mace with both hands and smashed it into Dandelion's back. The chain links clattered under the blow, several tiny pieces of twisted metal falling to the ground—but Dandelion paid it no heed, instead just backhanding Quentis across the face with stunning force. The Inquisitor's mace fell to the ground as he struggled to stay standing.

We can't keep fighting this lunatic as if he were a normal man. He doesn't care about being hurt.

I brought my left rapier down in a diagonal slash and drew a line of blood across Dandelion's face, and the distraction was enough to make him focus his attention on me. "Quentis," I said, "we can't win like this. Give me the bastard's neck."

Without waiting for a reply, I stepped in close enough for the Needle to reach me with his warsword, and exactly as I'd anticipated, he raised the weapon high in the air. *If that blade comes down, there are going to be two Falcios for the Gods to curse.* Quentis, bless his black Inquisitor's heart, leapt up behind the big man and reached around his chest, grabbing the collar of the chain mail shirt and yanking it down. It moved just enough to reveal an inch of our enemy's throat, and even though Dandelion drove an elbow back into Quentis's ribs, the Inquisitor hung on for dear life. In that gap of time and space he gave me, I lunged and drove both my rapiers into the center of our enemy's throat. The tips pierced flesh and then ground past bone to come out the other side.

The Needle looked confused for a moment, and then he opened his mouth, as if he had something funny to say, although nothing but blood came out. Even then, even with all the damage done to him, the madman strengthened his grip on his sword still held aloft and prepared to bring it down on me. I stepped in and using all my remaining strength, I pried my rapiers open like a pair of scissors, and tore Dandelion's throat apart.

His head hung there for a brief instant, suspended only by bits of bone and strands of flesh, while blood pumped out of the severed veins and dyed his chain mail scarlet, then it dipped low, as if he were bowing to me, conceding a match well fought among friends. I stepped back just as the God's Needle toppled to the ground and lay there among the remains of his victims.

There was silence for a little while. The remaining mist swirled around us as Quentis and I stared at each other, our dead enemy's body laying like a bridge between us. "So that's what they're like," Quentis said, his words punctuated by coughs, his otherwise refined features marred by blackening bruises. His own blood streaked his short blond hair.

The world felt strange to me, quiet and still in a way it hadn't been in a long time. The things I usually do without thinking at the end of a fight became conscious steps to follow: I took in a slow, deep breath, waiting for any signs of internal injuries to make themselves known to me—pain in the ribs or wetness in the back of the throat. When none came, I placed both my rapiers in my right hand and reached into my coat for a small cleaning cloth. There was no pain in my shoulders or arms. I carefully wiped the blades as Quentis watched, a little stupefied himself, I think. The rest of the pilgrims approached us, slowly, tentatively. I think they too were wondering what in hells I was doing.

I turned my head as I worked, surveying the scene, but also testing to see if my vision was blurry—that would have been a sure sign of either head trauma or loss of blood. My eyes caught sight of a bag, perhaps a foot wide, sitting not far from where the God's Needle had stood. *The nightmist,* I thought idly.

I replaced the rapiers in their scabbards. A lot of people were staring at me now, waiting for me to speak or fall down or do something useful. Maybe they just thought I was crazy.

"Falcio?" Quentis asked. "Are you all right?"

I wasn't crazy, though. My head was clear for a change. I wasn't hallucinating or injured; the surge that came from life-or-death combat had begun to fade, but not so much that exhaustion was overtaking me yet. I was perfectly balanced in that moment, and I wanted to take advantage of it.

A man shows up in the middle of a closed courtyard full of pilgrims. He's wearing chain mail and carrying a huge two-handed sword, but he isn't noticed. He might have come in with one of the carts that stood a little way along the road in front of the entrance to the courtyard, but that would have been too long a walk to hide a weapon that size.

I looked around a little more, not quite sure what I was searching for until the very moment I found it. There, a few yards away, was a heavy brown cloak sitting on a pile of wooden boards. *So, a laborer then, walking in with his materials.* He'd covered up his armor under the cloak and brought the sword hidden under the armload of planks.

Once inside the courtyard, he would have dropped the boards, then removed his pack containing the nightmist and set it off. Then he'd dropped the cloak and drawn his sword from where it lay hidden among the wooden planks and begun his work.

"It was perfect," I said aloud.

The plan had factored in the closed gates of the courtyard, the mental and physical state of the pilgrims, the way the guards would react—protecting the palace and their Lord rather than acting to defend those outside. *Pure chaos,* I thought, *manufactured, measured, and doled out precisely as someone had intended.* I could see all of it now, all except that one piece that kept eluding me: *who had planned it.*

"Falcio," Quentis said. He was pulling gently on my arm. "We should go inside now."

"Not yet," I said. "I'm waiting."

"Waiting for what?"

The thing about chaos and terror is, you don't create them just for the fun of it—not when you've got the kind of intellect capable of devising and executing a plan like this so well, so seamlessly. You do it for a reason. You do it to send a message.

"You can come out now," I called out into the courtyard. The pilgrims looked up at me, a sea of confused and frightened faces.

I kept waiting for one of them to break—to suddenly crack a lunatic's grin and tell me what all this had been about. They didn't, but instead, I heard the sound of a horse-cart creaking its way up the road toward the courtyard gates.

The mist was still thick in places, but I followed the sound until I stood at the outer gate and saw a young boy of perhaps eight years hauling on the reins, bringing the pony that pulled his cart to a stop. It was a simple, open-backed wooden box with wheels. Inside was a thin black length of fabric shrouding what I could already see was a body. The boy hopped down from the seat and walked to the back of the cart.

"Step away from there, son," I said.

He looked over at me through the iron gates, not a trace of fear on his face, innocent as the morning dew.

Please don't tell me the world's been set afire by an eight-year-old.

"Are you Falcio?" he asked.

"I am. What's your name?"

He looked unsure for a moment, then shook his head. "He told me only to give you the message. Nothing else."

Quentis appeared at my side. "Why don't you come inside and give us the message then." He reached out to open the gate, but it was locked and neither of us had the key.

Before I could turn to call for one of the guards, the boy stepped back and brought a hand up to his neck. I saw the glint of metal. It looked like a small iron thimble on his little finger, but there was a half-inch-long needle at the end of it. I heard gasps behind us and realized that many of the pilgrims had followed us. I glanced back and saw some of the guards with them now.

"He said it would be quick," the boy threatened, still holding the tiny needle at his neck.

"Don't," I said. "Just . . . don't move."

The boy seemed unperturbed. "He said you'd probably need to spend some time trying to figure out if you could talk me into giving myself up. Are you going to do that?"

"Why don't you tell us your name and we'll go from there?" I asked.

The boy shook his head. "He said I should tell you that I have a mother and a father. I have two older sisters and a baby brother, born last harvest. He said to tell you that they would all be dead if I didn't do as I was told."

I considered how fast I could draw one of my throwing knives, and whether I could hit the boy in the shoulder in time and not end up killing him by mistake myself. Then I wondered if perhaps Quentis's pistol might fire now that the nightmist was dying out. I glanced at the Inquisitor but he shook his head, evidently having had the same idea himself.

The boy looked up at me quizzically. "Do you need more time? Or can I give you the message?"

"Go ahead," Quentis replied.

The boy waited, unmoving, until I said, "Say what you came to say."

He reached back with his other hand and lifted the cloth to reveal a woman's corpse beneath. The body was naked, clothed only in dozens, maybe hundreds, of tiny red lines—the last faint traces of blood. She looked thin, withered. The boy removed the rest of the cloth so that I could see the iron mask covering her face. "He said to tell you that this used to be Saint Laina-who-whores-for-Gods, and that you probably shouldn't invoke her name so much anymore." The boy waited for a moment, then said, "He said you might find that funny."

"Then he doesn't know me very well," I said. "What can you tell me about the man who sent you?"

The boy's eyes narrowed for a moment, then he took in a deep breath and held it before letting out a long, preposterously theatrical sigh. "He said to do that if you asked about him. You've never met him. You never will. That's why you can't beat him."

The words my wife—or rather, my hallucination of Aline—had uttered came back to me. *He needs no mask of his own.* But was the boy telling the truth, or was this a ruse to keep me from seeking out my opponent among the plentiful enemies I already knew? *It might be a lie,* I thought, *but if so, it's a lazy one.* "What does he want?" I asked, knowing I wasn't likely to get an answer but unwilling be shamed into not trying by a child acting on the orders of a madman.

The boy perked up at that. "Oh. He said you'd probably swear some kind of oath or make a threat before you got to the point." He paused again, mumbling a bit as if rehearsing the words, then he looked back up at us. "He said to tell you that there aren't many Saints left now, but that he'll stop hurting people just as soon as he gets the one you've been keeping from him."

Ethalia. He wants Ethalia. "Tell him he can—" I stopped myself. *Enough. Stop playing his game.* There was only one thing I could hope to gain from this situation, which was some tiny shred of information I could use later. "If I agree, where should I bring her?"

"Oh, he said you don't need to take her anywhere," the boy said. "He has people who will come and get her. Lots and lots of them. If you keep standing in their way, all that's going to happen is more people will get hurt." The boy looked past me to the crowds of pilgrims. "You don't have to die, you know. Your crops don't have to wither. The Gods are very angry with you, but he said to say that they'll forgive you once the last false Saint is dead."

My fists gripped the iron bars between us. Here was the real reason why the boy had been sent, why the God's Needle had massacred these people. The message wasn't for me. It was for everyone else. *He wants them afraid so that they'll give up Ethalia.*

The sounds of grumbling started behind us, but I ignored them. The boy was still looking up at me. He still had the point of the short needle against his throat. "Do you think he'll really let my family go?" the boy asked, speaking for himself for the first time.

I looked into his eyes. I'd been wrong about him being an innocent. That had been taken away from him before he'd begun this journey. I thought about lying to him, giving some small hope to his last moments.

"He won't let them go," Quentis said, "for the same reason he told you to put that needle to your throat. You can't save them, child. Come inside. Let us help you."

The boy didn't move. "He showed me something before he sent me here, you know."

"What was it?" I asked, as gently as I could. We had lost this fight before it had begun.

There were tears in the boy's eyes now. "He showed me that there are worse things he can do to my family than just kill them." With that the child pushed the needle attached to the thimble on his little finger into his throat. He slumped back against the horse-cart and gently slid down to the ground.

CHAPTER FORTY

THE LOVE OF GODS

"Falcio?" Quentis said, for perhaps the fifth time.

I was still clinging to the gates even though one of the guardsmen had come and opened them. The boy was still lying on the ground, next to his ragged little cart. His skin was a perfect pale white now, his lips blue as a clear sky. The little pony that had pulled him all this way was looking over at its master, doubtless wondering when the boy would get up to feed him.

"Falcio, there's nothing more you can do here."

The wooden surface of the cart was clean, as were the wheels. The only dirt I could see had obviously come from the journey up the road to the palace. *He told the boy to clean it just before he got to the gates to make sure there wouldn't be any evidence to follow.*

"So many dead," a woman moaned, inching closer with several others of the pilgrims.

I looked around at the courtyard. Guardsmen had come to collect the dead, but the pilgrims were making them wait while they said final prayers over strangers and loved ones alike. They began surrounding us. "The Gods have turned against us," an old man said, stumbling forward, leaning on a crooked staff that matched the curve of his back.

"Because of you," a young woman added. She was pretty, with a flat nose and bright red hair. There was iron in her eyes. "You've brought this on us, you and your false Queen and your false Protector and your false Saint."

An elderly woman took my wrist in thin, crinkled fingers. She pulled me toward the bodies in the center of the courtyard. Not knowing what else to do, I followed. "There," she said, pointing to a man nearly split in two by the God's Needle's massive sword. "My husband," the words tumbled out in a single sob. "Why is he dead while the ones you love still live, Trattari?"

I said something then, something I shouldn't have. I must have known it was a bad idea because I'd muttered it so quietly that only Quentis had heard. "Falcio . . . don't," he cautioned.

A wiser man would have heeded the warning. I didn't. "Because I fight for the people I love," I said.

They heard you that time, I thought, as the pilgrims started constricting me. Quentis tried to grab my shoulder but I shrugged him off and drew my rapiers. "Have I offended you?" I asked the mob. "Have I offended your Gods? Is that what it takes to make you fight? Is that what was missing when one man came among you and began cutting you down, one after another? Should he have spat on a statue of Phenia, Goddess of Love? Or perhaps Argentus, God of Coin?"

The guardsmen were starting to inch forward, not yet drawing their weapons but I doubted they'd let me go on for long. *What good is this?* I asked myself. *What is there to gain? Do you want them to attack you?*

"Come on!" I shouted, "show me your vengeance." I spat the next word. "*Tristians.* 'The people of sorrows' the Avareans named us when they brought us here in chains to work the mines. Too bad they never took the chains off."

Somewhere in the crowd I saw a young man clasp his hands to the center of his chest the way one does when praying to Purgeize, God of War. "That's right," I said, "pray for the Gods to come down and smite me. Use the great power of your faith to make them strike me dead here and now." I spread my arms out to the sky and looked up. "I'm right here, you bastards! Come and get me!"

"That's enough, Falcio," Quentis said. His mace was in his right hand and I wondered if he was planning to protect me with it or knock me out. *He'd be doing me a favor if he did,* I thought.

I sheathed my rapiers. My voice was quieter when I said, "Keep praying. Bow before your Gods. Kneel before them." I started back to the palace entrance. "It's all you're good for."

I pushed past the guardsmen who had, I noted, finally drawn their weapons, and grabbed the heavy pack of nightmist the attacker had left behind. The last thing we needed was for some pilgrim to start weeping over it and set the damn stuff off again.

"You know," Quentis said, following me back to the palace, "people are quite wrong about you. You give really *terrible* speeches."

I felt something soft and wet hit the back of my coat. I didn't bother to see what had been thrown at me.

Quentis did glance behind us. "Not especially grateful to us for saving their lives, are they?"

"You get used to it," I said with a sigh.

CHAPTER FORTY-ONE
THE VISITOR

I paid little attention to what people said to me as I entered the palace and crossed the grand foyer. A servant, or perhaps he was a clerk, informed me with an upturned nose that the Ducal Protector required my attendance in the throne room. I told him I'd be there at my soonest convenience, which I was fairly determined would be never.

Quentis started on about wider concerns to address and the need to discuss the message the boy had brought—the clerical council who gave him his orders would be arriving tomorrow and they would expect action to be taken. I think he said something about this being a big, complex, changing world and that I needed to recognize that those who led the faithful would no longer be able to sit back waiting for a handful of Greatcoats to fumble about the countryside. This was the time, he informed me, to consider the future.

I said I'd get back to him on that.

By the time I reached the diplomatic chamber, I was being bombarded with questions about the fight outside: sensible questions. Important questions. I didn't answer any of them.

"We're leaving here," I informed everyone.

"To go where?" Brasti asked.

I glanced over at Valiana, who was still sitting on the sofa, waiting for someone to help her. "We need to get her up to her chambers for now. It's easier to protect her if we all stay together."

"And then?" Kest asked.

"In two days' time the troops Valiana sent for will be here. We'll use them to get all of us back to Aramor safely."

I started toward Valiana but Aline blocked my way. "She wanted those troops to help protect Luth, to show the clerics and the nobles here that the Crown was supporting Pastien—what's he supposed to do if we just abandon him here?"

I gently pushed past her and walked to the sofa. I leaned over and took Valiana's hands and helped her to her feet. "Pastien can go to any hell he wishes," I replied, "and he can take his Duchy with him."

"Can I make a suggestion?" Brasti asked as he and I led Valiana down the wide central hallway of the Ducal Palace, past the dozens of men and women gawking at the sight of the Realm's Protector trapped in an iron mask of infamy. We pushed past them all and made for the stairs that led to the private rooms Pastien had set aside for her.

"He still thinks we should kill Quentis Maren," Kest said, walking alongside us. He kept his left hand on the hilt of his sheathed blade, although even that seemed to hurt these days.

Aline led the way, her status as heir to the throne sufficient to make the servants and guardsmen stand aside, though they muttered to each other as they did so, and I saw more than one nobleman smirking at Valiana's condition. If I hadn't been holding her I would have been hard-pressed to stop myself from scraping away those gleeful expressions with my bare hands.

We passed by a long painting that portrayed all of the Kings of Tristia dating back several hundred years, riding together as they pursued a shining white stag in a very improbable hunt—a symbol, no doubt, for some glorious future they sought to achieve. *But you were wrong, oh Kings,* I thought. *I've become something of an expert on this and I'm fairly sure you were all just chasing a hallucination.*

"Quentis says he works for the Church," Brasti continued, "but there *is* no Church of Tristia, not really. You know why? Because religious zealots can't work together—it's as simple as that. Saint Zaghev's burning balls, how do you expect these people to unite behind one God when they've spent the last thousand years arguing over which one has the biggest cock?"

We reached the bottom of the grand staircase, and Kest said, "According to the *Canon dei,* it's Purgeize, God of War."

All of us stopped and looked at him. He was the only one of us who'd made any real study of Tristia's religious texts. "Seriously?" I asked incredulously. "You're telling me the oldest holy book describes a God's—"

"No," he said, noticing that we were all staring at him. "I was . . . trying to lighten the mood."

"You see?" Brasti said to me. "That's how stupid your theory is. *Kest* has started making jokes."

"He is right to do so," Ethalia said. "If these people see us looking frustrated or angry, then we defeat the purpose of Aline's plan."

Except we are angry, I thought as we carefully ushered Valiana up the stairs.

I pushed for waiting until dark and sneaking Valiana away, not exposing her to prying eyes, but Aline pointed out that the Dukes and their retainers already knew what had happened to her, and if we tried to keep her condition a secret, they'd step all over each other to be the first to blackmail us—or worse, make sure the information spread in the most damning way possible. The only answer was to neutralize their advantage, and to do that, we needed to escort her in full view of the palace. I was proud of Aline; she'd come to a perfectly sensible, logical conclusion.

I hated it.

And so did Tommer, who was even worse than me at hiding his anger at the way people were staring at Valiana.

"My, my. A new day brings many changes, does it not?" a tall, thin man in red and gold silks tittered, perfect teeth grinning down at us from the gallery where he stood bookended by elegantly dressed female companions, neither of whom looked old enough to be his wife nor young enough to be his daughters.

"I'm surprised at your fine mood, Viscount Thistren," Tommer called out, his young voice echoing up the wide marble stairway. "My father is considering revising the borders of your Condate—it's a shame that several towns and estates are likely to become part of Viscountess Hemmier's territory, is it not?"

The pretty nobleman practically fell over himself trying to block our way as we reached the top of the stairs. "I . . . I understood that my lands were to be expanded, not reduced—!"

Tommer, not half the man's height, pushed him out of the way so we could get by. "You said it yourself, Viscount: a new day brings many changes, and sadly, not all of them will necessarily be to your liking."

We left the man sputtering behind us. Had I not been holding onto Valiana I would have stopped to hug Tommer.

"Viscount Thistren is a wealthy and well-connected man," Aline warned. "Your father won't approve of you making enemies."

Tommer's eyes passed over those of every other noble lining the hallway. "A man who mocks my sister is already my enemy, though he might not know it yet."

Brasti craned his neck to study Tommer. "We seriously need to make this kid a Greatcoat," he told me.

I couldn't imagine a better way to turn Duke Jillard against us, but that was a problem for another day.

We walked down a narrow hallway that ended with an arched doorway, with Mateo leaning casually against the wall next to it, wiping a black cloth along the length of the curved blade of his fal-chion. "So how was the parade?" he asked.

"No corpses," Brasti replied, "so that's something."

"Any intruders?" I asked. Once we'd decided to bring Valiana to her rooms, I'd sent Mateo to check them first; he really hadn't needed my *very* specific instructions on dealing with anyone waiting inside for her.

"No assassins, mystical or otherwise. No spies or guardsmen, either."

"Good," I said, and reached for the door handle.

Mateo stepped in front of me. "There is *someone* inside, though."

"Then get rid of them. I told you to—"

"Yes, Falcio: you told me to scare off anyone looking to make trouble. Unfortunately, *she* doesn't scare all that easily, and she had some rather colorful suggestions about what I might want to do with my threats."

"'She'?"

Mateo pushed open the door and just inside, sitting decorously on the chair she'd no doubt placed in that exact spot to ensure she was the first thing I saw, sat the Tailor.

"Oh hells," Brasti swore. "The Gods really do hate us."

Her hair, usually wild and unkempt, was carefully tied back. She wore her own greatcoat, freshly cleaned and oiled. I should have had it burned months ago. Next to her, on the bed, sat a pair of thick red and black leather-bound books which I recognized as the two volumes of the *Regia Maniferecto De'egro,* Tristia's oldest legal texts dealing with the laws of royal ascension.

"Well, children," she said, "the Gods have abandoned us, civilization is on the verge of collapse, and the Realm's Protector is locked away behind an iron mask. I suppose it's time we discussed who's in charge, don't you?"

I kept my patience for a very long time, by my estimation almost an entire minute. The first eight seconds were spent ushering Valiana into the room and seating her in a tall wingchair near the hearth while the others crowded in behind us, leaving Mateo and Tommer outside to guard the door. I used another ten seconds to check the locks and set sharp steel caltrops on the floor, carefully extracted from their heavy leather drawstring bag in my pocket, just in case someone decided to break in. A few more ticks of the clock went by as Brasti and I hoisted a table onto the window sill to block any possible projectile fire from outside. I finished by letting a small knife slide down from the inside of my right coat sleeve into the thin slot inside my cuff.

The last twenty-seven seconds went like this: "Ah, see how diligently the shepherd guards his flock?" the Tailor said. "A pity it's so long after the wolf has already shat out the remains of the sheep."

"I get that I'm the shepherd," I said, "but I can't tell if you're supposed to be the wolf, the sheep, or maybe just the shit in this story."

She gave a gravelly laugh before rising from the bed and reaching out a leather-gloved hand to brush the collar of my coat. She patted my cheek with the other. "Ah, Falcio val Mond, the saddest man in a country born of sorrows. If only such noble suffering led to understanding."

"Oh, look," Brasti said. "Here's the part where she starts going on about knowing the length of every piece of string in the country."

The Tailor ignored him. "Valiana has done an admirable job keeping the Dukes in line, these past months." Her hands brushed idly at the shoulders of my coat as if I were a doddering old man who couldn't keep himself clean. "But the girl's time is done now, and you, Falcio, lack the—well, let's set aside our differences for now. One of us must lead now, and it can't be you."

That was about the time my sixty seconds of patience ran out, possibly because our "differences" included the fact that the Tailor had nearly driven the country into civil war and chaos as part of a perverse plan to ensure Aline would one day take the throne. *Not to mention handing me over to the Dashini.*

"Ah," she said, thin lips pulled tight, "there's that look I love so well."

"You picked the wrong time to push me," I said, my right hand on the hilt of my rapier.

"I'm a Tailor, Falcio. My timing is always perfect. You should know that by now."

"Falcio . . ." Kest warned.

What I'd assumed to be a caution against wasting time in debate with the Tailor turned out to be something else entirely. Following the line of Kest's eyes, I finally focused on the almost invisible steel thread now running around my neck, one end in each of the Tailor's gloved hands. The Tailor gave just the slightest of tugs on the thread and it bit painfully into my neck. Apparently she'd kept a few tricks back for her sole use when she designed our greatcoats.

"Long past time you took me seriously, Falcio," she said.

CHAPTER FORTY-TWO

THE GENERAL

Sometimes the hardest thing to do in a fight is to not react. Your reflexes, usually what save you, can also be what get you killed. In this case, my instincts were screaming at me to grab the steel thread from the Tailor, but if I'd tried, I'd've been dead long before my hands reached hers.

"I've changed my mind," Brasti said, the bend of his bow creaking behind me. "I'm going to kill Quentis Maren *second*."

"It wasn't long ago," the Tailor said conversationally, "that Kest could have drawn his blade so quickly that he'd have had my head before my hands could even clench. Now look at him: barely able to hold a sword without passing out in agony." She gave a tiny nod toward Brasti, and I belatedly realized she had positioned me so that I was blocking his aim. "On a good day, that fool could have fired an arrow that would have threaded the needle's gap between us—but see how his arm twitches, ever since the madwoman stabbed him." Her gaze came back around to me, and I could have sworn there was sympathy of a sort there, a sadness that belied our current relationship. "And you, Falcio: I remember when you were far too clever to ever let me wind my thread around your neck."

Aline, who was wise enough to keep from making any sudden moves, said, "Stop this, Grandmother. This is no time for dissent between us."

"On that score we agree, sweetling. The world is falling apart around us. Someone must lead." She paused, for just a moment. "The last time I failed to protect you. I won't let that happen again."

"Then perhaps you should remember," Kest said evenly, "that the man you're threatening is the one who saved her."

"And I love him for it!" the Tailor growled. "But the country turns against us." Her gaze fell on me. "I need you to see that you aren't the man you once were, Falcio. You can't beat this enemy."

"And you think you can?" I gave the question as much force as I could, hoping to mask the fact that I couldn't have cared less about her answer. I tend to lose interest in philosophical debates when there's a garrote around my throat. Instead, I raced through my meager possibilities of escape. I could try to head-butt her, since that wouldn't entail pulling against the razor-sharp wire, but then she'd fall backward and there was a strong possibility she'd yank hard as she did so, bringing my head with her. Mateo and Tommer were both outside the door, Aline had no weapon, and Ethalia—

A soft light glimmered off the steel thread. "None of us are who we once were," Ethalia said, "yet some of us still seek to do what is right rather than what is easy."

"Tell the whore to back away, Falcio," the Tailor warned. Her hands twitched, and I swear I felt a bead of blood drip down the back of my neck.

"'Whore,'" Ethalia repeated. "Do you think that word harms me? Do you think you can shame me for my years in the Order of Merciful Light?"

The Tailor gave a snort. "How can you even say that with a straight face?"

"We brought gentleness and the simple pleasures of the body to those whose lives drove them to anger and violence," Ethalia said, "and in this way we moved them, pace by pace, toward compassion. What have you done these past years, Tailor, save walk ever further down a path of rage and bloodshed?" Ethalia took another step toward us and the light glistening on the thread grew brighter. "Neither you nor anyone else will ever shame me over that time in my life."

"Do you suppose you'll feel regret when you see Falcio's head fall at your feet?" the Tailor asked. "Because that's what will happen if you take one step closer."

Ethalia's eyes, a still, fearless blue, caught mine. "Do you trust me?"

"Always."

"Fools," the Tailor growled, and the rage in her voice thrummed along the steel thread between us. "Dreamers," she spat. "You claim the mantle of a Saint—yet you couldn't even stop two halfwits dressed as guardsmen from attacking you. What makes you think you can stop me?"

Ethalia's voice, strident a moment before, became gentle. "Because your sorrow is so much greater, sister." She reached out a hand. "Because I know what scares you."

"Is that what you believe, little girl? I should point out I've known a lot of Saints in my time, and mostly they're full of shit."

"And you're no Saint, are you?" Ethalia's words held no mockery, no condemnation, just understanding. "You're the Tailor, who sees where the threads begin and where they end, who knows which to pull and which one to let be. So tell us, where is the enemy? What is his plan?"

"I don't know!" the Tailor shouted. "I can't . . . *I can't find him.*"

We stood like that for a long time, and I kept expecting the Tailor to say something caustic, that Saints and Gods were useless things, the poor invention of an unimaginative people. This was perhaps the longest she'd ever gone without delivering her usual speech about how clever she was, but instead, the frustration and fear she'd been hiding began to show in her eyes.

I still had the small blade in my right sleeve and the Tailor was distracted; I could take her out. I didn't, though, because Ethalia had asked me to trust her and because I knew now that she was right. "You aren't the only one who's afraid," I said.

Something broke inside the Tailor. The steel thread went limp as she let go of it and sat down heavily on the bed. Her gaze went to Aline, and for the first time in my life, I saw despair in her eyes. "How can I protect her if I can't follow the threads anymore?" she whispered.

We stood in silence, divided over what had to be done, united in the knowledge that we weren't the people to do it. Last year, maybe even last month—or even last week—the Tailor had been able to see the movements and patterns of the world in ways none of us could ever hope to match. Now she was just a mother who'd lost her son, a grandmother who feared losing her granddaughter.

None of us are the people we once were, I thought, *but maybe we never were.* What if all those victories had come only because we'd never faced an enemy like the one we did now?

I closed my eyes, trying to imagine what his face might look like. Was he young or old, a nobleman or a pauper? *Who are you? And why are you so much better at this than we are?*

I sat down on the Tailor's chair, suddenly exhausted, and realized everyone was looking at me. They were waiting for me to say something insightful, or maybe give some clever speech about how we just needed to be brave and everything would work out in the end. *I think the world has had just about enough of my speeches.*

For the first time in my life, I wondered if the time of the Greatcoats really had passed. *Or maybe Brasti's right, and I should just go and challenge the head of the Inquisitors to a duel. That's the only thing I've been good at lately.*

But the truth was, however much I hated the idea of the Inquisitors, I didn't really believe Quentis Maren was our true enemy. He was too obvious a target, too perfectly placed in our path: the kind of person we all despised and would naturally suspect. During my last hallucination, Aline had warned me: *the enemy fits his masks to others, and in so doing hides his own face.* And then King Paelis had said something else: *to strike the enemy you must first pierce his deceptions.*

And Duke Jillard's jibe came back to me: "Has it ever occurred to you that the people you're so driven to protect are always women?" I found myself looking around the room, at Aline, who'd nearly been taken by an assassin's blade, at Ethalia, attacked by the God's Needles last night, and finally Valiana, poisoned by blood from a madman's tongue . . .

Of course! "He's an *avertiere!*" I said.

"A what?" Aline asked.

"An *avertiere*," Kest said, giving the word its archaic Tristian pronunciation, "is a duelist who uses feints and false attacks to distract his opponent, aiming at those parts of the body his enemy will instinctively protect—like the eyes or the neck—and drawing out wide parries so that when the avertiere launches his true attack—"

"—the real target will be undefended," Aline finished.

"Oh, wonderful," Brasti said. "Another fucking fencing metaphor to describe exactly how we're being screwed. How does that help anything?"

Aline looked annoyed at his glib tone. "It tells us that the crises we've been dealing with aren't the real threat."

"The *real* threat?" Brasti asked. "You think that trying to kill the heir to the throne, the Saint of Mercy, and the Realm's Protector aren't real enough for him?" He began pacing the room and his voice rose in volume and pitch as he cried, "The damned Saints are being murdered! We're being infested with these lunatic 'God's Needles,' and even the bloody *Inquisitors* can't deal with them, and meanwhile there are hordes of whining pilgrims massing outside the palace. Even I'm starting to think the fucking Gods hate us—and I don't even believe in them!" He stopped and threw himself heavily down on the sofa beside my chair. "I swear, if this keeps up much longer I'm going to take up religion—and trust me, none of us wants that."

The sounds of scuffling from outside the door drew our attention. Kest's blade whispered from its sheath, and Brasti's bow creaked as he bent it.

"Tommer's out there," Aline said, rushing toward the door.

I held her back with my right hand and lifted my rapier with my left. "Wait," I said, and after I saw her nod assent I swept the caltrops aside with my foot and opened the door. On the other side I was greeted by the sight of Pastien, Ducal Protector of Luth, lying on the floor on his backside, a hand to his cheek. Tommer stood over him, his own fist raised. Mateo held him by the wrist while his own blade, held straight out at neck height, moved between Pastien's two guardsmen, who were looking very uncomfortable with their current choices.

"The first blow was for standing by while my sister suffered," Tommer said. "The second will be if you ever again *demand* to see her."

"What in the name of Saint Zaghev-who-sings-for-tears is going on here?" I asked.

"Do you suppose Saint Zaghev's still alive?" Brasti asked, sidling next to me to get a better angle on one of the guardsmen. "Because it would be just like this wretched country to have the worst Saint of all be the one who lives."

Mateo, still gripping Tommer's wrist, replied, "Lord Pastien requested an audience with the Realm's Protector."

"He *demanded* one," Tommer corrected.

"I am the Ducal Protector of Luth," Pastien insisted, "and I'll not be battered about by children in my own palace."

"Stand up," Tommer said to him. "Stand up so I can knock you down again."

"He really is going to make a terrible politician," Brasti commented idly.

I sheathed my rapier. "Everyone shut up and put down your weapons." I grabbed Tommer by the collar of his coat, Jillard's words from earlier coming back to me. *If my son dies, I'll make you pay for it.* "And you: hold your temper until there's a genuine threat to fight."

Reluctantly, the boy lowered his fist.

I leaned over and offered Pastien my hand. "Why are you here?" I asked.

The young man rose to his feet. He straightened his jacket and his back. "I need help."

"We're a bit busy killing each other," Brasti said amiably. "Try coming back later."

"Later may be too late," Pastien replied.

"Then tell me," I said.

He hesitated for a moment, no doubt searching for some way he might regain his dignity, but eventually he gave up. "The clerics I told you about . . ." He paused again. "Yesterday Valiana suggested that I send scouts ahead, in case anyone tried to attack the delegation."

Hells—tell me there aren't more dead at the hands of the God's Needles . . . I steeled myself and asked, "Was the delegation attacked?"

"No," Pastien said, then corrected himself. "Well, actually they were—my scouts say they spotted a dozen men preparing to assail the caravan, but they fled."

"A handful of priests scared off brigands?" Kest asked suspiciously.

Pastien shook his head. "It wasn't the priests who scared them off; it was the contingent of armored Knights accompanying them. A hundred of them. And Falcio, those Knights weren't wearing Ducal tabards. They wore white."

"*Church Knights?*" Brasti asked, incredulous. "There haven't been any of those since—"

"—since they were banned by Ducal decree a hundred and seventy years ago," Kest finished.

The Church, it appeared, had had enough of being pushed around.

CHAPTER FORTY-THREE
THE AVERTIERE

"A hundred Knights," Brasti repeated for the third time as our odd company sat staring at each other in Valiana's chambers. "Where in the name of Saint Laina's cold left tit did the clerics find a hundred Knights?"

"From Hervor," Kest replied. "From Orison and Luth and even the Duchy of Aramor itself." He turned to me. "From the broken remains of those whose loyalty was sworn to Dukes whose entire family lines now lie buried."

I thought back to all the men I'd seen standing so arrogantly in their polished armor, their entire self-worth built on serving a great lord. Take that away from them and what did you have left? Big men in steel suits desperate for something—*anything*—that would restore their sense of personal honor. *I think I hate Knights almost as much as I hate magic.*

"Valiana talked about restoring the Knighthood," Aline said, pulling me back.

I looked over at the chair sitting in the corner of the room where Valiana sat alone, waiting for one of us to shout into those little slits in the front of her mask and tell her what was happening. "Why didn't she?"

Aline started to answer then stopped. After a few seconds, she said, "There was a great deal else to contend with before dealing with something so—"

"It was you," the Tailor interrupted, favoring me with an angry stare.

"Me? She didn't even discuss the matter with me—"

The Tailor gave a snort. "Do you suppose she doubted for a second what your opinion would have been on the matter?"

"Well," Brasti began, a hard edge to his voice, "if it was going to be, 'not even over our cold, dead bodies,' then for once Falcio would have been right."

Brasti's law, I thought: *no more armor. No more Knights.* Only, it didn't work that way; there would always be second sons, men with money and swords who wouldn't inherit anything, and they would always be looking for some way to distinguish themselves in the world. If they couldn't find it from the Dukes, they'd search for it in religion. *Saints. Inquisitors. God's Needles. Church Knights.* Why now? *Why all of a sudden?*

"Is he losing it again?" Brasti asked.

"Leave him be," Kest replied. "He's sorting something out."

"Well, Falcio sorting something out looks a lot like an old drunk trying to remember where he left his cup."

The Saints start being murdered, and that brings back the Inquisitors. The God's Needles start sowing fear, and that forces the return of the Church Militant. And in the middle of it all are the common folk, already cowed by years of chaos since King Paelis died, desperate for order. No wonder so many of them were abandoning their farms and towns and turning to prayer and pilgrimage. *Brasti was right. Any more of this and we'll all be taking up religion.*

It was almost funny. *Except it's not a joke,* I realized with a start. *It's the target.*

"Brasti was right," I said.

"I was?" he asked, then, "How?" He turned to Kest. "And in future, please remember that the words 'Brasti was right' came out of Falcio's mouth, in front of several witnesses."

"You said there wasn't a real Church in Tristia because they've always been fragmented, belligerent about their individual beliefs. All this time we've believed someone was attacking them— murdering their Saints, destroying their holy places . . . but what if this isn't about destroying faith in this country. What if these aren't acts of desecration at all?"

"Then what else would you call them?" Kest asked, trying to follow my reasoning.

"Consecration," Ethalia said. Everything about Ethalia is in the eyes, and hers were cold and hard as iron now. "The Church isn't coming apart. It is uniting, for the first time."

"By killing each other?" Brasti asked. "How does that—?"

Ethalia cut him off. "They're creating a new religion—one untainted by division among the clerics, one free of interference by the living Saints."

The Tailor looked up at me suddenly: she could see the pattern as well now. I wondered if it pained her that I'd figured it out first. "It's not possible," she said. "It's too complex . . . all the threads that would have to be pulled at just the right time . . ."

Brasti held up his hands to shut everyone up. "Hang on a minute here. Okay, so let's say you're right: let's say the people being killed are those who might stand in the way of a new, united faith. But why destroy actual *churches*? Where are these new clerics supposed to preach?"

It was Aline who worked it out first. She'd moved over to sit next to Valiana and had been relaying everything being said, but now she rose and said, "They won't need churches. This new religion has no use for small, run-down roadside houses of worship or weather-worn sanctuaries." She spread her arms wide. "The churches they want have already been built."

I turned to Pastien. "How many guardsmen do you have at the palace?"

"Not even fifty," he replied.

So it would start here in Luth: a weakened Duchy led by an even weaker Ducal Protector. *A hundred Knights. That's all it's going to take.* From there, they'll restore order, give the lesser nobles a little more of the power they so crave in exchange for subservience to Gods they care nothing for. I thought about all those terrified, desperate pilgrims outside. They just wanted someone to protect them, and now they'd get it. "Our enemy isn't just creating a new religion," I said. "He's creating a theocracy. The Church is taking over Tristia."

CHAPTER FORTY-FOUR

THE WAR

Throughout that night we did the things you do when you know the conquerors are coming for you. We discussed strategies, we debated plans, we made preparations. Mostly, we found out just how completely screwed we were.

"So you decline then, Your Grace?" Pastien asked, seated on his throne in the great hall. He'd argued that the setting might make him more formidable. He'd been wrong.

Hadiermo, Iron Duke of Domaris, gestured at his two guards holding his massive warsword across their outstretched palms and repeated, "I'll not waste what few soldiers I have with me on a fool's venture that's just going to antagonize the churches."

"The Crown urges you to reconsider," said Aline, seated on a smaller chair next to Pastien's throne. Valiana in her iron mask sat next to her.

"What 'Crown'?" croaked old Erris, Duke of Pulnam. "All I see is a child on a stool next to a peasant girl in an iron mask." He turned around as if to address an audience that wasn't there. "Who brought that disgusting creature in here anyway?" His eyes finally settled on me.

Ah, I guess I'm the audience for this performance.

He smiled and said, "She belongs in a dark cell where no one will have to look at her."

Despite the provocation, I didn't draw my rapiers, I made no threats. I kept my hands in the pockets of my coat. This was all theater and I knew it. *Let's make the Trattari lose their tempers so we can feel justified in our cowardice.* I glanced at Quentis Maren, standing with two of his Inquisitors. I was saving any rash moves for him.

"Alas, Your Grace," Aline said placidly, "the Palace of Luth houses only a few cells, and only one is currently vacant, and that one we must save."

"Eh? For what?" Erris asked, bemused.

"For the next man who issues a threat against the Realm's Protector."

Jillard, Duke of Rijou, stood apart from his fellow Dukes, leaning casually against a pillar. I wondered why I hadn't noticed his fondness for leaning before now. "Perhaps we should calm ourselves and get to the point? Some of us have vital business in our own Duchies."

The vital business of which he spoke had come up suddenly, one might say miraculously, once word had spread that the clerical delegation was bringing a hundred armored Knights with them. *All of a sudden everyone is homesick,* I thought.

Mateo and I had snuck out during the night to inspect the barns, and sure enough, all three Dukes' groomsmen were busy preparing their horses and those of their entourages. Had the three of them agreed to stay and fight, we could have turned the clerics away. That fact was not lost on the Ducal Protector of Luth. "Your actions ill-become your station, Your Graces," the young man said, nearly shouting. "You would abandon your fellow—"

"Fellow what?" Hadiermo interrupted. "You're no fellow of mine, you base-born mutt. Why do you think the Viscounts and Margraves of this pathetic little Duchy put you in that chair? I'll tell you why—you'll be easy to remove when someone worthy wants the seat."

"And what happens when someone wants *your* seat?" Tommer asked. He was standing near his father, apparently still determined to run headlong into the first duel he could find. Jillard looked remarkably displeased. With me.

Hadiermo took no offense, instead breaking out into his idea of a hearty laugh. "You think some traipsing troop of clerics and a handful of landless Knights will come to *my* home? Domaris has never fallen, boy—Domaris never will."

It was, in fact, true: Hadiermo's Duchy had never fallen to any army . . . that's because a body can't fall when it's already sitting down. No enemy had ever had to fight the Iron Duke; he avoided confrontation by letting potential threats run roughshod over his lands—and his people—and persuaded the invaders to let him handle the bureaucracy. It worked like a charm for him and his; not so much for the common folk. But he'd always made his views on the peasantry quite clear.

"So what, then, Your Graces?" Aline asked. "You will simply walk away and let Luth be taken—and what then? Will you trade with its new rulers? Will you—?"

"We will wait," Erris said, leaning heavily on his walking stick. I had a profound urge to beat him senseless with it, especially now that I had some experience with using the cane as a weapon. "In all likelihood, whatever cleric sits the throne of Luth won't do so for long."

"And if they do?" Pastien asked.

It was Jillard who answered. "My brother Dukes are confident that there is no danger to our own Duchies. Despite recent events, the simple fact remains: we have more than enough troops to protect our own lands. Our minor nobles are well-heeled and our peasants well-fed."

I'd tried to remain silent, but I found I had to ask, "And you, Your Grace? Do you agree with their conclusions?"

Jillard looked straight at me. "I have been given no reason to believe otherwise, First Cantor."

The glib answer angered me, not because I expected better of the Duke of Rijou—he was, after all, still a vile man whom I fully planned to kill one day—but because he was right. We had spent half the night debating how the Church might take over the country. Aline had studied every day under Valiana, I had learned from her father, Kest had read everything that had ever been written on warfare, and the Tailor—well, she knew everything that hadn't been written. We could see any number of ways in which the Church might take over several of the Duchies—maybe even all of them, but we could see no means by which they could keep them. It's one thing to conquer and quite another to hold.

Duke Erris's cackle brought me back to the room. "He's not the First Cantor anymore," the old man said. He pointed to Quentis Maren. "The Inquisitors have the task of administrating the Law now. May they do a better job with it than the former holders of that office." He reached into his robes and drew out a rolled document fastened with an ostentatious ribbon. "This decree removes the Greatcoats from authority."

"May I see that, Your Grace?" Aline asked.

One of the old Duke's retainers took the decree and quickly ran it up the dais to hand it to Aline. She opened it, read it out loud, and then handed it to Valiana. There was a bit of fumbling, but once she had it securely in her hands, she tore the document in half and half again, and let the pieces drift down to the floor.

"What madness is this?" Erris demanded.

"It appears the Realm's Protector has elected to override your decree," Aline said. She looked at Quentis Maren and his fellow Inquisitors. "Your services won't be required, Cogneri."

Quentis locked eyes with me, as if asking what exactly I thought this would accomplish.

I shrugged amiably.

Duke Erris was trembling with rage. "There *is* no Realm's Protector. Look at her! She sits there, deaf, dumb, and blind behind an iron mask. She can't—"

Aline rose from her chair. "She can, Duke Erris, and she has." When Hadiermo started to rumble something about children overstepping their bounds, she stepped forward to the front of the dais and stood there alone, a girl of fourteen facing three of the most powerful men in Tristia. "We are done here, Your Graces. You have made your decisions, and we have made ours. Go back to your homes. Take your crowns with you, and enjoy them while you can."

"Careful, little girl," Hadiermo said, his usual barreling voice quiet, like a snake hissing before it strikes. "You live only so long as we allow it."

"Then I can't imagine that will be very long, Your Grace," she said, unmoved, "for my father ruled only five years before you took his life."

Erris coughed out a laugh. "And you think you'll sit his throne, child?" He motioned toward me. "Has this fool really convinced you that you'll *ever* take power?"

"The odds aren't good, I admit," Aline replied. "But you forget one thing, Duke Erris: people have been trying to kill me my entire life. They have all failed." She let her gaze fall on each of the three Dukes in turn. "Despite all your best efforts, it's just possible that I might surprise you all and sit the throne of Aramor one day soon. I suggest you keep that thought in mind when you call me *child*."

There was a brief moment of silence as they weighed her words, but Hadiermo, the Iron Duke, wasn't going to be cowed. "The hells for this," he said. "Make your threats, you little bitch. Were you a true warrior I would challenge you here and now."

Without missing a beat, she said, "Were *you* a true warrior, Duke Hadiermo, I might accept. Since neither of us appear suited to the task, take your leave of us." She turned to Pastien. "Unless you have further use of the Ducal Council, my Lord?"

It took a while for Pastien's tongue to come unstuck. "No . . . no further use, your Majest—I mean, My Lady."

I would have expected the Dukes to fume some more, perhaps make a few more threats, promise all kinds of retribution, but the truth was, these weren't stupid men; they'd said what they'd come to say and there was nothing left to discuss. The Dukes would leave Luth to fall, and hope we'd go with it. All of this had been a stage play, targeted at one man: Duke Jillard. He was the most likely to support us if we came through the next few days; we'd needed to show him that we weren't giving up.

"Good luck," he said as he walked by, a firm hand on the back of Tommer's collar. It actually sounded like he meant it.

Once the Dukes and their entourages had left, Quentis and his Inquisitors approached me. "We will remove ourselves from the palace for tonight," he said. He looked more than a little pained. "I want you to know that I wasn't aware of any plans to . . . I'm a man of the Law, Falcio. The Council of Clerics doesn't consult me on politics. I investigate what they tell me to investigate and I—"

His sincerity annoyed me. "You don't care that your Saints are being murdered to put your clerics in power? You don't care that the desecrated churches are—?"

"You're wrong, First Cantor. The men I work for . . . they may not be perfect, but they are devout. I truly believe they would never sully their souls with such acts."

"Sure," I said, "because no one's ever committed a crime in the name of the Gods."

He raised a hand. "We're not going to agree on this, Falcio. Out of respect for . . . well, out of respect, I'm pulling my men from the palace. We'll make camp a little ways down the road. But in a few hours, when the delegation comes, my Council is going to command me to help secure the palace, and I'm going to have no choice but to do so." He glanced down to the pistol at his side. "You're fast, Trattari, but you're not *that* fast."

It was strange. Against my better judgment I sort of liked Quentis Maren. We were both men of the Law, magistrates and duelists. We might not agree on everything, but we understood each other. So I really didn't hold any ill will toward him. I smiled and said, "You never know, Cogneri. Sometimes I surprise people."

CHAPTER FORTY-FIVE

THE REALM'S PROTECTOR

"Well, that was fun," Brasti said, descending from the gallery with his bow in hand. Kest, Mateo, Ethalia, and the Tailor followed him. We had decided that we probably didn't need to aggravate the situation by having more of us annoying the Dukes than necessary—also, it helps to keep a little surprise prepared, just in case things don't go to plan. "Anyone want to tell me what the point of that little performance was?"

I was about to answer when Aline cut me off. "It was a rehearsal," she said. Her eyes caught mine. "For all of you."

The tone of her voice took me unawares. "I don't understand. I thought we wanted to show Jillard that—"

Aline turned to Pastien. "Summon your chamberlain and the captain of your guards now, please."

The young Ducal Protector signaled for his page, who took off at a run for the door.

"What are you doing, sweetling?" the Tailor asked, looking not at all pleased.

Aline stepped down from the dais to stand in front of Kest. "What is the avertiere's weakness?" she asked.

He was surprised by the question. "In fencing, the avertiere's weakness is his reliance on the opponent trying to deflect the false attacks."

"Child," the Tailor said, "this isn't the time for—"

Aline took up an imaginary guard position against Kest, extending her right arm as though it held a sword. "And if his opponent doesn't parry? If he attacks instead?"

Kest shook his head. "It's not that simple: if you don't parry the attack"—he lunged with his left hand, touching her shoulder before she could react—"the avertiere will simply follow through and deliver the blow."

She reached out her other hand and held onto Kest's. "A sacrifice is made, but now you can no longer attack your true target, and I am free to counterattack."

"So long as you aren't dead," I said, not liking where this was going.

Aline returned to the dais and walked to where Valiana sat unmoving. She took one of her hands and helped her up. "Any attempt to permanently transform this country hinges on eliminating Valiana. She's the one who holds Tristia together."

"Sweetheart," Brasti said, taking a seat on the floor next to one of the pillars, "I know you look up to her, but—"

She cut him off. "Don't treat me like a child, Brasti Goodbow. It just makes you look like an idiot."

"She's right," Kest said slowly. "Not about Brasti being an idiot . . . well, perhaps that too, but mostly that Valiana's the one who's been building the relationships that have kept money flowing into Aramor and kept the Dukes from walking away from the Council. It's all been on her shoulders."

I looked over at this girl of barely twenty, standing a few feet away from me, trapped behind the mask. How could one young woman hold the weight of an entire nation on her shoulders? *With no help from you,* I realized bitterly. I'd been a selfish fool every step of the way, trying to prove the Greatcoats were still relevant, that *I* was still relevant, and all the while, our enemies had been plotting not against me or even Aline, but against Valiana, and through her, the entire country.

"Fine," Brasti said, "but she can't do the job now, so we need a new Realm's Protector."

Kest shook his head. "No, it's as I told you before, it doesn't work that way. The legal provisions in the *Regia Maniferecto De'egro* governing the appointment of a Realm's Protector are archaic. There's no mechanism for replacement, or succession, or anything else."

"So who's in charge then?" Tommer asked.

"I am," the Tailor said finally. "As the girl's grandmother, I am the only one who can stand as her regent while there is no Realm's Protector. That's a law older than the written word in this country."

"Hang on," Brasti said, getting to his feet. "Let me grab my bow again."

"My grandmother is right," Aline said. "There are going to be hard decisions that will have to be made and we can't afford dissension between us. Someone has to take charge if we are to be united."

The Tailor rose to her feet. "Wise girl," she said. "All right, here's—"

"Sit down," Aline said. She didn't wait for compliance, but instead spoke to all of us in a clear, steady voice. "I am the heir to the throne of Tristia. The Realm's Protector exists only to act in my stead. If she dies or cannot perform her duties, then by those ancient laws Kest was referring to, those powers revert to me." She glanced over at the Tailor. "Not to you, nor anyone else. To *me*."

"That's . . . one interpretation," Kest said.

"It's the only one that matters."

The doors to the throne room opened and the page returned with the palace chamberlain and the captain of the guards. Neither looked very comfortable. *It's probably hard to be cheerful when you know you're hours away from being attacked.* Pastien took two rolled decrees from his coat and handed one to each of the men awaiting him. "Captain Ciradoc, Chamberlain Matrist," he said. "As of now the Duchy of Luth is no longer sovereign, and thus it falls under the command of the Crown." He bowed to Aline. "The heir will give you your orders now."

The Chamberlain looked like he'd just choked on something. "But how can—?"

"Gentlemen, time is short," Aline said. "Captain Ciradoc, in a few hours the clerics and their Knights will arrive, fully intending on taking the palace. When they do . . ." She stopped and looked over at the rest of us before finishing, "You will let them."

"Wait, what?"

Aline gave a flick of her finger to silence me.

"You want us to lay down arms?" Ciradoc asked.

"More than that. You will place yourself and your men under the command of the clerics."

"I don't understand . . . are we to pretend—?"

"Don't pretend," Aline said. "Follow their orders. The people of this Duchy have already suffered enough chaos and confusion. The clerics are taking this palace. Make the transition as smooth as you can."

"The Viscounts and Margraves won't stand for this," Matrist said.

"Look around," Aline replied. "You'll find the palace in short supply of noblemen right now. Your job, Chamberlain, is to see to it anyone who needs to leave the palace can do so quickly. There might be some here to whom the Church won't take kindly, and it would be best they were gone before they decide to make use of the Inquisitors."

"Pardon my saying, My Lady," Ciradoc began, "but first among those would be yourselves."

Aline acknowledged the man's concern for her. "Don't worry about us, Captain. We'll be leaving in due course."

"Can I—? Some of my men could—"

"No, Captain. When the clerics arrive, I will depart with the dignity required of my station."

The captain looked uncertainly at the girl standing before him. "Excuse me for asking, but how?"

Aline smiled. "Through the front door, of course."

* * *

I managed to restrain myself until after the guardsman and the chamberlain had left, but then I shouted, "Have you lost your mind?"

Aline held herself very firm. "As of right now, First Cantor, I am taking on the duties of the Realm's Protector of Tristia. I need your support in this. Do the Greatcoats stand with me?"

I clenched my hands in frustration. Of all the problems I had to deal with, a teenage girl's naïve notions of how to run a country shouldn't have been one of them. Brasti, Kest, even Mateo would follow my orders. If I told them to ignore Aline and get her somewhere safe, lock her in until the danger was past, they'd do it. *After all, it's our job to protect her, even if it's from herself.*

I was about to speak when Valiana grabbed for my wrist. She took my hand and squeezed, and somehow I understood that she wanted me to trust Aline, a fourteen-year-old girl who was badly traumatized by the events of her young life. The sane, sensible thing to do would be to treat her that way—except that I'd thought the same of Valiana not long ago and she'd proved me wrong. *Maybe it's not enough to protect people,* I thought suddenly. *Maybe sometimes I have to trust them too.* "The Greatcoats stand with you," I said.

"Enough of this nonsense," the Tailor said, stepping up to the dais. She reached out a hand for her granddaughter. "Sweetling, I know you want to show you're brave, but this—"

"Silence," Aline said.

The command had been delivered with such force that it took me a moment to realize it wasn't Valiana speaking. Aline stood there, unflinching while the Tailor gave her a stare that I was absolutely convinced would stop a raging bear in its tracks, and I realized that Aline had probably been readying herself for this fight from the moment we'd entered the throne room.

"The laws don't exist for your convenience, Tailor. They weren't written to give you the means to exact your revenge on the world for all your grievances." Aline looked at each of us in turn. "You all think I'm a little girl, barely able to keep from falling apart at the seams." She stepped down from the dais and walked over to one of the tall windows that looked out to the courtyard. "Yesterday—yesterday that was true. Yesterday, I could afford to be a weak child who couldn't hold a sword properly and lived or died only by the whims of others. But today, when we know . . . we *know* the enemy seeks to use my weakness against us all? I can't afford to be that silly little girl anymore. So today I am Aline, daughter of Paelis, heir to the throne of Tristia, and until Valiana is free from that mask, I am also the Realm's Protector, and anyone who tries to dispute or ignore that fact will answer to me."

In tone, in style, in raw determination, it was like watching Valiana in action. *Valiana's been training her for this, for this moment, in case something happened.* Sometimes it took me a while to catch up.

Valiana squeezed my hand again, not seeking explanation of what was happening but more tenderly, and it suddenly occurred to me that *she* was trying to reassure *me.* I squeezed back, wishing I could say to her what was in my heart: *you are the woman fathers dream of bringing into the world.*

The Tailor and I looked at each other, two angry, broken creatures seeking only to protect Aline as we had failed to protect her father. Neither of us knew what to do next.

But at least we knew who was in charge.

For the next several minutes Aline proceeded to give us our orders in a whirl of words. This was her country now, for as many hours or days as she could hold it. She called for the rest of the palace staff, told them what was to come and instructed them on what they needed to do during the transition. I was amazed at how much she had learned in such a short time.

When she took Brasti aside and gave him his instructions, his eyes widened, and then he gave a smile. "For once someone gives me orders I like."

Shortly before dawn she ordered Kest to get Ethalia out of the palace; we'd all meet up later, a few miles outside the city. Mateo was sent through the servants' passage to the back of the palace with the bag of nightmist. The Tailor and Pastien went to pack up any vital documents that might be needed.

I was wondering what my last job in Luth might be when Aline announced, "I need you with me when I meet with the clerics."

"What for?"

"I might need you to intimidate them a little."

This is how it falls apart, I thought. *She believes I'm some grand hero who will chase away all her enemies with a stern glance.*

Seeing my hesitation, Aline said, "Of course I have doubts, Falcio, but I'm going to need you to have faith in me now."

Faith. The one thing I had never had much of. Even so, there was only one answer. "Whatever comes, I'll stand with you," I said.

She smiled faintly and returned to the endless preparations. There wasn't much I could contribute so I just waited until all her orders had been issued, then Aline joined me where I was sitting with my back against the wall at the far end of the dais.

"So what now?" I asked.

"Now we wait until the clerics arrive, and then we go out there to deal with them." She sat next to me and stretched out her legs. "It's all right, Falcio. It's just like Rijou during the Blood Week—all we have to do is fight our way out." She spoke with the perfect confidence of a duelist who has no idea what they're about to face.

Is she still Aline? I wondered. *Is she still the child broken by too much tragedy? If the rest is an act, a performance, how long will it hold?* In Rijou we'd faced Ganath Kalila and a city full of killers and thieves, men and women who would've traded Aline's life for a single black penny. That felt so long ago now. We'd accomplished so much, come so close—here we sat, in the middle of a Ducal Palace, on friendly ground.

"We were supposed to be safe here," I said.

Aline reached over and took my hand in hers. She closed her eyes and leaned her head against my shoulder. "Nowhere's safe, Falcio," she said sadly. "Haven't you figured that out yet?"

CHAPTER FORTY-SIX

THE DELEGATION

The hours slipped by unnoticed. Aline and I dozed off, leaning against each other like two vagrants snoozing against a tavern wall. At some point I heard shouting from outside and the door opened—some errant nobleman, probably demanding an audience with Pastien, had jostled his way past the guards. Whatever he'd expected to see probably wasn't Aline and me looking preposterous slumped together, having a nap on the floor. I wondered briefly if he'd been embarrassed, then went back to sleep.

I awoke some time later to a hand shaking me. "The clerics are here," Captain Ciradoc said. He really didn't look very happy. "Lady Aline, are you sure you won't let me—?"

"You have your orders, Captain: just you, and the men at the gate."

I rubbed at my eyes and then saw Aline holding a silver platter at arm's length, using it as a mirror. "This isn't quite the correct attire for welcoming dignitaries," she said, smoothing her dress, "but it's formal enough not to ruffle too many feathers."

"Ha!" I pushed myself to my feet, ignoring my aching joints. "Since most of the clerics I've met wore grubby robes so worn I was

lucky not to find myself greeting their private parts, I don't imagine we need worry too much about whether we're sporting rabbit
instead of ermine."

It turned out that I was quite wrong: the three clerics who awaited
us outside the palace gates looked as regal as Kings, their richly colored silk and brocade robes flapping in the breeze like the proud
flags of a conquering nation. They were made even more magnificent set against the field of spotless white tabards on the hundred
Knights standing behind them. The two hundred-odd pilgrims
in the courtyard looked upon them in awe. Even Quentis and his
Inquisitors had given their gray leather coats a bit of a polish. *Enjoy
your pretty clothes while you can, friend.*

Aline had cautioned me to remain calm and dignified, and I put
every effort to that endeavor, though the white tabards were filling
me with fury. *I am so sick of Knights,* I thought. *They're at the center
of every fucking problem this country ever has.*

"Open the gate, Captain," Aline commanded Ciradoc.

The man looked askance at the force assembled outside and tried
again to dissuade her, but she stopped him, saying, "Shush, Captain.
I won't be rude to our guests."

He gave the order unhappily, and the guards worked the winch
and raised the middle gate. The clerics were about to walk in when
Aline stepped out in front of them. "Welcome to the Ducal Palace
of Luth, Venerati," she said, respectfully. "I am—"

Before she could finish her sentence, a servant in trim coat and
matching trousers standing next to the clerics handed Aline a rolled-
up piece of parchment.

As she unfurled the document I was almost overwhelmed by
the grandeur of the thing: the thick, deeply textured material
of the sort used by Kings, not clerics. I had some difficulty reading
the calligraphy, Old Tristian inscribed with a rich black ink outlined
in gold. A wax seal at the bottom displayed an emblem I had never
seen before: nine tiny circles arranged in three lines, above which
shone six stars.

Nine Duchies under six Gods? The new religion looks a lot like the old one.

"Do you require help reading the document?" the first cleric asked, and it took me a moment to recognize him as Obladias, the priest from the martyrium. He'd been wearing heavily patched gray robes the last time we'd met; he'd apparently decided that silk robes in the rich crimson of the God Purgeize suited him better. *Are you the enemy?* I wondered. *Are you the man who set this in motion?* I felt a powerful urge to draw my rapier and end him then and there. *Just in case.* Instead I said, "This document is very pretty, but I note it lacks a signature."

The second of the three clerics, a heavyset man with Northern features sporting the more familiar greens of the God Argentus, or Coin, stepped forward, head bowed a little and eyes down. "It's . . . If you look at the first line, you'll see it says, *Voce omnius cericis en tatem,* which in the archaic form of Old Tristian means—"

"We aren't here to teach oafs and children how to read, Buther," Obladias said.

He seemed like such a humble fellow, the first time I met him. Not that I bought it . . .

"Forgive me, Obladias, I only meant—"

"The line reads, 'In the united voice of all clerics,'" Aline said clearly, and I couldn't quite stop myself from looking at her in wonder. Other than Kest I didn't know many people who could read even the simplified form of Old Tristian, never mind the archaic.

She smiled at me. "What was it you thought I did in my lessons, Falcio?" She turned back to the document and glanced through the rest of it before unceremoniously rolling it back up and handing it off to Captain Ciradoc. "Your scribe would benefit from lessons in verb conjugation. The way he's written the section on 'providing unto the faithful a just and Godly rule' is in the past perfect tense, suggesting such service has already been rendered." She looked up at Obladias. "Unless that was your intent, Venerati? If so, I thank you for the souvenir and wish you a pleasant journey on your return home."

Obladias looked neither impressed nor amused, but before he could speak, the third cleric, in the orange robes of the disciples of the God of Craft, gave a laugh and stepped forward. "Hello, My Lady. My name is Galbea. Please forgive our poor choice of scribe—events have moved rather quickly, and I'm afraid we chose a skillful hand over accurate grammar." He gave Aline a flicker of a smile that made the wrinkles on his forehead crinkle together. "The lettering is pretty, though, don't you think?" He was of the same age as the other two men, but the harder life of a village cleric was written all over his face.

"I wonder, Venerati," Aline said innocently, "have you come to declare war on Tristia's Crown?"

Both Galbea and Buther looked slightly aghast, but Obladias fully embraced the arrogance of a man who'd dedicated his soul to the God of War. "Child, I ask again: are you having difficulty reading the words on the page? It is a message of *peace*—we are here to lend our support to this troubled Duchy in its hour of need."

Aline didn't return his condescending smile. The first phase of the game was apparently over. "I understood every word on the page, Venerati, just as I recognize the full meaning and intent of your choice of escort. By what right do three clerics and a band of thugs in mail seek to overthrow one of our Duchies?"

Obladias bridled at that. "It is hardly *your* Duchy, little miss, now is it? I have a great deal of trouble imagining that the Kings of old intended this palace to be a girl's plaything."

"Obladias . . ." Buther said, horrified. He was looking at me.

I tried to calm myself and match Aline's expression; her face betrayed nothing, and yet I could sense a subtle gleam of satisfaction in her: she had made the cleric in red reveal something of himself—something she could use.

Damn it, why is even a fourteen-year-old girl better at politics than I am? I wondered, but this wasn't the time to ponder that further, for Coin's cleric was saying apologetically, "The Knights are for the protection of the faithful, My Lady." He motioned very slightly to the crowds assembled outside the palace. "There have been tales of clerics being murdered, and we have seen with our own eyes some of Tristia's oldest churches destroyed."

"None of which," interrupted Obladias, "is as despicable as the murder of Saints." He clenched his fist and I could see he was badly wishing for something to bang it against. "The Saints! How much more desecration will the Trattari commit before they are brought to heel?"

"Now, Obladias—" the priest in orange began.

"That man," the cleric in red shouted, jabbing a finger at me as if lightning might spark out of it, "that *man* has been responsible for the deaths of two Saints that we know of, and we now strongly suspect he was also responsible for the deaths of Birgid-who-weeps-rivers— and who knows *how many* more!"

I knew this was all going to be my fault somehow. "Is that how you're going to sell this?" I asked. "You accuse the Greatcoats of murdering Saints? Because, in my defense, Venerati, it was my friend Kest who killed Caveil-whose-blade-cuts-water. I just did away with Shuran-whose-Sainthood-didn't-last-very-long."

"Of course you bring up Kest, the *apostate*," Obladias scoffed. "He who spat in the face of the Gods' gift—while *you*"—again, he pointed at me, and this time I imagined a ball of flame—"this one murdered a chosen vessel, the new Saint of Swords—"

"He wasn't exactly your best Saint," I pointed out, but Aline took control of the conversation once again.

"The man Shuran, Venerati, was preparing to take Tristia for himself, with a thousand Knights in black tabards at his back. Speak softly, Venerati, for you have brought only a hundred with you." She smiled then. "Though I will admit that their tabards are prettier."

The Knights rumbled as if they wanted to kill her, but I could have kissed her. *And there's the reason why no one ever asks you to handle diplomacy, idiot.*

Aline stepped forward and pushed past the three clerics to face the assembled Knights. "Which one of you commands?" she asked.

Obladias spoke up from behind her. "They are the *Fideri*, girl. They are Church Knights, commanded by the Gods themselves."

"Really?" I asked, my voice light but my hand ready in case some-one made a move on Aline. "Do the Gods speak to them very often? If not, I expect they get a bit confused when it's time to fight."

One of the Knights stepped forward, a little too close to Aline for my liking, and towering over her, snarled, "Should we choose to do battle, you will see how smoothly we function."

I could see Aline's hands shaking, but she betrayed none of her fear when she spoke. "Excellent," she said. "Since you appear to speak for them, I will give you my instructions, and you can relay them to the others."

"Don't presume to give me orders, girl"—he turned to his men and laughed—"unless it is in your bedroom tonight!"

Okay, time for a different diplomacy. My rapier was drawn and I had the tip at the man's neck. "I'm going to consecrate that fuck-ing tabard of yours in bright red if you don't take a step back right now."

The Knights all reached for their weapons as I heard Quentis say, "Falcio, don't." I didn't bother to look at him; I was fairly sure his pistol was aimed at me.

"Please, gentlemen," Galbea, the monk in orange, said. "Let this not descend into violence." He motioned to the Knights. "Do as the Greatcoat says. We came here in peace."

Without looking back at me, Aline raised her hand, commanding us all to stand down. If I didn't obey her, I would be undermining her in front of the clerics.

I sheathed my weapon. The Knights didn't.

Obladias decided he'd won. To Aline he said, "This has been a pleasant diversion but there is work to be done now. You and the Trattari will be taken into custody pending a trial." He looked past us to Captain Ciradoc. "Your men will lay down their arms now."

The captain, looking very much as if he had a number of pre-ferred uses for his weapon at that moment, unsheathed his sword and laid it on the ground before kneeling. "The palace is yours."

"You see, Venerati," Aline said, "there is no need for conflict between us. You came for the Duchy and now you may have it." She made a show of beginning to walk toward the road leading away from the palace.

"Stop!" Obladias called out, and two Knights stepped in front of Aline. My fingers were twitching, and I had to fight to keep from drawing my blade again. *Wait*, I told myself. *Follow the plan.*

Aline's hands were shaking so badly now that she held them behind her back, fingers interlinked. She looked up at the Knights. "I wonder, Sir Knights, have you ever made a study of archery?"

"What is this foolishness?" Obladias asked.

Aline went on, "Would you like to see my bow?" She stepped back and then held out her left fist as if it held a bow. "I haven't been practicing lately, but it's still quite accurate."

The leader of the Knights snorted. "What's this, then? Has someone given you an imaginary bow to go with your imaginary crown, little girl?"

Aline laughed at the joke, then she said. "Sometimes imagination can be a powerful weapon, Sir Knight."

"Enough," Obladias said. "Take the mad creature inside."

One of the Knights reached for her but she stepped back and drew back her right arm, pulling at empty air. "Ah, ah, ah. I'm afraid I must warn you—"

The Knight stepped forward again, Aline's right hand opened and suddenly the shaft of a two-foot long ironwood arrow was piercing the armor on the Knight's thigh. He fell, screaming, to the ground. The Knight next to him raised his weapon; Aline turned to him and again drew back her string, and once again an arrow appeared, this one in the man's shoulder.

"That's odd," she said. "Those don't look like imaginary arrows, do they?"

Everyone's eyes went up to the ramparts. There sat Brasti, swinging his legs and playing with the arrows—dozens and dozens of them—that were lying next to him.

"Don't mind him," Aline said. "That's just my archery instructor, Brasti. He gave me this bow. I know it doesn't look like much, but he promised me it would never miss." She turned and faced the other Knights. "You know, there are so many of you all packed close together—I don't think it's a very big challenge."

Several of them started backing up, until their leader shouted to them to close ranks. Some had shields, some didn't. I counted enough crossbows among them that even with the problem of height, one of them would be able to kill Brasti soon enough. Obladias knew it too. "Play that little trick again and you'll be dead," he warned.

"Oh, very well—but I have plenty of other tricks, Venerati. For example, I do believe I can make fog."

At the signal Mateo Tiller, dressed as a pilgrim, stepped from the crowd and dropped a bucket of water on a black and gray patch of dirt where Quentis and his Inquisitors stood. The nightmist sizzled and an instant later the thick gray smoke filled the air. "Damn it all," Quentis said, holstering his pistol. "Draw your maces," he told his men. "Pistols won't fire in the nightmist."

Obladias coughed, but got himself under control. "There are more than enough of us to deal with you and your archer, girl. You won't escape this way." Already his words sounded distant, distorted by the effects of the nightmist.

"Perhaps," Aline conceded. She looked thoughtfully up at him. "But I suspect my aim is so good that even if I die, you'll lose an awful lot of your Knights." She looked out at the pilgrims staring at us. "Which is odd, don't you think? If the Gods truly supported your cause, surely they would make it harder for me to hit you with my imaginary arrows."

Despite the precariousness of our situation, I nearly laughed. *She's pulling a God's Line on them,* I thought proudly. It made sense, after all: if the clerics really did represent the will of the Gods, then surely one girl and a couple of Greatcoats shouldn't be able to kill a dozen or so of their chosen Knights? Aline held out her left fist again and mimed drawing another arrow. Her next words were spoken with deadly calm. "We planted a thousand black dahlias in the gardens of Castle Aramor a few months ago. I do believe that lilies would go better in this courtyard."

The leader of the Knights showed no signs of fear as he waved at the thick gray mist with a gauntleted fist. "You had a thousand archers when Shuran's troops attacked—"

"A thousand?" Brasti interrupted, shouting down at us, "A *thousand*? I had less than a hundred archers with me, you ass!"

Buther, his face now as green as his robes, tried to intervene. "I think we should all calm down, My Lady. You must understand—"

"No, Venerati," she said loudly, her words overpowering him. She might not have a deep voice, or one that could carry, but there was no denying the force of her next words. "Through treachery and betrayal you have come for this place, and if I resist you, innocent people will die. So you may have the palace, but know that it is only because I *choose* to give it to you."

She took a step toward the Knights. Their leader barked out, "Crossbows!" and a clump of men on the right flank raised their weapons and aimed the bolts at Aline. "Do you think you can fire your imaginary bow fast enough to stop them all, little—"

His words were cut off by a scream, strange and distant in the nightmist but whose source I could already see came from among the crossbowmen. The others turned, trying to see who had killed their fellow, then another shouted in pain and stumbled back, falling into the others. In the thickening fog they couldn't spot the attacker, who was weaving in and out of their midst.

"You have met the King's Heart and you have met the King's Arrow," Aline said to the leader of the Knights, then paused to wink at me. "Best that none of you try the King's Patience."

Darriana must have returned last night, and Aline ordered her to stay hidden for precisely this purpose. I tried to smile back before she turned away, but I couldn't: I was overwhelmed. Whatever these men had expected—whatever *I* had expected—Aline was something entirely different. Valiana had trained her these past months, she had nurtured her and helped her to find the strength I hadn't believed she truly had.

"These names you bandy about are those your father gave to *his* Greatcoats," Obladias said, his lips pulled thin as he spoke. "Your father's stature, borrowed by an insolent child long overdue a whipping."

Say the word, you bastard. Say the word and you'll be the first to see whether the Gods are real or just devices you and your kind use to fill your pockets.

There was a moment when I thought perhaps Obladias would command the Knights to attack, or one of Quentis's Inquisitors would lose their patience, or, hells, maybe Brasti would just fire again, by mistake. But no one broke the stillness. In the thickening mist Obladias's face was starting to take on the hue of his robes, but after a few moments he growled, "Go. Flee this place—but know that the Gods are not done with you."

"Enjoy the palace," Aline replied. "Take care not to damage anything, for there will be a full accounting upon my return." With that she walked past the Knights and through the crowd of pilgrims as casually as a young girl out for an afternoon stroll.

CHAPTER FORTY-SEVEN
THE HYMN

Once Aline and I were far enough down the road that I had stopped looking behind us, I said, "You didn't order the captain of the guards to stand his men down in order to keep them safe. You did it to make us look weak."

"I did," she admitted, "but it's more than that. When the clerics see palace guards, they see men who can be turned to their cause by money or by force."

"But not the Greatcoats," I said.

"Not the Greatcoats."

I shook my head in wonder. "Those clerics had no idea who they were dealing with," I said. *Nor did I, apparently.*

I expected Aline to look pleased, but she wasn't. She stopped walking and when she looked at me, her eyes were very far away. "Falcio, I need you to listen to me now. Those men, those clerics, they're absolutely right. They know exactly who and what they're dealing with."

"I thought—" She held up a hand and I shut up.

"In a few hours one of them will be seated on the throne of Luth. In a few days Tristia will have a Prelate ruling a Duchy for the first time in six hundred years. The Dukes are wrong to think it won't spread. The Church has money, and they'll use it make things better for the common folk—for a short while at least. They'll use it to bribe noblemen around the country, and things will begin to change really quickly, and soon the country—"

"—the Dukes would never allow it," I said forcefully, but she was shaking her head.

"The Dukes won't last the year. The lesser nobles are all sick of being stepped on by the Dukes; the clerics will offer the Viscounts and Margraves and Lords greater power and control in exchange for fealty to the Church, and they'll get it. Falcio, all of this? It's just a delaying tactic on my part, to show the clerics and their Knights that they should be afraid of moving too quickly. It's what Valiana would have done: make time so we can find a different way around the problem facing us."

"We have lot of problems, sweetheart. Which specific one are you talking about?"

She took in a breath, and I realized I'd really irritated her. Before I could apologize, she said, "Falcio, what I'm about to say to you isn't a request, it's an order. We need something beyond a few brave souls with swords, so you, Kest, and Brasti are going to take Ethalia to find a functioning sanctuary so that she can come into her power. We need that power, now."

That's simple enough, I thought. *Just tell me to abandon you here as the snakes begin to slither around the nest. I don't fucking think so.* "I'm not sure if anyone's told you this yet, but the Greatcoats don't actually follow the orders of the monarch."

"You followed my father's commands," she said, accusingly.

"We liked to think of them more as strongly-worded suggestions." I raised my hands, not wanting to argue. "Look, it's a big country, and we don't even know if there is an undesecrated sanctuary left—I wouldn't have the first idea where to look."

A mocking voice answered, "When did a Trattari ever know where to go without a Bardatti sending him?" Rhyleis, the musician I'd met at the tavern in Baern, was striding toward us. The cocky smile on her face was the perfect match to the swagger of her step.

"I spoke to Rhyleis earlier," Aline told me, "and now I want you to listen to her."

"I do indeed have a tune for you, First Cantor." She stopped in front of me and reached up with her index finger to trace a line along my jaw. "Ah, but poor Falcio. You look lovelorn. Are you still chasing after the Saint of Mercy, calling down the moon itself in the hope that it will shine favor upon your desire? Perhaps you should find a companion better suited to your ardor." She punctuated the last word with a wink.

I was starting to get mildly annoyed with the way everyone felt so comfortable discussing my relationships. "Lady, did you come with information, or are you asking me out on a date?"

Rhyleis was suddenly downcast, her expression almost heartbreaking in its sincerity, as if, here and now, for the very first time, someone had shattered her heart. Seeing that I wasn't entirely convinced, she seamlessly shifted to a haughtier and substantially more genuine stance. "You know, in days past when a Bardatti came bearing news, men and women greater than you would fall to their knees begging to hear it sung." She held out a slim hand as if examining it. "Rings and chains of gold and silver would have been thrust upon me, in those better days."

"And yet all you're going to get from me is a thank-you."

She smiled, for the first time looking normal; a moment of her life that was not a performance. "That will have to suffice, then. Very well, listen as I play you my little tune."

I looked back up the road at the Duchy that we had just abandoned to the Church, where the Inquisitors would soon be enforcing the new laws that Obladias and his tame clerics were no doubt busy writing. The Saints were dropping like flies, the Greatcoats were nowhere to be found, and somewhere out there an opponent who'd planned all of this so carefully was outmatching us at every turn. Even from here I could hear the pilgrims united in song that sounded both exultant and whiny.

"Please don't tell me you're really going to sing it for me," I said, turning back to Rhyleis, "because I think that might just be the thing that finally makes me slit my own throat."

"Silly magistrate," she chided me. "That's the news, right there— you need to listen for it."

"Rhyleis, that's enough," Aline said, apparently done with watching us fence. "Tell him."

The musician gave a very impertinent rendition of a bow and said, "Alas, My Lady, the Bardatti do not do the bidding of Queens and Kings."

Aline looked up at me. "Is there anyone in this country who does? Because I'm starting to wonder precisely what power a monarch is supposed to wield."

Rhyleis gave a second bow, and this one was a lot more sincere. "That, My Lady, is an excellent question for an heir to the throne to ask." She gestured up the road to the palace, to the singing pilgrims. "Do you like the song, Falcio?"

As a general rule, I dislike hymns; they always sound a bit pretentious, and you can't dance to them. But I was noticing something odd about this one. Tristian hymns are sung in harmony, with each line a different plea to the Gods, but this one had a strange countermelody; I hadn't consciously noticed it at first, but now it really stuck out.

Rhyleis had been watching my face. "I see you have something of an ear," she said approvingly, as if that suddenly made me more attractive. "Do you know what it's saying?"

Aline interrupted the show again. "You know he doesn't, so stop showing off and tell us."

"The first pair of notes are the Bardatti word for 'found,'" Rhyleis replied, relenting. "Nehra sent us searching for undescecrated sanctuaries, so that means one of us has found one. Listen: that descending fourth, up a fifth, then down a sixth? That's the Condate of Verderen."

I struggled to hear what she was talking about. "You can name every March and Condate in the country from a sequence of notes?"

"More the sequence of intervals between the notes, actually, but yes. We can specify all the way down to an individual estate if we want to, but it's hard to bury that inside a song without using instrumental lines."

Aline was tilting her head as she too, listened for the hidden message in the middle harmony line. "So are you saying there are Bardatti singing among the pilgrims?"

Rhyleis laughed at that. "Of course not! How would we ever get anything done if we had to go around masquerading as pilgrims? No, My Lady, it's much simpler than that: one of us constructs the melody, then sings it a few times here or there, wherever the pilgrims are to be found. They hear it and without even realizing, pick up the tune. It spreads quickly when we compose it properly—I could tell you which tavern a drunk was patronizing by the way he honks along to 'The Horse and the Straw.'"

"You can really do that?" Aline asked. "You can change a few notes in a song and others will pick it up and sing it without even realizing it?"

"I'm a Bardatti," Rhyleis replied, as if that answered everything. "But if you want to hear something really impressive, get Nehra to show you how she can make redlarks spread a tune through the skies."

It bothered me no end that orders like the Bardatti and the Cogneri had managed to preserve so much of their lore, while we Trattari had to pretty much make it up as we went along. *And I still don't like the name, even though I now know it's not the insult people believe it to be.*

"How do we know the information is correct?" I asked. "You want me to race off to the middle of Domaris on the basis of a few notes in a hymn to the Gods?"

"Our new Prelate is an impressive figure, don't you think?" Rhyleis replied, ignoring my question. "Such a strong voice. I find the deep roll of his consonants particularly fascinating."

It took me a moment to figure out what she was getting at. "He's from *Domaris*?"

"Anyone who isn't deaf could tell you he's from Domaris, Falcio. I'm telling you he's from *Verderen*. The rise in his vowels might be subtle, but it's a dead giveaway."

Back when he was pretending to be a humble monk, Obladias had told me some inane story about a man from his estates losing faith in the Gods after the death of his family. If he really was from Verderen, that might well be where this started—and where they kept the one remaining sanctuary. *It's thin evidence,* I thought. *Nothing but speculation, rumor, conjecture.*

Aline could see the look on my face. "Falcio, you're going to take Kest and Brasti, and the three of you are going to find a way to get Lady Ethalia into the Condate of Verderen. You're going to find a way to get her into that sanctuary and help her find the strength of her Sainthood. If she can stop the madness that's holding Valiana, then we might have a chance."

"But—"

She gave Rhyleis a meaningful look, and the Bardatti took the hint and sauntered down the road for a bit. "It has to be now, Falcio," Aline said, looking back at the crowds outside the Palace of Luth. "It's our only hope: that there's a reason why the enemy fears her so much."

"I'm not leaving you alone and defenseless," I said, with as much finality as I could muster. "Who's going to watch out for you and Valiana the next time—"

"I will," Darriana said, stepping out from the trees lining the sides the road.

Aline looked annoyed. "I specifically asked you *not* to spy on us, Darriana."

"And I ignored that request." She locked eyes with me. "Understand?" The message was as clear as it was simple: Darriana wasn't afraid to ignore royal commands. She'd do whatever it took to keep Aline and Valiana safe. I nodded once by way of reply, and Darri left us.

She glared daggers at me for a moment, then sighed. "As you can see, there's not much danger of me being left unprotected. I'll have the Tailor and Mateo too."

"Don't forget Tommer," I said. "He's probably slipped his father's leash by now. I'll bet he's already heading back this way."

I'd meant it sarcastically, but Aline gave a smile. "He loves me, or at any rate he thinks he does." She sounded like a woman of twenty speaking about an eight-year-old's first crush, not as a girl of fourteen, barely older.

"What happened to the half-crazed girl who pulled out her hair and couldn't last another day?" I wondered aloud.

Aline reached out and took my hand, then pressed it against her cheek. "That girl is hanging on by a thread, Falcio, trying to pretend she can hold the country together, though we both know it isn't true."

I didn't know what to do or say; Aline had just given voice to my deepest fears.

"I'm sorry," she said, "but I need you to know the truth. I have to keep up the act for the others—they need someone to believe in right now, but you . . ."

Now it was me reassuring her. "You've come a long way, Aline, you just need time for the Dukes to see that you—"

"I'll never get the time I need. There's only one person who can save this country and she's trapped behind a mask of iron. You need to find a way to save Valiana before we're all brought to ruin."

CHAPTER FORTY-EIGHT

THE WHIPPING BOY

I was the last one let in on the plan, which made sense, since I never would have agreed to it if I'd known about it first. It didn't help that my damned Inquisitor's coat itched like it was lined with tiny little demons scratching at my skin.

"Do you suppose it's intentional?" Kest asked, tugging at the stiff collar and noting the way I kept scratching the back of my wrist where the cuff was rubbing against it.

"How so?"

"Perhaps the irritation is a form of privation, to make the Cogneri resistant to secular temptations."

Brasti snorted. "Those sons of bitches we got the coats from seemed distinctly unsaintly to me."

We hadn't set out to confront the Inquisitors—in fact, we'd spent a good deal of time discussing how we might sneak into Domaris without having to deal with them at all—then we came across four of them outside a small church brutalizing a congregation of worshippers of the Goddess of Love. The Inquisitors had chosen a particularly demeaning form of punishment to inflict upon them.

"I still don't understand why I have to parade around with this useless device," Brasti went on, spinning the wheel lock around his finger by its trigger guard.

"Inquisitors don't carry bows," I said. "And stop playing with the damned thing. If you shoot yourself in the foot you might drop the pistol and break it. We're going to need it soon enough."

"Have I mentioned how much I hate your plan, by the way? Why couldn't we—?" He stopped, looking down the road. "Saint Zaghev's balls—"

We halted our horses before the oncoming horde of weary travelers. The shuffling of their feet along the dusty road kicked up such a cloud that it was hard to make out their numbers.

"How many?" I asked, trying to wipe the dust from my eyes.

"Must be a hundred of the poor bastards."

Kest stood up in the stirrups and surveyed the mass. "Closer to a hundred and forty."

Neither number made me comfortable. Today was our sixth day riding the northern roads, the second since we'd crossed from Aramor into Domaris. Every day we encountered pilgrims, a few here, a few there, sometimes as many as a dozen together: little flocks of determined men and women, their bellies empty, extending shaking hands toward us as we rode by, hoping we might drop some morsels of food. We gave what we could for the first few days, but after that, necessity reined in our charity. Those we encountered never complained or cajoled or threatened; more often, seeing our gray Inquisitors' garb, they praised us as we past.

"They're afraid," Ethalia said, tired eyes staring into the cloud of dust and dirt. "They're drowning in fear." Now that we'd left the Palace of Luth the fever was worse than ever. The paleness of her skin accentuated how tightly it was stretched against the bones of her face. She shivered during the day, even under the noon sun; at night I watched the sweat drip down her face and dampen her blankets. Always I sought for something to say or do that might ease her suffering, but the kindest thing I could do was to keep my distance.

"They're getting close," Kest said, his voice soft, as if that might somehow lessen the insult of what had to come next.

"I'm so sorry," I said to Ethalia. "You need to put the hood back on, and the bonds."

She nodded and reached down to the gray linen hood tied to the front of her saddle. She slipped it over her head and then placed her other hand back in the iron handcuffs dangling from one wrist. Now she looked every bit the heretic being brought to trial by three Inquisitors. I reached back and took her reins so that I could lead her past the crowds, all the while hating myself, and the world along with me.

We kept the horses to a walk, not wanting to look too eager to get by, but the crowds parted easily for us, bowing their heads as we went by, holding out their hands in case we had anything to give them.

"Falcio," Brasti said. His voice was low and even, immediately catching my attention, as he pointed to a bend further down the road. Several men were standing around a tree.

"What's going on up there?" I asked, my vision not being as good as his.

The crack of a whip filled the air, followed by a scream, and I was leaning forward in the saddle, trying to see what was happening, when a moan from behind me made me turn to see Ethalia leaning heavily to one side. She was barely keeping herself in the saddle.

"What's wrong?" I asked her.

"They're beating the hells out of some boy tied to a tree, from what I can see," Brasti said, but my attention was still on Ethalia, who was getting worse the closer we got.

"Is it the boy's pain?" I asked urgently. "Is it—?"

"That," she said, her words muffled by the gray hood, "but more the enjoyment of the men hurting him. The emptiness in them, the lack of—"

"The lack of mercy," I said, remembering my first encounter with Saint Birgid. *I've called out to you,* she'd said. *Always when the victory was won but before the final blow was struck.* Was that what repelled Ethalia—not the *necessity* of violence in my life, but my inability to stop when the fight was done?

Whether from my words or my thoughts, Ethalia nodded.

"Here," I said to Kest, handing him her reins. "Stay with Ethalia; we'll go ahead."

"Falcio, if you interfere . . ."

"If I don't interfere, Ethalia's going to be screaming by the time we get there, and that's going to raise even more questions."

He held my gaze for a moment, then said, "I know, but I would urge you to be a little . . ."

"Subtle?" I asked, and he nodded, his forehead furrowing and making him look a nervous mother about to send her child into the city alone for the first time. I found it oddly funny.

"I can be subtle," I said, kicking my horse into a slow trot through the crowds of pilgrims. "I'm the very Saint of Subtlety."

The big man's head snapped back as my fist collided with his mouth and the whip fell out of his hand as he stumbled back into his friends. The one who caught him saw the look on my face and promptly let go of him, watching helplessly as he slid to the ground.

"This is subtle?" Brasti whispered from just behind me, but I didn't bother replying. This was as subtle as the situation allowed. Three men had been taking turns whipping the boy, whose back was now as bloody as if he wore a scarlet cloak. I'd told the man to stop what he was doing, and he told me to go and fuck myself—I'd been about to give him a second chance when I remembered that we were disguised as Inquisitors. I'd never heard of an Inquisitor taking kindly to an insult, so I hit him.

A sharp pain in my right hand caught my attention and I held it up and saw something small and yellow protruding from the skin of my index finger. It was one of the whipmaster's teeth.

Okay, so maybe I didn't need to hit him quite that hard.

The man was struggling to get up without any noticeable help from his friends. Once he'd gotten his feet back under him, the first thing he did was run his fingers through his long, unkempt black hair. I thought it an odd gesture, but felt it would be impolite to comment.

"You lousy son of a bitch," he said.

I sighed, then punched him in the face again.

To his credit he stayed on his feet this time, shaking his head like a bull preparing to charge.

"Thank me," I said, my voice cold and made colder by the imperious accent I'd taken on. Inquisitors, from what I understood, were drawn mostly from noble families.

"Thank you? You stupid—"

I held up a finger, so close to his face he could have reached out and broken it. "Thank me."

"For what?" he asked, defiance slipping from his tone as he noticed his friends backing away. Some of the pilgrims shuffling by us were slowing to watch what was happening.

"For saving your life," I replied. "I instructed you to stop whipping that boy and you failed to comply. Your choices now are to walk away or, if you prefer, I will put you to the trial and see how pure runs your soul."

He looked from me to Brasti and back. "I—I was just doing what the other one said . . ."

"The other what?" I asked, with as much lack of interest as I could muster.

One of the man's friends spoke up. "The other Inquisitor," he said, and pointed behind me to a man in a gray coat much like mine— although I suspected his was earned the more traditional way— walking toward me. He had several white-tabarded Knights on foot alongside.

"Hells," Brasti said, thankfully low enough that I doubted anyone else had heard him.

Blind fool, I cursed myself. *You never checked to see if there were more than just pilgrims and priests in the crowd.*

The Inquisitor stopped less than two feet in front of me. He offered no greetings nor asked any questions, just stared into my eyes.

He's testing me. I'd feared something like this might happen. We knew little about the Inquisitors—they served and answered to the Church, so they had never been of much interest to the Greatcoats.

I didn't have the slightest clue about their rituals or protocols, so the next few minutes were going to be all guesswork and bluff.

I kept my eyes on his, but took note of his posture, the tension in his mouth. Was he waiting for me to speak, or to see if he should do so first? The first speaker perhaps had to be of higher rank. I saw no insignia on his clothes—I hadn't seen signs of status on any Inquisitor save for Quentis—but the way this man was watching me told me that just because they didn't wear any special markings on their clothes didn't mean there wasn't a hierarchy.

I caught a tiny movement in the man's mouth just as his eyes narrowed. He was looking more certain than when he'd first arrived. *He wants to speak first—which means the higher rank controls the conversation.*

I waited until he opened his mouth and immediately cut him off. "Silence," I said.

His eyes widened, and the Knights in white tabards beside him tensed.

Shit. I got it wrong. I let my hand drift toward the sword at my side, but the Inquisitor didn't notice. He was bowing his head low.

Oh thank you, Saint whoever-the-hells-deals-with-this-stuff.

I caught the gaze of one of the Knights behind him and stared at him until he knelt down. His fellows followed suit.

"You gave this man leave to beat this boy?"

The Inquisitor looked up. "The child is a heretic."

"And his heresy?"

"He invoked the Saints."

Behind me, Brasti said, "Since when does—"

I held up a hand to cut him off, but too late, unfortunately.

The Inquisitor rose to his feet. "Forgive me, Cogneri," he said, not looking apologetic in the least, "but I'm afraid I must ask your name and rank."

I decided to ignore the question and try to make the best of what Brasti had blurted. "Since when does an Inquisitor delegate the punishment of heresies to others?" I asked.

"I . . . appointed these men as *Servanti* to complete the trial." Then he added, "As is my right."

That pause, that tiny, beautiful pause almost made me want to sing. I had no clue how any of this was supposed to work, but I know when a man thinks he's been caught. I looked around at the three men, rough bully-boys all. "You felt the Gods' work could be left to such as these." I made sure it didn't come out as a question.

The Inquisitor looked a little pale now. "We . . ." He looked around at the Knights by his side, who were very focused on counting every pebble on the road. "I felt I could not delay our journey. My instructions were—"

I cut him off with a wave of my hand. "Leave us."

"What about the boy?"

Shit. Good question.

I looked over at the child. He couldn't have been more than nine or ten years old, and mercifully he was unconscious, most likely from terror and exhaustion. "You've made a mockery of the sentence," I said. "A beating by curs such as those you chose for your Servanti will have done *nothing* to purify him. He'll have to die now, by my hand, delaying my own mission, which I assure you is considerably more important than herding pilgrims."

For just a moment, the Inquisitor looked as if he might turn and begin the long march with the others. Then he paused and said, "Forgive me, but my orders came from one *above*."

One above. Okay, so they don't say the names of superiors unless they have to.

The Inquisitor went on, "He will demand the *name* of the one who . . . *corrected* . . . my verdict."

I looked at him. The Knights had evidently decided they no longer needed to concern themselves with the pebbles on the ground and were now staring straight at me.

Now he's wondering if I'm a higher rank than his superior—hells! Why does everything *to do with religion have to be so damned complicated?*

Now a good many of the pilgrims had stopped too and were watching our exchange. A tall, stoop-backed cleric in dirty gray robes, his hood down over his head, shuffled toward us, leaning heavily on his staff. I kept my eyes on the Inquisitor, searching for some sign of what would happen if I refused. The way he'd said "the *name*" made me think this wasn't a simple matter of making something up.

Well, when in doubt, stick with what works, I thought, and I backhanded the Inquisitor so hard he spun a quarter-turn and barely managed to catch his balance.

Damn, I swore, forcing myself not to hold my hand. *I've really got to start wearing gloves if I'm going to hit people this often.*

"My *name*?" I said, my voice loud enough now that everyone could hear it. "You want to know *my name*?" I took a step toward him and raised my hand again, and he flinched. "Call me Falsio-fucking-dal-Vond if it pleases you, you fetid little worm."

He looked at me, eyes wide with shock, then someone in the crowd laughed and it quickly spread to others. Even the old bent-backed cleric chuckled from inside his hood, "Falsio dal Vond! Well done, Inquisitor," he said. "You've found the Greatcoat hisself!" He stood there chortling as he tapped his staff on the ground three times, then twice again, a pattern that took me by surprise. I let it go though; I had more pressing concerns.

Even a couple of the Knights were laughing at the joke.

"That's right," Brasti said, "and *I'm* Brasti Goodbow!"

The Inquisitor looked up at us. "I'm sorry, who?"

Brasti swore under his breath behind me, "There is something deeply wrong with this country, you know."

"Did you have any more questions for me, Cogneri?" I asked the Inquisitor, keeping my voice light and pleasant, while still making it clear I would have no hesitation in dishing out significantly worse, should he choose to speak again.

He shook his head and turned, signaling his Knights to follow him, and they soon disappeared, leaving only the cleric standing there.

He knelt down before us and bowed his head low until it touched the ground; that at least I recognized as a plea to make confession.

"You may speak, cleric," I said. I had no idea what the proper words were, but I was fairly certain I could knock the man out before anyone noticed if he tried to raise the alarm.

"'Falsio dal Vond'?" he asked, his voice so quiet I could barely hear it. "Really do like to play it close to the edge, don't you, First Cantor?"

For the first time I took in the broadness of his shoulders and the ease with which he held his heavy staff. From under his hood I could now see a wide grin. I really should have recognized Allister Ivany from the staff, if by nothing else.

The crowd of pilgrims was slowly disappearing from view, but still I kept my voice low as I asked, "What in the name of Saint Forza-who-strikes-a-blow are you doing here, Allister?"

The King's Shadow was still kneeling on the road in front of us, his head bowed. "I'm afraid the God's Needles killed Saint Forza last week, Falcio, so you'll need to find someone else to swear by." He glanced back to the road. "Are they gone yet?"

"They're still too close," Brasti said. "Someone might see if you stood up now. Besides, you look good on your knees, Allister. Very natural."

"As soon as you and Falcio are done wrecking the country, Brasti Goodbow, I'm going to beat the pair of you so bloody people will think there are two Saints of Swords."

Brasti tapped the toe of his shoe against Allister's staff. "Won't you need to get yourself a proper weapon first?"

Kest appeared, leading his and Ethalia's horses. "How long have you been masquerading as a priest?" he asked as they joined us.

"About a week," Allister replied. "I was heading to Aramor and needed a way to blend in. I'm telling you, being a cleric is the easiest job I've ever had. You just find a few gullible fools along the road, spout a bunch of nonsensical pseudo-doctrine, and people will follow you anywhere." He looked up at me. "Kind of like what the King did to us, don't you think?"

"Leave it," Kest said.

But Allister wasn't done goading me. "Come on, Falcio, tell me I'm wrong. Enlighten me at last as to the King's grand plan."

My nerves were already on edge and the situation might have escalated had Ethalia not interrupted. "Please," she said, her voice muffled inside the hood, "this . . . isn't helping."

"Forgive me, Lady Ethalia," Allister said at once. "I promise, one smile from you, and I will be on my best behavior."

She reached up with her bound hands and lifted the hood just enough to reveal her face and give him a wan smile.

"How did you know it was Ethalia?" I asked, and Allister looked at me as if I were stupid, which I suppose I was.

"Wait," Brasti said. "Where's Talia?"

Allister pointed back the way we'd come. "Disguised as a pilgrim— didn't you see her? She practically waved to you as you went by."

"You're lying," Brasti said defensively. "I could spot her from a mile away."

"Don't feel bad, Brasti. You're getting old. They do say the eyes go first."

"Enough," I said, before either of them could continue. "We're a bit short on time, and in a somewhat precarious position here, so Allister, why don't you just tell us what you've learned about the God's Needles?"

He craned his head to look back at the road one more time, but even the dust cloud accompanying the pilgrims had disappeared now. He rose to his feet and stretched. "If you four are heading into Domaris then I'm guessing you found out the same thing I did: there are rumors of a working sanctuary in the Condate of Verderen— that's where they're making the Needles."

I felt a huge surge of relief at hearing confirmation of the Bardatti's theory.

"How well guarded is it?" Kest asked before I could.

"I couldn't get close enough to find out: the sanctuary is right in the center of his lands and I didn't think anything as lowly as a country cleric would gain entrance. But I've seen six more of those damnable God's Needles, and they do all appear to be coming from Verderen." He looked up at the unconscious boy tied to the tree. "What are you going to do about him?"

"Cut him loose and bring him to the nearest village," I replied. "We'll leave him with a few coins; he will have to make his way to safety from there."

For a second I thought Allister might protest, but then he said, "This thing with the churches? There's something off about it: the clerics aren't preaching about the Gods anymore, they're preaching about 'The God,' singular."

"Which 'God'?" Kest asked.

Allister gave a wry grin. "I swear, I don't think they even have a clue. All I know is that if one of the old priests starts talking to his flock about Purgeize or Duestre or any of the others, that priest ends up disappearing pretty quickly. I think there's a war going on within the churches themselves."

"I suppose it makes sense," Brasti said. "If you're trying to turn the country into a theocracy it's probably easier to do if everyone worships the same God. Too bad they couldn't have picked Love, though. She always seems the least annoying of the Gods."

Ethalia dismounted from her horse, but before I could say anything she said, "The pilgrims are far enough away now. No one can see us and the boy's wounds need tending." She slid her right hand out of the handcuffs and pulled one of her blue jars from her saddlebag.

"Keep an eye out," I told Brasti.

Allister rose to his feet as well. "So Obladias uses his money and influence to persuade as many clerics as he can to his side. Then he brings back the Inquisitors and goes out and recruits all those wayward Knights looking for something to believe in. He creates these foul 'God's Needles' to start desecrating any holdout churches and forcing the remaining clerics into line." He waved his hands in the air elaborately. "And just like magic, Tristia has a new religion."

"Clever," Brasti said. He turned to me. "How come we never come up with plans as clever as that?"

"We've been a little busy trying to keep the Dukes from destroying the country."

"That's the problem, Falcio," Allister said, his face tight; he looked genuinely angry with me. "You keep winning the battle, but you never get any closer to winning the war."

"Most of the time I'm just trying to figure out who the enemy is," I admitted.

He spread his arms wide. "Haven't you figured it out yet? It's *everybody*." He brushed down his robes and said, "I should rejoin my little flock before someone poaches them from me. Do you have any orders, First Cantor?"

I couldn't decide whether he used my title because he was remembering his duty or because he was just as scared and uncertain as the rest of us. Whatever the reason, I gripped his shoulder. "Get back to Aramor and keep her alive."

He nodded, then grinned. "Well, good travels, fellows. Odds are we won't see each other again on this side of Death's embrace—then again, maybe the One God has killed off Death too."

Brasti gave him a rough hug. "Try not to trip over your stick."

Allister set off down the road, but after a few steps he paused and turned back to us. "The boy—he's going to tell people, Falcio. Even if he swears to keep his mouth shut, he won't keep quiet. They never do. These heroics you're so fond of are going to get you killed, and then where will we be?"

I thought about that, and only then considered the fact that Allister hadn't stopped the men from whipping the boy. "Would you have really let them do it?"

He didn't look at me, but when he answered, his voice was harsh and full of self-loathing. "To complete the mission? To stop what's happening out here? You're damned right I would, and so would Talia. So would Quillata and Tobb and most of the others. You better get ready, Falcio, because this is a war. And right now, the other guys are winning."

CHAPTER FORTY-NINE

THE DEMESNE

The Duchy of Domaris is split into three Condates and four Marches, the latter bordering the neighboring Duchies. The Condate of Verderen is larger than most, comprised as it is of half a dozen demesnes, each around fifty square miles. It was in one of those demesnes that we found Obladias's family estates, although I had to admit the search hadn't been that difficult. Whatever subterfuge had been used to hide the would-be Prelate's activities over the past months or years was apparently no longer necessary. The average farmer or villager might not know precisely what was going on, but they couldn't miss the steady stream of clerics, Inquisitors, and Knights clogging the roads, and everyone knew where the travelers were coming from.

"They glint in the sun," one old cart driver told us when he'd stopped to see if we might exchange a few coins for some of his supplies.

"They glint?" I asked, paying him a somewhat exorbitant price for a few apples and a wheel of cheese that I strongly suspected weren't his to sell. "You mean from the armor?"

The driver pocketed the coins and looked at Ethalia, lying tied across her horse. At first we'd told anyone who inquired that she was a heretic being brought for trial, but the closer we got to Verderen, the more the talk of Saints made it more plausible that we'd captured one who was too sick from the fever to fight back. "Nah," he said finally, as if only then remembering what I'd asked, "the shine comes from 'em flecks—they get 'em on their boots, 'aven't ya noticed when you been there with 'em other Inquisitors?"

I didn't respond; whatever the old man knew wasn't worth the risk of being discovered for fakes. Instead I gave him the look as Kest and Brasti took a step closer to him. The driver bowed his head and snapped the reins to get his horse to start moving.

Our disguises and the occasional threat were enough to get us into the heart of the demesne, where the question of where to go was quickly solved when anyone caught sight of Ethalia.

"Found another one, eh?" a white-tabarded Knight said, waving us forward into what could have passed for a small village constructed in the middle of an otherwise dense forest. He pointed down the path to an open-air building where smoke was rising from several chimneys and the sounds of hammering echoed out toward us. "Take her to the blacksmith, same as the others."

I nodded and started to go by. As Ethalia's horse passed by, he stopped it and reached up to put a hand on her leg. "Which one did you get? I imagine she's pleasing to the eye once you get the rags off her." Then a thought occurred to him and he added, "Hope she's not one of the dangerous ones."

Kest replied, "Only to a man who puts his hands on her."

I was grateful for his intervention—and, not for the first time, that my rapiers were strapped to the side of my horse and not within easy reach.

The Knight took his hand off Ethalia and backed away, and as we rode by, I wondered at his attitude. Did the Church Knights see themselves as *equal* to the Inquisitors? That hadn't felt like the case on the road. Perhaps here things were more . . . *collegial*?

The question lost significance when we got closer to the blacksmith's shop. There were no walls, only a roof held up by supports recently cut from trees, the bark still hanging off them. Within the space I counted six separate forges, each being worked by one or two men, all with the big, brawny frames required for such work.

"Over here," the one closest to us called, even as he picked up something I couldn't see with his heavy tongs and then dunked it in a barrel of water. Steam hissed up in the air between us. "Who's that you got there?" he asked.

At first I just stared at him, but my expression didn't appear to put him off; evidently he wasn't particularly in awe of Inquisitors. "Does it matter to you?" I asked at last.

He shrugged. "Not especially, but you'll want a mask aligned to her sympathies." I had no idea what he was talking about, but that didn't appear to matter; the blacksmith put down his tongs and walked past me. He reached up and passed a hand across Ethalia's still form, tied across the horse. "Ah," he said. "Love and Regret. Two of my favorite Gods." He stopped himself and gave a chortle. "Well, false Gods now, I suppose."

The blacksmith went back inside to a large wooden bin stacked with iron masks. He rummaged around for a few moments before retrieving one. "This should do just fine."

I had to shove the wave of disgust and rage back down my own throat, fearing it might trigger something in Ethalia. I badly needed to know more about how this worked. "Wait," I said, grabbing the blacksmith's arm, and when he looked down at me questioningly I asked, "Are you sure you have the right one?"

His eyes narrowed, but more from irritation than suspicion. "I've been at this longer than you, I reckon." He flipped over the mask, revealing the misshapen features and strange lines across its surface. "There, see? Love and Regret, both right there." He caught my expression but mistook it for doubt. "Look, it doesn't matter that much, anyway. Any mask of infamy will hold back their Awe. Like the Blacksmith says, getting the alignment right"—here he grinned and gave me a wink—"just makes the desecration sting a little deeper, eh?"

My chest was tight, and I couldn't stop myself from breathing in deep, the way I do before a fight. I hoped the man wouldn't notice, and fortunately, Brasti drew his attention away. "I thought you were the blacksmith."

The man in front of me looked over at his fellows inside the shop and laughed. "Hear that, boys? I'm the Blacksmith now!"

The others laughed. Our man turned back to us. "I'm *a* blacksmith, all right, but I'm not *the* Blacksmith. He's off doing something more important, I imagine."

I was trying to make sense of all this when Kest, recognizing I wasn't thinking clearly, took the mask from the man and examined it. "Hard to believe, isn't it?" he said, smoothly, "that all you need to do is put an iron mask on a Saint and they become as easy to kill as anyone else."

"Well, sure," said the blacksmith, "but it's not as if any old iron will do, is it?" He waved an arm down the path. "It's only our mine here that's got the right ore to make the masks—you haven't been down there yet?"

Kest shook his head. "We've been dealing with heretics in Baern for the most part." He motioned toward Ethalia's still form. "We only came here because we caught this one half-dead outside one of the old churches."

"You sure she's weak?" the blacksmith asked. "They come out of the Fever unexpectedly sometimes."

"Not this one," Kest replied. "She's been out of it for six days. When she does talk it's just to moan and beg us to help her."

The blacksmith smiled knowingly. "Funny how Saints are just like little children that way. They'll just keep screaming and screaming till they get to play in their little sanctuary." He glanced over at Ethalia again. "Well, the clerics have been bitching and moaning for a fresh one for the past two days so best we get this done, and you take her down to the mine." He took the mask from Kest's hand and walked back to Ethalia.

I started for him but Kest caught my shoulder. We locked eyes and he gave the slightest shake of his head. We had talked about this, all of us. I'd known since we'd started this foolish plan what we might have to do and Ethalia hadn't just agreed to it; she'd *insisted*.

I'd had two weeks to prepare myself and I still wasn't ready.

The blacksmith grabbed the back of her head with one hand and put the front piece of the mask over it. Then he held it there and released the back of her head and swung the back plate over, snapping the locks in place with practiced ease. The moan that escaped her destroyed some last piece of whatever love I had left for myself.

The blacksmith raised his voice and spoke into the holes in the front of the mask. "You wanted a sanctuary, little girl? Well, you wait until you see what we've got down there for you."

Even before I took the first step past the heavy wooden frame that opened onto the sloping path into the mine, I could sense something deeply wrong with this place. My fingers twitched, desperate for the comforting grips of my rapiers, which I'd had to leave with the horses in order to maintain my disguise; I still had no idea why they favored maces. It hardly mattered, though, as my arms were fully occupied with carrying Ethalia. Looking down at her, I could no longer tell whether she was pretending to be unconscious or whether the Saint's Fever had finally overcome her.

Unless it's the mask that's doing this to her.

"A plan would be nice right about now," Brasti said. It was going to take one hell of a trick to get us all out of here alive once this was done.

Kest finished pouring the rest of our water into a heavy skin inside his pack. "I thought we'd agreed to a Snake in the Soup."

"You two agreed to it," Brasti lifted his own pack in the air. "I'd rather not rely on luck and this shit to keep us alive."

"We could try a Flock of Swallows," Kest offered.

"Forget it," Brasti replied. "Maybe if I had my fast bow"—he looked dismissively at the pistol in the holster at his side—"but this bloody thing takes too long to reload."

"Inquisitors don't use bows," Kest said, then pointed to the mace hanging from his belt. "Besides, if I have to carry this thing . . ."

Brasti made a show of examining the mace. "I don't see what you're complaining about. It's not that different to a sword, is it? It's still just a big stick you wave at people." He turned to me. "Come on, Falcio, can we at least consider a Cloak and Tickle?"

"No," I said, barely paying attention. Ethalia was so light in my arms—when had she gotten so thin? She was barely heavier than the pack I carried on my back. Had she been eating at all since becoming a Saint? *Focus! Find out what's down there—find a way to prove Obladias is behind this and put a stop to his machinations.* "We stick with the Snake in the Soup," I said quietly.

Brasti swore and took the first step into the mine. "Fine, but I never want to hear you bitching and moaning about how much you 'hate magic' again after this."

"Well," Brasti said quietly, his voice lightly echoing inside the shaft as we walked along the rough stone floor, "I always knew you'd lead us into some hell eventually."

"Shut up," I said.

Ethalia's body twitched just as the light of the lantern Kest held in front glinted on something embedded in the walls. "Iron ore," he said.

"It's an iron mine," Brasti said. "What did you expect?"

Kest stopped for a moment and reached out a hand, his fingers almost but not quite touching the tiny fleck of ore in the wall. "It's . . . *different.* It feels not unlike when I was in the sanctuary of Saint Forza, only stronger . . . *deeper.*" He turned and looked down at the mask covering Ethalia's face. "I think it's something about the ore that holds back the Saint's Awe."

Brasti pressed his own hand against the wall of the mine. "I'm not feeling anything. Must be a Saintly thing."

"We need to keep going," I said, and Kest nodded and continued down the passageway. The roof of the shaft was much higher than I'd expect in a mine, and all too soon we found ourselves in what appeared for all the worlds like a massive underground city. Rough-hewn corridors illuminated by lanterns hanging from hooks every twenty feet or so were peopled by men and women carrying tools and supplies, sometimes dragging a body along the ground.

I tried to focus on the plan, on what might lie ahead, but every step I took increased my feelings of dread.

Imagine what it's doing to Ethalia.

Every few minutes her limp body in my arms would twitch or shiver and it took all my will not to set her down and strike off the mask, to see if she was all right. But we were committed now, for good or ill, so I just kept going, counting the number of steps down each hallway, memorizing every turn. I forced myself to close my eyes, to picture the space in front and behind me, to pay attention to the smells of sweat and fire, when I could feel a breeze and when it disappeared. I couldn't count on my sight to help me if things went to hell.

Things always go to hell.

"Falcio?" Kest said.

I stopped walking and looked up as he motioned ahead to where some two dozen people waited in a line. They were very different, dressed not in work clothes but in white robes, clean despite the dust and dirt all around them, the fine cloth almost shimmering in the torchlight. When they noticed us coming, several of them ran over and began to crowd around us.

"Let's have a look at her," one man said, excitedly. The simplicity of his robes was at odds with the elegant cut of his hair, the manicured nails of his hand as he reached out to us. This wasn't a poor man.

"Let me, Papa," begged a boy by his side, also dressed in white. "I want a taste."

A taste?

Others tried to get close, but the man shoved them away and placed himself firmly in front of me. The heat of his breath washed over my face as he leaned in. "Come on," he said, pulling out a small blade barely long enough to shave with, "let's see what she's got for us."

My hands were busy holding Ethalia so I gave the man my best Inquisitor's look—the one I'd used to such great effect over the past few days, driving doubt into those who tried to get too close. The man looked afraid, to be sure, but his fear was vastly overshadowed by the hunger in his eyes. "Please," he said, "I've done everything—killed a dozen heretics, even the boy's mother." He held the tiny little blade over the exposed flesh of Ethalia's calf. "I've *earned* this."

"You have," I said, and his eyes came to mine, expecting to see approbation—until I smashed my forehead into his nose. He stumbled backward into the others, his son trying unsuccessfully to keep him standing. Kest and Brasti immediately took up position in front of me before anyone else had a go at slicing into Ethalia.

"What is this blasphemy?" a voice shouted from down the corridor, and the crowd parted silently to make way for the cleric who'd spoken. He, too, wore white robes, but unlike the others, his were draped in layers that perfectly fitted his lean body. There was a subtle inlay on the front, symbols I didn't recognize. Two Knights in white tabards followed behind, heavy warswords in hand.

"Take this one," the cleric demanded, pointing to the man who'd accosted me as he rose to his feet and tried to back away. He didn't get far before the Knight drove a gauntleted fist into the man's face, filling the corridor with the cracking sound of the shattering jaw. The boy screamed and tried to stop the two Knights from dragging his father away, but the cleric stopped him. "Your family's wealth has bought you passage to greatness, little Lordling. Will you forgo that, as your father has done, or will you await your turn?"

The boy looked from his father to Ethalia in my arms. "I'll wait," he said quickly. "I'm sorry, Venerati, I'll wait my turn."

As the two Knights dragged the father away, the boy's eyes remained on Ethalia, and he licked his lips. "I'm going to be the Saint of Righteous Vengeance," he said proudly to me. "I've made a list of the people I'm going to punish first—do you want to see it?"

My throat tightened in reaction to the bile rising up from my stomach. *Is the promise of power all it takes to turn men into beasts?* I thought, trying to hide my shudder. *Are we truly such cowardly beings that the promise of strength to quench that fear is all we need to do such horrible things?*

This wasn't the time to sink into despair. "Don't just stand there, Cogneri," the cleric ordered. "Bring her inside."

Once again the crowd parted, and for the first time I saw what lay at the end of the hallway: a pair of massive white columns either side of two wide doors, larger and grander than the entrance to the most powerful Duke's own palace. It looked as if it had all been newly made.

What in all the hells have they built here?

"Fascinating," Kest said when we were about fifteen feet from the massive doors, and as I caught his look, I cursed myself for getting so caught up in my fear and anger that I had forgotten what we were here to do.

"A moment, Venerati," I said. "I just need to rest my arms for a few seconds."

I knelt down, resting Ethalia's body on my thighs as I slipped off my pack and tossed it against the cavern wall.

"No point in carrying these in with us, I suppose," Brasti said, and tossed his on mine. It landed perfectly on top.

Kest put his down as well, reaching inside to remove an overly large skin of water. He took a small sip and offered it to me. I shook my head, and he placed it back inside the bag without bothering to close it. I reached into my coat pocket, pulling out a rag and wiping my hands with it, then tossed the rag onto Kest's pack.

"Time grows short," the cleric said, and I sighed and got back to my feet, carefully lifted Ethalia, and followed him. At the massive doors he stopped and turned to face me. "Have any of you been inside before?"

"No," I replied.

"Well, I advise you keep your wits about you. Whatever trials you've endured as an Inquisitor, whatever . . . punishments you've enacted upon the heretics—this is *different*. This will *feel* different. Remember, what takes place inside is *ritual,* even though it might look otherwise." He looked down at Ethalia. "Do you know which one she is?"

"I think so," I said.

"Those inside will know, at any rate." The cleric reached into his robes. I expected him to pull out a key but instead, he held a tiny iron bell between his thumb and index finger. He shook it, and it gave only the barest tinkle—there was no way that sound could have penetrated the massive doors, but a moment later they opened, the bottoms scraping against the bare stone. The cleric motioned for us to enter. There was a hallway, perhaps ten feet long, then it widened out into a vast circular chamber, and there, we saw what Obladias had kept secret, what Birgid had found before us.

A cathedral! They've built their own damned cathedral inside the depths of a mine.

Then I saw what else awaited us within, and I was startled by a heartfelt moan. It took me a moment to realize it had come from my own mouth. Kest spoke to me, his voice low, words of warning to stay calm, or perhaps some adjustments to our plans, but I took no note of any of it. I was trying not to retch at the sight in front of me. Brasti's words as we'd entered the mine suddenly took on the weight of prophecy: *I always knew you'd lead us into some hell eventually.*

He was right. I had. Then a darker thought took me. *I've brought Ethalia to the demons.*

CHAPTER FIFTY

THE CATHEDRAL

The chamber's perfectly smooth walls rose high above us, making the massive chamber feel oddly small, somehow. There were no altars, no religious symbols of any kind, only weapons of all shapes and sizes hanging on the walls. The ground was divided by circles of rough-hewn stones, each containing two pillars rising all the way to the stony roof. Heavy iron bands with six-foot lengths of chain ending in iron cuffs hung from spikes bolted into the top and bottom of each pillar.

Most of the circles were untenanted, the chains dangling loose to the floor, but inside one of the circles a man was held suspended a few inches from the floor by the chains. His naked chest was covered in blood moths, their bodies bloated and crimson from feeding on his wounds. The little of the man's skin I could see beneath the insects looked pallid and withered. His mask of infamy was carved to represent a young man about to kiss his lover.

Around this lone victim crouched seven men and five women, dressed in the same white robes as the crowd waiting outside. As we watched, three of them plucked blood moths between trembling fingers, opened their mouths wide and consumed the living insects

whole. Behind each supplicant stood three more, impatiently awaiting their turns.

Brasti, bless both his heart and soul for however much longer we
would live, vomited on the floor.

A cleric approached us carrying a long, curved knife in one hand
and a whip in the other. "It's not as uncommon a reaction as you'd
think," he said affably.

"Forgive us, Venerati," I said, my mind unfreezing and turning
to all the ways I would tear this smiling, friendly cleric apart when
the moment allowed.

"Not Venerati," he corrected, holding up the knife. "*Admorteo.*
Mine is not to preach to the mind, but to free the spirit."

"Of course." I bowed my head so he couldn't see the anger I was
struggling in vain to hide. "Admorteo."

The cleric came to examine Ethalia, and only then did I feel the
exhaustion in my arms, shaking as I held her; I wondered if the cleric
thought it was from fear of his presence. His eyes narrowed as
he placed a hand gently against her arm. "She is . . . Oh, my! You've
done well, Inquisitors." He looked back up at me. "Do you realize
who you've brought us?"

"We've brought you the Saint of Mercy, Admorteo."

Brasti, in an effort to cover his own revulsion, said, "Does that
mean we get first taste?"

The cleric gave a small, forbearing smile and pointed toward the
white-robed men and women eating the blood moths on the dying
Saint. "Only if you want to end up like them." He paused and looked
at Brasti. "I would have expected an Inquisitor would know better."

"Forgive us, Admorteo," I said, my mind racing to understand
what this meant. "We have been a long time on the road." I looked
down at Ethalia in my arms. "Her . . . presence is sometimes difficult."

"Of course," the cleric replied, and pointed to a circle. "Let us
bind her there."

He led us to the pillars, but I stopped and looked at the men and
women who'd been plucking blood moths from the dying Saint's
wounds. Another cleric had arrived and was now beating them with

his whip, shouting, "Slowly, fools! Do you wish to lose your minds before you come into your strength? Or worse, for him to die before we have drained him fully?"

Once the men and women had backed out of the way, the cleric reached into his robes and withdrew a small flask which he held to the bound Saint's mask of infamy. He dribbled the liquid into the slots that led into the funnel forced in his mouth, then held the Saint's head back for several moments before letting go. I loathed the self-satisfied smirk on his face.

I'll bet that's Adoracia fidelis. So Jillard had been right: they were forcing it into the Saint and diluting the madness that came with it.

The cleric led us to the circle of stones and knelt down to move one aside. "Make sure the cuffs are firmly attached before I set the prayer-stone in its place," the cleric said, sounding deadly serious. "Once the sanctuary is formed, her fever will pass; only the mask will protect us from her Awe, so it is imperative the prisoner cannot reach the mask, nor smash her head against the floor or one of the pillars—that's how this one's predecessor escaped."

"I heard," I lied, feeling some small shred of joy that Birgid had managed to get out of this place; that she'd died surrounded by love, far away from this hell. "I was surprised to hear she'd overcome you all."

If the cleric was insulted by my tone, he gave no sign of it. "You wouldn't be if you'd faced Birgid's Awe." He looked at Ethalia. "Odd, isn't it? One would have thought that Mercy would be the weakest of the Saints, and yet she was quite possibly the most powerful."

He motioned for me to enter the circle, and Kest followed me, then he told Brasti, "You can bind her to the chains now."

"Now?" Brasti said.

The affable cleric's mask slipped and he looked slightly annoyed. "Yes, you fool, *now.*"

I set Ethalia on her feet, hanging onto her to keep her from sliding to the ground. "Forgive him, Admorteo, he wasn't talking to you." I nodded to Brasti. "Yes, now."

He cocked his right elbow and smashed it into the side of the cleric's head, grabbing his long knife before he went sprawling to the floor, and before he had any idea what was happening, Brasti had knelt down and pushed the stone back in place, completing the circle. Kest drew a short chisel from inside his coat and with perfect accuracy, smashed the locks of Ethalia's mask in two quick strikes. The pieces fell away and her hands wiped at the hair, slick with sweat, that was matted to her face. "Gods, Falcio . . ." she croaked, "the masks . . . they're worse than we could even begin to guess . . . we *must* save Valiana from this . . ."

"We have to save ourselves first." I pointed to the other cleric, across the room, who'd noticed us; he was shouting and gesturing at the entranceway, but Brasti was already running toward them. Brasti dropped the heavy bar across the double doors with a clang. I doubted anyone was going to be breaking in any time soon.

I looked back at the cleric; he was pulling weapons down from the walls and handing them out to the twelve men and women arrayed around him. They brandished them eagerly as they faced us, their eyes feral, their mouths open in expressions of ecstasy.

I looked into those faces full of hunger, madness, and sheer joy at the thought of what they had done to the Saint and what they were now about to do to us.

I was smiling too.

In a better world, the God's Needles inside the cathedral would have been newly made and weak; unfortunately for us, these men and women were, if anything, even faster and deadlier than those we'd encountered before.

"This isn't going too well, Falcio," Brasti shouted, swinging his sword at a man coming at him with daggers in each hand. Despite Brasti's lack of finesse, his blow landed just fine, slicing a deep gouge across his opponent's face. The man grinned, splitting the wound even wider.

"Don't fence with them," I reminded the others. "Pain doesn't bother them and they're not afraid of dying—we've got to disable them." To emphasize my point, I brought my mace down with all my strength on the skull of a man who looked oddly familiar. He was close to my age, with aquiline features that had probably been considered handsome, at least up until the moment my weapon broke his head open. That's when I realized that I'd just killed Viscount Tuslien.

"I can't . . . keep this . . . up . . . long . . . Falcio," Kest said, swinging his mace left-handed, still with his astonishing speed and precision, but every swing was causing him more and more pain.

He'll kill himself from the effort before the damned Needles even get to him. The thought terrified me. I tried to get closer to him but a woman, possibly the Margravina of Selez—or was that my perverse mind punishing me?—leaped at me. In her right hand she held a long, thin blade, much like the one used by the first God's Needle we'd encountered. I wondered whether these people were being trained in weaponry before undergoing the ritual, or if the Adoracia made them so fast and powerful they didn't need training. Something to ponder . . .

I shook my head furiously and cried, "Brasti, help Kest!"

"I'm trying not to die here, Falcio," he shouted back, kicking out hard at the second woman, who was now grabbing at him with her bare hands. "You know, Ethalia, this Awe of yours would be helpful anytime now."

"I . . . can't . . . not yet . . ."

I sidestepped, letting my opponent's thrust go by me, and wrapped my arm around her blade, praying the sleeve of my Inquisitor coat would protect me, then smashed the mace down hard close to the guard. The blade broke off, vastly reducing the weapon's reach.

I sneaked a look at Ethalia. Her eyes were closed, her face taut with concentration. I glanced at the captive Saint, hoping against hope that perhaps he might have freed himself somehow, but he simply hung limp from the chains.

The woman attacking me dropped the hilt and instead locked her hands around my neck. Instantly my windpipe felt the crushing pressure. *Damn, but these people are hellish strong.*

A choke hold requires leverage, and I broke hers by bringing both my arms up between her hands, trapping her forearms under my armpits and driving my right heel into each knee in quick succession. I stepped back and let her fall forward, both her knees shattered, yet still she crawled toward me, that same unearthly smile on her face. "I am the God's Needle," she said. "*His* will calls me forth."

"I'm Falcio," I said, bringing the mace down on her skull. "And a terrible fear of death commands me." I shouted to the others, "Get in close around Ethalia—form a circle."

"Watch your left!" Kest shouted and I swung around just in time to see the other cleric coming at me. I'd expected a weapon, but instead he threw the contents of his flask at me—I couldn't imagine what pure Adoracia would do to me if it got into my face and I threw myself backward and sideways, falling into one of the pillars. The liquid splashed over the ground at my feet.

Hells! Just what I need, to become even crazier than I already am— But before the cleric could try again I knocked the flask out of his hand with the mace and drove my foot into his knee. I don't think I broke it, but the pain on his face told me he wasn't going to try to get close to me again.

At least you're not immune to pain, Admorteo.

I drew back inside Ethalia's circle. A grunt from Kest drew my attention. I turned and saw that he'd downed his opponent but he had a nasty wound on his forehead, and blood was dripping into his eyes. Around us I counted five of the God's Needles either dead or so badly wounded all they could do was drag themselves on the floor toward us.

That still left seven. "Hey Kest," I said.

He wiped the blood from his eyes with his right arm even as he drove his mace into his opponent's head, smashing his eye. "Yes, Falcio?"

"How would you rate our odds now?"

He reversed the mace and plunged the stick end into his opponent's other eye. "I'd rather not say. I was rather hoping, this being a holy place, a miracle might be forthcoming."

"Saint Laina's tits!" Brasti shouted and I heard a clanging sound as his knife hit the floor. His hand was now covered in blood. "That's my *draw* hand, you bastard," he said, kicking out at a man who'd lost half his jaw and didn't look at all bothered about it.

"There is no Saint Laina anymore, Brasti," I reminded him.

Kest's eyes narrowed as he worked through our chances. "Then we need another Saint, Falcio, because they're about to swarm us."

"Ethalia," I said softly, not even sure if she could hear me, "it has to be now."

I could hear her labored breathing for a few brief instants as the God's Needles, their victory clearly in sight, rushed as one toward us. Then I heard a long, slow exhalation and felt my legs fall out from under me. For a moment I thought one of the God's Needles had somehow gotten behind me and hamstrung me, but then I felt the weight *inside* me: a heavy sadness made from my own anger, my own need for violence. Tears of regret filled my eyes as I sank down, barely able to muster the strength to check on Kest and Brasti, who were on their knees too, also afflicted—and then I heard the sounds of our enemies falling to the ground. They gazed up at Ethalia, standing behind me, and their eyes, moments before filled with madness and lust, had suddenly turned soft and uncertain, begging forgiveness. Then I looked at the woman I'd loved and lost, standing in the center of the circle and shining white as the sun. What I felt in my heart was, I knew, shared by every one of us in that room: we were in awe of her.

CHAPTER FIFTY-ONE
THE ESCAPE

I don't know quite how long we stayed that way, all of us kneeling, bound by Ethalia's Awe, but after a while I felt it fade enough that I could get back to my feet. Kest and Brasti followed.

"The God's Needles don't seem to be moving," Brasti remarked.

"I am focusing my will upon them alone," Ethalia replied, her eyes closed. "It is rather difficult. You should bind them now."

Kest looked down at them. "It would be . . . Forgive me, Ethalia, but it would be safer to kill them—"

"Use the chains," she said.

It wasn't a command, but I didn't get the impression that we had a choice, so we dragged the God's Needles one by one to the pillars and bound them there. If they felt rage or sorrow, nothing of it showed on their slack-jawed faces. I wondered what would happen once Ethalia left this place. Jillard had not mentioned any cure for Adoracia poisoning; were we leaving them to a slow, agonizing death?

I left the question aside and pulled out the chisel I'd kept secreted in my Inquisitor's coat. My hands were shaking from the aftermath of the fight, and it took me several tries to break open the locks on the old Saint's mask to reveal an undistinguished man with skin the color of parchment; he looked to be in his late sixties.

"I . . . am grateful," he said, his hoarse voice barely louder than a whisper.

"Who are you?" I asked, working at the chains holding his ankles.

"Erastian," he replied weakly, and at Brasti's querying look he grinned. "Erastian-who-plucks-the-rose, Saint of Romantic Love, if you can believe it."

"I believe it," Ethalia said, joining us, just as the sound of hammering at the doors started echoing around the great cavern.

"We don't have much time," I said to the old Saint. "That liquid the cleric was forcing into your mouth—"

"Foul stuff," Erastian said. "It brings madness long before it brings power, but a Saint's will is strong enough to hold back that madness. When the Needles drink our blood, they too can withstand the adverse effects of the toxins, for a time at least. I suspect it kills them eventually."

"But it doesn't actually make them Saints, does it?" Brasti asked. "Because that would really dim my views on religion."

He shook his head. "No, the Adoracia just makes them worse sinners."

As I gazed around the room, wondering at all that had been done in this loathsome place, Kest asked, "What troubled you?"

"This cathedral . . ." I motioned to the pillars and the chains. "The elaborate ritual. The masks. The chains. All of this is just to create assassins?"

Brasti leaned down to pick up a shortsword from the floor. "Damned strong assassins who nearly killed—" His words were interrupted by more hammering from outside. "Should we be doing something about that?"

Kest was already examining the doors. "They could spend a week trying to break down those doors and it wouldn't do them any good."

"Terrific," Brasti said, his eyes on one of the God's Needles we'd bound to the chains. She was looking at him with an unhealthy interest.

Ethalia knelt beside Erastian. "Sancti, there's more to all this than assassins, isn't there?"

He sighed. "It's . . . complicated to explain, but, in essence, what you are witness to is an act of Desecration."

"'Desecration'?" Brasti asked. "Who gives a shit about that?"

The Saint of Romantic Love looked a trifle annoyed. "Desecration doesn't just mean pissing on an altar, you damned fool! I'm talking about removing the very sacredness of a thing. When a Saint dies, that essence passes on to the person most attuned to the force that our Sainthood held."

"But if you die here," I said, my flesh creeping, "when they do . . . the things they were doing to you . . . your essence is lost?"

"Not lost," Erastian spat, "*returned*. The faith or power or whatever you want to call it, well, you could say we stole it from the Gods, I suppose."

Brasti looked unconvinced. "Doesn't look like you stole all that much, old man."

The Saint of Romantic Love drew himself up a little. "I've been getting my fucking blood poisoned and drained for the past month, boy. It wears a body down."

"So this is a war, then," Kest said, his eyes far away. "A war between Gods and Saints."

I started thinking about what Birgid had said, weeks before. "This mine was one of the originals, wasn't it? Where the first groups of Tristians were brought as slaves, to mine the iron ore. This is where they prayed in the nights, passing the prayer-stones and begging for Gods to come and save them."

"We always were a people prone to begging," Erastian said, "until we became powerful enough to build armies and make war against our enemies. We decided we could strive to be greater than the limitations of our ancestors." He shook his head. "We are a vain and corrupt people, I'm afraid."

"Including the Saints?" I asked.

"The Saints worst of all." Erastian looked up at Ethalia and smiled. "There were a few exceptions, though—Birgid was different, some of the others too." He reached out a hand and stroked Ethalia's cheek. "She loved you so, child, but there was no other way. She held on for so long. I was hundreds of miles away, and yet I felt her passing. I don't think the Sainthood could have passed to anyone else, but it must have broken her heart to force this upon you."

Ethalia glanced back at me, though only for a second. "I accept the burden."

"It's always been my experience that burdens are made lighter through love," he said. He was staring at me.

What are you trying to say to me, old man? Are you offering me hope? Are you saying there's still a chance for Ethalia and me? Or are you simply reminiscing? "You loved Birgid, didn't you?" I asked.

Erastian laughed, and in that laugh I caught a glimpse of what he must have been not so long ago: handsome, charming, full of passion. "What man could fail to love Birgid? What woman, for that matter—she was wind and fire and joy. She was certainty itself."

"That doesn't sound much like a Saint of Mercy," Ethalia said, surprised.

"Mercy isn't *passivity*, my girl. It isn't *inaction*. It is the decision that heals the vanquished and the victor; it is far more powerful than most realize. It is mercy we call out for in the darkest hour; it is mercy we summon to protect us." He gazed up at her for a long time, then said quietly, "It saddens me that you should be its Saint and yet not understand that."

Something heavy pounded hard against the doors. Kest might be right; they could hold forever, but I was done with this place. "It's time to go," I said, reaching down to help the Saint of Romantic Love to his feet.

"I thank you, Trattari, and the Gods know I would dearly love to not die in such a foul place, but I'm afraid this little victory of yours is next to worthless. There are dozens of Knights and clerics, and men darker even than they, roaming these corridors."

I looked at Ethalia. "Can you use the Awe again?"

"She can't," Erastian interrupted before she could reply. "She hasn't come into her full power yet. Her strength comes from being inside the sanctuary itself, and once you leave this room, the Awe will fade until she has time to—"

"Fine, fine," Brasti said. "Then it's back to the original stupid, horrible plan."

Erastian looked doubtful. "You really think you can get past all the men guarding the mine? I should think the odds rather slim."

Brasti did at least grin at that. "Old man, we're the fucking *Greatcoats*. Beating the odds is what we do for a living."

I pointed at his hand, clumsily bandaged and already showing blood seeping through. "You sure you're ready for this?"

Following his rather lengthy reply, paired with a series of obscene gestures, he removed the wheel lock pistol from his holster and raised his arm.

Kest went to the door and removed the bar. The hammering was growing louder and the doors were shaking. "Don't miss, Brasti," he said, and opened the door.

As the doors opened, three Knights holding a heavy log as a battering ram stumbled into the chamber. Brasti fired the pistol and an instant later, the metal ball shattered against the cavern wall a few feet from where our packs lay.

"You missed," Kest said as he smashed the pommel of his sword against the helmeted head of one of the Knights.

"It's that damned pistol," Brasti explained. "Bloody toy made for children who can't draw a bow."

"Just load another ball," I said, facing off with another of the Knights to stop him going for Brasti. I swung the mace and promptly missed, which just pointed out how exhausted I was; the others probably were too.

The Knight noticed too; he hoisted his broadsword in preparation to cleave my skull. "And here I was expecting a real battle, Cogneri . . . or should I say, *Trattari*?"

The blade came down and I leaped backward, nearly tripping over the body of one of the slain God's Needles. I threw the mace at him and was absurdly pleased when it struck him dead center in his chest. Mind you, it wasn't a strong enough blow to do much damage, unfortunately, but at least the Knight found it funny. "I'm afraid you're without a weapon—should I lend you one of mine?"

"Don't bother," I replied. "I'm not planning on staying long. Brasti?"

"Coming, coming," he said. We'd made him practice a hundred times on the road and though he professed to hate it, he was actually fairly fast now. He lifted his arm and took aim.

At first the Knight thought he was the target, and when Brasti fired and the bullet harmlessly flew past him he turned and smiled through the slits in the front of his helmet. He started, "You miss—!" before the ball from Brasti's pistol found its target and struck the piece of amberlight I'd laid on top of Kest's pack. The shower of sparks set off the pistol powder, which then exploded in a pleasant little fire that sent people scurrying.

"That was your brilliant plan?" Erastian asked. "A distraction?"

"Wait for it," I said.

It didn't take long: the modest explosion from the black powder broke through the heavy flask of water, which then poured down over the insides of my pack, which was holding the rather large supply of nightmist I'd taken from the dead God's Needle back in Luth.

The strange mixture of chemicals and magic inside the powder soon filled the corridors with gray smoke so thick it choked even the light of the lanterns hanging from the walls. I handed Ethalia and Erastian pieces of cloth we'd prepared. "Cover your mouths and noses and stay between Kest and me. Don't bother trying to see— there won't *be* anything to see except gray soup—so just close your eyes and hang onto us."

Brasti shook his head, tutting, "Falcio val Mond using magic! What is the world coming to?"

"It's a changing world," I said, pushing him forward. The five of us entered the billowing clouds. "I'm just trying to adapt."

CHAPTER FIFTY-TWO

THE CHAPEL

The mine became an endless ocean of gray into which we swam blind as all the other fish. We had the advantage, however: we'd known this was coming.

Twenty-two paces forward, I whispered to myself, *then a left turn, followed three paces later by a slight bend to the right.*

People were shouting and screaming all around us—apparently all those nobles and their families waiting to become God's Needles had little experience of being trapped in a mine. Having the Knights running around barreling into people with their heavy armor probably didn't help, either. It's one thing to be underground with nice bright lanterns every few yards; it's another thing entirely to suddenly discover you can't see *anything.*

The screams became ghostly and confusing, muffled and distorted by the esoteric properties of the nightmist. I found the effect oddly soothing, which worried me. *Some new-minted Saint strike me down, I think I'm starting to like magic—*

A clawing, desperate hand grabbed my arm and, guessing at where their face would be, I struck out with the palm of my hand. It wasn't a very solid strike, but it got the job done. I continued striding along the corridor, feeling Ethalia's hand gripping the back of my coat. "There are stairs up ahead, about six paces," I said. "I'll pause when we get there. Then we'll find three steps going up, each one shallower than you'd expect, so be careful."

I wasn't sure if she heard me, but somehow we got up the few steps and down the next passageway. By my reckoning we were less than three minutes from the exit now. Despite my earlier confidence, the nightmist was starting to play havoc with my sense of direction. I stumbled into a wall, regained my balance and pressed forward, counting my strides until we should reach the next staircase, the long one that led up and out—but suddenly I felt Ethalia tug at me, then her hand disappeared. I stopped and turned, reaching out for her but feeling nothing. I heard a shout so loud I thought it came from inside my own head and was starting to head back the way we'd come when I heard the sound of shuffling.

"It's all right," Kest's voice loomed out of the darkness. "I've taken care of it."

He sounded as if he were miles away, but a hand grabbed onto mine and I knew instantly it was Ethalia's. I turned and resumed our slow trek down the passage and a few moments later, we reached the stairs.

"Thirty-six stairs," I announced. "They get taller near the top."

My warning turned out to be unnecessary; the open air ahead was far enough away from the source of the nightmist that the smoke became only a light gray haze through which we could clearly see the exit.

Chaos had erupted outside the mine, but this was the *good* kind of chaos, the sort in which our enemies were scattered and confused. Half had gone into the mine to start the rescue attempt while others were scrambling to find water, thinking that a fire had broken out deep inside—and none of them knew we weren't the Inquisitors we appeared to be, nor did they know what we'd done. "Get down there," I commanded a group of men standing with an odd mix of weapons and pails of water, neither of which was going to do the least bit of good. "When you get to the cathedral, the clerics will instruct you."

They nodded and ran past us, clambering down the stairs into the mist. Once they were gone, Ethalia emerged, followed by Kest, carrying Erastian in his arms.

"I can stand, you silly fool," the old man said.

"Are you sure you're the Saint of Romantic Love?" Brasti asked, bringing up the rear, "because you sound much more like the Saint of Grouchy Old Codgers."

"We need to get out of sight," Kest said, pointing to a path that led into the forest. "That way we can circle around and make our way back to the horses."

We traveled deep into the woods, leaving behind the noisy confusion we'd sown. The undergrowth made it slow going, and after ten minutes of walking I called a halt. I pointed at a little trail that cut across our path. "Let's take this. It shouldn't be more than two hundred yards to the horses."

Kest and Brasti were several yards down the trail before we noticed neither Erastian nor Ethalia had moved. They were staring into the distance, a strange look on their faces.

"What is it?" I asked.

Erastian looked at Ethalia. "Do you feel it?" The two of them started moving deeper into the forest, completely ignoring me.

"Wait!" I cried, and when they still didn't respond I set off after them, gesturing for the others to follow. *Perfect,* I thought. *The one time a plan actually works and now the damned Saints feel the need to ruin it.*

Brasti, close behind me, tapped my shoulder. "I see something— through that copse—"

I saw it now too: a building of some sort, about twenty feet away, the dirty white stone walls barely visible through the barrier of thick leaves. I drew my Inquisitor's mace and pushed past the Saints, in case there was trouble waiting for us. After a few minutes of forcing a way through the heavy undergrowth, we entered a small clearing with a circular chapel not unlike the one at the center of the Martyrium of Baern. Like that one, it had six doors around its circumference, and also like that one, six statues, one for each of the Gods of Tristia, worn and broken by time and neglect. That's where the similarities ended, however.

"Saint Zaghev's balls!" Brasti swore. "What in all the hells—?"

Beside each ruined statue was a tall gibbet made of a recently felled tree and thick new rope. From each hung an emaciated figure dressed in robes so filthy it took me a moment to see that each of the six wore a different color—the colors of the Gods. Their faces were obscured by iron masks.

We entered the grisly grave site with caution. "More murdered Saints?" Kest wondered aloud, "or clerics, maybe? Perhaps this is some kind of ritual punishment for heresy?"

"Killing priests?" Brasti asked.

One of the cracked wooden doors of the chapel creaked open and a deep baritone voice answered, "You think priests should be immune to paying the price of heresy?" The barrel-chested man who stepped out wiped thick hands against his heavy leather apron, then hooked his thumbs into the wide belt. His tools—a hammer, tongs, several files and hand-punches—hung from loops on either side. "Ah, there you are, Falcio," he added, as if we were old friends.

"Who is this?" Kest asked me.

I shook my head, unable to speak. I had never met this man, never seen him before, and yet in that moment I knew *exactly* who he was.

"*You have never met him,*" the boy had said—but I'd had clues, many of them—simple things, *obvious things*: the carefully designed metal clasps on the iron masks; the complex triggers on the Inquisitors' pistols, each detail a kind of metaphor for the perfectly crafted way each event had unfolded.

It was as if the whole world had become a machine built to this man's specifications.

"What's going on?" Brasti asked. "Who is this arsehole, and what's he doing with a bunch of dead priests?"

"I am a blacksmith," the man replied.

"He's lying," I said, though it was a small lie, buried in one letter.

How many times had we asked ourselves who could so perfectly manipulate the country? The Dukes couldn't do it; even Trin, who was vastly cleverer, couldn't. I'd only ever met *one* person with the brilliance and cunning to pull something like this off. *"I'm a Tailor,"* she'd told us, so many times. *"The last true Tailor in all of Tristia."* She'd been right, of course.

"Well, who is he then?" Brasti asked.

"He's . . . Whatever the Tailor is, he's like her. He's not *a* blacksmith. He's *the* Blacksmith."

"Clever," the man said, stepping out of the doorway of the chapel to face us. "It's a shame to see a mind like yours go to waste, Falcio. I'll bet even the old woman never figured it out, did she?"

"She leaves the little things to me," I said smoothly, trying to stop my voice shaking.

"Don't underestimate yourself. It is a remarkable thing to unwind the plans of those of us like the Tailor and me. Did you know, it turns out there's a word for us? *Inlaudati*: the Unrecognized. It's not an especially grand name, I grant you, but I suppose that's because our nature is to remain hidden."

"And yet here we are."

The Blacksmith spread his arms wide. "And you should be proud. You *found* me." His eyes showed genuine delight: the secret desire of every murderer to have someone admire his handiwork. But there was something else there, too: he was curious about me, whether I was going to figure out what he'd done.

I already had. I looked up at the figures hanging from the six wooden gibbets, swaying gently in the soft breeze. "These aren't priests and they aren't Saints."

"No . . ." Ethalia whispered. She and Erastian already knew what I had just now deduced. And then Brasti and Kest's expressions changed as they too understood what we had found here in this little chapel.

I'd always been the least religious of us all, so I felt it was up to me to say it out loud. "This man killed the Gods."

CHAPTER FIFTY-THREE

THE HERETIC

When you come upon a corpse, it's important to set aside emotion. Rage won't help you understand death, nor sorrow, and if there's one thing the dead deserve, it is for their true story to be told. As a Greatcoat, I'd seen no end of corpses in my time; it comes with the job. I'd seen bodies in every state of decay, from the still-warm victim whose eyes stare back at you, demanding answers, to desiccated skeletons picked clean by scavengers until the bones fairly gleam. What surprised me most, staring up at the dead Gods of Tristia, was how ordinary they looked.

"How can you kill a God?" Brasti asked. There was a brittleness in his voice, an almost childlike uncertainty that was unusual for him. I'd never really thought about Brasti and Faith in the same sentence; I'd never considered that deep down he might actually be religious.

"The same way you kill anyone else," I replied, my eyes still on the withered corpses hanging above us. "You take out your victim when he's at his weakest."

"Correct," the Blacksmith said, as if a favored pupil had answered a difficult question. "Although I confess I was disappointed when I found them so enfeebled—there was barely any Faith left inside them with which to do my work." He pointed toward the mine. "They huddled like beggars in the tunnels, trying to get what warmth they could from half-remembered prayers."

Though far out of my normal domain, it made a certain sense: faith in Tristia had been declining for centuries—for all the piety-by-rote you'd see on high days and holy days, I didn't think many people really gave much credence to the Gods anymore. *Well, not until the Saints being murdered set off a religious panic.* "You didn't start with the Saints," I said. It felt like I was slowly taking apart a clock, holding up every tiny wheel and pinion and spring; seeing for the first time how they connected to each other. "You killed the Gods first."

He smiled. "Again, you impress me, Falcio: such a simple deduction, and yet one that would have eluded most people, so blinded are they by what passes for belief in this broken country." He reached up a hand and squeezed the foot of the one I assumed was the hanging corpse of Duestre, God of Craft. "We worship them, we pray to them—so what does it tell you when no one even notices when they die?"

Even Kest looked troubled. "But the risk of facing a living God . . ."

I was pondering the same question. I looked up at the iron masks covering their faces. *Forget the fact that they're Gods and stick with what you know.* "You make sure the victim can't fight back," I pointed out. If the masks were made from the ore from the mine, and it was the ore that had long ago transformed prayer into power, then it stood to reason that the Gods might be just as vulnerable to the effects of the masks as the Saints were.

"Right again. It's a shame we cannot help but be at odds, Falcio, when we share the same goal."

I hated the raw confidence in the Blacksmith's voice, the way he could say such things without sounding smug or arrogant. I wanted to take the mace in my hand and shatter his skull for all the things he had done—but I had to *focus*. *He's an avertiere, remember?* These thrusts and feints cost him nothing; they were intended to pull me off balance. "What goal is that?"

"We both want to make this a better country." His sincerity unnerved me.

"You son of a bitch," Brasti spat, and drew a long knife from inside his Inquisitor's coat, but I held up a hand to stop him.

"Wait," I said.

The Blacksmith shook his head. "You see? This, right here, is the difference between us: you're all posture and preening. You seek to change the world through grand acts of daring and cleverness." He gestured at Saint Erastian. "You came all this way and risked your lives—in an admittedly brilliant gambit—for what? To rescue the doddering remains of a nonentity: an old fool clinging to a fading romantic dream the world long ago forgot."

"Better a fool dreaming of love than a butcher who commits atrocities to satisfy his own perverse religion," Erastian said.

"'Religion.'" The big man repeated the word as if it were an insect he'd spat from his mouth. "I'm a *craftsman,* not some pious preacher selling false hope. I make *tools.* I forge *weapons.*"

"Fine," Brasti said, "you're a blacksmith, we get it." He looked at me. "Can I kill him now?"

"No," the Blacksmith replied, "I don't think you can." He signaled with his hand, and a figure stepped out from the chapel. The man stood a little taller than me. I could make out broad shoulders and a warrior's build beneath draped white robes like those the nobles had been wearing in the mine. The man was hooded, but I caught a hint of a smile that made me cold inside.

I forge weapons, the Blacksmith had said.

Brasti was unimpressed. "Go ahead, tell your little God's Needle to make his move. All you've shown us so far are madmen, and we're getting pretty good at killing those."

The Blacksmith ignored him and looked at me, visibly disappointed. "*Really,* Falcio? You haven't solved the last piece of the puzzle yet? You must have figured out by now that the Needles were just a means to an end?" He stepped behind the figure in white. "This, I think, will impress you."

"I thought you said they couldn't make Saints," Brasti said to Erastian.

"They can't," he replied, his eyes narrowed as he looked at the figure in front of us.

"The old man is right," the Blacksmith said, reaching his arms around the front of the figure's white cloak and unfastening the clasp. "It turns out making Saints is much harder than it's worth— that's why I decided to go for something considerably more ambitious. Rejoice, for I have forged our salvation!"

The Blacksmith drew back the hood and dropped the man's robes to the ground. The figure wore armor underneath: a sculpted, gold-rimmed steel chest-plate that left his powerfully muscled arms bare. His face was that of a hardened soldier; his eyes were dark, as if he were staring down at his enemy dying on the blood-soaked ground. When he lifted his hand, it held a great axe—and I knew that weapon better than I knew my own rapiers, just as I knew the lines of this man's face more clearly than my own. I had seen the man only once before, fifteen years ago, and yet his features were etched into every nook and cranny, every scar on my soul. This was the man who had come on that fine spring day to the little farm Aline and I had built together; this was the man who had urged his Duke to take Aline from me.

The man's name was Fost, and he belonged in hell.

"Say hello to your new God," the Blacksmith said.

CHAPTER FIFTY-FOUR

THE GOD

It was Kest who spoke first. His voice was quiet, as it often was when he was saving the air in his lungs to prepare for his first attack. "How is this possible?"

The God didn't reply, but the Blacksmith did. "The way you make any great work: by finding the proper materials. That was the difficult part, of course."

Ethalia was still gazing up at the bodies hanging from the gibbets. "You discovered the Gods were too weak to give you what you needed, so you pursued the Saints instead."

"I knew that power like that couldn't simply fade away—it had to go somewhere," the Blacksmith said. "Then I made my most important discovery: Saints like Erastian and—and I know you will forgive me for saying this, My Lady—yourself are nothing but spiritual thieves, pilfering Faith from the Gods like back-alley pickpockets. I have simply stolen it back."

"Why *him*?" I asked. I was trying not to tremble as I stared at Fost. "Why, of all the faces in the world, *his*?" My hand fumbled for the mace hanging at my belt, but my fingers were trembling so badly I knew that if I tried to lift the weapon, it would only fall from my grip.

The Blacksmith looked at his God, then back to me. His eyes were oddly sympathetic. "Tell me what you see, Falcio."

I didn't want to give him the satisfaction of an answer but the words came out anyway. "I see the man who buried the blade of his ax in my wife's skull, a man deserving of a thousand deaths at my hand, not *reverence*—not *Godhood*."

Brasti swung around suddenly. "What! Have you gone blind?" He pointed at the God. "It's exactly what I told you when this whole mess started: it's fucking *Trin*."

"No," Kest said, "neither Fost nor Trin stand before us—and nor is it the man I see." He was blinking furiously, beads of sweat dripping from his brow into his eyes.

"Who do you see?" I asked, my voice suddenly gentle.

"I see Caveil-whose-blade-cuts-water. I see every detail of his face—his gaze, his smile, the way he stood when I faced him . . ."

"Mortal eyes were not meant to gaze upon the Gods," the Blacksmith said, "and so we each see what our minds will allow."

And what do you see, Blacksmith? I wondered.

"How many of my brethren did you desecrate to make this pretty toy of yours?" Erastian demanded, but the Blacksmith was unaffected by the Saint's anger.

"No more than was necessary," he replied, offhand. "Perhaps a hundred."

The old Saint looked stricken. "*A hundred* . . . but there were never more than twelve score of us. You killed—?"

"I did. I killed them," the Blacksmith confessed. "The first one was Anlas, Saint of Memory. He was always the cleverest of you all—do you know there's remarkably little written about Saints? They aren't even mentioned in our oldest scriptures, but from his screams I tore the truth: that the power you wield is stolen from the Gods. Better yet, with his wheezing final breaths, Anlas told me of this old cult of wealthy zealots who believed they could take that power for themselves by drinking the blood of Saints." He shook his head with feigned disgust. "Isn't it odd that the richest among us are such petty creatures?"

Every time he spoke, Ethalia looked pained. "You speak of murder as if it were nothing more than—"

"Nothing more than melting down old horseshoes in order to make new ones," the Blacksmith finished. "And that, of course, was the *real* challenge: how to harness the power of Faith once a Saint has been properly desecrated."

He was trying to make it sound simple, but that too was a ruse meant to deceive us. *The perfectly executed murder of Saints, drawing in followers to create the God's Needles, tricking the churches into bringing back the Inquisitors without his own identity becoming known . . .*

"The Pilgrims," I said, my voice sounding faint to my ears. "You did all this to spread fear throughout the country, convincing people that the Gods had turned away from them so that you could—"

The Blacksmith's composure broke for the first time. "The Gods *did* turn away from us!" he shouted.

I looked into his eyes, searching for some sign of weakness, for despite his rough appearance, this was a man of the purest intellect. *Show me how to wear you down.*

"You are in agony," Ethalia said to him, her voice gentle, probing. "I can see it in you." I could see she was seeking out some shred of humanity with which to draw him back, but it was a mistake.

The Blacksmith took in a slow, deep breath, and when he looked back at her, his eyes were dead. "You know *nothing* of pain, My Lady, but do not worry, for I will rectify that ignorance very soon."

"I really don't think you will," I said, but even before I'd finished the sentence, I knew he'd tricked me.

"Ah, Falcio, you never fail in your consistent inability to surprise me. You want an enemy: a cruel villain you can hate and fight and kill, but I am not he, I'm afraid." He ran the back of his hand across his brow like a laborer coming to the end of a long day's work. "People laugh at you, you know. Everywhere you go in this country your Laws are met with disdain. When a peasant farmer thanks you for risking your life in a duel to get his land back, do you think he cares one bit about which Law was broken or restored? Of course not; he just wants his land. Our countrymen don't wish to obey your Laws." He walked back to stand behind the man with Fost's face and placed his hands on his shoulders. "They want to obey their God."

"Then maybe you shouldn't have murdered the six we had," Brasti pointed out.

"Those half-remembered fools? Their era was long past. Our people want a new God: one strong father to lead them." He turned to admire his creation. "Look at what I have made; tell me he isn't beautiful beyond all things."

"What I see," Erastian said, stepping forward to stand between us and the God, "is an ass, standing next to another ass, both of whom are deserving of a fine beating."

The God opened his mouth and spoke for the first time.

"*Blasphemer.*"

The word made no sound—it was a shadow wrapping itself around my heart, forcing a scream from so deep inside me that it threatened to shatter my inner ears. The word was the scent of death and decay, worming its way into my nostrils; it was the weight of defeat, settling upon my shoulders. I realized that it wasn't just me moaning, and I dragged my head around to see Kest and Brasti had both succumbed to the same sensations I had.

"Tricks," Erastian announced, reeling but somehow unbowed. "Is that what you have to offer our people?"

"You show a remarkable lack of Faith for a Saint," the Blacksmith replied.

The old Saint planted his feet a shoulder-width apart and faced the God square on, though he spoke to the Blacksmith. "That Faith of which you speak so glibly came from men and women fearing the darkness of the night, the yoke of their oppressors. It is from that Faith that the Gods were spawned." To the God he said, "You did not create us. We created you."

The Blacksmith waved a hand. "Does the mother of the child who becomes King get to ignore his rule? Why does it matter *how* a God is created? All that matters is that you *obey* him."

Through the fog of my own terror, I managed to say, "It matters when that God was created through fear and manipulation—"

"No," he countered, "I am the Blacksmith. I do not *manipulate*, the way your Tailor does. I *forge*. I *shape*. I *create*." He looked at me without ire or hate. "Don't you see, Falcio? You and I both know how weak this country has become, how corrupt its citizens, from the highest noble to the lowest peasant. You and the Greatcoats . . . for all the honor and decency you've tried to bring to these people, how have they repaid you? With derision, betrayal. You've given your lives to save a country that is nothing more than a rotting carcass being fought over by venal noblemen. You know what I say is true, Falcio; you know Tristia can't survive as it is. We must make it strong again—it will *thrive* under a God's rule."

Erastian gave a bitter laugh. "You fool. Our ancestors were full of hate and rage at the world. They sat there night after bitter night, praying for someone to come and kill their enemies. Our Gods are little more than demons cloaked in deceit."

Of course, I thought, *because this is Tristia, where even the Gods we worship turn out to be petty and cheap.*

"And what are Saints, then," the Blacksmith asked, "but petty thieves seeking their own glory?"

"We show people they can aspire to something greater," Erastian replied. Then he turned to me and grinned. "Of course, that wasn't our original purpose." He turned back to face the God. "When the people of Tristia crafted their own laws to live by, the Gods became enraged: they sought to make us kneel before them, to swear on our souls to obey their commands. Some of us didn't; some of us stood firm. *That* is our purpose: the Saints exist to stand against the tyranny of Gods who would make their worshippers into slaves."

The God smiled then, and spoke for the second time. "*You. Exist. To. Serve.*"

The sentence was a mountain falling on our shoulders, and we all sank to our knees, even Erastian and Ethalia. There was no way for us to resist. Nothing I'd felt before, not even Birgid's Awe, could compare to this. This wasn't mere command; it was *revelation*: we were tiny, insignificant things, born to serve, fulfilled only in genuflection.

Beside me I could hear Kest, grunting like a pig struggling to escape a mud pit that was slowly sucking him inexorably into its depths. I could almost feel the vibrations in the air from his trembling body, from his desperate desire to stand. He made me so ashamed of myself, for not being able even to try, and I hated him then, for having so much more strength in whatever passes for a soul in our miserable flesh than I ever had.

Someone spoke, and it took me a moment to realize who it was until Erastian-who-plucks-the-rose, Saint of Romantic Love, said, "Right, well then, I guess the time for talk is over."

With all the effort I could muster, I brought my chin up enough that I could see him as he rose to his feet, dusted himself off and extended a hand to Ethalia. "Remember when I told you that Mercy wasn't the same thing as passivity? It's time to fight now, sister. Even the Gods are bound to trial by combat."

Ethalia looked at me, her eyes wide with pain, as she slowly pushed herself to her feet, and I tried desperately to rise, to join her, to fight by her side.

I couldn't.

I guess we aren't all meant to be Saints.

CHAPTER FIFTY-FIVE

THE APOSTATE

If you've never seen two Saints fighting for their lives against an incarnate God, it looks like—well, nothing, really.

"Are they doing anything?" Brasti asked. The three of us were still on our knees, still unable to rise. "Because right now it looks an awful lot like they're all trying to stare each other to death."

Kest's labored breathing told me he too was fighting against the force that held us to the ground. "You . . . aren't *seeing* it," he tried to explain. "The battle's happening beyond this place."

I tried to see what Kest saw, to bear witness to the war between God and Saints unfolding before us, and for a long time it was just as Brasti had said: the almost comical vision of the three of them facing each other, staring intently into each other's eyes—then my vision blurred, as if I'd stared at a flame too long, I felt a stabbing pain in my temples, forcing me to close my eyes, and at last I saw the way such duels are fought. There's no fire, no lightning, no giant serpents swallowing their victims whole. This was something different. This was much, *much* worse.

"You . . . see?" Kest asked.

I see a big man with a back made strong and shoulders made broad from long days working the mill, baring his teeth as he brings his fist down upon his child's jaw, again and again: a brutal, endless rhythm as he punishes the boy over and over . . .

Two young women hold an old mother down while a third kicks her in the stomach, the leg a swinging pendulum keeping time, once, twice, thrice . . .

A bird lands on a windowsill, drawn to a small pile of seed, but before it can eat a hand comes crashing down to grab it and squeezes until the tiny bones of its ribcage crack and give.

"Hells," I whispered. I had seen all that, and a hundred hundred more such horrors; worse, I knew every one was real and happening right now somewhere in the vast distances of this country. *This is who we are as a people. This is what we do when no one is watching.*

Erastian's glib voice pulled me out of the blood-soaked visions. "Is that really all you've got, you dumb son of a bitch?" The old man's brow furrowed in concentration and I closed my own eyes and saw—

—a girl, young, her cheeks alight with the first bloom of womanhood. She climbs up the mountainside, although it's dangerous; everyone knows it, and she's always been afraid of heights. But not today, because there's a blue rose that grows there and she plans to pluck it. She'll hold it between her teeth by the stem and smiling confidently, she'll stride into town, to the young traveling musician who'd played the song for her on his violin, the song about a rose that couldn't be found. But she knew where it was, and she would find it: a gift. A promise . . .

"Fascinating," the Blacksmith said, standing apart from the conflict, apparently quite unaffected by his God's terrible will. "Such remarkable intensity from a man whose Sainthood is little more than a childish fantasy."

"*Kneel,*" the God said, and a rushing filled my ears—*a thousand moans escaping the lips of a hundred terrified men, hanging onto the sides of a boat even as the storm tears it apart, begging for the lightning to stop.*

"See, this is the problem with Gods," Erastian said, and when I turned, I saw him grinning, his jaw set tight. "The only thing they understand is whatever single-minded, half-witted emotion bound itself into their form."

Suddenly, the moans disappeared, replaced by whispers—

—two lovers, their breath warmed by the early morning sunlight. They make promises together, tell each other tales of the improbable life they will share, full of adventures and embraces . . .

"*Stop,*" the God said, smothering the lovers' song.

"You laugh at romantic love," Erastian said, "but it is the path that leads us beyond mere survival and greed. Mercy is the healer, but also the protector. She is the blessing and the sanctifier, the sword and the shield. What we bear is seven hells more powerful than your petty nightmares."

"What do you know of nightmares?" the Blacksmith shouted, pacing back and forth in front of his God, then he stopped and screamed, "Show them what a true nightmare looks like!"

—a man walks through the fields on the way home from a long day at the forge. He comes upon a patch of beautiful yellow flowers growing behind the old church. He hasn't seen their like before. He brings them home to brighten his family's evening in these hard times . . .

"What is this?" Erastian asked. "What are you—?"

—the man watches as his eldest boy screams, suffering such terrors, such insanity, that even after he binds him with heavy ropes, the child bites off his own tongue so he can choke on it—

"You . . ." I was barely able to summon breath. "You were the one Obladias talked about—the man who lost Faith after his family died. The flowers you found were Adoracia. That's what caused—"

—the second child has it now; her suffering is even worse. She clacks her teeth together, over and over, until they shatter, and with the remaining shards she chews herself until—

"Give them more," the Blacksmith shouted.

"No," Ethalia cried out, "don't—"

—the man watches his wife cradling their smallest child, not even a month old and too tiny to be able to hurt herself, but the pain never

stops. The mother prays over and over to every God and every Saint ever known, and none listen—

"All save one," the Blacksmith spat, his eyes on Ethalia. "She came—and she did *nothing*. She gave us *nothing*. Her Mercy was as useless as a breeze against a raging fever."

The God opened his mouth wide and let forth his next words: "*No Mercy.*"

—the wife looks up at her husband, feeling the illness come upon her at last. She's so grateful that she won't have to watch her man suffer first—

"You survived," I said. "The toxin—"

"I prayed to the Gods to grant me my own death, and even that was refused. I thought I would go mad with grief. I suppose I did." He looked down on me. "We are all mad in this fallen country, Falcio. The only question is what shape that madness will take."

"You became like her . . . like the Tailor."

"That's what it means to be Inlaudati," he said. "When my mind shattered, I didn't find the peace of oblivion or even the purity of endless agony . . . instead, I began to see the deep patterns of the world around me—I saw how that world might be changed. We Unrecognized, like your Tailor, like me, we do not become Kings or Queens or Saints—instead, we shape events. *We* decide who will rule and who will die."

"Such power," Ethalia said. "You could honor your family's loss with this skill; you could use it to help save this country—and instead you bring us ruin!"

"Have you not listened to a word I have said?" the Blacksmith scolded her. He looked upon the God he had made. "Not ruin but *order,* not tyranny but *efficiency.* This country has been tested over and over again, and it has been found wanting. It is tired, enfeebled: a country of women in a world that demands the strength of men."

"He takes an unnecessarily dim view of women," Brasti muttered.

"And of the country," Kest added.

The Blacksmith wandered beneath one of the gibbets and reached up a hand to set the corpse of the dead God of War swinging. "War is coming, Falcio. Your King knew this; you know it. Avares will cross those mountains one day soon, and this time they'll destroy us. And what good will all your petty little laws do us then?"

"*No laws save mine,*" the God declared, his words transforming into a wild dog made rabid by pure rage, tearing at our minds piece by piece. It appeared the time for talk really was over: now the God brought forth his nightmares and set them on us one after another—

—*the boy can't see, his eyes too swollen. He smells his own urine as it runs down his leg and pools on the floor. His hand slips in it as he tries to crawl away, sobbing, "Please, Father, please. I'll do anything you want, I promise. Anything!"—*

—*the old woman coughs, and blood fills her mouth. The scent of bile fills her nostrils as the two girls holding her cheer for the third to kick harder. "Please," the old mother says, "please, I'll give you anything you want. Anything"—*

—*the bird's hollow bones crack under the crush of the mighty hand. It smells the morbid scent released into the air as its internal organs split apart under the pressure. It has no words, no song with which even to beg—*

Erastian coughed, and the thin, wrinkled skin on his face started splitting from the strain of holding back the foul images. Blood began to trickle from his nose, then his mouth, then his eyes.

The Blacksmith sounded almost disappointed. "Your Saint has failed his test, Falcio."

"No!" Ethalia cried, and she took Erastian's hand. "Tell me how to help."

Despite the intense pain he must have felt, the old Saint smiled at her. He winked, and the blood clung to his eyelashes. "It . . . gives me strength just to be near you, my dear, but if you could summon a little love in your heart, that would be of great help."

She turned her gaze on me, and I realized she was searching to find that brief moment we had shared, when we'd truly been in love; it was like watching someone try to break apart stone with their fingernails. I have never felt more pathetic.

"Erastian can't hold on much longer," Kest said, growling; he was still pushing against the ground, trying to rise. "I do not have the strength to break free," he added.

"Then what *are* you doing?" Brasti asked. His own attempts were obviously just as weak and useless as mine.

"I am . . . searching inside myself for the strength to do so."

"And if you do? What good is a sword going to be against a God?"

"The man I see wears armor."

Brasti managed to move his head barely an inch, but it was enough. "So what? Trin's wearing armor too."

Then I realized what Kest meant: though we saw different versions of the God, there was one similarity . . . *Why would a God need armor unless he had some vulnerability to the physical world . . .*

"Kest," I said slowly, "as First Cantor of the Greatcoats, I am *ordering* you to get on your feet and kill that son of a bitch."

The Blacksmith chuckled as if we were sharing a joke. "I would have expected such an experienced duelist to know the difference between strength and false hope."

Erastian appeared to have redoubled his efforts, for the blood was now dripping constantly down his face. "We fight with dreams," he pointed out. "There's a difference."

Ethalia turned away from me, trying to fight back against the God with her own strength.

—a mother comforts her child, "It will be all right, my dearest, just—"

The vision faltered, like a kite without enough wind to let it fly. A bead of sweat trickled down her forehead.

—a soldier saves the life of a defeated enemy. He wraps the wound—

"I can't do it!" Ethalia cried.

"You can, and you will," Erastian said, gritting his teeth. "Don't just make things up: find something *real*. It's out there somewhere."

She closed her eyes, and then . . .

—a girl steps out from behind the table where she's been hiding. Her father yells at her, tells her to get to her room, even as he reaches down to grab the boy by the neck. The girl starts to leave, but then

stops, turns and steps in front of the father, keeping him from her brother—

"That's the stuff," Erastian said, "give me more of that."

The Blacksmith's God countered, bringing his own foul visions down like an ax upon them, and Erastian and Ethalia leaned against each other, struggling to withstand the onslaught. The sights, sounds, and smells swirled around us: a war fought on a hundred different planes against the endless power of a God, while all I could do was to kneel on the rough ground, a spectator.

Then something odd happened: the visions slowly began to turn; the sounds of gloating started fading beneath music, sweet and daring, the stench of despair began to flee in front of clean ocean air.

"*Stop,*" the God commanded.

"Fight, damn you," the Blacksmith shouted at his deity.

"He's weakening, I think," I said quietly, but Kest didn't reply. I could see his arms shivering as he fought to push back the earth itself so that he could rise.

"*Stop!*" the God repeated: a wave crashing down on us, tearing our flesh and our souls.

Erastian, bloody as he was, showed no signed of relenting. "Your God isn't as strong as you hoped. I guess your faith isn't—"

The old man's voice was cut off, replaced by a groan of pain, and I dragged my head around to see the Blacksmith, standing over the Saint of Romantic love with his blade deep inside the Saint's belly. "Here is your *faith*," he spat, and Erastian fell to the ground.

The God regained his footing and I watched him smile at me, first as Fost, then Trin, then Caveil, and now his features were shifting back and forth between theirs and the faces of every other monster I'd met in my life.

"No!" Ethalia screamed, and in that battlefield that was a thousand places and none at all, I could see she was pushing back with a ferocity and strength I couldn't have imagined.

It wasn't nearly enough.

"I'm sorry, My Lady," the Blacksmith said, pulling the dagger from Erastian's body and turning to her. "You did nothing to deserve this."

She set her Awe upon him and for just a moment, he stopped—but now the God was focusing his will entirely on her, and in my mind I saw—

—*a child, trapped in the narrow confines of a well, water covering his chin, still rising, over his mouth, and now his nose—*

Now, I told myself, *it's time to get on your damned feet before he kills her.* I had my own vision then, of a young and foolish husband who knelt on the ground of his own farm while his wife sacrificed herself for him. *No, not again.* Never *again.*

But I couldn't stand, however badly I wanted to; my flesh was too weak. I lacked whatever spirit lets a man face his Gods. In desperation, I begged Kest, "Please! You have to save her."

My oldest friend looked at me with eyes forced so wide from pain and inexhaustible effort that I didn't think he could possibly have heard me until I saw the almost indistinguishable dip of his head, though the muscles in his neck were so taut they looked as though they might snap.

"*Now!*" the God exulted, and suddenly the Blacksmith was free from Ethalia's Awe. He drew the dagger back and I saw the still-bloody tip of the blade that was about to bury itself into Ethalia's heart.

A cry of anguish filled my ears, and for a brief instant I thought it another vision in the battle between God and Saint—but then I saw a miracle happen: Kest leaped into the air, and in that same fluid motion, drew his sword from its scabbard. The blade crashed down on the Blacksmith's wrist and I heard the bones break. The heavy gauntlet held, though, and the Blacksmith switched the dagger to his uninjured hand and went to stab again, but Kest knocked the blade out of his hand even as he brought his own weapon back in a swing to strike at the God.

"*Cease,*" the God commanded, and Kest fell back.

The Blacksmith scrambled for his dagger and snatched it up from the ground. He lifted it back up, preparing to strike at Ethalia, but the old Saint of Romantic Love wasn't done, not quite. He had one hand pressing down on the wound in his belly, but with the other he reached out and touched the Blacksmith's leg.

The big man stumbled back as if he'd stepped in fire.

"Your God isn't looking too good," Erastian said, spitting blood and rising to his feet.

The Blacksmith saw his creation struggling to stay standing. Kest was finding his balance again. We might even be winning.

"You should be proud," the Blacksmith said to Kest. "You renounced your own Sainthood and stood in defiance of a God's will. It is a remarkable thing to do. Take comfort from that thought." He looked back at the God he had created; it was obvious that he was severely weakened, thanks to the strength of Erastian and Ethalia and Kest.

But the God spoke a single word: "*Apostate.*" There were no visions this time, no sounds of terror, no slithering sensations or vile scents attacking us. Even Kest gave no sign that he'd heard, at first. He just stood there as if he were planning his next strike.

"Kest?" I asked.

He opened his mouth wide, as if not enough air was getting into his lungs. His sword slid from his hand and he reached up and clutched at his heart.

"There is a price to be paid for challenging a God," the Blacksmith told him, not ungently. He glanced at me. "I feel sorrow for you, Falcio. You find good men and women to do what you think is right, but the world you once believed in is long gone—it might never have been what you were told." He hesitated for a moment, then said, "I offer you this gift, Falcio val Mond: go back to Aramor. Take your people away—find a country worthy of your courage. Leave this one to those who might yet be able to redeem it." He turned and led his God down the path away from us.

"No," I said. "No, don't do this. You don't have to—"

Kest's eyes caught mine as he began to slip to the ground, and I could see that he understood what had been done to him. There had been no blow, no injury, no illness. At the command of a God, Kest's life had simply ended.

CHAPTER FIFTY-SIX
THE BROKEN HEART

Kest fell to the ground, landing so hard on his back that dust and dirt flew into the air. Even an unconscious man would have made a sound as the wind fled from his lungs, but Kest was completely silent, though the emptiness was filled by someone screaming his name. I think it was me.

"What in hells just happened to him?" Brasti asked.

Ethalia knelt by Kest's side. "His heart has stopped." She placed both hands just below his chest and pressed down hard, then repeated the gesture several more times before stopping briefly to listen for his breath. When none came, she said to Erastian, "Help me . . . I can't make it start again!"

The old Saint, still on the ground, was looking more than half-dead himself. He held a hand to his wound, and I saw a faint glow around it, the pink of a rose just beginning to bloom. "Damned knife wounds," he muttered, then crawled one-handed toward Kest and looked down at the already pale features of the friend I'd forced into a fight he couldn't win because I'd been too weak to do it myself. "A God's curse weighs heavy on a mortal life," Erastian said, then added, "Sons of bitches."

"Do something," I begged.

The Saint took Kest's hand in his. "Did Birgid teach you the calling?" he asked Ethalia. She nodded as she repeated her motions, and Erastian looked both confused and disappointed. "So she taught you how to heal but not to fight? What was the woman thinking?"

Ethalia's eyes narrowed. "That I had committed enough violence for one lifetime."

Violence? Ethalia was the most peaceful person I had ever met.

Erastian was neither shocked nor impressed by the heat of her gaze. "Don't give me that look, woman. I've been stared down by Gods." He placed Kest's palm against Ethalia's heart and gestured for her to hold it there. "Come on then, perform the calling. Show me what a coin with only one side can buy."

She held Kest's hand to her heart and placed her other hand against his chest. Her eyes closed, and the skin of her face tightened as if she were trying to push a boulder up a mountain. She started whispering, so softly that it took me a moment to hear that she was calling out Kest's name, over and over.

"The boy's death isn't natural," Erastian explained. "This isn't a stab wound or an infection. His heart simply stopped beating. If she can call him back—"

"Call him how?" Brasti asked. "From where? Will someone please tell me how—?"

He shut up when Ethalia began to glow, the light first manifesting as a sheen as sweat started dripping down her face, then pushing outward until her entire body looked as if it were cut from polished ivory.

She's so pale, I thought, and Erastian's jibe about her being a one-sided coin filled me with dread. *Prove him wrong, sweetheart. Prove to us that there's some purpose to magic and Saints beyond just ruining the world.*

"What can I do?" I asked.

"You can shut up," Erastian replied, his hand still covering his own wound. The old man didn't look optimistic. Brasti and I stared at each other, utterly miserable in our helplessness: there was no enemy for us to fight, no daring action we could take to stop the blow that had already fallen.

"The beat of my heart to yours," Ethalia whispered. "You hear me, Kest, son of Murrow. You must answer." The glow around her grew brighter as her words became more desperate. "The beat of my heart to yours," she repeated. "Kest, by the love you bear this world, you will answer me."

"Is she really supposed to be glowing like that?" Brasti asked.

"No," Erastian replied, his eyes still fixed on Ethalia. "She's got to stop now." He raised his voice. "You've got to stop now, Ethalia. It's over. Enough now, girl."

Ethalia's eyes opened briefly and there was such cold fire there that even Erastian-who-plucks-the-rose knew to stop talking. "The beat of my heart to yours," she repeated, her voice stronger now, though her whole body was shaking as if the earth beneath her was breaking apart. "The Saint of Mercy calls you, King's Blade, and you will answer."

For just an instant I thought Kest had moved, but it was only Ethalia, twitching under the strain of whatever invisible forces she was struggling with. "Something's wrong," Brasti said. "That glow of hers is dimming."

"Enough," Erastian said, reaching out to grab at her wrist. "You'll kill yourself."

Ethalia held firm, but she cried out "Birgid, help me! I can't bring him back!"

The old Saint finally managed to tear her hand away from her chest. "It's done, girl," he said softly. "Let it be done."

Ethalia began to slump forward, but she stopped herself. Her eyes went to me. "I'm sorry—I'm so sorry—"

"I can thump on his chest," I said, moving to his side and trying to replicate her movements from earlier. "He's strong. He can come back." *You don't go out this way, Kest. With a blade, maybe—with ten thousand masters of the sword rushing down the hillside at us, maybe. Not like this. We don't go out just because some fucking God says so.*

"Falcio, stop," Brasti said. "You're going to break his ribs. It's not doing any good. Let him—"

"No." I resumed pushing his chest up and down, though I had no damned clue what I was doing. Ethalia had been doing it, so it must've had some purpose.

Erastian sounded sympathetic as he explained, "His heart won't beat for hers."

The words held such a small, simple truth, that all the strength drained from my body and I found myself repeating them. *His heart won't beat for hers.* I looked over at the old man, at this useless sack of flesh who called himself a Saint and was doing me no good whatsoever. "Why?"

Ethalia's eyes were full of pleading, as if she were begging me to forgive her. "He won't follow my heartbeat—he won't come to my call."

I grabbed Kest's hand and put it on my own chest. "Then show me what to do. Maybe he'll come back—"

"You don't have the power, Falcio," she said. "It's part of the Sainthood. I can't . . . I don't even know how to explain it to you."

"Just tell me how to save him, damn you!" I reached out and grabbed her arm. "There must be something else you can try. *Anything.*"

"You can't!" she cried, "not without . . . You just *can't*, Falcio."

She turned away from me, too quickly for it to just be guilt. I've been a magistrate for a long time, and when I look for it, I can tell when someone's lying to me. "Tell me," I demanded.

"He has a right to try," Erastian said, his voice wheezing as his own wounds threatened to overtake him. He turned to me. "How far are you willing to go to save your friend?"

It took me a while to understand what he was asking. "Oh," I said finally. "I suppose that makes sense."

Ethalia grabbed me by the shoulders, and I could see her eyes were filled with tears now. "No, you don't understand—there's no assurance I can bring you back."

"Just tell me how."

Misery and uncertainty clouded her face, but she knew me well. Even with all that had already been lost between us, she knew I wouldn't back down from this fight. Finally she said, "Lay down next to Kest and place his hand over your heart. Then we must . . . Falcio, I can't be the one to do it."

"I know," I said.

"Would someone *please* tell me what in all the hells is going on?" Brasti asked plaintively.

Saint Erastian sat back heavily on his haunches. "You aren't going to like it, that's for sure," he muttered.

I rose for a moment and held Brasti by the shoulders. Before he could speak I shook him. "Brasti Goodbow, listen to me. I'm not your friend right now. I'm not a fellow Greatcoat. I'm the First Cantor. Do you understand? Do you still remember what that means?"

"What in the name of Saint Zaghev is *wrong* with you, Falcio? Of course I—"

"No questions, no debate. I'm giving you an order now, so you either follow it, or you walk away. For good."

He finally understood what was coming next. He looked down at Kest then back at me. "Please, Falcio, don't ask me to do this."

"I'm sorry," I said gently.

I let him go and laid down next to Kest, placing his hand on my heart, then I looked up at Brasti and said, "Kill me."

Brasti knelt over me, squeezing his hands into fists, trying to build up his courage. *Or whatever it is you need when one of your best friends tells you to murder him.*

Ethalia's voice was gentle. "We're running out of time. He can't go without—"

"Brasti," I said, locking eyes with him, "it's going to be all right. I swear to you, I'm not going out like this. *Not like this.*"

He nodded then, placed a hand over my mouth and with the other squeezed my nostrils shut as I told myself, *It's fine. You can do this. You've nearly gone to your death dozens of times. Just go a little further this time.*

At first it was no different to holding my breath, then it started to burn, like diving too deep into water and waiting too long to come back up. Then the first convulsion hit me and my body struggled to take in air, resisting Brasti's grip. He let out a great racking sob and held me down even more firmly.

Part of me was thankful that for once in his life, Brasti was following orders. The rest of me was panicking. *No,* I screamed silently, *no, it's a mistake! This won't work! You're killing me!* My eyes betrayed me as they tried desperately to lock onto Brasti's, pleading for him to stop, to see that I was dying, to see that he was killing me.

The second convulsion was worse and now I was fighting back with everything I had, but Brasti was now kneeling on me, holding me down and crushing me under his weight.

I cursed him then, cursed how stupid he was. *Damn you to every hell there is, Brasti Goodbow, bastard—traitor—*Then a sudden inspiration hit me and my eyes sought out Ethalia. She would understand—she would put a stop to this. But her own eyes were closed as she held one of my hands against her heart. I could feel the beating there. I hated it.

Bitch. Whore. This is what you wanted all along, to be rid of me. You tricked me into this!

I wish I could say I was a better man, that in those last moments I found my courage again, found my Faith.

I didn't.

I went to my death afraid and cursing everyone I had once loved.

CHAPTER FIFTY-SEVEN
THE LAND OF THE DEAD

Every duelist knows that the only God who really matters is Death. His is the damp, grasping hand you feel reaching into your heart every time a wound cuts a little too deep or a fever rages a little too hot inside your skin. Death is the opponent whose challenge we all must eventually accept, and his is the duel that in the end can never be won no matter how skilled the fencer or how noble the cause. All our tricks and techniques are stripped away when we step into his courtroom for that final trial.

Shit, I thought, looking down at myself. *I'm naked.*

I had always assumed that the land of the dead, if such a place existed at all, would be an endless expanse of darkness and shadows. Instead, what I found was a landscape carved from bone: roads, trees, mountains in the far distance, even the sky above: they were all the same sickly ivory color. There were no lights, nothing that glowed or burned, and yet there was no darkness, either, only an endless dead whiteness.

Except me, I thought, once again taking stock of my less than impressive figure. *Because when you're dead and naked what you really want to do is stick out.*

"And people claim my royal staff was of modest proportions," King Paelis called out and I turned to see him walking up behind me, his robes glistening seven different hues of red. *Even in the afterlife the rich get to dress better than the rest of us.*

My wife, walking alongside him, wore armor that glistened against the drab surroundings. It was so perfectly shaped to her that were it not for the ridges and buckles it would have looked as though molten steel had been poured over body.

"That's an odd look for you," I said.

"Really, husband? Was I not always a fighter?"

The King snorted. "Enough, Falcio. I've gone along with your imaginings as long as I could, but this is too much. You really envision your wife as a great warrior striding across the land?"

"She was to me," I said, wishing she were real, wishing this wasn't simply the hallucinations that came whenever I slipped too close to death. "None of this is real, is it?"

Aline stepped close to me and reached out with a gauntleted hand to smooth the hair away from my face. Her touch felt strangely soft. "Do you remember the oath I gave at our wedding, Falcio?"

The question made me uncomfortable. "It was something about loving and sharing, but to be honest, I was so busy trying to remember my own vows at the time, it's possible I wasn't paying attention."

She took both my hands in hers. "I said you were a silly man, too awkward and earnest to make his way through life in a country that fed on such things." She squeezed my palms and now I could feel the steel of her gauntlets. "I said I would always protect you."

Something felt like it broke inside me and a shuddering sob escaped my lips. "No—that's not what you said. The cleric gave us our vows. I was the one who was supposed to say—"

"How would you know?" King Paelis asked. "You already said you weren't paying attention."

"It was *my* job to protect *you*!" I turned away from them, wishing them away. "You aren't her. You're a delusion made from fractured memories and broken dreams."

"Look at me," Aline said. I felt her hand on my arm and she repeated the words more gently this time. "Look at me, Falcio."

I did. I'd never been able to refuse her.

"Do I look like a delusion to you?" she asked. Her smile was neither soft nor stern, her features not plain, but nor were they particularly beautiful. For the first time in a very long time I saw her as she had truly been in life: a village woman, a farmer. Pretty, but mostly in the way she grinned when she had something wicked to say. Sensuous, but mostly when she danced. You could see in her eyes how brilliantly clever she was—not for its own sake, but because her sense of practicality demanded it. Beyond and above all those things, however, Aline always had an unwavering determination about her. "Whether dream or memory, Falcio, I said I would protect you. I always will."

"It's supposed to be me," I said. "I was the swordsman. I was supposed to—"

The sky cracked, the sound crashing down on us while the world around us shook and shivered in its wake. Everything went black then, ended, then a moment later the darkness disappeared, to be replaced once again by the endless bone whiteness of this place.

"Ha!" the King roared. "Did you see that? That was—"

"Let him figure it out for himself," Aline said.

I thought about it for a moment, until I realized I'd mistaken the source of the sound. "It wasn't thunder," I said. "It was a heartbeat."

"One of your last, if you don't get on with it," Paelis said. "Hurry. Kest is hiding in this place and you must find him."

The sky shook again, another heartbeat, and again the world went black before returning. *The darkness lasted longer this time. Time to go.*

"Who is Kest hiding from?"

King Paelis put a hand on my shoulder. "From you, Falcio."

"But why? Why would—?"

"He's your dearest friend," Aline chided me. "Do you truly know him so little? Go. You must find him now."

I started to move, then stopped. "It should have been you," I said. I didn't trust myself to be able to leave if I looked back at her. "You should have been the first Greatcoat."

She gave no reply, but King Paelis laughed in that reedy tone of his. "Don't you get it, Falcio? She gave up everything to protect you. She made an oath that held despite fear and death and the Gods themselves. Aline *was* the first Greatcoat."

I'm not sure how long I chased Kest in the endless pale shadows as he weaved and ducked around and behind everything that might shield him from me. The sky shook twice more, the final desperate beating of his heart, or mine. *Or maybe none of this is real and this is just the last defiant flicker of my life fading away.*

Every time I came close to grabbing Kest's shoulder he darted out of the way, and the chase continued anew. *This isn't real,* I thought. *There is no world of bone for us to race through. We're lying on the hard ground. Damn you, Kest, just breathe, and get us out of here.*

I shouted for him, again and again, and no sound came from my lips, but he appeared to hear me—not that it did me much good. Every time I called out to him, he looked up at the sky instead of at me, and then turned and ran even faster.

I heard the crack of thunder again and this time, the black clouds began to gather together, expanding until they became too big for the sky. They descended upon the countryside, taking on a thick, oily form as they began to smother everything in sight. Breathing became harder and harder as I tried to outrun them.

"Kest!"

He didn't turn now, just kept on running, always ahead of me.

"Kest!" I tried to force a shout from my lips. The clouds were all around us, as though the nightmist we'd unleashed in the mine was pursuing us, even here. I started after Kest again, but pulled to a stop when a shape began to push its way out of the black mists, burning them away with an angry crimson fire. He carried a sword, and spun it so fast I couldn't see the steel, only the trail of flame it left in the air.

Caveil-whose-blade-cuts-water, I thought. *The Saint of Swords is coming for me.*

Birgid's words from months before came back to me, reminding me that *I* had been the one destined to face Caveil—the one destined to die at his hand.

Instinctively, I reached for my rapiers, but the world of the dead has as much justice in it as the world of the living and so I was still naked and unarmed.

Caveil whipped his sword through the air and I felt the tip striking me a hundred times before I could even draw the breath to scream. By the time I looked down at my flesh, a thousand little cuts were bleeding, and tiny flying insects descended on me, attaching themselves to my wounds, sucking at them like human mouths.

The Saint of Swords brought his blade up high in the air and I saw the very moment where it reached its zenith, and the immeasurable fraction of a second where it held before it began its descent toward my skull.

A pale blur leapt between us: a flash of steel came alongside and knocked Caveil's sword from its path.

"Don't worry, Falcio," the figure said, taking up a position between me and the Saint. "I'll protect you!"

It was Kest, but not the man I knew. Instead, the boy I had first known, barely twelve years old, grinning from ear to ear as he struggled to hold up a warsword far too heavy for his size, and far too slow to stop the Saint of Swords. Caveil gave out a soundless laugh and struck out with his own blade, stabbing Kest over and over until a dozen holes in his body revealed the black-smothered world behind him.

Caveil's gaze returned to me and he smiled as he sent his blade shooting out toward me. But again, Kest managed to bring up his sword and strike, ignoring the fact that he was far too wounded for such a feat even to be possible. He kicked out with a gangly leg and hit Caveil in the stomach, knocking him back into the black clouds.

Kest turned to me, still grinning even as he bled from his wounds. "Boy, that sure wasn't easy," he said.

"Kest, come with me," I said, extending a hand toward him. "We have to go."

He shook his head and pointed back to the clouds. "We can't, Falcio. There are still more people trying to kill you."

A second figure emerged from the mists, this one taller and broader of shoulder than Caveil. The armor covering his body was made of thick steel plates. The sword he carried was nearly as big as I was.

Shuran.

Even before Kest could lift his sword up in defense, Shuran knocked him aside and began marching toward me, heaving his massive sword back and forth as though he were cutting the space between us apart. His helm covered his face and yet I could see him smiling, his hard jaw set in preparation for the single blow it would take him to cut me in half.

I looked around for something, *anything* with which to fight back. There was nothing on the cloud-covered ground of use but little black rocks, but when I tried picking one up, intending to throw it at Shuran, even though it was barely bigger than my fist it refused to be lifted, sticking to the earth as though welded there.

Great. Even the rocks in this country are cowards.

I rose back up to my feet. I thought about running away but now my own feet wouldn't obey my commands. Shuran stopped then, barely three feet away from me, and raised his sword overhead.

"Goodbye," he said.

Just as the heavy sword started down for my head, Kest rose up and parried the attack with his warsword. Shuran grunted in response and lifted up his weapon, just a few inches, before bringing it back down and severing Kest's hand at the wrist, sending it along with his sword crashing to the ground.

The boy Kest ignored the loss of his hand and dropped to his knees. Picking up his sword in his left, he prepared to attack, but Shuran was faster and with a single stroke he took Kest's other hand, leaving him without the means to hold a sword.

"No!" I screamed.

Shuran tried to knock the boy aside to get to me but Kest ducked and came back up after the blade had swung past. He kicked out with his bare foot, striking the Knight in the hip, sending him stumbling backward. "I'd better go after him," he said, before turning to run into the black clouds.

"Kest, no!" I shouted. "You can't fight now. He's too—"

"Don't worry, Falcio," the boy shouted back, grinning, "I've still got two legs to lose, and then my head after that!"

The thunder cracked once again. How long had it been since the last time? Surely this had been the longest gap between beats? With a force of will that was far beyond what I could have imagined, I reached into the clouds and grabbed Kest by the shoulder, hauling him back before he could disappear into the blackness.

"Stop!" I said, not just to him, but to the world around us. "*Stop!*"

My command had an odd effect: the landscape shifted again, returning to the unlit white I had seen when I first arrived. I could move again without strain. I was so furious with the boy's reckless desire to protect me that I spun him around to shake him, but when I did, he had become the Kest I knew again, with a man's form and a man's face, his limbs returned to him except for the right hand I had severed months before. He was crying.

"What in hells are you doing?" I demanded.

"Please, Falcio," he said, the tears streaming down his cheeks. "Please . . ."

I let go of him. "Please what? What is it you want?"

He wiped a bare arm across his eyes, then held out the stump toward me. "Just let me die."

The thunder that came next was softer than the others, the last tired rumbles of a fading storm. My limbs felt exhausted. I looked down to see that they too were taking on the tired white of the landscape around us.

"I don't understand," I said, not for the first time.

"Of course you do," Kest said, his voice devoid of any emotion, even the ambition to sway me. "You just prefer to pretend that you don't." He walked a few feet away where a dim shadow of his war-sword lay discarded on the ground. He knelt down and picked it up in his left hand, the muscles on his face contorting with pain. "Look at me," he said, holding the sword out, tremors running along the length of his arm as he struggled to keep it from falling back to the ground.

"It's only been a few months," I said. "The healers warned that you might experience ghostly pains—"

Kest laughed at that, a cold, bitter sound. "'Ghostly pains'? Falcio, this isn't *real*. You and I aren't made of flesh in this place. This sword isn't made of steel, it's not made of anything. It's just a hallucination."

"Then why—?"

"Because it still hurts!" he screamed, and threw the blade to the ground. It landed without a sound. "Don't you see what's happened to me? It's not the sword that gives me pain, it's the very thought of holding it!"

Another echo of thunder, this one barely a stutter, with no sign of lightning following it.

"We have to go, Kest."

He looked away from me. "I spent every day of my life since I was twelve years old trying to become the best swordsman in the world, trying to protect you, trying to fight for the things you believe in."

"The things *we* believe in," I said, but the words sounded hollow even to me. All my life I'd wanted to be a great swordsman, someone who defended others. Instead, they had all been protecting me.

Kest shook his head. "I would do *anything* to go back and stop her from dying, Falcio. When you met her, those first couple of years . . ."

"Don't," I warned.

He ignored me. "I thought maybe you would set aside all your talk of Greatcoats, of fighting the horrible things of this country. I thought you would be happy, that maybe I could find a way to be happy for you. Then . . . Then they took her. A few vicious men in a tavern do the kinds of things such men have been doing for a thousand years and just like that, they broke the world." He turned back to me. "Do you think, in whatever hell Fost now occupies . . . do you think he marvels at what he unleashed on the world?"

"Don't blame this on Aline," I said. "And don't blame it all on me. It was the King's dream we all—"

He waved me off with his remaining hand. "Don't start with that shit all over again. There isn't a man alive who loves you as much as I do, and even I can't stand to listen to you anymore."

The words stung, a leaden weight as if my heart was too busy trying to push out one last beat to be worried about such trivial things as discovering your best friend can't abide your presence. I looked at his sword lying between us like a line meant not to be crossed. "So what, then? If you can't be the greatest swordsman in the world then you can't be bothered to live?"

The tears were still streaming down his cheeks. "Is that so wrong? I've practiced every day of my life, read every book, trained with every living master. I've studied everything from fencing to dancing to research every possible way of moving, of perfecting my skill with the blade, all so I could become someone who *mattered*. Something other than just your . . . I don't even know what to call it." He held out the stump of his right hand to me. "What am I now, Falcio, if I can't be who I was?"

The sky sputtered for a moment—barely a sound now—and I wondered that Kest could feel such pain when there was so little life left in us. I glanced around me: the stillness of the landscape was broken by terrified men and women, scurrying to hiding behind rocks and trees, their hands clasped in prayers that would never be answered.

"Go," Kest said, "before it's too late. Do me this one service, this one favor in exchange for those I did you. Live your life and fight the Gods and shout at the oceans; just let me be."

I waited a moment before replying. I knew my answer, but it was a dangerous thing to say. "You can be less," I said at last.

He just stared at me for a long while. Then, "Less."

I knelt down and lifted up his warsword. It felt weightless, insubstantial. "You'll never be the swordsman you once were. Hells, maybe you can't ever hold a blade again at all." I tossed the weapon away. "Maybe you never were as good as we all thought; maybe Caveil whose-blade-cuts-water just had an off-day when you met him."

"This is not helping," Kest said.

I didn't care. "We're all less than we were, probably less even than *we* believed we were." I pointed to the fading landscape behind us, the cold white slowly turning to an empty gray. "And our enemies are worse than we thought, and stronger. There're more of them, and I don't think it's ever going to end. We're less than we were, less than we believed, and less than the world needs. Ever since this started I've been haunted by the fear that maybe this time we can't win."

"You really do save your best speeches for other people, don't you, Falcio?" He snorted then, an uncharacteristic action that made me wonder if all this really was just in my head. *But it doesn't matter if it's real,* I thought. *It still needs to be said.* "Maybe I don't have any good speeches left. But there's this one question that's been nagging at me every day, even when I've discovered how badly I've screwed things up, even when we're outnumbered, even when they send a fucking *God* against us."

"What's that?" he asked.

I pointed to hazy figures in the distance, looking around themselves and discovering that in the growing emptiness, there was nothing left to hide behind. "If not us, then *who*? Who's going to stand when everyone else kneels? Who's going to argue for the law even when there's no justice to be had? Who's going to try even when the trying is too damned hard?"

We looked at each other a long while before Kest finally said what he'd been holding back. "They're going to kill you, Falcio. Please don't make me watch while it happens. I won't be able to save you this time."

I nodded. He was probably right. "Fair enough. Chances are I'm going to lose my head, my life, and my country. So just answer me this: if you're beside me, are my chances of failing more or less than they would be without you?"

"Less," he said. After a moment he smiled, just a little. "Son of a bitch. I can't believe I fell for that."

A feeble crack barely lit the sky before fading into a sigh.

"Come on," I said, reaching out a hand. "It's getting harder to hear Ethalia's heartbeat and it will be peculiarly embarrassing if this all ends up being for nothing."

Kest took my hand in his. "Where are we going?"

"Follow the thunder," I said. "That's usually where the trouble is."

CHAPTER FIFTY-EIGHT
THE AWAKENING

I woke to the sound of crying. Oddly, it wasn't Ethalia.

"Hello," she said, leaning over me.

My head was in her lap, she held one of my hands over her heart. I looked to my right and saw my other was still on Kest's chest. He was breathing slowly but steadily. When I looked back up at Ethalia I said, "My heart beats for yours."

She nodded. "Apparently so."

"So I must not entirely dislike you."

She smiled at me, the little crinkles appearing around the edges of her eyes, and I felt a little better. "And it's possible I don't entirely detest you, Falcio val Mond." She held that smile a long time, long enough that had I blinked or looked away for just a moment I might not have seen how it faded. But I'm clever sometimes, so I knew what to watch for, and so I saw the illusion break.

"I hear her when she talks to you," she said at last. "Sometimes she speaks to me too."

"My wife is dead," I said, trying to keep the shame and resentment I felt from creeping into my voice. "Those are memories—hallucinations. How is that even possible?"

"I don't know," she admitted. "Perhaps you're right. Perhaps I simply imagine her too." She looked into the distance, as if she could see someone calling to her. "I'm sorry I can't love you the way Aline did."

I've never asked you to, I thought, but I didn't say it out loud. I'm no Bardatti but I know the ending of a song when I hear it. I couldn't resent Ethalia for concluding that our time together had reached its end almost as quickly as it had begun. Love is supposed to take time to build, but ours had been a bright spark that we had mistaken for a flame, until it had been smothered, over and over, by death and violence and, finally, this Sainthood that was more curse than gift to her. But none of that was the true cause; I knew this. I had loved a woman once who had been taken from me, who I refused to let go. I didn't know if Aline was a ghost, or a memory, or just a dream of a woman who, like the King, had never really been who I thought she was. None of that mattered, though: she was going to be with me always. I was as defined by her loss as I was by the shape of my face or the sound of my voice. I was a widower, still married.

So when Ethalia looked back down at me and we found ourselves staring into each other's eyes, I blinked, to signal my acceptance. Very gently, she moved my head onto a pillowed blanket. "I should look to Kest," she said.

I turned over and very slowly got back to my feet. The sound of weeping caught me again, and I looked around to see Brasti, sitting on a tree stump, his face in his hands.

"Sorry," I said, as I got close to him. "I'm afraid Kest and I are both going to live."

Brasti sniffed and rubbed his nose on the sleeve of his coat. "Erastian's dead, in case anyone cares. *He* isn't coming back." He gestured to the Saint's body. When I looked down, I saw what I could have sworn was a smile beneath the blood and dirt.

I extended a hand to Brasti. "Get up," I said.

"Why?"

"Because I'm going to hug you, you idiot."

He turned and looked up at me, his eyes and nose red. "They've got a God, Falcio. A fucking God."

"They do at that."

"They've got a God who can snap his fingers and Kest—*Kest!*—drops dead in his tracks."

"Just a little death," I said. "He's fine now."

Brasti slapped my hand away. "Oh, well then, I suppose I should just forget the fact that the actual living God of this shithole of a country is out to get us. I mean, it's not like I didn't know you had a unique ability to piss people off, Falcio, but even I underestimated just how truly skilled you are at making powerful enemies." He sniffed again, an embarrassing sound that would have made both of us laugh were it not so full of anguish. "You made me *kill* you. You made me hold your mouth closed and pinch your nose until your heart stopped."

"I'm sorry about that," I said.

"'Sorry'? You arsehole! You've got the church, the Inquisitors, the God's Needles, and now an actual God after us. Oh, but it's okay because Falcio val Mond is *sorry*. Great, now fuck off. I can't think of one reason why I'd want to hug you."

"I can think of one."

"Yeah? What would that be?"

"Because if you don't get off your ass and stand up so that I can hug you, I'm going to kiss you right on the mouth."

Brasti looked up at me, eyes narrowed for a moment, then he said, "Hells. I suppose there are some things worse than death." He rose to his feet and I pulled him to me. His breath came in big, sudden bursts, as if he were laughing. It took me a moment to realize he was crying again.

"This isn't going to help our reputation one bit, you know."

I expected a joke in reply. What I got instead was, "I'm going to destroy him, Falcio. I swear it. Before this is done, I just want one chance. I don't care if he kills me afterward but with the last arrow I fire I'm going to murder a God."

We carried Saint Erastian's body with us for more than twenty miles until we were free of the Condate of Verderen. We knew the old man well enough to be sure he would not have wanted his mortal remains left in that particular hell.

Eventually we decided to lay him to rest behind the ruins of a little church dedicated to Phenia, one of the many names of the Goddess Love. We spoke no prayers as we dug Erastian's grave, being fairly confident the Goddess could no longer answer them.

"He really was an ugly old codger," Brasti said, wiping the sweat from his brow. Lacking proper tools for grave digging, we made do with branches broken from the copse of trees that had grown through the broken stones of the church.

"Perhaps someone else should compose the eulogy," Ethalia suggested. She was standing in the three-foot hole we'd dug, using her cupped hands to remove the loose dirt.

"It's the truth," Brasti insisted. "Foul-tongued. Mean spirited. Hard to imagine how he ever inspired anyone to fall in love."

Kest pushed the edge of his branch deeper into the dirt to loosen it. I'd told him to leave the work for us, given that he'd been on the wrong side of death only a day ago, but he'd insisted he was fine. "Perhaps for some romance is about more than just beauty."

Brasti snorted. "Speaking from all your expertise on the subject, are you? Do you know, you're the only person I've ever met who, when he says he's going off to polish his sword, really means he's going to polish his sword!"

"I'm not sure I follow the distinction," Kest said, then gave a slight smile to show he had, in fact, understood. Despite the awkwardness of working with only one hand, Kest stood tall, easy. He looked more like his old self than he had in months. I knew it for an illusion, though. He was simply clinging to the pretense of normalcy the way a man being pulled down a raging river hangs on to any branch he can find.

My stick kept hitting more and more rocks beneath the soil. "That's probably as deep as we can go," I said, turning to Ethalia for her consent to place Erastian's body in the grave.

"Kest is right," she said, lost in her own thoughts. "Romantic love isn't merely attraction and pretty words." She stepped up out of the pit and knelt next to Erastian's body. "I never understood until . . ." She stopped and looked up at me. "He was the Saint of Romantic Love not simply because he embodied its virtues, but because he above all others understood its strength, and because he was willing to fight for it."

Brasti looked dubious. "I still don't see—" He stopped talking when he caught Kest's look, clearly telling him to let her be.

Ethalia spoke as if she'd forgotten the rest of us were there. "Birgid was always so kind . . . so full of serenity. I thought that's what it meant to be the Saint of Mercy."

It made sense, but on the three occasions I'd met Birgid-who-weeps-rivers she'd never evoked much of that "perfect serenity" for me. *Perhaps now's not the best time to mention that.*

"I was such a fool," Ethalia said, rising to her feet so that Brasti and I could pick up the body and place it in the grave.

"There is nothing foolish about seeking to bring peace," Kest said gently.

She began picking up handfuls of dirt and tossing them onto the body. "Peace has no currency in this world. Even Mercy must be paid for with violence."

We passed the next few minutes in silence, heaping dirt down upon the still form of the dead Saint, giving whatever last thoughts we could to the strange man we'd known for such a short while. Brasti was right: Erastian looked nothing like how one would picture the Saint of Romantic Love—in fact, nothing at all like the statues made in his honor that adorned the gardens of wealthy and sentimental nobles. *You were rude and disagreeable and shockingly unhandsome for a Saint of Romantic Love. But if I knew how to pray, I'd pray to you, old man.*

We rode south to Castle Aramor and whatever hell awaited us there. We three were back to wearing our proper greatcoats again, as we'd seen no more no hordes of shuffling pilgrims—only the signs of their passing mocked us: the long tracks left by their wagons, the abandoned remains of their fires by the side of the road, the hastily dug toilets they didn't bother to cover up. *This is what you do when you stop giving a shit about the world because you're so convinced a God is going to solve all your problems for you.*

At night we rested the horses, and ourselves, talking through plans, debating strategies. Kest theorized about whatever force it was that acted upon our will, preventing us from rising up against the Blacksmith's God. Brasti suggested traps, like digging a pit deep enough that the God might fall in and we could just bury him there. I tried to envision ways we could force one of the masks of infamy onto him, in the vain hope that that might make a difference. It's not that we thought these suggestions would do any good—none of us had a clue how to defeat a God—but you can wallow in defeat for only so long.

Ethalia sat alone through all our nonsense, meditating and trying to summon the strength to do what Erastian had done: to face down a God.

The last night out from Aramor, Brasti said, "There's something I don't understand. How can a Saint of *Mercy* be expected to fight? Isn't it a paradigm?"

"He means 'paradox,'" Kest corrected.

Brasti grimaced at him. "You know, sometimes I actually do use the word I mean to use."

"Are you sure this one of those times?"

"Shut up," I told them, because "paradox" was tickling at the edges of my thoughts. I stood up and walked over to the deserted road.

As I stared out at the dark horizon in the distance I wondered aloud, "Why did the Blacksmith wait so long?" Our timing couldn't have been so perfect that we'd just *happened* to arrive at the Cathedral at the precise moment when his God had become material—he couldn't have *meant* us to find him there when we did, could he? And Erastian and Ethalia had come close to defeating the God; they'd certainly weakened him enough that the Blacksmith had been forced to flee with him, rather than risk the Saints getting a second wind. If, as we surmised, the God's strength really did come from the worship of his followers, why not get him to them sooner? *Why wait to take power?*

"Saint-Zaghev-who-sings-for-tears," Brasti groaned. "He's doing that thing again—you know, where he stares off into the distance and mumbles to himself for hours."

"Shut up, Brasti." Oddly, it was Ethalia who spoke that time. She rose and joined me on the road. "What do you see?" she asked me.

I see a hundred victories, I thought. *I see a Prelate in control of Luth already making a move on other Duchies. I see almost all the Saints murdered, and a new God who can stop a man's heart with a word. And yet the Blacksmith isn't ready . . .*

"He's afraid," I said.

"Yeah, he's terrified," Brasti said, kicking dirt on the remains of our fire. "He's only got God's Needles and Church Knights out there killing anyone he wants. The heir to the throne is probably hiding in a barn somewhere with the Realm's Protector who, in case you forgot, is still trapped behind an iron mask herself. That leaves the Dukes to write whatever decrees the Church tells them to, which really don't matter all that much now anyway, because now the damned Inquisitors are in charge of administering the King's Laws—oh now, they're not the *King's* Laws anymore, are they? They're the *Church's* Laws!" He turned to Kest. "See, now, *that's* a fucking paradox."

I chuckled at his comment and then stopped myself. *And there it is.* The answer was so simple that it could only have been the result of a thousand individual equations. *So it really is a paradox of sorts.* "I know what weakens a God," I announced.

"What?" Kest asked.

"The Law."

During the long silence I looked at their faces: Kest was trying to see if I'd actually lost my mind this time. Brasti was reaching for a joke. Only Ethalia started to look as if she understood. I explained, "During the fight, Erastian said, '*When Tristia crafted Laws to live by, the Gods became enraged.*'"

"So the Gods are petty," Brasti said. "That's hardly a revelation."

But Ethalia was shaking her head. "Rage is simply a mask to hide fear and weakness. If the Gods were created by the Faith of their followers, then it stands to reason that when men and women began to live by their *own* Laws, the Gods were weakened. Faith is a finite force—so if the Blacksmith wants his God to be all-powerful, he needs to destroy all Faith in the Law first."

"You realize how insane this sounds?" Brasti asked. "You're talking as if the Law is some kind of living thing he's trying to kill."

"Maybe to a God, the Law *is* a living thing," Kest suggested. "I can see there is a certain perverse mathematical element to it." His gaze became distant, the way it does when he's calculating our odds of surviving a fight. "The Blacksmith begins murdering Saints and unleashes his God's Needles to make people fear that their deities have turned against them. Then pilgrims begin threatening the palaces, and the Dukes withdraw their support for the Realm's Protector. The Churches move to take power, and suddenly the Greatcoats are replaced by the Inquisitors." He looked up at me suddenly. "You were wrong about the Blacksmith, Falcio. He *isn't* an avertiere. He hasn't been using feints and false attacks to draw us out. He's a *delusor*."

"What's a delusor?" Ethalia asked.

"Oh, God, come back and kill me now," Brasti moaned. "Another pointless term you've found in some old swordplay manual that no one's used in a hundred years—"

"In fact," Kest corrected, "the word 'delusor' doesn't appear in any of the old fencing texts—it's not so much a style of fighting as a strategy—the simplest one of all, if you think about it: *defeat the enemy before the fight begins.*"

"I don't understand," Ethalia said. "I thought a duel couldn't start until both parties entered the court circle. So how can you—?"

"It's actually quite simple," I replied. "You want to beat an opponent before the fight starts? Send thugs to rough him up in a dark alleyway the night before—not too badly, mind you—just enough that in the morning he'll be a little slow, a little too injured. Or maybe you bribe the tavern master to put a little something in his drink the night before—not to make him sick, just enough to make him a bit nauseous and blur his vision a bit the next morning."

"Fine," Brasti said, "so the Blacksmith is a delusor, and this whole thing has been one long duel against the Law." He pointed at me. "You're the First Cantor of the Greatcoats. Why not just kill you when he had the chance?"

"Because the Greatcoats *champion* the Law," I said, already running to saddle Arsehole. "We don't *embody* it, not the way the Blacksmith needs. *I'm* not the one he has to kill."

"The Realm's Protector," Kest said as he and Ethalia brought the rest of our packs. "To make his God all-powerful, the Blacksmith is going to execute Valiana."

CHAPTER FIFTY-NINE
THE CASTLE

We rode through that night and well into the morning, stopping for just long enough to keep Arsehole and the other horses from breaking legs or expiring from exhaustion. The curses I was muttering to myself had become a rolling, endless chorus: why had I let Aline send me north? We'd found the place where Saints were being killed, only to discover it no longer mattered; the Blacksmith already had what he'd wanted from them. We'd rescued one old man, only to have him die saving us. Mind you, at least *we'd* been saved. Ethalia had come into the power of her Sainthood, only to find out she needed to be a warrior to wield it—so was she supposed to sacrifice herself, the very *essence* of what she believed, on the altar of our need? *Why am I taking orders from a fourteen-year-old girl anyway? I should have stayed behind to protect them: it's my damned job.*

"Stop," Kest called out, and I yanked hard on Arsehole's reins, then looked back to see I'd left them all in the dust behind me.

I was about to press on, leaving them to catch up when they could—and only then noticed the bend in the road ahead. We were much closer to the castle than I'd realized. *And of course the smart*

thing now is to race ahead into the middle of whatever army is wait-
ing for us.

I forced myself to slow my breathing as I walked Arsehole back
to the others. Kest had already dismounted. "I'll circle around the
other side and see what's our best point of entry."

"I'll go," Brasti said. "I'm quicker, and I can fire the pistol if I run
into trouble."

Ethalia looked out past us. "There's so much dust, it's hard to see."

"Blame him," Brasti said, jerking a thumb at me. "He's the one
who practically ran his horse—"

"It's not dust from the road," she said, eyes narrowed. "It's gray,
not brown."

We walked a few steps along the road, trying to make out the
haze. "It's not nightmist," I said. "It is definitely dust of some kind . . .
what does it mean?"

"It means you're too late," Darriana said, emerging from the trees.
She was unsteady on her feet, but I saw no wounds save for a bruise
on her forehead. Her greatcoat was almost completely covered by
the same greyish dust, and tiny flakes of rock. "It means it's over."

Brasti ran to her and threw his arms around her. "Are you all
right?" he demanded.

She started to push him away but he clung to her, and she relented.
"Where did this come from, Brasti Goodbow?"

He leaned back but kept his arms around her. "Nothing. This is
how I greet all of the Greatcoats."

She smiled through the dirt on her face, and it would have been
a nice moment, if we'd had time for such things.

We didn't. "Tell me what's happened," I said.

She pushed Brasti aside more firmly, and this time he let her. "It's
better I show you," she replied, and started walking toward that last
bend before the castle.

"Wait," I said. "The pilgrims—"

"Oh, there are plenty of pilgrims. Inquisitors, too," she said, walking away from us. "They won't bother with us. No one really gives a
shit about us anymore."

Darriana's assurances weren't filling me with confidence. I drew my rapiers as she led us to the path up to Castle Aramor. I hadn't had my own weapons in hand since we'd left for the cathedral in the mine; it gave me some small comfort to know that if I had to fight, at least I wouldn't be swinging a damned mace anymore.

"I suppose I should tell you to prepare yourself," Darriana said.

"For what?" I asked, trying to wipe the blinding dust away from my eyes. It was getting thicker the closer we approached. "You still haven't told us what's waiting for us."

Ethalia walked next to me, watching Darri. "She's in pain, but she isn't afraid," she said quietly. "It's sorrow . . . loss."

"Keep out of my head, whore," Darriana said, quickening her pace, as if to hide the tears I now glimpsed in her eyes.

The clouds of dust kept getting thicker until it became hard to breathe, and I could barely see ten feet in front of me. But once we got to the top of the road it no longer mattered: you don't need to be able to see clearly to see what isn't there.

Years ago, when the King was still alive and willing to pay whatever exorbitant price was asked to acquire books for the royal library, Kest and I tried to figure out exactly how many different fencing manuals existed in the world. We got to somewhere in the neighborhood of two hundred and twenty-six: an impressive number, given that you'd be hard-pressed to find two hundred and twenty-six books on any other subject.

The odd thing, we realized one day, was that while there were any number of texts describing how to fence, we only ever found *one* book on the specific subject of *dueling*. Oh, there were no end of treatises on trial by combat, but they all focused on the rules, the weapons, the *politessi dan guerita*: the "what to say" and "how" and "when." Only one book, the somewhat depressingly titled *You Are Sure to Die*, by an obscure author named Sen Errera Bottio, described how to actually fight and win a duel.

Kest's theory was that while fencing masters wanted to show off their skills to get students, no true *duelist* would wish to reveal his techniques, for fear they might be used against him. As Bottio had developed a painful wasting disease, he'd apparently decided he'd now be quite happy to have someone kill him quickly, rather than slowly fade away.

So each chapter details a different aspect of the mental and physical preparation required for the various duels one might face over the course of a (presumably short) lifetime. The first chapter, "On The Morning Of Your First Duel," opens with a full description of what to expect the first time you're forced to engage in trial by combat.

It was Bottio who coined the term "delusor," in the chapter entitled, appropriately enough, "On the Night Before Your Death," in which he detailed all the different ways an opponent might weaken you in the days and hours leading up to a duel so as to ensure your failure and subsequent death. Bottio believed the most devastating attacks weren't on the body, they were on the mind. He wrote, "The body can recover from many different wounds, often with surprising speed. The soul, once broken, can never be repaired, and there lies the final target where the skilled delusor will strike—and always on the very eve of the fight."

Bottio was right, I thought as I surveyed the scene in front of us.

For ten years Castle Aramor had been my home. I knew every one of her nine towers, every inch of her battlements. I'd been in every room at one time or another, read most of her books, and pissed in every one of her privies. Most days I can't recognize my own face in a mirror, but I could draw Aramor's fortifications, and more accurately than any of the craftsmen who built her.

I loved that place. I had come there seeking to kill a King, and instead became his most devout follower. The Greatcoats had been reborn there, and it was there that I had hoped one day to see my King's daughter take the throne: the physical manifestation of all my foolish dreams.

Maybe that's why I could still visualize it rising high above the endless throngs of pilgrims kneeling on the greensward, singing their hymns of joy into the thick gray clouds of its broken remains, scattered across the earth like a child's toy shattered by a mighty hand.

We had been standing there for just a few seconds before Darriana started wading into the pilgrims. "Come on," she beckoned, "they won't attack us."

I followed her like a sleepwalker, quite unable to convince myself that what I was seeing was real. I'd seen castles destroyed before, but none so *completely*. Only one tower still stood among the rubble, the shattered remains of stone and mortar.

Darri led us through the kneeling crowds until we reached the castle's great entrance: the very place where we had waited boldly to dictate terms to the Ducal Council. That had been just a few months before, after the battle of the Black Tabards. It felt like a lifetime ago.

"How was this done?" Kest asked, looking past the ruins and around the periphery. "I see no siege-engines, no armies."

"Like this," Darriana said. She held up a hand and snapped her fingers. "That's it. Tristia's one true God came and waved his hand, and the towers began falling."

"That's not possible. It would take—"

"Oh, there was a fine speech," she said, her eyes on me. "You would have liked it, Falcio. They held a trial, if you can believe it. *A fucking trial.* That Prelate of theirs—Obladias?—he came out and declared that the Church had deemed the rule of King's Laws to be corrupt and in violation of God's will. God. Singular." She pointed to a small patch among the ruins that had somehow stayed clear. "He had his little deity stand right there, listening to *hours* of testimony—from clerics, peasants—oh, and you'll *love* this: fucking Duke Hadiermo, the Iron Duke of Domaris himself, testified that the Dukes themselves were traitors to the country."

"Why go through the sham of a trial?" Brasti asked.

It was a fair question: why the formality? Why the performance?

"Did the trial follow the Laws of Jurisprudence?" I asked. "Was everything done according to the rules of evidence?"

"You think anyone cares about that?" Darriana demanded. "You think anyone but you—?"

"Answer the question," I said. "Was this a legal trial or not."

"Yes! Everything was nice and legal—does that make you feel better?"

I didn't bother to answer. I understood Darri's pain—I shared it—but I didn't have time for it. "This is how you destroy the Law utterly," I said to Kest. "In a trial."

"What happened next?" Kest asked, and she turned and pointed to the far left side of the ruins. The dust-haze was so thick that what I'd mistaken for the remains of a wooden beam standing on its end turned out to be a tall gibbet. When I squinted, I realized that wasn't a pile of broken stone underneath, but broken bodies. "Then the executions started."

Executions—Oh, Saints, no—"Aline—*Valiana*—" My heart was about to shatter. "Please, *please,* tell me you didn't let them come here..."

The look on her face was so full of rage I thought she might cut me down there and then. "Religious zealots were taking the castle—*of course* Valiana and Aline were here. They ordered us to escort them here so they could face the charges."

I moved closer to the bodies by the gibbet, trying to find them, praying to who knew whom that I wouldn't see them.

"Falcio," Ethalia said, a hand on my arm, "they aren't there. They must have escaped." She turned to Darriana and ordered, "Stop torturing him."

"I told you, bitch! Stay out of my head—"

Kest stepped in front of her. "You don't care about this castle, so if Aline and Valiana aren't dead, why are you so angry with us?"

Darriana let out a breath. "Your little whore-Saint is right. The Prelate ordered the Inquisitors to bring them to the gibbet. Quentis Maren refused."

"Quentis Maren *refused*?" Brasti asked. His voice echoed my own disbelief.

Darriana nodded. "He gave his own little speech about following the Gods—the Blacksmith explained that the Gods Quentis had worshipped were all dead, of course, but the Inquisitor said, 'Better to follow a dead God than an evil one.'"

"So he helped them escape?"

"We all did."

I looked at the destruction all around us. "How was that even possible?"

"And why aren't the pilgrims tearing us apart right now?" Brasti asked. "Why aren't there soldiers waiting to capture us?"

Darriana gave a bitter smile, devoid of anything resembling joy or hope. "Because after everything went to seven hells and the first blood was shed, Aline had the bright idea of demanding trial by combat. Apparently that's something the God gives a shit about, because he agreed. So until the duel tomorrow, no one is allowed to touch us."

"So we run," Brasti said, looking at me. "We get everyone the hells out of Tristia."

"Aline won't run," Darriana said, "and neither will Valiana."

"Why not?" Brasti looked astounded.

Darriana waded out into the pilgrims, then stopped and stood there like a single living tree in the middle of a gray desert. She spread her arms wide and at last I saw that the men and women and children kneeling all around her and singing their hymns were also coughing and choking, and among them I now saw the bodies of those who had already succumbed to the clouds of dust rising from the ruins. "The God has commanded that they remain here and sing his praises until Aline and Valiana return to face his judgment."

CHAPTER SIXTY

THE CHURCH

With Darriana once again in the lead, we marched through the streets of the city of Aramor, which looked impoverished without its castle looming in the background, winding our way between the two- and three-story buildings of brick and stone, the shops and homes built one by one over hundreds of years and clinging to the hillside like barnacles to a ship.

A ship that's now drifting to the bottom of the ocean.

What surprised me most was how many people were going about their daily business as if it were a normal day, mostly ignoring us, except for the occasional sneer as we passed. No doubt the Greatcoats had proved to be just what they'd always believed: a fantasy, a feeble joke played upon the people of Tristia by a King who understood nothing of their real struggles. But there were some whose heads turned as we passed, whose eyes followed us as if waiting for some sign that this must be some temporary feint on our part that was going to precede our counterthrust against the forces arrayed against the country. I avoided their gaze the most. They were the greater fools.

There was no plan, no feint, no counterattack left to us.

"We're here," Darriana said, gesturing down a long, narrow alley in the dirty riverside district of Ponte Calliet to a plain wooden door beneath a broken, poorly lettered sign that read THE BUSTED SCALES. It was a tavern, of sorts.

The Busted Scales had been our informal gathering place, back in the day—the King had provided us with all the space we needed at the castle, but most of us were from poorer backgrounds and didn't feel entirely comfortable in opulent surroundings. Within these dilapidated walls we could talk and drink and tell our stories without ever feeling too grand.

"I'd never even been here before," Darriana replied. "Talia and Allister said this was the best place to prepare. They called it 'the Greatcoats' church.'"

"Well," Brasti said after a moment, "it's certainly as close to a church as most of us ever got."

As I moved to enter, Darriana grabbed my arm. "You want to know why I'm angry with you?" she snarled. "Because this is *all* your fucking fault, Falcio. You should *never* have filled Valiana's and Aline's heads with all this useless idealism of yours. They should have run the second that monstrosity appeared at Aramor . . ." She stopped for a moment. "We got them out, but not everyone made it."

"Who?" I asked.

She pushed open the door. "See for yourself."

The light was dim, but I could see Greatcoats sitting around the same old battered tables, tending wounds or talking quietly. Talia and Allister were poring over a torn map and arguing with Nehra and Rhyleis, the Bardatti.

The Tailor sat in a corner, pulling a heavy steel needle through a greatcoat; I recognized it at once as the one the God's Needle had stolen from Harden. It's odd that I remember coats more easily than faces.

Antrim Thomas was kneeling by the old trapdoor to one of our hidden caches of weapons—one of Brasti's first innovations, years ago. He'd pulled out a pile of swords and spears and was hauling up a shield. I smiled wryly at that; I remembered the King offering it to one of us once, and we'd all made a joke of it; what would a Greatcoat need with a shield?

I caught sight of Mateo Tiller, sitting at a bench changing the bandages on a man's shoulder. It took me a moment to recognize Quentis Maren. "It turns out our coats aren't quite as good at protection as your own," he said, seeing me.

I walked over and looked down at the small, almost perfectly round wound. "You were shot."

"Apparently being leader of the Order of Inquisitors is insufficient to prevent one's own men trying to kill one on occasion."

"Tell me about it," I said.

He laughed, then caught his breath. "Don't. It hurts."

Mateo looked up at me and rolled his eyes. "I offered the man all the alcohol he wants. He keeps refusing."

"Inquisitors don't drink," Quentis said. "It offends the Gods."

I really wasn't sure how to answer that.

"Oh hells," he said, catching my expression, "you mean it's *true*? I was hoping that the Blacksmith and his demon were just bragging."

"Sorry," I said, "but I'm afraid there's been a change of ownership over our souls."

"In that case," Quentis said, motioning for a flask on the table, "give me that."

Mateo grinned. "I knew I was starting to like you, Inquisitor."

I felt someone at my side. "Falcio," Ethalia said softly, and I followed the line of her extended hand to where Aline sat in the shadows with Valiana. I couldn't help myself; I ran to them.

"We're fine, Falcio, let go," Aline said, struggling to breathe as I crushed her in one arm even as I reached out with my other to take Valiana's hand.

I ignored Aline's protestations for a while, but then I realized how stiff and awkward she was, and guessed she was trying hard trying to hold herself together. Valiana was squeezing my hand, but it felt wrong somehow, sorrowful. Then I felt Ethalia's hand on my shoulder.

"What happened?" I asked.

"Come with me," Aline said. "There's still a little time, and he'll want to see you."

She led me into a windowless room at the back of the tavern. It was lit with only a couple of candles and I could barely see anything except for a small figure lying on a pair of tables that had been pushed together in the center, and a taller figure standing over him.

"Damn you to every hell, I told you to leave us alone!" Jillard, Duke of Rijou, shouted. "We don't need your sympathy and we don't want your caterwauling Bardatti laments—"

"I've brought Falcio," Aline said gently, and he stopped his ranting. After a moment he gestured imperiously. "Bring him."

I entered the room, Ethalia close behind, her hand resting on my arm. When I reached the table, I found Tommer lying on his back, looking up into the darkness. His breathing was ragged. He still wore his long leather coat, fashioned to look like one of ours. But his wasn't a proper greatcoat, of course; it didn't have the dozens of hidden pockets with tools and tricks to help us survive. It didn't have the thin bone plates that might have stopped the weapon that had pierced his stomach so deeply that even through the layers upon layers of bandages the crimson of his blood stood out against the darkness.

Ethalia stepped past me to examine the wound, but it turned out there was more than one and I could see in her eyes that there was nothing she could do. This wasn't a briefly stopped heart; there would be no calling young Tommer back from this.

She looked up at me. "Falcio, this wasn't done with a blade."

Jillard spoke then, his voice quiet, steady, but quite unable to hide the unquenchable rage I could see shivering through his body. "Two of the Inquisitors got hold of the Realm's Protector during the chaos. They dragged her to the gibbet, and my son—*Tommer*—ran in front of her and tried to duel the God. But before Tommer could issue the challenge . . ." He paused then, and I heard him take two slow breaths before he spoke again. "The God drove his fingers into my son's stomach."

"No," I said, and then I said it again, as if repetition could stop the steady clock that was marking off Tommer's death, one ragged tick at a time.

"First Cantor," the boy whispered, the words broken by coughs that spurted blood from his mouth. His father wiped it away with a silk handkerchief.

I started to reach for his hand and then stopped and looked at Jillard. I didn't need to see his eyes to know he blamed me for this; I already knew that he despised me and even now in his grief he was probably constructing a lifetime of punishments. Despite all that, I needed his permission.

He gave me the briefest of nods, then went back to wiping Tommer's mouth.

What do you say to a twelve-year-old boy as he awaits death? Do you tell him he's brave? Do you make promises of an afterlife in the arms of the Gods whom you know are already dead? Do you kneel and blubber over life's injustice?

"Greatcoat, report," I said.

The boy's eyes opened a little wider; he swallowed. "Tommer, sir."

"You seem a trifle under the weather, Tommer."

"I had a spot of trouble, First Cantor."

"'A spot of trouble'? Is that what you call it when you attack a God?"

He coughed, and blood spurted from his mouth. He had to swallow several times until he could catch his breath. "The fool tried to lay hands on my sister, First Cantor."

I smiled then, and held it there like a lantern for him, because I knew he could still see me even if no more sounds could make it through the blood filling his mouth and throat, and because I knew he had held on this long so that those would be the words we remembered.

A little while later the Duke left, carrying his son's body with him, still wrapped in the long leather coat. There was a silent promise between Jillard and me; there would be a reckoning between us.

Had I not encouraged Tommer in his dream of becoming a Greatcoat, had I shunned him or mocked him, or done any of the dozen things you do when a boy doesn't understand the dangers of this stupid, stupid life we lead—

"Falcio," Aline said, cutting through my misery, "Tommer saved Valiana's life. He may have saved us all."

"He didn't," I said curtly. "The God could have killed her if he'd wanted. This is all theater: a performance. He wants her coming to him on her hands and knees so he can shatter the Law for all to see."

I heard the sound of an arrow and saw Brasti drawing another as Allister looked on. "Off your target, almost an inch," he said. "Pay up."

"I told you," Brasti complained, "these are new arrows. I need one free shot to get used to the weight first."

Of course, I thought, *because this is what you do when you're Brasti Goodbow and the world is falling apart around you: you pretend everything's just fine.*

Aline caught my attention. "You're wrong, Falcio. The Blacksmith was going to hang us—when Tommer came, when he tried to challenge the God . . . It was like it scared them, somehow. That's how I got the idea to demand trial by combat. Maybe there's some way that—"

"Enough," I said, practically shouting. "This isn't a tale told over wine and song. There's no virtue in pretending that foolish daring and useless valor mean anything to anyone—"

"What?" Brasti interrupted, "Daring and valor are falling out of fashion, you say? I'll not hear such blasphemy inside these sacred walls."

I strode up to him, my hand closed into a fist. Brasti's glib tone had struck a nerve in me. I could still feel the sticky wetness of Tommer's blood between my fingers where I'd held his hand. Aramor was in ruins. A God had walked among its broken stones and still-falling towers, and the Blacksmith had proved once and for all that the Greatcoats could no more bring justice back to Tristia than we could bring back the dead.

"Falcio . . ." Kest started, but I ignored him. Brasti stood in front of me, his smug grin still on his face. I was so sick of his jokes, his pranks. I was tired of his drunkard's advice, his admonitions to "just be a man" about it all. I needed to hit someone, and there was no one else strong enough to punish for my failures.

"Do it," he said. His expression hadn't changed. His smile was intact and his tone was light and easy, almost as if he were challenging me to a fight, but his eyes held a softness in them that made me see what this was: he *wanted* me to hit him. He wanted me to unleash my useless anger on him. I looked around at the others. They were as tired and heartbroken as I was.

He wants you to hit him so that you won't loose your rage on anyone else.

I unclenched my fist and turned away from him, from all of them. I stared at the bare boards of the building, at the dank green moss that had intruded between the cracks. How long did it take for such things to worm their way inside the places that humans built, to slowly weaken them until they would fall from the slightest breeze? It had taken King Paelis a lifetime to devise his great strategy to save this country. Had the Blacksmith needed even ten years to bring his scheme to fruition? Five? One?

I guess it's easy to bend a people to your will when their nature is to kneel.

"Falcio?" Aline's voice was distant, muted; it was only the touch of her hand on my arm that caught my attention, and it was only then that I realized someone had asked me a question.

"What is it?" I asked.

"She asked what your plan is, *First Cantor*," Rhyleis replied from where she sat strumming her guitar. She gave my title weight, as if to remind me of the responsibility that came with it. I was really starting to dislike the Bardatti.

The word "plan" sounded absurd to my ears just then, and I caught myself chuckling. The sound was at once freeing and terrifying: the first tentative step into madness. I'd been mad before, after the death of my wife. I'd become a crazed thing, wandering the roads from a tiny village in Pertine that no one had ever bothered to name all the way to the home of a King, killing every man responsible that I could find along the way. I longed for those days again.

I forced myself to look up, and saw my fellow Greatcoats waiting for me to speak. Allister, Talia, Mateo, Kest, Brasti, Darriana—even Quentis Maren. They had given up their lives to try and do the right thing and where had it gotten them? I looked at Aline, the heir to a throne that was now worthless; at Ethalia, a Saint whose brethren were pretty much all gone. But it was Valiana who held my gaze longest: my chosen daughter, trapped behind an iron mask from which we had no means to free her. "*Take your people away,*" the Blacksmith had said. "*Find a country worthy of your courage. Leave this one to those who may yet be able to redeem it.*"

It was the best advice I'd heard in a very long time.

"Find what supplies you can, if there's anything left here," I said. "In the morning we'll buy horses, or steal them, or do whatever it takes and ride south."

"We're doing no such thing, First Cantor," Aline said firmly.

I ignored her. "Start packing up now."

The others stared back at me, confused. "What's in the south?" Mateo asked.

"Ships," I replied.

Nothing had changed since the moment the Blacksmith had spared our lives: we still didn't have the means to fight him, and chances are we never would. This wasn't a duel we could win, which meant there was only one strategy left—the one I hated most.

The *fugidatist* isn't really a fencer; it's just the word we use for a man who's found himself in a duel he can't win. Lacking any other means of survival, he just runs around the dueling circle, desperately avoiding his opponent's blade, crying and begging for mercy, hoping against hope that his opponent will, out of sheer embarrassment, call a halt to the whole affair. It rarely works, but *rarely* is better than *never*. I would give Aline what little life there was to be had—I'd give them all what life I could. That would have to be enough.

"We're leaving Tristia," I said.

CHAPTER SIXTY-ONE

COURAGE

"Are you out of your fucking mind, '*First Cantor*'?" Antrim shouted.

I didn't know him particularly well; the King had made him a Greatcoat while I was on the road, and our paths had never really crossed until recently. It hadn't taken him very long to take a dislike to me, all things considered.

"Let it go, Antrim," Talia said, her voice so calm that it made me wonder if she had any idea how much fury and disdain was in her eyes as she stared back at me.

He turned on her. "No, I don't think I will. I gave up my home and my life to become a magistrate, and I gave up being a magistrate to try and fulfill the King's last asinine command. And after all that, after we come to this point"—Antrim rounded on me—"I was ready to die for Paelis's dream because I thought it might make this rancid shithole of a country just a little fairer, a little better. And now you're telling me it was all for nothing?"

"For less than nothing," I said. "You wasted your life, Antrim."

His jaw clenched and I could see his teeth behind the snarl of his lips. He wanted to hit me almost as much as I wanted him to do so;

I was craving physical pain to match the pain inside me. Maybe this was why Brasti had goaded me.

"That's enough," Ethalia said, and suddenly we were all struggling to stay on our feet.

"I don't think so, Saint of Mercy," Talia said. She was resisting the Awe, her hand wrapped around her spear and raising its point. "Maybe if you weren't so damned 'peaceful' you might have helped us prevent this disaster."

"Don't," I warned. It looked like I was having more trouble standing than the others.

Aline shouted "*Stop!* Lady Ethalia—all of you! Cease this madness!"

Ethalia looked down at her hands, and the pressure was gone. "Forgive me. I simply couldn't stand the rage in this room any longer."

"No, I'm sorry," Antrim said, bowing his head. "I meant you no harm, My Lady."

"Oh for the sake of whatever Gods remain, Antrim," Brasti said, "don't you start hitting on Falcio's woman too."

"She's not—" I closed my mouth when I realized Mateo, Allister, and I had spoken at once.

"What in all the hells is wrong with you people?" Antrim asked, and despite everything, that caused the lot of us to laugh, if only for a moment. Ethalia walked over to the bench where Valiana sat silently in her iron mask. She took her hands, and once again tried to calm the madness inside her.

Once we'd settled down, Talia said, "Fine: let's talk about it. Let's say we run: we board a ship bound for the Southern Islands or to Dieram, anywhere. We flee. What then?"

"We live," the Tailor said. It was the first time she'd spoken since I'd arrived and she sounded different, and looked different too: sadder, older. Diminished. I wondered what it must be like to be so brilliant, to be unique, only to discover that you aren't unique at all, and that there's someone out there better at what you do than you are. She caught my look and returned a scowl. "We live, and we give the Blacksmith and his God time to fail and hope that the people of Tristia aren't quite so willing as he believes to enslave themselves once again."

"One would think you'd never lived in this country," Darriana said, scowling. "Of course they'll take to this new theocracy. It gives them what they've always wanted: a new master to serve." She locked eyes with me. "One who doesn't complicate their lives with notions of laws and justice and the responsibility that comes with those things. One who tells them when to rise, when to work, and when to die."

I felt someone take my hand. Aline said, "Falcio, I don't want to run. If my father's reign stood for anything, it was the hope that we could be better than our pasts. But if you believe that's the only choice left to us, if you've lost faith then"—she looked down—"then I won't ask you to keep fighting for me if it will only bring us more bloodshed."

Her words carried no accusation nor repudiation, but I felt Tommer's death between us now. "There's nothing else we can do," I said to the others. "Don't you understand? Our choice is to live or to die, that's all there is. There are less than a dozen of us—they've got an army. They've got their crazy God's Needles. They've got a fucking God. What do you want of me?"

Ethalia spoke first. "Falcio? I can feel . . . Valiana's trying to say something."

I sat down next to Valiana while the others scrambled to find something she could write with. After a few minutes, she had a pen dipped in ink and was scrawling on what had once been the tavern master's book of accounts.

"I can't read it," I said.

Aline took it from my hands; she didn't need to do more than glance at it. "You know exactly what this says, Falcio."

Valiana reached out and Aline placed the book back in her hands. She wrote more, filling the page with jagged lines: *I gave my oath to defend this country. I am the Realm's Protector and I will not flee my duty for any man nor God.*

And then, beneath it, the same line she'd written at the beginning: *Take off the mask.*

"You'll go mad the instant that mask comes off," I yelled at her. "You'll rip at your own flesh, and when we hold you back, you'll tear your muscles and break your bones trying to break free—and when that fails, your mind itself will snap and you won't last five minutes before your heart bursts in your chest."

She tore off the page she'd written and began writing anew. *Then for those five minutes I will fight.*

"You stupid, *stupid* girl!" I shouted. "It won't do any good, don't you see that? What difference does it make whether we die on our feet or on our knees?"

It was Aline who replied, "When the dying is all that's left, Falcio, it makes all the difference in the world."

I gazed around the room, searching for one of the others to step forward and tell Valiana how foolish she was, how wasted this death would be, but no one spoke a word. One by one they nodded, as if their assent held any meaning, as if their admiration mattered, as if Valiana's noble act would even be remembered. Maybe they were right: maybe some last futile act of bravery was as worthy an ending as we could hope for, but I was tired of fighting, and even more tired of losing. Nothing I had done—nothing *any* of us had done—had made the country one jot better. I lacked the courage to do what they wanted and hadn't the strength to face down their stares. In the end, I simply turned and fled.

CHAPTER SIXTY-TWO

THE BOY AND THE CAT

Every turn I made as I walked through the city streets set me more and more at odds with myself. I kept expecting to be attacked, by God's Needles, Church Knights, the God himself—hells, I wouldn't have been surprised to find a pair of Dashini assassins waiting for me around the next corner. But despite the fact that I wanted the mercy of a quick death, my body was rebelling: every time a man or woman in the crowded streets glanced at me, my hand went reflexively to my rapier. I kept watch on every shadow-filled alley I approached, my heart pumping fast, readying my muscles for combat. I might have given up on the world but my instincts had not.

Find a riverboat, I told myself, *or a barge—hells, even a decent-sized log. Get them the hells out of here and figure out the rest later.*

Despite the grand events playing out in the world at large, the shops and market stalls remained open; families loitered around butcher shops and fruit stands, negotiating prices and going about the daily business of life as though nothing had changed. A traveler from a foreign land might have been forgiven for thinking that what he was seeing was simply the normal ways of this country; that he had come to a place where people lived and died and perhaps prayed a bit too much, but were otherwise a simple people.

He would certainly not have believed they were in the process of trading what little freedoms they had for the relief of servitude, or the ease with which they were slipping into their shackles. I wanted to scream and rage at my countrymen, but lacking the will, I just kept walking until finally I found myself staring at a bridge spanning a narrow point in the canal about thirty yards away; hawkers selling passage on the river boats sometimes plied their trade here.

A group of boys were playing on the bridge, shouting to each other, laughing and giggling as they tormented a large orange cat they'd trapped. The creature struggled against them, scratching and clawing, hissing and spitting even as they forced it inside a cloth sack and tied it closed. For a moment they dropped it on the stone surface of the bridge, chortling as the bag tumbled around on the ground as if possessed. One of the boys wasn't laughing, though. He was smaller than the others, and I realized he was trying to reach for the bag, but one of the larger boys was holding him back, a big hand on his forehead. That, too, was prompting merriment from the other boys.

A small part of me thought about intervening, but I quickly lost the will to do anything. Children torturing cats—how many times a week did some nasty little wretch come to this very bridge to drown the kittens they'd found starving in some back alley? How many boys in other cities were, even at this very moment, repeating this same cruelty, this odd, almost ritualistic act of devotion to their own desire to watch things struggle and die. What purpose would it serve for me to stop them when they were acting in accordance with the natural order of this world?

Creating fear was, it appeared, the only way any of us knew how to cope.

Finally the bag stopped moving. One of the bigger boys kicked it and got a few more laughs when the cat inside struggled once more, but they'd grown bored. One of them picked it up and tossed it in the canal and it bobbed along on the surface for a few moments as the boys shouted angrily and threw rocks at it, trying to drive it down. It was the currents running along the canal that finally dragged the bag down, taking the cat to its final destination.

I turned away, disgusted by my inaction. Piece by piece the Blacksmith had been working to destroy our faith in justice, and he'd succeeded.

A shout caused me to turn just in time to see the smaller boy kick his captor in the shin. One of the others clubbed him across the face, a massive blow that sent the boy reeling, but he managed to wriggle free. Before anyone could stop him, he'd dived into the canal.

You're wasting your time, kid. Even if he did manage to bring the bag back up, the other boys would simply take it from him and toss it back in the canal. If anything, his attempt at valor was only prolonging the creature's suffering.

The other boys shouted insults at him, promising retribution on an almost mythical scale, but they too were wasting their time. The boy couldn't hear them under the water.

I was transfixed by the scene: it was as if the Blacksmith's God had staged the perfect performance for me: a metaphor of my life, of the futility of the Greatcoats and everything we'd striven to do.

Suddenly the boys on the bridge stopped their shouting. One of them saw me and shouted to the others, and they all pelted across the bridge and scattered into the mean little streets. It took me a moment to understand why: the smaller boy hadn't resurfaced. He was drowning, and they weren't going to be caught at the scene.

My feet pounded against the cobblestones as I raced for the bridge. My hands reached up of their own accord and tore off my coat, discarding it on the street even as my eyes searched for some indication of where the boy had ended up.

The currents in these parts didn't travel especially fast, but the water was deep. I sucked in air as I leapt over the stone railing, realizing too late that I probably should have removed my boots before diving into the canal.

Cold water—far colder than I would have expected for this time of year—embraced me, pulling me down under the surface. I forced my eyes open and the world became a blurry haze of green and brown mist, dirtied by silt and the filth of the waste dumped into the canal. I could barely make out their yellow tendrils but the water-whips rising up from the river bottom were stinging my cheeks. I let myself sink down a little further, wondering if I might even now be mistaking the boy's filthy clothes for the grimy bottom of the canal bed.

I felt the first stirring of my lungs wanting air as a discarded piece of fruit drifted by me. *Damn it—the currents! He'll be further down the canal by now.*

I swam out, following the flow of the water, searching for any sign of the boy, cursing my poor vision underwater, but after the third return to the surface to take in air I was beginning to tire. I had to let the current carry me for a few moments before trying again. I passed a heavy stone pillion that had to be one of the supports for the next bridge. Heavy rocks covered the bottom, covered in some kind of brown plant that shifted and waved in the current.

There, I realized, *that one's not a rock—*

A few feet ahead of me was the boy, on the floor of the canal, struggling to lift something. I kicked harder, pushing myself lower, until my feet were touching the ground. *The boy's clothing must be stuck between the rocks,* I suddenly realized. *How long has he been without air?* I reached out and grabbed his hand and started to pull him up, but he tried to yank his hand free: he was still pulling something from under the heavy rock—it wasn't his trouser leg after all. His wrist slipped from my grip as I recognized the sack: he was trying to pull up the bag with the cat inside.

You're going to die, you fool—leave the damned cat! But he wouldn't; I could see that. Then suddenly the boy turned to me and nodded, I grabbed his arm and pushed off from the bottom as hard as I could. My own lungs were trying to force me to suck in the canal water, but I managed to hold back the need, though the burning in my chest was moving up to my eyes, and I could no longer see.

A moment later we broke the surface. I tried to breathe too quickly and ended up swallowing a great mouthful of water, which set me to coughing so badly I began to slip back under the water, pulled down by the weight of my sodden clothes and boots. The boy had already grabbed onto the stones lining the canal and heaved the bag onto the bank and was now hoisting himself up, but he reached out a hand for me and kept me from sinking back under until I could anchor myself on the side of the canal.

After several minutes of hard coughing I finally had enough strength back to pull myself out of the water. The air tasted crisp and sweet. *It appears it doesn't matter how little the mind thinks it cares about life—the body is going to fight to hold onto it.*

"You bloody fool," I shouted at the boy, trying to wipe my eyes. "Were you trying to die?"

"Of course not, Falcio," he said. "That would be silly, don't you think?"

I looked at him, seeing his face clearly for the first time.

It was Tommer.

CHAPTER SIXTY-THREE

THE PRAYER STONE

I scrambled backward, scraping my palms against the rough cobblestones. I reached first for my rapiers, then my throwing knives, but all my weapons were with my coat, lying discarded several hundred yards upstream.

"That's a bit of an overreaction, don't you think?" said the boy who looked exactly like Tommer as he busied himself untying the bag.

Can I really have lost my mind so easily?

"You'd think someone who's been around insanity as much as you have would have developed a more refined sense of it by now," the boy added. "But hey, if you want to see something really mad . . ." He opened the bag and the cat leaped out, soaked fur flying in the air, and hissed at me with a fury that would have sent a bear running for its cave.

The boy with Tommer's face grinned at her. "She's a beauty, isn't she?"

I had no idea how to respond to that, so I answered honestly, "She is quite possibly the ugliest cat I've ever seen."

The boy ignored the slight and pointed behind me into the streets. "There was a little puppy in the alley back there yesterday.

Those other boys were throwing rocks at it for fun, trying to see who could get it to bleed first. Suddenly *she* was there, growling at them, forcing them back." He reached out to pet the cat, who promptly swatted his hand. He pulled it back: a line of red blood was appearing on his palm, and it apparently set him to grinning.

"You're hurt," I said, quite possibly the stupidest thing I've ever said.

"It's funny, don't you think?" the boy asked, "a cat protecting a dog? But there she was, like a mountain lion protecting her own cub." He looked over at the bridge and sighed. "The boys came back today and trapped her. She could have run if she'd wanted, but she wouldn't leave the puppy."

The cat, satisfied that she'd removed any question as to who was in charge, ambled toward me. She gave me a perfunctory hiss and then sat on my lap and went to sleep. "She's . . . very brave," I said.

The boy looked surprised at that. "Brave? No, no—don't you get it, Falcio? Those weren't her kittens she was defending. It was a dog: a completely different kind of animal, completely unrelated to her. It was something she had no *need* to protect."

"I don't understand—isn't that bravery?"

He threw his hands up in the air. "That's not mere *bravery,* Falcio; that's *valor.*" He smiled in wonder. "Who would have thought that *that* would be the last missing piece I needed?"

"Needed for what?"

"To *be,* Falcio. Come on, I know we've never met—well, to be fair, there was no way we could have met before today, but still, don't you recognize me?"

In the past weeks I'd been stabbed, beaten, and tormented, and I had watched as everything I cared for slowly disappeared. So I really wasn't at my best. But I wasn't stupid, either.

What if the Blacksmith deceived us . . . what if the Gods aren't dead . . . if those bodies we found hanging outside the chapel were just . . . bodies.

"You . . . you're a God?" And when he grinned, I asked, "Which one? You aren't War, and I can't imagine you're Coin or Death or even Craft."

"I am none of those," he said.

I thought about his story of the cat protecting the puppy. "Are you Love?"

He shook his head. "Nope. You're running out of guesses, Falcio."

"Regret?" Even as I said the word it sounded odd to me; I'd always pictured Regret as an old man, weary of the world.

"Nope, wrong again. Regret died with all the rest of them."

"But—" The implications of what he'd just said were beyond my mind's ability to comprehend. For a moment I couldn't bear to look at him, so I looked down at the cat instead. The creature was purring as it slept, as normal and natural a sight as you could imagine. "I'm hallucinating this," I started. "I drowned down in the canal and now I'm imagining all of this."

"That's a bit melodramatic, don't you think?" The boy was starting to sound a little bored. "Come *on,* Falcio. Has the Blacksmith really gotten you so twisted around that you believe Faith can't lead to anything but darkness?"

"Then how?" I asked, my voice breaking. "How can anything *good* come from a place where all I can see are cruel, petty men ruling the world?"

He shrugged as if the question were irrelevant. "A grouchy old cat leaps to the defense of a frightened pup. A boy faces down a God to protect a woman he knows isn't his sister." He reached over and tapped me on the forehead. "A brokenhearted man rushes into every fight, every duel, still trying to save a woman who died years ago."

I felt the tears trickling down my cheeks. "That easy, is it?"

"It's the hardest thing in the world, Falcio, and that's why it matters so much. Now come on, finish the game. Who am I?"

I understood now why it was Tommer's face I saw, but it took me a long time before I could say out loud, "You're the God of Valor."

I'm not sure how long we sat there, drying out in the sun, while the cat alternated between purring and growling on my lap, before I heard voices calling out for me.

"There he is!" Brasti shouted, running toward me with my coat and scabbards in hand, Kest hard on his heels. The cat, evidently deciding that it was now sufficiently dry and that five was a crowd, leaped off my lap and went loping toward the alley.

Kest's eyes narrowed as he approached. "How can she be here?" he asked.

At first I thought Kest was referring to the cat, but then Brasti said, "What do you mean 'she'?" He nocked an arrow, then shifted his aim between me and the boy. "Which one is real?"

"Wait," I said, rising, "this isn't what you think."

Brasti turned his arrow toward me, though his eyes were still on the boy. "Kest . . . which one is Falcio?"

"Fascinating," Kest said.

It took me a moment to understand what Brasti was seeing.

Saints . . . whoever would have believed it? He always acts like I'm such an ass. Eventually, he figured it out, too, though he didn't lower his bow. Finally he said, "Oh . . . well, this is all sorts of embarrassing."

"Who do you see?" Kest asked me.

I turned to look at the God of Valor. "I see Tommer."

"Ah. That makes sense."

"You?" I asked.

"Valiana. Without the mask."

Brasti put down his bow. "Yeah. I see Valiana too."

I walked over and hugged him, knowing it would only make things worse for him. I don't get that many chances to torture Brasti.

He pushed me away. "Will you stop grabbing at me every time you see me? And will *someone* please tell me what in all the hells is going on?"

Kest walked over to stare at the God of Valor. "Apparently the world isn't limited to the Gods we knew."

"Don't get your hopes up," I said. "This particular God was busy trying to drown himself saving a cat when I found him."

Brasti looked at first at the God and then at me, then he burst out laughing. "But that's *exactly* the kind of thing you would do, Falcio!"

I turned to Kest for support but then he too had started laughing.

"All right," the God of Valor said, gesturing for us to sit. "We should get to business."

"Are you sure?" Brasti asked, still giggling. "There may be pigeons in need of rescue!"

"You do recall that the world is falling apart?" I asked.

"Good point." He turned to Valor. "Okay, God of Drowning Cats, what are we doing here?"

The God stared at Brasti for a moment, looking annoyed. "Evidently my Awe isn't very powerful yet."

"Have you tried it out on kittens? Or maybe start with something smaller—mice, perhaps?" Brasti turned to me. "I think I like this one: he's exactly as inconsequential as I'd expect a God of Valor to be."

"It's not about *me*," Valor said testily. "It's *never* been about the Gods. When you saw me down by the stones, it was because I was trying to reach *this*."

He reached into his pocket and pulled something out which he held out to me. I leaned forward and saw a small piece of stone, a few inches long and an inch around. Flecks of rust marred the smooth gray surface.

"That's an unusual shape," Kest said, looking interested.

"It's a prayer-stone," the God said.

Brasti leaned over to peer at it too. "Looks more like iron ore."

"It is." The God of Valor held it up and rubbed it between the palms of his hands. "When the first Tristians came here as slaves, they had no religion, no Gods. They sat together in the night doing this for hours, sometimes days on end. They'd take a rough piece of ore and slowly work it in their hands until it was perfectly smooth, praying all the while. They passed it from person to person within the tribe, each uttering the same prayer, over and over, as they rubbed the stone into this shape." He handed the stone to Brasti. "Here. You're going to need this."

"For what?"

"For later."

"What did they pray for?" Kest asked.

"For the Gods to come and save them, of course."

"I thought you told me they had no Gods," I said.

"They didn't. That's what you need to understand: the first prayer came before the first God."

The first prayer came before the first God.

"I don't get it," Brasti said.

The God of Valor rose to his feet. "Of course you do. You've always understood, deep down. It's why you fight, even when the cause is lost. It's why the King sent you all traveling across the country, spreading your verdicts and virtues, repeating them, over and over, like—"

"Like prayers," Kest said.

The God nodded. "Just like prayers."

"'The first prayer came before the first God,'" I repeated.

That was why the Blacksmith had engineered all these events to take place the way they did—why it was so important to destroy faith in the Law.

I looked at the God with Tommer's face and saw a thin red line of blood on his cheek. It hadn't been there before. "I should go now," Valor said, as a second wound appeared, this one on his forehead above his left eye.

"What's happening to you?" Kest asked.

"The Blacksmith knows I exist, and so does his God; even now we fight." Valor recoiled, suddenly, as if someone had just struck him hard across the face. I reached out to grab him, to try to protect him from this invisible enemy, but he backed away from me. "You can't fight for me, Falcio."

"Then protect yourself, damn it! He's killing you! Why are you—?"

The God of Valor smiled, even as his lower lip split and blood dripped down his boy's chin. "Nothing lasts forever, Falcio. Not people, not castles, not even Gods."

I thought about the boy whose face the God had taken, who had thrown away his life to buy Aline a single day. I was so sick of losing at every turn. "Then why fight?" I asked. "What's the point?"

Valor looked up at me. "Because that's how we pray, Falcio." He mimed an en garde position, pretending he held a sword in his hand.

"Because in those moments—those brief, tiny instants where some- one like you or Tommer or Valiana rises up—just about *anything* is possible."

With that, Tristia's newest God, one who would live shortest of all of them, turned and set off skipping down the street, heading toward the alley he'd pointed to earlier, like a boy dreaming of great and grand adventures.

Because every act of valor is a prayer . . .

After he'd gone, Brasti said, "Just so I understand correctly, Tom- mer died and helped create a new God, which is great, because he's not an arsehole like the other one, except that this one is too weak to fight the arsehole God, which means we're right back where we started from—"

"No," Kest said. "Everything has changed."

"How?" Brasti asked.

"Look at Falcio's face."

Brasti stared at me. "What about it? He just looks drunk and confused . . . Oh—you mean he has a plan now."

CHAPTER SIXTY-FOUR
THE RETURN

The three of us returned to the Broken Scales to find the others making preparations for our departure, but as soon as I came through the door, Aline signaled for the others to stop. "Something's changed," she said, looking at me.

Saints, no wonder I never win at cards if I'm this easy to read.

I went to where Valiana was still sitting on the bench next to Ethalia. "Can you hear me?" I asked.

Darriana strode over to us, her eyes narrowed, but I ignored her.

"Can you hear me?" I repeated, "or do I need to shout into the slits?"

Valiana nodded that obscene iron mask of infamy.

Everyone else had gathered around us now and they were all waiting for me to speak. I took one of the knives from my coat and handed it to Kest. Only he had the skill to do what had to be done without simply breaking the blade.

"Do you still want me to remove the mask?" I asked Valiana. "Do you still want to fight?"

She nodded, but I grabbed the tavern master's book and the pen and placed them in her hands. *I'm not afraid to die,* she wrote.

"Not good enough," I said.

Darriana took a step closer to us, hand on the hilt of her sword.

"Either draw your blade or back the hells up," I said.

She did neither.

"*I am the Realm's Protector,*" Valiana scrawled.

"No, you aren't," I interrupted her. "A madwoman trapped behind a mask can't be the Realm's Protector. So what's left? Are you still a Great-coat, or are you just the spoiled girl who thought herself a princess?"

"Falcio . . ." Aline said, but I turned her away with a hard stare. This wasn't the time for gentleness. "Answer the damned question."

She wrote again. "*I am a Greatcoat.*"

"Then report."

She hesitated, so I shouted at her, "I'm the damned First Cantor of the Greatcoats. When I ask you to report, you report: are you a Greatcoat or not?"

She scratched the answer on the page in jagged strokes that got harder and harsher with every word until by the end the pen tore through the paper. "*I am Valiana val Mond. I am the Heart's Answer, and either in the living or the dying, I remain a Greatcoat.*"

"Good," I said. "Hold on to that thought, and let's find out which it is."

I gestured to Kest, who walked behind her. Darriana grabbed at my shoulder and growled, "You son of a bitch! She's still got that poison coursing through her veins—you take that mask off and you'll send her headlong into madness!"

"Of course I will," I told her, but my eyes were on Ethalia, who had already guessed what I planned to do next. "I'm going with her."

"Falcio, I don't know if what you want to do is possible," Ethalia said. "This isn't like what happened with Kest. It's madness, not—"

"Just try. *Please.*"

Ethalia took my right hand and placed my left in Valiana's. I looked at Kest, and he hesitated, just for a moment, but he didn't bother asking me if I was sure. We don't play such games, he and I. So when he caught my glance he drove the knife blade down against the iron mask covering Valiana's face. The edge of the blade, brought down in a single, perfect strike, shattered the two thin metal locks, the mask fell open and behind it I saw Valiana's pale skin and the fluttering of her lashes as she opened her eyes to the world around her. "Oh," she said.

I watched as the first tickle of madness began to take her. I felt it as it wormed its way inside my own mind. With what little command of my own voice I had left, I said, "Speak the oath."

The movements of Valiana's eyes were small, the twitches of her cheek barely noticeable, and yet each one reached deep inside me, dragging me down into her insanity.

"I'm here," I said, though no sound came from my lips. All I could do was hope that Ethalia could keep us tethered together as we tumbled into the endless pit of our shared madness. The skin of my face itched. My fingers shivered; I was already trying to let go of Ethalia so that they might scratch that itch, remove the layers of fear one after another, taking away the pain by taking away that which contained it. That was the answer, of course: I just needed to break apart the jar holding the horrors and then they could flutter away and leave me alone.

No! I thought, trying desperately to focus. *Fight it! Show her how to hold it at bay.*

I had done that once, years ago, after Aline had died: I had taken all the madness the world had to offer and locked it inside myself, burning it like coal to fuel my every step, my every duel on that long road that stretched from Pertine to Aramor, from the village where I'd found my wife brutally dead to the castle where I'd met a strange skinny man with a dream that, even though it wasn't real, was still worth fighting for.

"Speak the oath," I said, but I felt Valiana pulling away, slipping down further and faster than I could follow.

Stay with me, I begged. *You're the bravest person I've ever met. You* can *do this. You're a Greatcoat!* Speak the oath!

For a moment I felt her hand tighten around mine as she fought the madness, struggling to stay with me, but then her descent began anew. I opened my eyes and saw tears in hers even as her mouth began to open for a scream that, once begun, I knew would never end.

No—please, no. I closed my eyes and reached for memories, for hope, for *Faith*: there was strength in such things, strength that even the Blacksmith and his damned God couldn't erase from the world entirely. *But it's not enough,* I realized, feeling myself begin to slip as well. A sudden cowardly impulse made me want to pull away—it was too late for Valiana, but I still had a chance. Didn't I deserve a chance to live? What good would it do if both of us were lost?

Suddenly I realized those thoughts weren't mine, they were Valiana's: her last desperate effort to save me, and I reacted as strongly as I could. *No, damn you—if you fall, I go with you.*

Again I reached, harder this time, drawing from every moment of bravery I knew, mine and Valiana's, pulling them to us and wrapping them around us like a coat to resist the icy-cold of our madness, but nothing changed.

I felt something, intangible as wind, fleeting as memory, and I grabbed at it with every ounce of will I had inside me. For a brief instant, I held it in my hands, then it slipped away. "The oath," I shouted. "*You've got to speak the oath.*"

But she didn't, and the darkness became absolute. I heard Ethalia shouting, "No! You've got to come back now. It's too—"

Down, down I went, until I struck something hard: I had reached the bottom. My body shivered endlessly. So ends Falcio the fool: a death well deserved for a life so futile.

"Falcio?"

My eyes opened to see Brasti kneeling over me, shaking me.

"Brasti?" I said. The others were standing around me as well. "I'm . . . ?"

He shook his head. "Not completely fucking crazy? I'm sorry. You most definitely are."

"Valiana . . ." I said.

Brasti stepped back and I saw she had fallen to her knees on the ground next to me. Her fingers were clenching and unclenching as if she were trying to tear up the floor with her nails. Her eyes were blinking too fast, her mouth twitching as unrelenting insanity twisted and turned inside her. I watched in horror as she reached out and clutched the remains of the iron mask, bringing it up in painful, slow increments toward her face. Her lips began to tremble and she said, "I was . . . born of nothing and to nothing I will return."

I failed, I realized with a great wash of sadness. *The madness still has her.*

For the briefest moment Valiana held the mask over her face, and I knew she was lost to us—but then her hands kept rising, until she was holding the foul thing high over her head. With a sudden violent motion and more strength than I would have thought possible, she brought it crashing down against the flagstone floor with such force that I had to shield my eyes from the shards of iron flying in all directions. When I opened my eyes, the iron mask had been shattered into pieces.

Valiana's jaw was clenched tight, as if her own body was trying to keep her silent. "But until the day I die, I will stand for the laws of this country. I will stand for the King's Laws." She let out a ragged sound, part angry growl, part despairing sob. "I will ride these roads and see those Laws enforced." Her head turned, too hard, too fast, and I thought her neck would snap, but she was looking at Aline. "I will protect you for as long as there is strength in my arm to fight and blood in my veins to bleed." Valiana's whole body was shaking now, her hands thudding against the floor as she tried to push herself to her feet.

Enough, I thought, *it has to be enough now.*

But she wasn't done. With all the madness of the Adoracia still burning behind her eyes, pulling at her, tearing at her soul, my daughter rose to her feet. "I. Am. Valiana val Mond. I am the Realm's Protector of Tristia. *I am the Heart's Answer.*"

There was no cure for Adoracia poisoning, I knew that—but here was a will too strong to succumb to it. And she would be fighting against this madness for the rest of her life. Valiana reached down to help me up. "I *am* a Greatcoat," she said.

CHAPTER SIXTY-FIVE

THE OATHS

"Okay, what now?" Darriana asked, leaning over me as I slumped on the bench against the back wall. Ethalia sat next to me, looking as worn and exhausted as I felt.

"Are you all right?" I asked, reaching out a hand to take hers. Her skin was cold.

"I abide," she said, smiling weakly. "That was . . . a dark journey."

"Yeah," I said, trying to suppress the shivering in my hands. "I probably should have warned you that the inside of my mind is not a nice place to visit."

"Not so bad as all that," she said, then she looked up: Darriana was still waiting for an answer.

"What do you want from me?" I sighed. "I can barely remember my own name right now."

"You're Falcio val Mond, you're the First fucking Cantor of the Greatcoats, and the world is still fucked. Now kindly get over yourself and tell us how we win this thing, because right now it's looking pretty hopeless."

I glanced over at Valiana, standing tall, even as she fought back the madness in her veins. She tried to nod reassuringly, even though

I should have been the one reassuring her. *Then do it, idiot. Tell her.* I'm usually embarrassingly terrible at these things, but I forced myself to my feet and stood before her. I placed my palms on her cheeks. *Whichever Gods remain, please let me say this without bursting into tears in front of the other Greatcoats.* "All the hope I will ever need is in the endless courage of my daughter's heart," I said.

Valiana put her hands over mine. "It's the oath," she said, smiling up at me, though her voice was still tight, almost stilted. "If I . . . if I hold onto it I can . . . I think the oaths are more than just words."

"*All* words are more than just words," Rhyleis said, then added mockingly, "When will you Trattari finally learn that?"

"Don't goad them," Nehra said.

But there was a kind of truth in Rhyleis's derision that I was finally coming to understand. Back at the Palace of Baern, when Birgid had come with her Awe blazing, I had made some comment about Greatcoats not kneeling, but I realized now that the *deeper* truth I'd been hanging on to at that moment was my oath. I turned to the others, trying to decide who to start with. I chose Antrim. "Why did you become a Greatcoat?" I asked.

"What? Why are you—?"

"Just tell me."

He looked around at the others briefly, looking a little embarrassed. "I . . . well, I come from the middle of Orison. The Viscount Drance ruled there. He . . . he had these rules about taxes: anyone who failed to pay the *instant* the collector came around was forced to burn his own lands, all their goods, and livestock—no one was allowed to intervene and no one was allowed to take them in, on pain of suffering the same fate; no one could even feed them. So you either watched your neighbor struggling to live off whatever roots and berries they could find, knowing they would starve once winter came—or you joined them."

"You couldn't pay your taxes?" Talia asked. "I thought your family was wealthy."

"We were," he admitted. "But I tried to sneak food to a family who'd been forced to destroy their home. I was found out, and I paid the price."

"How did you survive?" she asked.

He gave a soft snort. "I killed a Knight, stole a horse, and rode like seven demons were at my heels. By the time I got to Aramor I was nearly dead, and the men chasing me finally caught me. The King's guards intervened and brought me to him. The King asked me what I'd do if he gave me clemency. I guess I must have been a little delirious because I said, 'I'll make damned sure no lousy Viscount makes a man burn down his own home ever again.'"

"So that was your oath?" Kest asked.

Antrim gave a little shrug. "I like to think it came out a little more eloquently, but yes, that was basically it." He turned to me. "Why did you make me tell that story?"

"How long ago did you take the oath?" I asked.

He didn't hesitate, not even a second. "Six years, three months, and seven days."

"Swear it again," I said.

"Falcio, the King is—"

I pointed to Aline. "Swear it to her."

I expected him to argue, but he didn't. He picked up his short-sword and took three steps to stand before Aline. He said, "I have known wealth and I have known deprivation. I have seen the power of charity and the vicious theft of the only scrap of bread from a child's mouth. The Law says no man or woman can be made to starve at the whim of another. I *will* ride the roads of this country until that Law holds true." He gripped his sword tighter. "I am Antrim Thomas of the Condate of Drance, and I am—"

Aline stopped him before he could finish. She reached up and placed her hands on the side of his face and pulled him close. I thought she was going to kiss him on the cheek, but instead she whispered something into his ear. She let him go and he looked down at her. "I think I can live with that," he said, grinning from ear to ear.

I didn't have to ask Talia; she had already picked up her spear and now she took Antrim's place, standing before Aline and speaking clear and true. "Where I was born, in the Duchy of Pulnam, a girl of ten could be forcibly wed to a man of fifty. Her sisters and brothers could be killed for trying to protect her from her abusive husband. The King said that no child could be forced into marriage, that everyone had the right to love of their own free choice. I will ride these roads and I *will* see that Law and all the others enforced. My name is Talia Venire and by whatever Gods and Saints are left, I am—"

Again, Aline stopped her. She reached out to the taller woman and pulled her close into a hug that made Talia look remarkably uncomfortable. Aline whispered in her ear before letting her go. "It'll do," Talia replied. I'm not sure I had ever seen her smile quite like that before.

"Well you all know what I think of the Laws," Brasti said, evidently deciding it was his turn. He started strutting around the room like an actor walking the stage, spinning an arrow between his fingers, then suddenly he stopped, making the arrow freeze in his hand as he turned to the rest of us. "It's all shit, if you ask me." The arrow started spinning again and Brasti continued his swaggering gait. "But there are a lot of arseholes in this country: big men. Rough men." He turned and tossed the arrow to Kest. "Swordsmen, mostly." He paused for a laugh that never came and shrugged before going on, "And I suppose if a few Laws here and there can keep those men from making life even worse than it already is, and if being a Greatcoat means people can rest a little easier, live a little better, well then I'll ride these roads. I'll be a Greatcoat. I'll be the very paragon . . ." He paused and looked to Kest.

"Surprisingly, that's the right word," Kest admitted.

Brasti grinned. "I'll be the very paragon of Greatcoats." He turned then, having perfectly timed his words and his steps to arrive in front of Aline. "My name, little girl, is Brasti Goodbow, and I—"

She reached up for him as she had with the others, but just at the last instant he pinched her cheeks gently between thumbs and forefingers and kissed the top of her head. Before she could speak, he whispered something into her ear.

"You are rather impertinent, Brasti Goodbow," she said, once he let her go, "and I still can't believe my father ever chose you for the Greatcoats. But I consent."

He spun back on his heel. "Of course you do, sweetling. What choice do you have? I'm invaluable."

Mateo went next, then Allister, and then even Darriana managed to summon up just enough humility to retake her oath. When Aline whispered in her ear at the end, Darriana grinned. "Oh, I think that will do nicely."

When Kest began to take his own oath he almost passed out from the pain of trying to keep hold of the hilt of his sword, until Aline whispered, "Enough," and gently lifted his hand away. "You have to be more than a sword from now on." She leaned forward and whispered in his ear as she had the others; his expression was more dubious, but he too nodded acquiescence.

When I had finished my turn, she smiled at me but said nothing. "What?" I asked. "No secret message for me?"

"You are his, Falcio. You have and always will be my father's heart." She took my hand and squeezed it. "I'm glad for that."

Before I could reply she let go and walked over to the others and stood in front of Quentis Maren, who sat with his bandaged shoulder, watching the proceedings in fascination. The Inquisitor rose to his feet. "I'm sorry, My Lady," he said, startled at her presence. "I meant no offense . . . I'd heard of the Trattari rituals, but never witnessed one. I should have left the room."

"And how do you find our 'rituals,' Inquisitor?"

"Odd," he replied, candidly, "and—and forgive me for saying—a little sloppy compared to those of the Cogneri."

"That's it," Brasti said. "Now I'm definitely killing him."

Aline smiled. "We are a rather sloppy company, aren't we? Here I am, heir to a throne that appears to come with precious little authority over anyone."

"Precious little throne, either, now that the castle's in ruins," Brasti added.

I should have hit him when I had the chance.

Aline ignored him. "My lineage does come with one privilege, though. It is my right to choose those who will administer the Laws of Tristia." She waited just a second to see if he'd understood, and when it was clear he hadn't, she added, "Quentis Maren, I name you to the Greatcoats."

The Inquisitor looked shocked, and slightly aghast. "My Lady, forgive me, I am a Cogneri, I—"

"How's that been working out for you?" Mateo asked.

Quentis shook his head. "Not well, I suppose." He looked at Aline. "But I'm a man of the Gods—even if those Gods no longer live. I cannot swear to—"

"Give the oath you would give," Aline said.

He started to kneel down in front of her but she took his arm and made him stand. "The Greatcoats don't kneel."

He swallowed, visibly the most uncomfortable recruit I had ever seen, and then said, "I believe we should serve the Gods," he said.

"You know they're all dead, right?" Brasti asked.

"I know, but I still believe there is something greater than our own self-interest, than what lies before us in field and forest, village and city." He paused for a moment, then went on more firmly, "But I also believe that Faith cannot be born out of fear or enslavement. Only if we are free can we find that Faith. I will not stand by as anyone, man or God, seeks to use terror to command obedience."

Aline spoke to him quietly before kissing him on the cheek. He brought his fingers to the spot where she'd kissed him, looking oddly touched by her simple gesture. The Tailor rose silently, holding Harden's coat—and I finally understood that she'd been adjusting it to fit the Inquisitor's body.

"Is that it?" Quentis asked, pulling on the coat. It was a perfect fit. "I'm a Trattari now?"

Talia walked up to the man in her brother's coat, her fierce eyes appraising him. After a moment she punched him in the shoulder— the *uninjured* shoulder—hard enough that the former Inquisitor flinched. "We really prefer the term 'Greatcoat,'" she said.

Mateo raised a glass in the air. "Welcome to the Greatcoats, Quentis. The pay is lousy and the chances of survival are even worse."

"Remember something else," I said grimly, dampening the cheers that'd followed Mateo's toast. "Your oath isn't worth shit if you're on your knees."

He didn't look that convinced—none of them did. They had seen the power of the new God and they all knew no amount of effort would keep us from falling before him.

"I don't know anything about magic," I said, "except I hate it. I know even less about Faith. All I know is that this world is full of chaos and corruption, and we Greatcoats stand against that. We stood and we delivered our oaths and—well, maybe oaths are just words, but they didn't feel that way to me, not when I heard Antrim speak them, or Talia, or any of us. When we speak our oaths, when we bind ourselves to them, the words feel like—"

"Magic?" Brasti offered. For once he wasn't smirking.

"Greatcoats' magic," Talia said, her hand gripping her spear. She was practically glowing with pride.

"Words," Darriana said, her tone mocking, "foolish words and foolish deeds—is this all that's left to protect this shithole of a world?"

"Why not?" Kest asked. "It's the only thing that's ever worked before."

"There's only a few hours before dawn," Mateo pointed out. "We should prepare if we're going to meet the God in the ruins of Aramor."

He was right and I was about to start giving orders when Aline stopped me. "I'm not finished, First Cantor."

The Tailor came forward again, holding another bundle in her arms. I had never seen this coat before: the brown leather was tinted with subtle hues of red and copper. On the breast was inlaid a dove. "Are you sure about this, sweetling?" the Tailor asked. "It seems a terrible idea to me."

The heir to the throne sighed. "Grandmother, will you please stop contradicting me? And stop calling me sweetling."

"Never!" The old woman grinned, and for an instant she actually looked like a doting grandmother. I found it strangely terrifying.

Aline took the coat, and for a moment I thought she was about to put it on herself. But she didn't; she walked to where Ethalia was standing by herself in the shadowed corner. "Ethalia-who-shares-all-sorrows, Saint of Mercy." The room went deathly quiet. "I name you to the Greatcoats."

There was a great deal of yelling, most of it apparently coming from me. "You can't ask her to do this!" I shouted.

"Why not?" Aline asked, her calm an irritating counter to my loud frustration.

I turned to look at Ethalia, who still hadn't said a word. "She's dedicated her whole life to peace—to compassion. All we do is fight. We fight and we die and—"

"I accept," Ethalia said, quietly.

"You don't have to do this," I told her. "Birgid forced you into becoming the Saint of Mercy; don't let yourself be forced into this too."

Ethalia smiled at me for a moment. "No one *forces* me into *anything*, Falcio. Have you not learned that one simple thing about me yet? I chose to accept Birgid's burden, though I didn't understand it at the time."

It was a perfectly sensible and brave thing to say, and it annoyed me. "We're *duelists,* don't you understand that? For all our talk of laws and justice, most of us are nicknamed after the weapons we carry—swords and spears and arrows, all used to kill."

Ethalia took the coat from Aline's hands. "And you are named for these, too, for the protection they provide, not only to you but to those you defend." She reached out a hand and placed it against my chest. "Perhaps we can all be more than just one thing."

I put my hand over hers and held it there a while.

"It's time," Aline said. "I would hear your oath."

Ethalia turned to her then, and I wasn't in the least bit surprised when she said, "I am the friend in the dark hour. I am the breeze against the burning sun. I am the water, freely given, and the wine, lovingly shared. I am the rest after the battle, and the healing after the wound..." She paused for a moment, and then said firmly, "And I am the sword against the sword, the spear against the spear. I am the answering voice when torment cries out for mercy. I am the friend in the dark hour," she repeated, "and I am a Greatcoat."

This time I overheard what Aline said, and despite how furious I was, I had to admit that the name fit. I found myself looking around the room, at Kest and Brasti, with whom I'd started the first step of this journey, so long ago. They were smiling like idiots. I found the reason in the faces of the men and women around us: Antrim, Mateo, Allister, Talia, Quentis, Valiana, and Ethalia. There were less than a dozen of us left, fools one and all, protected by nothing more than leather and bone and a few desperate words. It was impossible not to love these people.

Aline went over to where Nehra and Rhyleis were sitting together, mumbling and occasionally scrawling notes in a little clothbound book. *No doubt writing down the story and getting the details all wrong.*

"Lady Nehra," Aline said, "do you have the means to get a message to the Blacksmith and his creation, wherever they might be right now?"

"I'm a Bardatti," she replied. "Yes. What would you have me say?"

"Kindly inform the God that the Greatcoats are coming."

CHAPTER SIXTY-SIX

THE PLAN

In the penultimate chapter of Sen Errera Bottio's treatise on trial by combat, he describes seven vices that can lead even the most expert duelist to his death. The first, Bottio argued, is believing the praise of one's supporters: *Their testaments to your skill and brilliance will be delivered with such eulogistic grandiosity that you risk forgetting your own weaknesses. Your enemy will not.*

Sage advice, although in my case it really wasn't necessary.

"Congratulations," Brasti shouted from where he sat opposite me on a chair in the surprisingly spacious second floor bedroom I'd taken. "After a lifetime of trying to come up with the worst possible plan ever conceived, you've finally succeeded."

"You have a better one?" I asked, trying in vain to rub away the headache forming just behind my eyes. Brasti wasn't the first one to make that particular observation.

He threw up his hands in disgust. "Sure, how about you just construct a giant ballista and hurl us one by one at the God, shouting 'Injustice! Injustice!' because I'm telling you, *that* plan is at least as good as yours."

I turned to Kest, who was leaning against the back wall. Up until now he'd stayed very quiet. Now he said, "Your strategy is . . . *inventive,* to be sure, but it's based on conjecture about magic and Faith, things none of us understand. If you're wrong about even one small part of it, we'll all be dead before Brasti can even say he told you so."

"Which would have been the *only* redeeming part of this plan, by the way," Brasti said. He pointed to Aline. "And after everything we've seen, you're expecting the heir to just—"

She cut him off. "We're fighting a God. We have to have a little faith in each other."

Faith, of course, was not a virtue to Bottio's way of thinking. *The second trap set by those who love you best is that they will try to convince you that your victory is inevitable; that the Gods themselves demand your success. Remember that such sentiment was no doubt expressed with equal enthusiasm to the last man you fought, most likely just minutes before you killed him.* Bottio's suggested solution to this vice was for the duelist to mutter under his breath the phrase, "I am sure to die, I am sure to die!" over and over while friends and family were cheering his imminent triumph.

"I'm not sure how someone as pig-headed as you ever lived this long," the Tailor said as she finished up her repairs to my greatcoat, "but this time you're good and screwed for certain." She tossed the coat to me. "Try not to get too much blood on it. I'd rather not have to clean it again before I give it to the next fool."

"You think there's going to be anyone left to wear it if I lose?" I asked.

She rose from her stool and headed for the door. "That's the beauty of Faith, Falcio. There will always be some idiot determined to live up to the bald-faced lies we tell of the past." She stopped and gazed at me for a moment, then gave me what I believe was her best approximation of a sympathetic smile. "May that thought give you comfort when the God rips your throat out with his bare hands."

I really don't think Bottio had the Tailor in mind when he wrote his caution regarding the faith of one's supporters. After she left I took off my boots and lay back on a bed that was uncomfortably soft and smelled suspiciously of mildew. I closed my eyes, so certain that I wouldn't have to worry about Bottio's third vice that I nearly slept through the quiet knocking at my door.

"Is there any way someone could just kill me and be done with it?" I asked as I opened the door.

I was surprised to find Rhyleis, the Bardatti musician, leaning against the doorway, yellow hair glimmering in the faint light of the candle she held. "I suppose so," she said, one side of her mouth turned up in a smile. "But it's only the little death I seek tonight."

That may just be the most dangerous smile I've ever seen. "What are you doing here?"

She straightened up. "Nehra got a message to the Blacksmith and he sent one of his little Needles to reply. We face the God's trial at Aramor when the light of the sun first shines upon its ruins."

"I know," I said. "Nehra told me herself an hour ago. You were there."

"Oh, was I?" Rhyleis asked, looking not at all surprised. "Then I suppose I must have come here to bed you."

"I . . ." It's only on very rare occasions that I wish I had Brasti's way with words; however, this turned out to be one of them. "I'm . . . er . . . flattered?"

"Of course you are," the Bardatti said, reaching out a finger and tapping my nose. "I'm very fetching, in case you hadn't noticed."

She was at that, and there are times in your life when you just want to feel something other than despair. On the other hand, I could almost hear Errera Bottio screaming in my ear, "*While there are few good reasons for losing a duel, there is at least one spectacularly bad one.*"

It was looking awfully like Rhyleis was delighting in my hesitation. "You know, it's rumored that making love before a duel steadies the hand and steels the nerves, Falcio."

I chuckled, embarrassingly. "I've read almost all of the books on fencing ever written, Rhyleis, and never once have I found that particular suggestion."

"We Bardatti are the keepers of mysteries," she said, and stood on her toes to kiss me. "We know any number of things that others do not."

"And apparently there are a few things you don't know that everyone else *does*," Ethalia said from behind her.

Neither of us had heard her come up the stairs—or at least I hadn't. "Ah, forgive me, Sancti," Rhyleis said without a trace of sincerity. "I'm so terribly embarrassed by my wanton behavior. You must find me truly reprehensible."

Ethalia came forward into the light of the candle. "Rhyleis, I'm not quite sure if you're trying to mock me for being too prudish or mocking me because I was a prostitute."

"Can't it be both?" she asked archly. "Or perhaps it's simply that I don't understand a woman who thinks it proper to discard a delightful puppy by the side of the road and then resent someone else for wanting to pick him up."

The two of them stared daggers at each other and I remembered how Brasti liked to regale Kest and me with tales about the times when two beautiful women had fought over him. We had always assumed he was making those stories up . . . *because, in fact, he absolutely was making them up. Hells.*

"Drop the act, Rhyleis," I said, irritated.

Rhyleis looked up at me, eyes full of innocent confusion. "My darling?" She kept it up for a good long time before she broke out laughing. "It's not entirely deception, First Cantor. I promise I would, in fact, give serious consideration to spending the night with you . . . were circumstances otherwise."

Ethalia's eyes narrowed. "This was a performance. You made sure I saw you coming up to Falcio's room."

The Bardatti gave a small bow. "And now, my sacred work is done." She looked up and winked at me. "I leave you to your very important spiritual consultations." She skipped down the stairs, leaving us alone.

"And people say *my* plans are stupid," I said.

"Perhaps we should be flattered," Ethalia said. "Don't the stories say that when the Bardatti interfere in matters of the heart it is because they foresee a romance for the ages?"

"Really? Who is it who tells those stories, I wonder."

She smiled. "That would be the Bardatti, I believe."

It was, I supposed, a kindness on Rhyleis's part, an attempt to bring some small joy into our lives before everything went to hell. "I'm sorry she disturbed your meditations," I said.

Ethalia stepped past me into the room. "If I am to be honest, I . . . wanted to come."

"Really?" I asked.

What followed was an unimaginably awkward series of furtive glances and half-begun words back and forth, until eventually we managed to establish that Ethalia had not meant she was coming to sleep with me, and I had not intended to imply I wouldn't want to see her otherwise.

"We appear to be quite hopeless at this," she said at last with a laugh.

"Being hopeless at things is one of the few skills I've mastered lately," I said.

Ethalia took one of my hands in hers and suddenly the laughter was gone. "Your plan, Falcio . . . it will all come down to you and me at the end."

"I know."

She looked up at me. "The others . . . For all their courage, they don't believe we can win. They fear the will of a God cannot be withstood by mere human beings."

"I know that too."

We stood there, staring at each other for a long time. Everything about Ethalia is in the eyes, and that's why I suddenly found myself barely able to breathe. It wasn't fear or doubt or even compassion I saw there. It was pure determination.

"Then we will show them just how dangerous the two of us can be."

CHAPTER SIXTY-SEVEN
THE FALLING TOWER

Bottio begins his chapter on the deaths of expert fencers with this: *On the morning of your last duel, your opponent, like a brilliant and battle-tested general, will first gain advantage of the terrain.*

I remember reading that line for the first time, wondering if I'd mistakenly picked up a book of military strategy. Everyone knows a dueling court has no topography—there's no "terrain" to benefit one side or the other; it's just a floor. But in the next paragraph, Bottio explains himself. *Look not to the ground, poor fool, but to the air all around you. Are there ladies in the courtroom who just happen to be wearing the very scent your enemy has learned you are allergic to? Listen. Do the musicians play songs of sorrow that are making you weary and fearful? Has the enemy set sights before you in the court, like pieces on a game board, that will make you feel trapped, like a fox in a cage as the dogs circle around, waiting to pounce?*

Say what you want about Bottio's prose, but the man understood dueling.

As we approached the remains of Castle Aramor for the last time, it was clear the Blacksmith understood it too.

Thick clouds of gray dust still drifted listlessly across the ruins, covering the pilgrims as they knelt, coughing and choking out their hymns in praise of the same God whose demand for reverence was slowly killing them.

A massive wooden platform had been assembled over a bed of broken stone and mortar, unshaded from the sun except by the lone tower that stood precariously against the remains of the curtain wall, looking rather like a tired old man leaning on his cane. I did wonder if our enemy had left that tower standing just so he could later drop it on our heads.

Knights in white tabards and Inquisitors in gray coats stood at the back and in the center, between dozens of prettily dressed noblemen, was the empty throne of Aramor.

"Lucky for the God that the throne wasn't crushed when the castle fell," Brasti noted. "Otherwise he'd've had to find a different prop."

"Why would a God give a damn?" Darriana asked from behind me.

It was Valiana who answered. "Because this is theater. The Blacksmith wants to use this moment to create the illusion of legitimacy."

"Everyone stop worrying about the damned chair," I said. My attention was focused on the assemblage of nobles, who looked perfectly normal except for the feral glee in their eyes and the weapons at their sides. Husbands and wives stood together, apparently united in the desire for petty power at the expense of their souls. Boys and girls barely tall enough to hold a sword stared out with mad grins at the crowds of pilgrims, hungry to mete out revenge for every petty slight they thought the world had dealt them. In Tommer I had seen the very best of youthful enthusiasm; here stood the worst.

How much of your souls did you trade away for a little power, you great lords and ladies? I wanted to shout. *How long do you expect it to last?*

"At least the Dukes aren't among them," Kest observed.

"Because they're hiding away in their little palaces," Brasti countered.

Jillard isn't, I thought. *If he hasn't already joined up with the Blacksmith it's probably only because he has worse things in mind for me.*

Brasti nudged me. "It's not too late to have Aline taken out of the country, Falcio."

I glanced back at the others: fewer than a dozen Greatcoats and the fourteen-year-old heir to the throne, come to challenge a God to a duel. I was sure Brasti knew just how tempted I was to take his advice. *And maybe I would run, if I thought there was somewhere we could hide from a God . . .*

"We're not running," Aline said. "This ends here, today."

What do you say to someone who, even while her hands are shaking with terror, stands there still, awaiting death bravely? Had her father been on that field, even just in my imagination, I was confident he'd have made a joke, so I tried to come up with one, but I failed. Staring out at Castle Aramor's broken remains, I thought, *Some things just aren't funny, your Majesty.* Ever since my King had died I'd fought and bled trying to bring back a past that probably existed only in my imagination. But others had their own notion of what a golden age should look like: a nightmare worse than this country had ever seen.

"They're coming," Kest warned.

"Last chance," Brasti said. "If we go now we can st—"

The Prelate Obladias emerged from the gray haze resplendent in robes in a hundred shimmering shades of white. The Blacksmith walked close behind, wearing his plain leather apron and the wide belt holding the simple tools of his trade. His plain appearance was a mask, though, hiding the most devious and dangerous mind the world had ever known. I needed no more evidence of that than the sight of the figure at his side: Tristia's one true God.

"It's too late to run," I said.

Unlike the Prelate, the God wasn't dressed in finery, and unlike the Blacksmith, he made no pretense of being a simple craftsman. He still wore Fost's face. Over his chest he wore the same steel and gold breastplate; his powerful arms were bare save for thick golden rings around his biceps and forearms. Cuisse and greaves covered his legs. And every part of him glowed as if all the sun's light were reflected from him.

The voices of the thousands of pilgrims rose at his presence in a haggard crescendo of awe—even I felt like praising him. How had I ever convinced myself I could fight him? I wasn't a Tailor or a Blacksmith; I couldn't twist events to my liking. I was a *magistrate*. I was supposed to enforce the Law, that was all.

So do that, I reminded myself. *Stop making this about magic and Gods and the fate of the world.* I glanced over at Ethalia. Her eyes were closed as she struggled to find the strength to live up to Saint Birgid's legacy.

This began with a murder. Let it end with a trial. "You shouldn't have killed Birgid-who-weeps-rivers, you son of a bitch," I muttered out loud. I looked at my army and saw the effect of the God's presence on their faces. "He's just like every other criminal we've had to arrest, only unimaginably powerful and especially venal," I said loudly. "Fuck him and his Awe."

That got me a chuckle, and some of the Greatcoats even looked like they might believe I was as brave as I tried to sound.

"It's starting," Aline said as Prelate Obladias stepped to the front of the dais.

"The time has come, false Queen," he boomed. He was really playing to the crowd, who were watching, enraptured. "It is time for you to make your confession."

Aline led us to the dais, then bade the rest of us to stop once we reached its foot. She turned to me and took my hands. "You have your orders, First Cantor?" she asked, very seriously.

"Put the pointy end into the bad man?" I replied.

"Did my father ever point out to you that you have a distinct lack of reverence for the monarchy?"

"Only twice a day, sweetheart."

She let go of my hands. "I'm about to die for the cause you and he started. Don't call me 'sweetheart.'"

"Anything you say, poppet."

She shook her head at me and walked up the three steps to the dais. "I am here," she said, speaking not just to Obladias but also to the pilgrims, "to meet on this field. To settle the future of this nation. I am Aline of Tristia, and I stand before you without—"

"*Kneel,*" the God said.

Without even a moment's resistance, as if a thousand chains had suddenly clamped around her limbs, Aline dropped to her knees.

"Hells . . ." I heard Mateo mumble behind me.

"You've killed her," the Tailor growled in my ear. "You've sent her to her death and now there's—"

"Shut up," I said, holding back the overwhelming urge to run to her, to try to get her out of there. "Now is when we see."

"See *what?*" the Tailor demanded. "She didn't last even a second. His Awe is too strong."

I looked at the fourteen year-old girl in whose hands I had just placed the fate of the world. "Now we see if Aline deserves to be our Queen."

The first part of our plan was based on a hunch. Every other deity was made from a single, fundamental human drive: the need for Love, the greed for Coin, the impulse to wage War. The Prelate wanted us to believe that this was the One God, the True God above all others—but I had a different theory. The Blacksmith had made the only God he could with the materials he had to work with. He had used murder and terror to unleash panic upon the population because that was the easiest metal to shape. People were *always* afraid in Tristia, so the Blacksmith had brought forth a God of Fear.

"Hold to your oaths," I said, looking around, making sure I caught everyone's eye. "When the time comes, remember the words."

"We have a bigger problem than just dying," Brasti pointed out, and when Talia looked worried, he explained, "It looks like that damned monk is going to give a speech."

Obladias stood tall and raised his arms wide so his flowing robes caught the wind. *I bet he practiced that.* "People of Tristia," he said, as if the entire country was listening to him and not simply the crazed few massing outside a ruined castle. *Mind you, maybe he is talking to the whole country,* I thought; his voice was echoing with perfect clarity across the expanse of dirt and rubble.

"That's a clever touch," Kest noted.

"Why does the Blacksmith look bored?" Quentis asked.

"His labors are complete," the Tailor said, her eyes on the big man. "He has put all the pieces in place and hammered them into the shape he willed. He cares nothing for this pomp and ceremony; for him, there is only the work."

Inlaudati: that's what he had called those like himself and the Tailor. *Please let there be only the two of you.*

"People of Tristia," Obladias repeated, "the Church comes not to rule you but to free you."

"That's nice. Can we go home then?" Brasti asked.

"Shhh . . ." I was curious about where he was going with this.

Obladias stepped in front of Aline and loomed over her. "This nation has lived under the heel of tyrants for too long." He knelt down and lifted a handful of her hair.

My hands twitched, desperate to draw my rapiers, to drive a blade through the bastard's throat. *Wait,* I told myself. *Have faith for once in your damned life.*

"A child, with a child's ambition and a child's arrogance, comes to command you." The Prelate let Aline's hair fall back down to cover her face. "And why? Because the Law says so—because *words in a book* dictate that we should allow a foolish girl to rule over men."

"Is it me, or do these people really dislike women?" Brasti asked.

Obladias strode along the front of the dais toward us. "There!" he shouted pointing, "you see there? You see what this heresy of 'Law' has brought us? Saints and Trattari and Bardatti and Dashini and every other kind of hateful creature place themselves above you, above those who live righteously, according to nature."

And there it is: "according to nature."

"See how these heretics look down on you? See how they consider you lesser beings for all that you live and toil and do as your natures command? These . . . *magistrates* . . . seek to tell you what laws you must obey. There is only one Law: live according to your nature!"

There's that phrase again.

"Those who live in humility live in *happiness*," he crowed. "Those who live in humility live in *decency*. They live under the one true Law." Obladias turned to gaze upon the Blacksmith's God. "We have brought you that one Law made manifest. Today we free you from the bonds of the traitors' false laws. Today we give you back the right to live according to your nature. We give you back the joy of humility. We give you back the most precious right of all."

The God said, "*Kneel.*"

Every single person in the crowd fell to their knees. So did we.

Well, shit.

Obladias, completely unaffected by the God's voice, walked back to Aline and reached down to grab her by the jaw. "I will hear your confession now, little girl." When she didn't speak he looked out to the crowd, an expression of mock bewilderment on his face. "What, no grand declarations? No proclamations of your laws and your rights?" He motioned to the empty throne. "Why do you not rise and take your rightful seat, oh mighty Queen of all Tristia?" Obladias made a show of scratching at his chin, then he stopped and tapped the side of his head. "Ah . . . I see. Is it perhaps because we need no Queens here? Is it perhaps because you are naught but a spoiled child badly overdue for proper punishment?" He reached down a third time and grabbed her hair, this time pulling hard and forcing her chin all the way back. "Is it because you are *afraid*? Come now, girl, *confess!*"

"I am afraid," Aline replied, the words so softly spoken I was surprised we could all hear her. "I am always afraid."

"He's doing something to her," the Tailor growled. "He's making her—"

"Wait," I said.

As if suddenly overcome by compassion, the Prelate placed a hand gently against Aline's cheek. "There, there. You are only a child, and it is right that a child should fear her betters." He leaned forward and spat on her head.

Okay, I'm killing you first, you bastard.

He started to rise, but Aline reached out with trembling fingers and grabbed his hand. "If only I had a child's fears, Venerati. If only my fears were the kind which could be banished by a mother's arms, or would fade with the day's first light."

"Enough," the Prelate said, tearing his hand away. "Do not seek to beg for—"

But Aline wasn't finished. "You were right to call me a child, Venerati. I begin each day as one. I sit in my bed each morning, my eyes full of a child's tears, waiting in vain for someone—*anyone*—to take away those fears. No one does—no one can. Do you know what I've learned about being a Queen, Venerati?" She looked so small, kneeling there, shaking beneath the gaze of a God.

"Something is happening," Quentis Maren said, an odd sound in his voice that took me a moment to recognize as awe.

Aline glanced back at me, just for a moment. "Every day a Queen must conquer her fear." Then as the crowd looked on, and in defiance of the God of Fear himself, the daughter of my King rose to her feet.

The Prelate's face went as pale as his robes. "That's not possible."

Moving so slowly I thought she might fall back down at any moment, Aline stepped past Obladias to stand before the God of Fear. "I am Aline of Tristia, daughter of Paelis, heir to the Throne of Aramor." She squared her shoulders. "Now get the hells out of my castle."

CHAPTER SIXTY-EIGHT

THE IRON

For the longest time, no one moved or spoke. Then the God's Needles stepped back, shocked by what they'd seen, and the pilgrims stopped singing their hymns. The God of Fear stared down at Aline, and she stared right back.

He spoke, a single word: "*Blasphemy.*"

It was like a wind, hot and humid, crushing down everything in its path—but not Aline. "I am done bowing to fear," she said.

The Blacksmith had been quiet, almost disinterested, throughout the proceedings. Now he walked to the front of the dais and looked down at me. "And was this your great stratagem, Falcio? You intuited that because the girl had known fear her whole life she could resist my God's Awe?"

I didn't reply. Bottio calls the fourth deadly vice of the duelist *canto anticipato,* or unintentionally revealing one's intentions for the final attack. The Blacksmith was vastly smarter than I was, and anything I let slip he would use against me; any plan I made, he could map out in his mind and find a way to defeat. Sometimes silence really is the best parry.

"Clever," he said to me, still not bothering to address Aline her-self, "but you forget that for all the girl's courage, she is merely flesh and bone." He turned and gestured, and two of the Knights stepped forward and grabbed Aline by the arms.

I heard the other Greatcoats behind me grunt as they tried and failed to rise.

The Blacksmith reached down and drew the heavy hammer from his belt. "Flesh and bone will always give way before iron, Falcio." He walked back to Aline and looked down at her with an almost sorrowful resignation. "My daughter was almost your age," he said. "She was brave too, for a while."

"Damn it, he's going to kill her," Allister said. "I still can't move, can you?"

"Wait," I said again.

"I grieve for you," Aline said to the Blacksmith. I could hear the quivering in her voice. "You have suffered a father's loss, and that loss has cost you your Faith."

He gave her a wan smile. "Look about you, little Queen. I have shown you all the Faith there is in Tristia. I have shown you how power flows from man to God and back again. It is all mathematics, engineering. There is nothing else."

"There is this," she said, and very softly, she sang, "'The First Law is that all are free. For without the freedom to choose, none can serve their heart, and without heart they cannot serve their Gods, their Saints or their Queen.'" Her voice was sweet and clear and true.

The Blacksmith turned to look back at me. "You see the foolish-ness you inspire, Falcio? The child could have run—she could have lived! Damn you for making me—"

"Speak to *me*," Aline said. "You *will* listen to me, Blacksmith, for I will see your Faith restored, and your blackened heart broken by it."

"Sing then, little girl, sing as the hammer falls."

She turned to look at us, and we struggled to stand, but the weight of the God's stare kept us down. *I'm so sorry, sweetheart . . .*

Aline smiled. "The First Law has been broken, Magistrates. In the name of that Law, I bid you rise and render your judgment. Greatcoats, report."

She can't see that we're still trapped, I realized, horrified. The second part of our plan wasn't working.

I tried to scream to her, but before I could she turned to the Blacksmith and said, "Come and show me the strength of your iron and I will show you mine."

With a roar born as much from anguish as rage, the Blacksmith raised the hammer high above his head. As it reached its apex, a blur of movement caught my eye, and the weapon was stopped in its downward arc, frozen in midair by a pair of slender hands wrapped around the Blacksmith's thick wrists. With strength born of the Adoracia she still fought inside herself, Valiana wrenched the weapon out of his grasp and sent it smashing down to the floor of the dais.

"Impossible," he said, as he realized who she was and what she had survived. "There . . . there is no cure for the Adoracia. Without the mask you should be—"

She backhanded him so hard he stumbled backward, dazed. "I am done with masks, you son of a bitch. I am Valiana val Mond, Realm's Protector of Tristia, and *I am the Queen's Iron.*"

It would have been nice if the Blacksmith had given up then, or if the God had magically faded away and all his followers had fled back to their homes. Unfortunately, and despite a lifetime of my wishing it were so, the world is never so accommodating.

The Prelate took charge again, declaring, "This is witchcraft! A violation of nature!" There was not a trace of irony in his voice. He ordered the God's Needles, "Make them scream for God's mercy!"

One of the Needles, a young man of perhaps twenty wearing a silver-trimmed Viscount's frockcoat and wielding a sword that, by any rights, ought to have been far too heavy for him, ran at Aline with a reckless glee. The blade caught the light of the morning sun as he swung it overhead, preparing it to come crashing down on her. The hem of a greatcoat whipped against my cheek as a second figure leaped past me. I saw the God's Needle blink and sparks fly in the air as his blade collided with the shield that now protected Aline's head. The God's Needle growled in frustration at being denied his prey, but Kest withdrew the three-foot steel disc and smiled. For the first time in months there was no pain on his face.

"I am Kest Murrowson," he said, "and I am the Queen's Shield."

The God of Fear, enraged at the sight of the man he'd consigned to death just days before, stepped forward and cast his gaze upon Kest. "*Kneel*," he commanded.

Even as Kest, mouthing his oath, struggled to remain on his feet, another of the God's Needles—a big bearded man wielding an eight-foot-long ax-headed halberd—ran forward with surprising speed and swung his weapon at Kest's neck.

With a single fluid motion, Kest spun around, deflecting the ax blade with the shield, ducked under a second attack, bridging the distance between the two men, then drove the edge of the shield down on his opponent's skull, knocking him to the ground. "Fascinating," Kest said, looking first at his attacker and then at me. "It doesn't hurt *at all* when I hit people with *this*."

"Great," Brasti said, grunting with the effort of getting to his feet and nocking an arrow to his bow. "Now we get to listen to him telling us how the shield is the most elegant of all weapons from now until—well, we're probably all about to die, so maybe it's not so bad."

"End this!" the Prelate shouted to the Needles. "*Now!*"

They came for Aline like a pack of wolves, the *Adoracia fidelis* and the blood of Saints coursing through their veins. There was not even the slightest trace of humanity on their mad, grinning faces. We met them on that field, terrified, tired, repeating our oaths, over and over as we struggled to resist the will of the God. And whenever it threatened to overcome us, we would cry out our names.

Darriana, driving her sword through the neck of the former Margrave of Therios, shouted, "I am Darriana, daughter of Shanilla." She withdrew the thin blade and held it high so that a sliver of sunlight breaking through the dust glimmered on its crimson surface. "I am the Queen's Fire."

Antrim, his own weapon fallen to the ground, held back an opponent's blade with his bare hands, gritting his teeth as he grunted, "I am Antrim Thomas, son of Margarite of Lanjou . . ." He kicked out, breaking his attacker's knee, who then stumbled to the ground, losing his grip on the sword. Antrim had been holding the blade over the man's skull; he flipped it back and knocked him unconscious with the pommel. "Be thankful, for I am the Queen's Charity."

Quentis, noticing one of the Inquisitors taking aim at Antrim's back, fired his own wheel lock pistol, declaring, "I am Quentis Maren, and I am the Queen's Prayer."

One by one, we used our oaths to break away from the Blacksmith's God's control, fighting against odds that would have brought a smile to the God of Valor's face, were he not likely already as dead as his predecessors. We might have been mercilessly outnumbered, but now we understood the God's Needles and we used their own ferocity against them. Darri was masterful at baiting her opponents, drawing them away, only to slip past before they could catch her, leaving Talia to use the greater reach of her spear to stab them through the back of the head. Mateo used ferin powder—we use it to remove rust; it's *incredibly* itchy if you get it on the skin—throwing it into the faces of several of the God's Needles. They might not have felt pain, but itchiness turned out to be another matter: they tore at their own eyes, blinding themselves even as they pursued him.

"Damn, but we're good at this," Brasti said, firing his third arrow and dropping a thin man who'd been coming at us with a heavy mace held almost negligently in his right hand. I looked around and saw that he was actually right. It was easy to forget, especially in all the relentless madness of recent days, that we had each been trained to duel any sort of opponent, from a Knight on the field to an assassin in a shadowy alleyway, and there were precious few who could beat us when we were ready for them.

"Help Valiana protect the heir!" Quentis Maren shouted, driving an elbow into the jaw of one of his former fellow Inquisitors and then neatly grabbing the pistol out of the man's hand before turning and firing on a second Inquisitor who'd taken aim at Aline. Quentis dropped the pistol and then took two steps up to the dais and jumped onto a Church Knight's back, knocking him forward to crash into two of his comrades who were converging on Valiana as she stood in front of Aline. Quentis Maren's martial skill and unwavering resolve in battle were daunting.

Brasti fired two arrows, each of which found their target through the back of the Knights' helmets, then he and I took up position around Aline, who was still singing softly over the din.

"What in the name of Saint—Hells," Brasti swore, "there really aren't any Saints to swear to anymore, are there? What's Aline doing?"

"Singing the Laws," I replied, crossing both my rapiers above my head to stop the blow of a heavy warsword and then kicking my attacker in the belly and knocking him into Talia's spear.

"Wouldn't it be more helpful if she threw rocks at our opponents or something?"

"Don't you feel it?" Valiana asked. Her own blade flashed like a hummingbird, keeping an Inquisitor from being able to aim his pistol at her. "She's reconsecrating the Laws!"

Something *was* happening—the air felt different, *charged,* like the moment just before lightning strikes. The Prelate Obladias was screaming at the Needles to fight, but there were fewer and fewer of them left. The God looked troubled for the first time—and even Brasti noticed. "So old Saint Erastian was right? The Laws do bind the Gods?"

"Let's hope so," I replied. The third part of our plan was based on our theory that the new God's creation had been made possible by the weakening of the rule of Law since King Paelis's death. If there really was something spiritual about the Laws, having the heir to the throne reconsecrate them might weaken the Blacksmith's God.

"Well then, can I suggest she sing louder?" Brasti ducked the swing of an Inquisitor's mace, came up the other side and drove an arrow into the man's chest.

"Someone *is* singing louder," Talia said, taking a moment to catch her breath.

I hadn't really noticed until then; I'd been making a point of ignoring the pilgrims' annoying hymns. But now that Talia had pointed it out, I could make out another song that had slipped inside the one they were singing; it had started as a gentle harmony but it was gradually spreading through the crowd, taking over the melody and words. And suddenly we all recognized the King's Third Law. *But how is that—?*

"It's Nehra and Rhyleis," I said. "They're using that unfathomable Bardatti ability of theirs to sneak the Laws inside the hymns!" There was a strange beauty to the melody and I could see it bringing strength and joy to the other Greatcoats, even as it drove the God's Needles more nuts.

"That's it. I'm quitting the Greatcoats," Talia said, driving the blunt end of her spear through a Knight's open mask. "I'm joining the Bardatti so I can sing people to death."

"You do just fine with that spear," Antrim said as he withdrew his blade from the neck of a God's Needle. He turned to me. "Falcio, is it possible that we're actually winning?"

I looked around at the chaos. We were keeping our enemies from organizing themselves, which worked perfectly for me. *We've never fought so well,* I thought. For so long it had felt like our time had passed, but now I saw what we could still do if we worked together, and I felt a relentless elation that I had never expected to feel again.

Which makes it all the more unfair that we can't win.

I didn't need Kest to tell me that the odds were too great: there were simply too many of them and too few of us, and sooner or later, the remaining God's Needles and Church Knights and Inquisitors were going to overwhelm us. Besides, we still had a bigger problem to deal with.

"You damned fool!" the Blacksmith shouted, standing next to his God. "I could have *saved* this country. I could have given us—"

"Oh, shut up," Brasti said, and fired an arrow at him. It would have been nice had it struck, but of course the God's influence made the shaft fly harmlessly away. "I really need a way to get through that," he commented.

"I'm working on it," I said, but stopped, my gut clenching, and watched in horror as the God lifted his arms and all the pilgrims rose as if a thousand nooses had descended from the sky and were slowly hanging them: men, women, and children, their mouths gasping for breath, their heads beginning to loll to the side as their eyes rolled into the back of their heads.

"This is your doing, Falcio," the Blacksmith shouted, his voice so full of righteous rage that for a moment I almost believed him. "If you won't let me give this country the God it needs to be strong, then I'll destroy it all and begin again!"

Allister raced into the crowd and grabbed a little boy who was on the very tips of his toes and struggling to escape the constriction around his throat. He lifted the child in his arms, but nothing changed. "It's not working!" Allister shouted, "there's nothing to free him from!" He called to me from across the distance, "They're dying—someone tell me how to save them!"

"Falcio," Ethalia said softly, her hand on my arm.

I turned to her and saw she'd taken a cut to the forehead. I reached out to wipe away the blood, but she stopped me. "It's time, Falcio. The God acts out of weakness. Aline has shown them that his will *can* be resisted. The others have stood in defense of the Law. Now the Faith of the pilgrims is fading, and along with it the God's power."

"Then how is he doing this?"

"He is still a God, and these are his followers." She took my hand. "There is only one way this ends. It's up to you and me now."

I turned to look back at the God standing among the ruins of our home, his armor glowing in the light of the sun. He looked majestic, perfect . . . unbreakable. "All right," I said, and followed Ethalia. "Let's go kill God."

CHAPTER SIXTY-NINE

THE CHALLENGE

I'm usually the reckless one, but this time it was Ethalia who launched the first attack. Even as we ran up the stairs of the dais, the glow of her Sainthood was flaring around her. "I know you, God of Fear," she called out to him, "and as the Law binds you, so too do I. You will be named Ingnavus, God of Cowardice. Others will know you as Relinquere, God of Despair. The rest will call you Timidus, Master of Cravens."

The words seemed to shake him. "*I am your God,*" he thundered, sending a shuddering wave of fear crashing down on us.

I started to fall backward, unable to keep my balance, but Ethalia grabbed my hand and steadied me. "*A God, perhaps,*" she said, "but you are no God of mine."

"Whatever she's doing, it's working," Brasti shouted suddenly. "The pilgrims are breathing, although just barely."

I spared a glance back and saw them still standing on tiptoes, as if they were being stretched out. "Let them go," I said to the Blacksmith. "You want to end the Law in this country? There's a way to settle this."

"You're a fool, Falcio. Do you really believe you can chain a deity by invoking a set of rules no one even remembers, let alone uses, and then threatening us with . . . what? A futile act of valor?" His eyes drifted to Ethalia. "Posture and shout all you want, My Lady, but you and I both know you lack the spirit for this fight."

She smirked—an unusual expression for her. "I brought all the spirit I need, *Inlaudati*. Set your God upon us and let your black heart feel what burns hotter than fire and shines brighter than stars."

What's happened to her? The glow around her was making it hard for me to see. The wind was picking up, swirling clouds of dust through the ruins. *I am so incredibly far out of my depth,* I thought, *I might as well throw stones at the moon to knock it out of the sky.*

"*You will bleed,*" the God declared, throwing his Awe against Ethalia.

For an instant we were lost, drowning in a pool of blood and filth, then we were scrambling, grabbing for something, *anything,* to pull ourselves out. I started running through my oath again, clinging to the words like scraps of driftwood. *I will ride these roads . . . I will judge fair . . . ride fast . . . fight hard. I will carry the law on my back if I have to.* I reached inside my coat for my piece of amberlight and leaned over to trace a wide circle on the floor of the dais. The small piece of rock flared against the wood, sparks flying as the black line grew.

"Have you decided to take up magic tricks?" the Blacksmith asked. "Is that what you brought with you to this fight?"

"You know," I said, completing the three-yard-diameter circle, "the funny thing is, I think I might be starting to like magic." I planted my feet outside the line and looked up at the God on the other side, steeling myself against his gaze. "I am Falcio val Mond, First Cantor of the Greatcoats and Chief Magistrate of Tristia. I find you guilty of the murder of Birgid, Saint of Mercy, and of Anlas, Saint of Memory. I find you guilty of a hundred other deaths and a thousand other crimes"—I looked out at the wreckage all around us—"including several counts of vandalism. Do you submit to my judgment, or will you plead for trial by combat?"

The God lent a moment of his attention to me, drawing away some of his attack on Ethalia, who was struggling against his Awe. *I will ride the roads,* I murmured under my breath. *I will find my way inside every castle and palace, every filthy hovel and rundown pigsty. I will judge fair and ride fast and fight hard.*

"*Marked,*" the God said, beginning a ritual as old as the country itself. He reached a hand back to the ax strapped on his back and brought it forth. The wide blade of the head was made of the smoothest steel I had ever seen, the long shaft wrapped in the most beautiful tracings of silver and gold. The grip itself was made of raw iron.

Ethalia joined me on my side of the circle. "Marked," she said, her forehead slick with sweat, leaving me to wonder how long she could hold out once the true fight began.

The Blacksmith shook his head in disgust. He sounded almost sick with disappointment. "You could have *lived,* Falcio—you could both have found happiness somewhere far from here. Do you truly believe you can fight a God with those rapiers of yours?"

"No," I confessed, and I tossed them aside. I walked over to a fallen Knight's warsword lying on the ground. I picked it up in both hands, and it was just as heavy and clumsy as every other broad-bladed weapon I'd ever used. I aimed it at the center of the God's gleaming breastplate. "This will make a bigger hole."

The opening of a judicial duel begins with both opponents walking the circle. As they trace each other's steps, they look for the opportunity to attack. Errera Bottio says that no matter how good an actor he might be, every fencer reveals his weaknesses in those first sluggish movements. He wrote: *Find your enemy's fears—seek out his hesitations as he walks, and there you will uncover the means to defeat him.*

Ethalia, the God, and I all moved around the circle in agonizingly slow steps, like dancers waiting for the music to start, but I was fairly sure that my opponent wasn't going to be revealing any weaknesses to me.

"I suppose it is fitting to end it like this," the Blacksmith said, standing a few feet away from the circle. "When I first heard about you and your penchant for dueling, I thought, 'Here is a man with only one tool in his belt, one weapon he uses for every purpose.' It led me to make a bit of a study of the subject, a way to better anticipate your actions."

"I'm flattered," I said, keeping my eyes on my opponent and making sure not to bump into Ethalia. Once the pacing has begun, either opponent can enter the circle and the other must meet them there within the beat or forfeit the duel. The idea is to wait until your opponent is slightly off balance, or a little distracted, and then you begin the fight with the advantage.

"I found it quite fascinating, all those *sanguinists* and *avertieres, persegueres* and *ludators*—it made me curious. A man of your profession must spend a lifetime mastering just one style—knowing that for every strength it holds a weakness, however did you decide which one to choose?"

For a moment I almost laughed; only a real amateur would ask that question. I gave it the answer it deserved. "That's simple. I mastered them all."

With that, Ethalia and I stepped into the circle and claimed the center ground. As she set the Awe of her Sainthood against the God's will, I met him, steel for steel.

The moment our weapons touched, I knew I couldn't beat him.

CHAPTER SEVENTY

THE DUEL

As that first *clang* of clashing weapons shook the air, I found myself crouched in a field of tall stalks of corn. I felt small, skinny, and there was a chain around my ankle. *I'm a slave*, I realized. The God was my owner, screaming at me in a language I couldn't understand as he whipped me over and over, on my face, my chest, my back, with a thick loop of rope. I tried to grab the rope away from him, but before I could—

—I sat across the table from the Blacksmith. Between us was a board with strangely colored pieces of all different shapes and sizes. He picked up a boar, but when he set it down it became a Knight on a massive charger.

"Your turn," he said.

I looked down at my pieces, now tiny, pale bits of bone carved to look like emaciated, terrified men and women cowering before an endless shadow. "I don't know the rules."

The Blacksmith smiled. "Of course you don't. That's the point."

I reached down, picking up one of the pieces at random, hoping it would counter his Knight, only to find—

—that I was no longer one man, but many, a dozen—no, *a hundred*. We hunched over small fires on a cold night, rough wooden clubs at our sides, praying the night would pass quietly, but suddenly horses came at us from all sides, men in armor riding them with swords held high. With a roar, we grabbed our clubs and turned to face them, knowing the fight was already—

—*lost,* I thought, finding myself back in the dueling circle. My arm hung heavy at my side, the point of the warsword trailing on the ground. Ethalia was trying to keep me standing, even though her own legs could barely hold her upright. The God didn't look as if he'd even moved.

"I'm disappointed," the Blacksmith said. "I wouldn't have expected a master duelist and a Saint to tire so quickly."

How long had we been fighting? Time moves unnaturally in the dueling circle, sometimes racing by, other times grinding to a halt as an enemy's blade comes for your belly. *Five minutes,* I guessed, *maybe seven?*

"Just give me a second to catch my breath," I said. "I'll be happy to beat your God senseless in a moment."

"Catch your breath?" the Blacksmith chuckled. "Falcio, the fight just began. You only parried one blow."

Hells. This isn't going to work. I looked at Ethalia, wondering if there was some way I could distract the God long enough for her to flee—the others could protect her while she gathered her strength or found a way to help them escape. She caught my eyes. "Stick to the plan," she said, her voice haggard, her breathing labored.

"Sure," I said. "How about a kiss for luck."

It was a stupid thing to say, the kind of glib remark that comes out of your mouth when you're desperate to hide the fact that you're terrified.

"I would," she replied with a weak smile, "but of late neither your kisses nor mine have been particularly lucky, have they?"

Before I could respond she drew her shoulders back and once again turned her Awe against the God. I saw shining, shimmering images of a man crawling across dry sand, his lips so parched and cracked they glared an angry red, only to have a young girl, the daughter of the enemy who sent him there to die, give him water.

The God's eyes wept, just for a moment, and the head of his ax dropped, and immediately I leaped at him, swinging my warsword around in a horizontal arc as if felling a tree. He batted it aside easily, the force of his parry sending me stumbling backward to the edge of the circle.

He started coming for me, but Ethalia bound him with the vision of two miners climbing down a deep shaft to save a dog that had fallen in and broken its leg. The dog whined, but its tail wagged as one miner held it close to his chest, and the other helped pull them back up.

I needed to separate the God from his weapon. I flipped my sword around and holding it by the blade, I smashed the pommel like a hammer against his hand, all the while wondering if Gods had bones that could be broken. It turned out the answer was no, and an instant later I watched the blade of his ax sweep up from the ground, aiming for my throat. He missed, though, stumbling forward as Ethalia drove him off balance with another vision.

This one I recognized: a broad-chested man with big, merciless hands and a jaw that could bite through bone stares down at the prisoner he's been ordered to torture endlessly—this is his job; this is what he knows and what he does. But this time he hesitates. He looks down on the foolish prisoner, who is singing in a broken voice of the Laws of a long-dead King. And the torturer leans down and lifts his victim in his big arms, carrying him down the hall and up the stairs to freedom: an act he knows will cost him his own life. A foolish act. An act of Mercy.

I never thought I'd say this, but I really miss you, Ugh, or whatever your real name was.

"Falcio . . ." Ethalia said.

I thought we might be winning, but then I saw how pale she was, the way her mouth was hanging open as if she no longer had the strength to keep it shut.

The God gave a roar that banished her visions and shook the ground beneath us. "*No. More. Mercy.*"

Ethalia fell against me and I tried to hold up my blade, but it felt so heavy that I couldn't get the point into guard.

The God walked toward us, the wood of the dais bending under the weight of his steps.

There was an expression of pity on the Blacksmith's weathered face. "I warned you, Falcio. I *begged* you not to begin this fight." He signaled to the God, and as the full force of his will struck us, the images he'd been holding back—the true blade that would cleave our souls—overwhelmed us.

"No . . ." I said, as I saw the vision sweep over me. Something tugged at my wrists and I saw that my arms were tied high above my head, against twin posts. My muscles screamed as dozens of needles were stuck in, all the way to the bone. There was something holding my mouth open, and a slight, strong man dressed in dark blue slid a small knife inside and tore strips from my tongue. I tried to remember the words of my oath, but they were drowned out by another voice. "Shall we begin?" Heryn asked, over and over again.

I heard a scream sounding over my own: Ethalia was caught in the vision with me.

"Do you know how Gods execute mortals for their crimes, Falcio?" the Blacksmith asked as his creation knocked my blade aside. "It's . . . Well, let's just say it's very different from any punishment you or I could ever render. There is no release when a God traps your soul. It becomes a plaything, a toy that can be shaped, a box that holds you inside, forever. The box my God has made for you and your woman is the Lament: over and over, Falcio, repetition without end. This is the death you've brought her to. This will be her eternity, and yours."

"No," I said, my voice pleading as every inch of my body started shaking. I couldn't even try to imagine myself somewhere else now. "Please, no—I'm sorry, I'm—"

"Do not ask for mercy, Falcio. There is none left for you. I gave you a chance to flee, to let me complete this great work to restore this broken country, and instead you came at me with your tricks and your clever insults and your childish Laws." For the first time I saw the cold, empty hate behind his eyes as he turned his gaze to Ethalia. "I warned you, My Lady: it takes more than a Saint's power and a kind heart to challenge a God."

Ethalia's hair was falling across her face as she raised her head slowly and said, "And I told you, Blacksmith, that I brought all the spirit with me that I need."

There was no fear in her voice, unlike mine, and I looked at her to see what was happening. Everything about Ethalia is in the eyes, and that's why I finally understood what she had done, and how she planned to fight back. Her words outside the cathedral echoed in my mind: *I hear her when she talks to you, Falcio. Sometimes she speaks to me too.*

Ethalia looked at me. "I've been carrying her for a long time, I think," she said in that last moment before the pale blue ocean of her irises gave way to the dark brown of fresh-turned earth. "No one else could love you the way she does."

CHAPTER SEVENTY-ONE
THE SPIRIT

Time moves in strange ways inside the dueling circle. Sometimes it's too fast, sometimes impossibly slow. Errera Bottio calls the latter "the grace before the blade."

The God walked toward us, coming to rip apart our souls, and yet nothing seemed to move. I stood there holding onto a woman whose eyes belonged to another.

"Well, husband," Aline said, her voice coming from Ethalia's lips. "You appear to be losing quite badly again."

"It's been a rough couple of months," I replied.

"Poor darling. It will all be over soon."

I glanced around at the scene before us, though I knew I wasn't moving. "Am I already dead?"

She looked up, the way she used to when calculating how much seed we could afford to buy for the spring planting. "Not quite yet."

I sighed. I had really thought I was done with living. I'd fought so long and so hard, for a dream that was doomed to failure—you'd think I'd be grateful to end things. Instead, I heard myself say, "I don't want to die."

She wrapped her arms around me, and never has anything felt so real in my entire life. "Have you forgotten what I told you?" she asked. "Do you not remember the oath I took?"

"You said you'd protect me."

"And haven't I done so?"

I was going say something funny, but it was a sob that escaped my lips. "Every day."

She let go of me and patted my cheek with Ethalia's hand. "Poor Falcio. For a dueling magistrate who leaps at every chance to risk his life, you really are quite sentimental. Do you know, I think you wept during our entire wedding ceremony?"

I took in a breath, about to explain that the tears had come from the realization of just how cold-hearted my future wife was going to be, but the air in my lungs suddenly felt very different—*cold*. Real. Aline put a finger to my lips. "Hush now, Husband, save that breath. It's about to begin." She patted the sword hanging loosely in my hand. "Time to stick the pointy end through the bad man's heart."

Everything speeded up again as the heel of the God's foot met the floor of the dais and the blade of his ax came for the center of my skull. But the blow never landed; instead, he fell backward as a dozen visions of mercy and valor smashed into him with the force of a hurricane.

I brought my sword up into guard and glanced at Aline standing next to me, that wicked grin of hers on Ethalia's face. I felt a moment of perfect joy, as though the greatest failure of my life, the unpardonable sin of having failed to protect my Aline, had been erased. She was here, alive. We were together, and together we would stare down the Blacksmith and his God and every foul thing the world had ever made. It was foolish, I knew—a desperate child's fantasy—but it was nonetheless, for that one brief instant, glorious.

The God's ax whirled in the air, fast as ever, but now each time he tried to strike, the force of Aline's will channeled through Ethalia's Sainthood knocked it aside. "Did you think I would let you have him?" she cried out, her voice a symphony of rage and mercy, of love and tenacity. "Did you believe something so small as death could withstand a wife's vow, you feckless, callow creature?"

The God reeled from the force of her Awe: the weight of an ocean crashing down on the tiny wooden boat of his strength. *This* was why the Saints had been born, I understood finally; this was how we had resisted the yoke our own Gods had tried to force on us.

"*Stop*," he said, and he started pulling in the Faith of his followers, winding it around and around the blade of his ax until it became so pure and full of power that I knew it would pierce Aline's will and kill Ethalia.

"No!" I shouted, striking with the warsword, interrupting him and drawing his attention back to me. He swung the ax in a wide horizontal cut, so much raw fury behind it that I knew even if I managed to parry it, that blade would smash right through my own weapon. I fell back, feeling the edge slice through the top layer of leather on my coat.

Aline redoubled her efforts, and he slid backward in the circle, but sweat was flooding down Ethalia's forehead. "I'm so sorry . . ." she panted, "he's just too strong . . ."

The God roared with joy as he felt her will slipping and turned his attack on her, his ax whipping through the air like a scythe, shredding the visions that were shielding us. "*You may carry the powers of a Saint*," the God crowed, "*but you are still just a woman.*" He backhanded her across the face with such a force that I thought her neck would break.

I ran for him, trying to throw myself at him, but he knocked me aside effortlessly and stepped forward to grab Aline. Wearing Fost's face, his grin, his rapacious hunger, he flooded her with a thousand cries born of her own terror. "*Look upon me*," he commanded.

She did, and suddenly the corners of her mouth turned up in a wry smile. "You see, this is why the Gods can never rule," she said, suddenly no longer panting for breath. "You're all so *very* gullible." She reached out with both hands and the air around us ignited, becoming a pure, white light that lit the world and, just for an instant, made it as clear and beautiful as the memory of first love.

The God of Fear turned away, blinded by it; Aline turned to me and shouted, "Husband—now—!"

In one of his more poetic passages, Bottio insists that at the moment of the final blow, the mind simply ceases to be: there are no more thoughts or choices to be made so the body, of its own volition, becomes a single, unstoppable weapon.

The heel of my left foot pressed against the floor of the dais, my calf clenched, and then the muscles of my back leg exploded, driving me forward. My hips carried the force up into my torso, transferring the energy into my arm as it extended into a straight, perfect line. My weapon suddenly became weightless in my hand; there was no sword, not really. *I am the blade.*

A spark skittered along the God's breastplate as the tip of the warsword struck against the hard steel and for just a fraction of a second it stopped there, metal against unyielding metal—but then the surface of the armor gave way, bending then parting, and a screeching sound filled the air. Tiny fragments of steel went flying in all directions and the blade slid with the ease of a lover's tongue into the breech of the God's armor.

He looked down at the sword sticking into his chest and we stood there, bonded together like a sculpture meant to last forever. "We win," I said, then I twisted the blade hard, widening the hole in the breastplate as I withdrew my sword.

But the God only smiled.

CHAPTER SEVENTY-TWO

THE SHOT

Valiana stepped onto the dais with the heir to the throne beside her. "The duel is ended. Your champion has lost. Your so-called 'God's Needles' are dead. You will withdraw from this place, from this country, from this world."

And that should have been the end of it. If life were fair, even to the smallest degree, my blade piercing the God's heart should have sent blood gushing from the wound and a gurgle from his throat as he died at my feet. *And just what, in your miserable life, has ever convinced you that you were that lucky?*

The Blacksmith came forward, his expression one of shock and disbelief. I don't think that even with all his Inlaudati genius, his ability to see all the patterns of the world, that he'd foreseen any way we could have won. "Remarkable," he said, sounding so much like Kest after a fight we should have lost that I almost broke out laughing. He met my gaze. "What you have done is wondrous. You should be proud. Alas, I'm afraid Gods aren't killed by a simple stab wound."

The God, despite the gaping hole into nothingness in his breastplate, lifted his ax and stepped back into the circle, waiting for us.

"Shall we call this round two?" the Blacksmith asked.

"Wouldn't that be cheating?" Brasti asked, stepping onto the dais along with Kest.

I tried to lift the sword again, but it was hopeless. There comes a point when, no matter the odds or the stakes, you just can't go on. I tossed the weapon aside. "Forget it," I said. "I'm done with you."

The Blacksmith signaled to the God, who raised the ax up high overhead. I felt entombed in its shadow, but I looked up without fear.

As the ax came down, Kest stepped in front of me and knocked it aside with his shield. "That would definitely be cheating," he confirmed for Brasti. "Though I suppose it's to be expected. Fear is an especially venal sort of deity."

The God growled and swung again, and once again Kest saved me. On the third attack, the shield broke.

"It is over," the Blacksmith said. "You have failed."

"Possibly," Kest conceded, "but in fairness, I was only the distraction."

Even the God's eyes widened as Kest stepped aside, revealing Brasti brandishing an arrow, an oddly shaped stone tip attached to its end, aimed at the hole in the God's breastplate. "My turn," Brasti said, smiling.

I could see the Blacksmith understood what we'd been planning now—that we'd figured out why a God so powerful would still choose to wear armor.

"No!" the Blacksmith screamed as Brasti fired the arrow.

A crack of stone striking against steel plate was followed by the snap of the arrow's shaft. The God looked down at the broken remains of the arrow on the ground.

Brasti had missed.

CHAPTER SEVENTY-THREE
THE ARROW

Everything we'd planned for was undone in that moment. Brasti Goodbow, the man who swore he always shot true when it counted, had just missed his target.

We all watched in horror as our last, best hope fell apart.

"What?" Brasti asked. He looked at me. "How many times have I told you this? When you're shooting with new arrows, you have to test-fire one to get the weight. *How many times?*" He sounded exasperated.

All of us looked down at the arrow on the ground. That's when I noticed it wasn't tipped with the prayer-stone.

"*Stop!*" the God shouted.

"Oh, do shut up," Brasti said, and with a single fluid motion, a perfect illustration of the beautiful harmony of the archer and his art, he nocked the second arrow—this one glittering at its tip—and loosed it.

The thrum of the bowstring was the only sound as the arrow found its target, burying the prayer-stone deep inside the hole within the God's armor.

The God of Fear looked down at the arrow embedded in his chest, the shaft still shivering with the last vibrations of its flight. He stared at us, and all of a sudden he looked different to me. I couldn't say I recognized his face now, but I'd seen that same expression on the face of hundreds of men who'd met their end in battle. His was a mask of fear: a mask of infamy.

The man who had just killed him stared right back at him. "My name is Brasti Goodbow," he said, "and I am the Queen's Jest."

The God fell slowly to his knees on the ground before us. He clasped his hands together as if in prayer.

Who do you pray to? I wondered.

Then what was left of his consciousness faded as he slid down on to the dais and into whatever hells await those Gods we no longer need.

CHAPTER SEVENTY-FOUR
THE SURRENDER

If I'd ever given any thought to the dying of Gods, I suppose I would have imagined it would be different from the ways of men.

"Not all that impressive, is he?" Kest said, coming to stand next to me as we looked down at the dead God.

Brasti joined us. "Fear becomes ever smaller, the longer a man faces it."

Kest turned to look at him. "That's actually quite astute . . . did you prepare that line ahead of time?"

Brasti grinned. "Been working on it ever since Falcio told me the plan. I want the stories to give my shining victory the weight it deserves."

"I suspect you probably shouldn't have added that last part, then," Valiana said.

He shrugged. "Well, a man can only be so glorious, I suppose."

What was left of the God of Fear looked up at us, his dead eyes disbelieving. I wondered what the others felt now, for I was surprised that I felt neither rage nor even relief at his passing. I had no desire to humiliate him, or to comfort him in his passing, so I simply turned to the Blacksmith and said, "It is done."

He nodded to me. I thought perhaps he might try to attack me, or raise some tiny blade to his own throat to end his life, but he didn't. He just knelt down on the ground before us and said, "I surrender."

People surprise you, sometimes.

CHAPTER SEVENTY-FIVE

THE AFTERMATH

It's strange how the world organizes itself after it's been upended. I half thought that the thousands of people in the crowd—the clerics, the soldiers, the noblemen, the peasants and well, everybody, really—would have gone completely mad. I wouldn't have blamed them.

A God was dead; worse, we had learned that the Gods were, for the most part, as small-minded and petty as we were, their natures aligned to the basest instincts of a people whose response to coming here as slaves was forever to seek out new masters. Maybe we were simply born to kneel. The crowds appeared to agree as they wallowed in the disquieting silence that filled the open air, shuffling from foot to foot, uncertain and scared, with no idea what might come next.

Actually, not everyone, I thought as I looked over at the daughter of my King.

Aline stood before the throngs, barely fourteen. She was just as afraid as the rest of us—in fact, she was probably more afraid—and yet it was she who had given us the chance to fight against the God, showing the rest of us how to rise in the face of fear.

It's just possible that there are wonders yet in this country that are worth protecting.

Someone in the front, a young nobleman, shouted out, "The Queen stands before us!" He knelt down on one knee and bowed his head.

"The Queen!" another shouted, and he too knelt.

People began to cheer and shout Aline's title, and a wave passed through the crowds from front to back as men and women, the youngest and the very old, knelt before the girl I'd first met dirty and coughing in the ruins of a burned-down house in Rijou.

"The Queen!" shouted a wheezing Duke Erris of Phan.

"Oh, and *now* the Dukes show up," Brasti said, pointing to a heavyset man further back in the crowd. He was not nearly so grandly dressed as I'd seen him on previous occasions, but he made up for it with his boisterous cheers of "Aline the First!" Hadiermo, Iron Duke of Domaris had magically found his humility.

No doubt the two of them hoped that a show of enthusiasm might save their heads from the block when the time came for a reckoning.

I should have been happy in that moment: the Dukes would have no choice now; there would be no further resistance. The daughter of my King was standing among her people and they were kneeling before her. But somehow the sight made me empty inside.

You're just tired, I told myself. *You've won. Stop complaining about it.*

But even as people shouted and cheered for Aline, the emptiness remained. I couldn't spot Jillard, though I imagined he was somewhere close by, waiting to exact his due from me for my part in Tommer's death.

I was pulled from my morbid thoughts when Aline cried, "Enough!" Her voice wasn't very loud, but when she raised her hand everyone became silent. "Enough."

Nervous whispers filled the crowd. Though they were thousands strong, and we only a handful, I could almost hear their thoughts. *Now we'll be punished. Now the new Queen will set examples of her enemies. Better keep low and quiet and hope she takes the next man and not me.*

It would be her right. The Law allowed her the right to execute each and every one of them if she so chose. When she turned to look at me, I saw the temptation in her eyes. She'd been the target of murder and conspiracy every day of her life and that wasn't likely to end any time soon. How better to banish fear and pain than by killing those who brought it to you?

Then she nodded to me, as though I'd asked her a question.

"Why are you kneeling?" she asked the crowd.

The nobleman who'd done so first looked up. "You are our Queen!" He said the words as if he'd just crowned her himself.

"One day," she replied. "Not today."

"The Queen of our hearts, then," the nobleman ventured, and others mumbled in enthusiastic agreement.

"Perhaps that too, one day," Aline said. She looked around the crowd. "It's not a job I ever wanted. Perhaps not one any of you would want me to have."

That was too much for the young nobleman. "We are your loyal servants! We are yours to command!"

"Servants," Aline said. Abruptly, she strode into the crowd, walking through the kneeling masses. I thought Antrim might have a heart attack as he rushed to follow behind her. She stopped in front of an old man who was shaking as he kept one hand on the shaft of his short staff. "Why do you suffer, Grandfather?" Aline asked.

"Forgive me, your Majesty," the old man replied, his head still bowed. "My knees ain't so good. They ache whe—"

Aline extended a hand and placed it under his chin. "Then why are you kneeling if it hurts so?"

The old man's eyes went wide. "Because . . . because we—"

"Rise," she said.

For a moment I thought the old man might refuse, but his fear of disobeying her overcame his uncertainty about standing in her presence.

"Is that better?" Aline asked.

"It . . . yes, your Majesty. It don't hurt so bad once I'm off my knees."

"Really?" she asked. "Imagine that. I wonder if that's why the Greatcoats don't kneel." She turned to gaze back at me. "Is that why, First Cantor?"

"I've found that it's hard to stand for anything when you're on your knees," I said.

"How odd. Perhaps it is time we all gave it a try." Aline, daughter of Paelis, heir to the throne of Tristia, gave her first royal command.

"Rise," she said.

"Am I wrong," Allister asked, "Or did the heir just overturn a thousand years of royal prerogative?"

"Sixteen hundred and twenty-seven," Kest corrected. "The first reference to the requirement to kneel before the monarch appears in the *Ediacto Regiae Principe,* though it's likely that the practice was common even before—"

"Kest?" Allister said.

"Yes?"

"Please shut up."

Then necessity took over: people had to be moved, the injured treated, the dead buried. After a quick consultation with the Dukes, Antrim retook command of the Aramor guardsmen present, and they in turn took command of the other troops. If anyone had any sliver of a thought about resisting this, they gave no sign. Sometimes people just know when it's time to give up. Sometimes I wished they knew that more often.

The crowds, still in shock after Aline's sole command, dissipated gradually, many of them helping their fellows where they could, but some just stood and stared, and a few started crying bitterly—maybe for their dead, or maybe for themselves as they began to realize all they'd given up or sold to get here. It would be a difficult return for them.

It was going to be a difficult return for all of us.

I leaned against my horse, Arsehole. We had left our mounts tethered outside the Busted Scales, but Arsehole had broken free somehow and made his way here, to me. His copper-colored hide was covered in gray dust and I was trying to clean him off in a slow, haphazard way. He didn't seem to mind, even giving me an encouraging snort now and again. "You're a damned good horse," I said, and feebly brushed at his side. There were probably more important things I was supposed to be doing right then, but I was too exhausted to care.

"You really do cut an impressive sight, my love." The voice was feminine but strong, soothing yet a little mischievous.

I looked over Arsehole's withers to see Ethalia—except the eyes staring back at me were still brown instead of blue. The lips belonged to Ethalia, but the words were those of my wife.

"I've had something of a day," I said.

She came closer and placed her palms against my cheeks. "Perhaps if you didn't insist on throwing your life away at every opportunity, you would fare better. How many more times will you set your blade against the world, Falcio?"

Everything breaks if you hit it enough times. "Until I save you," I said, and felt the tears slipping down my cheeks and onto her fingers.

She shook her head sadly. "Ah, Falcio . . . That's not a story that can be told. Don't you understand yet? *I'm* the one who saves *you*."

The tears were flowing faster now. "Every time," I managed. "*Every* time."

She smiled then, as if we'd just made a beginning: a new start for me, for her, for both of us. *Only life doesn't work that way.* "You have to go now, Aline," I said.

She pulled away and stared at me for a long time. "Husband, when did you become so very full of useless principle?" She waved a hand. "You might fool all these others but you and I both know you weren't at all like this when I was alive. Or perhaps you were, but you were also a little selfish, a little too easily cowed, more than a little lazy." She smiled. "And now, here you are, this . . . hero. Is there nothing left of the foolish young man I married?"

"Silly woman," I said. "I can be more than one thing."

I expected her to laugh, but she didn't. Instead her face grew deadly serious. "Ethalia doesn't love you, Falcio. Whatever you had before, it left when she took the Sainthood."

"I know that. But it's her life, and her choice."

"It was also her choice to give herself over to me—she knew the consequences, and she accepted them willingly, without reservation. Ethalia has given us this chance, to have the life together that was denied us."

"She has," I agreed. I took a deep breath and held it, hoping somehow it would strengthen my resolve. "And now you have to go."

Aline sighed as she leaned in and whispered, "Very well." Then she smiled. "I will settle for one kiss, for old times' sake. Let me feel my husband's lips on mine this last time."

I wanted the taste of that kiss more than all the wine in the world. I wanted that one moment, a tiny fragment of her love to carry with me for the rest of my days—hadn't I earned it?

But . . . "They aren't your lips," I said, before I could fall into that abyss from which I would never want to climb out. "Ethalia would not want this."

Aline groaned. "*Really?* You think she would begrudge you this one *tiny* thing? Is she so selfish a woman as that?"

"She isn't selfish at all, and that's why we can't do this."

Aline removed her hands from my cheeks and stood silently for a time, giving me a chance to change my mind, but when she finally said, "As you wish," the eyes staring back at me were Ethalia's, and she turned and walked away without saying anything else.

I stayed there a long time, wallowing in my own loss, but eventually I had to move. I made my way into the ruins of the castle. There were still debts to be paid.

The steps below the wreck of the seventh tower were crumbled in places, but there was enough of the staircase left to reach the basement. The door to Aramor's death house was open.

"I knew you would come," Jillard, Duke of Rijou said. He stood over the body of his son, his back to me.

"This is a bad place to keep him," I said, looking around. "The ceiling may not hold."

Jillard ignore the warning. "Did you come to pay the debt?" he asked.

"I did."

The Duke of Rijou shook his head several times, like an old man suffering from a palsy. "Then come back tomorrow, or next week. Come and see me a year's hence, in Rijou, where I will take you down to my dungeons and we can pay our debts to each other."

I walked to the other side of the table and looked down at the boy who'd given his life, and in exchange, helped to make a God. I wanted to tell Jillard how I'd met Valor at the bridge, saving a drowning cat, but I didn't think it would ease his pain, not yet.

"I could have you killed," he said, conversationally, no ire in the words, only fact. "I imagine you must think you're invulnerable to such things, with the luck you've had. But I promise you, I could have it done."

"You've tried on more than one occasion, Your Grace," I pointed out.

He looked up and I saw the dark circles under his eyes. "On those occasions, I was not quite so invested."

I understood his pain, and if anything, it made him more human. But even I have my limits when it comes to being threatened. "If there is some price you expect from me for Tommer's death, speak it."

He nodded, as if this had been the question all along. "I have to take his body to be buried, properly, in his home. That will take some time. There are arrangements to be made, political matters to be attended to. Of course, the country will be in jeopardy again by then and no doubt killing you would only make matters worse. So I will have to wait."

"If you're waiting until the country is safe, you might be waiting a long time."

"I know," he said, "but I'm a patient man. It will be years, perhaps decades. The world needs us as we are, you and me, doing the things we do. By the time the country has met its future, you may not even be alive. But if you are, if, when all this is done, you still draw breath, I will send for you. Will you come?"

I looked down at Tommer's face, at all that promise of youth and courage taken from the world. "I will," I said.

Jillard made no acknowledgment of my willingness to make myself his prisoner; it felt as if we were merely going over the items in a long-agreed contract. "You will come in secret, telling no one. I will choose the time and I will choose the place and you'll come to me." He opened his mouth to continue, but then stopped, and I saw the pain twisting inside him. Then he went on, "You will give up whatever weapons you have with you. You will give up your coat. My men will bring you to a room and chain you there, and I will come."

"Torturing me won't—"

He cut me off. "Then, Falcio val Mond, First Cantor of the Greatcoats, I will tell you about my boy, about my Tommer. I will tell you about the look of wonder on his face the first time he opened his eyes, smiling, not crying as other babes do. I will tell you about the way he stood up and walked, long before other boys. I will tell you about the silly things he said and the strange questions he asked. I will tell you all of this until your heart shatters in two, Falcio val Mond. I will tell you this so that you might know one tenth of the pain I will feel every day from now on. And when I am done . . ."

I waited for him to finish but he couldn't seem to find the breath. This, I understood, was a torture for him greater than he had ever known.

"Say it," I urged him.

He studied me, then said, "When I am done, you will tell me the stories of the Greatcoats you heard as a boy—the ones the minstrel, Bal Armidor, told Tommer. You will tell me the tales that made Tommer the way he was, that led him to the death he chose. You will tell me this so that in my final days I can try to become one tenth the man my boy deserved for a father."

"Marked."

We shook hands then, though there was no need. Jillard was a monster, a master manipulator, everything I loathed about the

Dukes. I, in turn, was everything he hated about the Greatcoats. But no man is all one thing; none of us are pure in our beliefs or our devotions. We are all bound by the frailties of our humanity, some of which feed our hatred, some of which, very occasionally, make us want to be something better.

CHAPTER SEVENTY-SIX

ON THE EVE OF
YOUR LAST DUEL

You would think that after everything that had happened, after the weeks of duels and deceptions, after fighting an actual God, that I would have slept like a newborn babe that night. I didn't.

In the wreckage of the castle I'd found the old Greatcoats' wardroom was still standing, though somewhat dustier for the rubble. I stripped off my filthy clothes and righted one of the old couches to use as a bed, but no matter how much I tossed and turned, sleep eluded me. Eventually I conceded defeat and, having nothing better to do, dressed, righted the fallen weapons rack, picking out an old rapier, and set about practicing the eight fundamental forms.

You can never get too much of the fundamentals, I thought, trying to pretend that this wasn't a completely preposterous time to be training. I gave myself ten rounds to get the forms out of my system, hoping that would leave me exhausted enough to sleep, and when that didn't work, I gave myself another ten, then another. After a while I could barely keep my sword arm up, and yet I couldn't stop, either.

There is something very wrong with you, Falcio val Mond. You're a sick, sick man. I was so wrapped up in my thoughts that it was some time before I noticed the knocking at the door. I listened more closely, as much to make sure I wasn't imagining it as anything else; after all, no one had any reason to believe I wouldn't be comatose by this point.

The knock repeated, and now I knew who it was. I opened the door to Ethalia, who wore a simple gray dress, a little drab, I thought, then wondered whether that was for my benefit. She was holding a long wooden case in her hands. The black leather covering was wearing off at the edges where I'd forgotten to glue it back down.

"You brought me my rapiers?"

She held out the case to me. "I thought you might be lonely without them." There was no discernible disdain in her words, so I decided none was intended. I took the case, walked back into the wardroom and placed it on the table. Ethalia took a step, then stopped, just inside the doorway.

"I suppose it was as hard for you to sleep with them in your chamber as it was for me to sleep without them," I said. It had sounded cleverer in my head.

"They're pieces of metal, Falcio. They don't make me sleep better, or worse. I just knew you'd want them."

I couldn't decide whether I was offended, or glad that she'd known how uncomfortable I would be without them. In the end I just said, "Thank you."

She looked around the wardroom. "If you're going to make your home here, you should really have someone put in a proper bed."

"Do you have a better . . ." I was going to say *a better suggestion*, but I stopped myself. I had a terrible feeling in my gut. "Ethalia, what I did, sending Aline away . . . it doesn't mean you should feel . . ." I stopped. This wasn't coming out right.

She leaned back against the doorway and crossed her arms, then raised an eyebrow and, tilting her head, said, "Go on, Falcio. What is it I shouldn't be feeling?"

I was just about bright enough to know I was treading in dangerous waters, but I couldn't quite put my finger on what I was doing wrong. "You shouldn't feel as if you have some obligation to me," I said after a moment. *Okay, that was definitely the wrong thing to say.*

She laughed then, with more of a mocking tone than I liked. "Really, Falcio? You're worried that I might feel obliged to—to what? To *love* you? Because you sent Aline away? Because you were so noble as to *not* allow her to use my body as her own?"

"You let her in," I said, a little defensively. Now I was fairly sure I knew where I'd gone wrong, and just as sure that I couldn't retrieve the situation.

"To save your life, and this country." She shook her head. "I swear, Falcio, you are the *strangest* man I've ever met. On the one hand you are determined to save the life of every woman you stumble over; on the other, you imagine that just because you had the basic common decency to *not* let your dead wife take control of me permanently, that I would react by coming here and throwing myself at you."

"See, when you say it like that, I don't sound very gallant."

She stared at me for a long while, then said, "Put on a shirt and come with me."

"Where?" I asked.

"Brasti's asked us to meet on what is left of the southern ramparts at midnight." She rolled her eyes. "Apparently he wants us to refer to him as 'Brasti Goodbow, the Queen's Godslayer' from now on."

Saints save us from Brasti's ego. "What did Aline say to that?"

"I think she's just relieved that he hasn't asked for actual churches to be consecrated in his name. Right now, though, you and I need to take a walk to the town square. I haven't had supper yet. I suspect you haven't either."

"You want to have dinner with me?"

"I do."

"Why?"

Ethalia let out a long breath. "Because I'm hungry. Because the stars are out and the air is warm." She came into the room and took my hand. "Because the truth is, you and I don't know each other very well. We thought we did, and what was between us was real enough, but that's passed now, and maybe it's a good thing. Perhaps we can get to know each other properly, as a woman and a man who both need to eat and who might like some of the same foods, as two people who might even have other things in common too."

I stood there for a while, enjoying the softness of her hand in mine, thinking about the need to put on a shirt but not wanting to let go, not yet. Then it felt awkward to be silent so I opened my damned mouth and said, "You know, you sounded a bit like Aline just then."

Oh, Gods . . . why do you let *me open my mouth at times like this?*

Ethalia's eyes narrowed. "You really aren't very good at this, are you, Falcio val Mond?"

Somewhere beyond the veil of life, Saint Erastian who-plucks-the-rose was doubtless laughing his head off. "I'm fairly sure I'm absolute rubbish at it," I admitted.

"Well, that's something anyway. Shall we?"

I picked up my shirt and looked at it. For a moment I wished I had something clean with me, then I decided that Ethalia knew who I was, and more often than not whatever I was wearing would be covered in dirt and dust and more than a little blood. I looked down at the case of rapiers on the table. "Ethalia . . ."

She covered her eyes with her hands. "For the sake of the Gods old and new, you're really not going to speak again, Falcio, are you?"

I knew there was a risk, but to hold my tongue just to keep her from leaving? That would have been no better than an outright lie, and she deserved better from me. "These swords . . . I know you think they're tools of violence, and you're right, of course." I leaned down and flipped open the lid. "But they're also the means by which I saved the life of a young girl who turned out to be the King's heir. They've helped defeat tyrants and assassins. I know there's a line between valor and violence, but sometimes being a swordsman is the only thing that lets me protect the people I love. I'm not going to apologize for who I am anymore."

I waited for her to walk away, but instead she came to stand next to me and slid her fingers around the grip of one of the rapiers.

"Good," she said. "Then *don't* apologize. Be who you are, and I'll be who I am, and let's see if we can get through a whole meal without the world ending."

She lifted the rapier from the box and handed it to me. I attached the scabbard to my belt. "I thought . . . I thought, what with you being a Saint now . . ."

"I *am* the Saint of Mercy, Falcio, and I have to honor that, and Birgid's faith in me."

"Then—"

"But I've come to realize that I'm also a woman of this land, of this country, and it's as much my duty to protect it as yours."

"That doesn't sound very Saintly," I remarked, but she took my hand again and pulled me toward the door.

"Silly man," she said. "I can be more than one thing."

That night I ate a simple meal in a simple restaurant with a very complicated woman. For the first half hour or so the two of us paid close attention to our food—venison stew, the contents of which spurred a good deal of comment and discussion on our part. Between courses we talked about the paintings of forlorn-looking farm animals on the walls, and argued over which of the cook's relatives had likely been the artist. Other patrons, a mix of obviously wealthy merchants and less well-clad men and women of assorted trades, drew our scrutiny and speculation too. This was, so far as I could tell, the way normal people spent time in each other's company.

Eventually we trod a wine-influenced, weaving path back to what little remained of the castle. Ethalia didn't stop to kiss me or confess to holding back a tide of love for me, but neither did she launch into a speech on the need for restraint in our relationship, or I the need for action. We didn't particularly discuss the state of the country, but we didn't shy away from the subject when some passing reference made it pertinent. We simply let the moments come and go as they chose. I wanted more, of course, but I didn't want a return to the way things were. I was content to believe the future was a set of doors; though none were yet open, none were locked, either.

Just past midnight we walked up the long flights of steps to the southern ramparts. We heard the music long before we arrived, and I recognized Nehra and Rhyleis's touch. We paused at the top of the stairs to hear Brasti emphasizing the importance of no one mentioning how badly the two of us had botched our relationship. His hearing is rather extraordinary, so I was fairly sure he knew we'd already arrived.

"Ah, there you are," he said, once we came through the arched doorway to the ramparts. "Making us wait for you as usual, I see."

Ethalia shocked me when she responded, "In our defense, we were having rather a lot of sex."

I realized that was oddly similar to something I'd said during my duel with Undriel—was it only a few weeks before? I *really* didn't know her as well as I thought.

Brasti pursed his lips and puffed out his cheeks in a fair impression of a man about to vomit. "Please," he said, after a rather lengthy performance, "there are children about."

"I assume you're referring to either yourself or Kest," Aline said tartly. "As I will soon be your Queen, it's probably best you not antagonize me further than your unsavory nature makes absolutely necessary."

"His unsavory nature accounts for a great deal of annoyance to everyone, your Majesty," Darriana said.

Brasti ignored them both, picked up an impressively heavy jug of wine and proceeded to fill a collection of shabby pewter goblets. I took a seat on a low section of wall, and Ethalia joined me there, not so close as to be intimate but enough to indicate she was there with me.

"What shall we drink to?" Valiana asked. Doctor Pasquine had done an impressive job of healing Valiana's face, but there were new scars there to match the others she'd acquired over the past year.

She's a warrior, I reminded myself, *by choice now, not just by chance. Warriors get scars.*

"We shall drink," Brasti said, "to a remarkable fellow, though one too often forgotten in the wake of his great deeds. A man of vision and of valor. A man some would call a legend and all know as a hero. A man who—"

"To Falcio!" Aline announced loudly.

"No, I meant—" Brasti's efforts to speak over her were cut off by boisterous shouting of my name, none of it for my benefit, of course, but I was happy to play my part in taking Brasti down a peg.

"Oh, I'm sorry," Aline said, after the noise had died down. "Were you referring to someone else, Brasti?"

"In fact, I was—you know, this is why this country goes to rot all the time. The sheer *unfairness,* the way those who do the *real* work of protecting it get—"

"To Valiana!" I shouted, and everyone else joined in, "To Valiana!"

"Gods damn you all!" Brasti said, and he was about to launch into a further tirade when a young man interrupted us with a cough. He held a small silver platter in his hands upon which sat an envelope bearing a Ducal seal imprinted in red wax.

The seal had already been broken. The clerk looked rather nervous.

"What is it, Claiden?" Valiana asked.

He held out the platter as if the letter itself were too hot to touch. "I bring a message, Realm's Protector, news from the North. There have been some—"

"Stop!" Brasti said.

"Sir?"

He walked over to Claiden and looked down at the envelope resting on the silver salver. "Have you read the letter?"

"I ... um ... it is my duty to do so, sir. The Realm's Protector—"

"I asked Claiden to review all letters," Valiana interrupted. "I trust him."

"Good," Brasti said. "So, Claiden, you already know the contents of this letter?" And when the hapless clerk nodded, he said, "I take it there are dark tidings? Trouble brewing? Dangers and dilemmas and catastrophe right around the corner?"

"That ... that is a reasonable assessment, yes, sir."

Brasti rubbed his jaw. "And will any of these calamities befall us tonight?"

"Tonight? Well, no sir, not exactly—but perhaps if I could deliver the message to the Realm's Protector—?"

"No."

"Er . . . *no,* sir?"

"Brasti," Valiana said, "leave the poor man alone and let him deliver his message. If there is urgent business—"

"*Of course* there's urgent business," Brasti said, throwing his hands up in the air. "There's *always* urgent business. Haven't you all figured it out yet?"

"Figured out what?" Kest asked, looking puzzled.

"That the entire world is out to get us. Whatever's in this letter? It's just the first volley from whoever is next in line to make our lives miserable. So I say, let's leave it for tomorrow."

"And you've decided to make such decisions on behalf of the Crown, have you?" Aline asked, her eyes narrowed.

Brasti made a show of examining his fingernails. "Someone has to run this country. Clearly it's too complicated for all of you."

"So what," she said, rising to her feet, "are your commands, oh wise and mighty archer?"

He grinned wickedly. "Dancing."

"*Dancing?*"

Brasti signaled to Nehra and Rhyleis. "I want to see Kest Murrowson, once Saint of Swords, once King's Blade, currently Queen's Shield, and by far the most dour son of a bitch ever to walk the earth . . . *dance the grandanza!*"

Nehra had clearly been prompted beforehand, because she launched into the first chords of a grandanza, a dance in an odd time signature that changes tempo between verse and chorus. It's a dance performed almost exclusively by experts.

All of us, the clerk included, turned to stare at Kest.

"Come on, swordsman," Brasti goaded him. "Time to show you're brave enough to fail at something for once."

Kest rose to his feet and looked around at all of us. His expression was inscrutable, and I began to wonder if he had taken genuine offense.

"Kest, you don't need to—"

But I was cut off when he turned to Ethalia and extended his left hand gracefully to her. "My Lady, if you would?"

Ethalia rose, Kest placed his right arm around her and then gently took her right hand in his left. He extended his right leg very far back. As the song came back to the opening beat of the measure, he stamped his back foot down and began drawing Ethalia into the odd, circular steps of the dance. Brasti roared with laughter, and the rest of us chuckled, but as the song progressed—none of us were experts at dancing, so it took a while—

"*Saint Zaghev's scorched balls,*" Brasti said. "It's not possible—"

"The evidence appears to suggest that it is," Aline said.

"No!" Brasti shouted, waving unsuccessfully at Nehra to stop playing. "He *can't* be fucking good at *everything.*"

In fact, Kest was a remarkable dancer; he was twirling Ethalia through the complex forms as though he'd spent his whole life at court. "What?" he asked, even as Nehra continued playing. "A number of treatises on swordplay commend dancing as excellent training for a fencer's footwork. In fact, the grandanza is mentioned in numerous texts as one of the—"

"Son of a bitch," Brasti swore. "There really is no justice in this world, is there?"

"Not much of it," I said, rising and extending an invitation to Valiana to dance with me. "But we're working on it."

The rest of us, never having practiced this particular dance, made a terrible mess of it and when Nehra shifted to a fast country reel we only got worse. But it didn't matter. We danced because we were together, because we loved each other, and because tomorrow was inevitably going to bring more strife and sorrow.

Aline joined Valiana and me, and the three of us spun each other around, the music filling the air as the world whirled by us. With every turn I saw Claiden standing there patiently, the envelope resting on the tray in his hand, waiting for us to acknowledge this new threat. I found the lightness of my heart at odds with that dark premonition, because for the first time since the King had died, I *finally* understood what he wanted from us. The Greatcoats hadn't been formed to bring back the past. King Paelis wanted us to protect the *future*.

The contents of that envelope would doubtless herald the next tyrant who thought he could take that future for himself.

I looked over at Ethalia, still dancing with Kest, then at Brasti and Darri, at all of them, and finally back to the letter on the tray.

You want our country? I thought. *Then you'd better bring more than just Gods and armies with you.*

My foot slipped and I felt myself losing my balance, tumbling back onto the stones of Castle Aramor's ramparts. Valiana and Aline rushed over and knelt by me. Someone said something, but I couldn't hear what it was over the music. Then Nehra stopped playing and a moment later all of them were standing around me. I looked up and saw the people I loved best in the world, ringed by more stars in the sky than there are demons upon the earth. I tried to speak, but it came out as laughter.

"What did he say?" Aline asked.

Ethalia leaned over and put a hand on my cheek. "I think he said, '*The Greatcoats are here.*'"

THE END

The story of Falcio, Kest, Brasti, and the
Greatcoats continues in *Tyrant's Throne*.

ACKNOWLEDGMENTS

THE AUTHOR'S LAMENT

My eminent editor and publisher, Jo Fletcher, insists that at no time did she promise me that the third book in a series would be easier to write than the second. Well, gentle reader, who are you going to believe? The woman who helped bring you books from giants of the field such as Ursula K. Le Guin and Terry Pratchett, and who now brings you new stars such as Naomi Foyle, Snorri Kristjansson, and Sue Tingey? Or will you instead put your faith in an author whose own narrator's memories of the past are sometimes suspect? Wait . . . don't answer that.

Making this my favorite book of the series was hard going. Fortunately, when the going gets tough, I turn to . . .

THE SAINTS

Supernatural intervention sometimes requires the spilling of a lot of Saints' blood:

Christina de Castell-who-reads-and-reads-and-reads, Saint of Literary Tolerance

Jo Fletcher-yes-that-jo-fletcher-even-though-she-lies-about-books-getting-easier-to-write, Saint of Editing

Kim Tough-who-knows-Tristia-better-than-I-do, Saint of Emergency Skype Calls

Eric Torin-who-sees-what-isn't-written, Saint of Narrative Philosophy

Heather Adams-who-keeps-writers-employed, Saint of Agents

THE INQUISITORS

Relentless, fearless, and happy to torture the truth out of authors and their stories:

Wil Arndt (@warndt)
Brad Dehnert (@BradDehnert)
Sarah Figueroa
Kat Zeller
Jim Hull (www.narrativefirst.com)

THE INLAUDATI

Some people help make books successful in secret, working their magic upon an unsuspecting world:

Nathaniel Marunas, who went farther than any publisher should ever have to in order to get the right cover for the US edition

Nicola Budd, who remembers the things everyone else forgets

Andrew Turner, whose tweeting we all miss

Olivia Mead, who's getting the Greatcoats back on the road

Patrick Carpenter, with whose covers we'd never know what to pick off the shelf

Dave Murphy and Ron Beard, the sales kings

Frances Doyle, the ebook queen

THE BARDATTI

I've said it before, I'll say it again: the heroes of the publishing world in the twenty-first century are the bloggers, booksellers, librarians, readers, and sometimes even fellow authors who go out of their way to share books they've discovered with the world. They're also the people who make being an author fun. Here are just a few of the wonderful folks I got to interact with this year:

* Mieneke van der Salm of www.afantasticallibrarian.com who is a delightful dinner companion and kindly pretended my Dutch wasn't awful.
* Walter & Jill of White Dwarf Books who are relentlessly supportive of fantasy and sci-fi authors.
* Cindy of draumrkopablog.wordpress.com who I got to meet at Nine Worlds in her dazzling steampunk outfit.
* Conn Iggulden, who reminded me to let the characters decide where the story goes.
* David and the fine crew of Goldsboro Books who put out lovely first editions of the series.
* Margo-Lea Hurwicz, who writes some fine Greatcoats poetry.
* Robin Carter of parmenionbooks.wordpress.com, who really deserves a greatcoat.
* Wendell Adams of bookwraiths.com who probably also deserves a greatcoat at this point!
* John Gwynne, who is incredibly gracious and has the nicest family on the planet.
* Sam Sykes, who says nicer things about the Greatcoats books than I do.
* Bob Milne of beauty-in-ruins.blogspot.com who wrote one of my favorite reviews of *Knight's Shadow* this year.
* Eon (Windrunner) who drove out to Capetown so we could have coffee and chat about books.
* Annika Thomaßen of lesekatzen.blogspot.de who is my only means of knowing if the German editions of my books are good!

*   Nazia Khatun, who randomly runs up to strangers and tells them to read my books.

And, of course, to all of you kind readers who take the time to write me e-mails with thoughts, questions, and comments about the Greatcoats. Reading your e-mails is one of the highlights of my day.

With gratitude,
Sebastien de Castell
twitter: @decastell
web: www.decastell.com
The Hague, Netherlands
January 2016

P.S. Anyone who takes the time to read a book's acknowledgments deserves to know some of its unwritten secrets.

In one of the inside pockets of Tommer's greatcoat, his father, Duke Jillard, found a carefully folded letter.

Aline,

You may be wondering why I've just handed you this letter, written years ago when I was just a foolish boy of twelve. As you read it, imagine me as I was then: not yet a man, small of stature (though I hope I've grown taller by now) and lacking in accomplishments (though that, too, I hope to have rectified these past years.) Think back on that boy who chased after you (subtly, I hope), and always sought to be by your side, sword in hand. Understand that he knew full well how silly he looked. He knew he was as much encumbrance as protector in those early days. He knew he had no chance to win your heart.

If you are reading this now, it is because I am once again standing before you, no doubt with a long line of suitors waiting impatiently for me to step aside. These will be good men, I am sure, each with virtues and qualities that outshine my own: Lords, Margraves, Dukes, doubtless even foreign Princes will have come seeking your hand. I picture them holding gifts for you: the finest jewelry, the greatest works of art, chests upon chests upon chests of gold and silver. This will be their one mistake, and my one chance. I will bring no jewels, no money and no title, for I intend to renounce my father's Ducal throne.

When I stand before you, Aline, it will be holding only this letter. When you read it, you will know that I loved you even before I was a man, and that you were my Queen even before you wore a crown. You will know that I have spent every day since I first met you trying to become a man worthy of your esteem, and if after finishing this letter you look up at me and smile, it will all have been worth it.

Your
Tommer

Duke Jillard read the letter three times before sending it to the flames of his hearth fire.

ABOUT THE TYPE

Typeset in Minion Pro Regular, 11.5/15 pt.

Minion Pro was designed for Adobe Systems by Robert Slimbach in 1990. Inspired by typefaces of the Renaissance, it is both easily readable and extremely functional without compromising its inherent beauty.

Typeset by Scribe Inc., Philadelphia, Pennsylvania.